PINSTRIPED PREDATORS

PINSTRIPED PREDATORS

Roger Kryss

The Book Guild Ltd.
Sussex, England

The Book Guild Limited
Temple House
25 High Street
Lewes, Sussex

First published 1991
© Roger Kryss 1991

Set in Baskerville

Typesetting by Dataset
St Leonards-on-Sea, Sussex

Printed in Great Britain by
Antony Rowe Ltd
Chippenham, Wiltshire

British Library Cataloguing in Publication Data
Kryss, Roger
Pinstriped Predators
I. Title
823. 914 [F]

ISBN 0 86332 681 1

To John

"I count myself in nothing else so happy
as in a soul remembering my good
friends."

William Shakespeare, Richard II,
Act II, Scene iii, Line 46

1

Martin Chandler took a sip of his whisky and water. Across the room Angela French unfolded her dramatically long legs, refolded them letting her negligee fall open to the top of her thigh, and continued reading *Homes and Gardens* as if oblivious to the effect upon Martin. It had its effect but not quite what Angela might have hoped and thought. Martin was sated sexually. At fifty-seven there was not only a physical limit to his ability to perform sexually but also an almost intellectual limit. Gone were the days when physical conquest was all, and the more frequent the better. He still enjoyed the conquest but frequent repetition at short intervals had lost its appeal, except when the excitement of his job really got his adrenalin flowing.

The sight of Angela's thigh accordingly did not arouse him but instead gave him a feeling of contentment and well being. This was not to say he did not take in the view appreciatively. The contentment and well being arose as much as anything else from the sense of freedom he had. A luxurious apartment in Eaton Square and an Angela, Fiona, Nicola, or whatever the flavour of the month happened to be, was a far preferable combination of place and person for the weekend than his boring stockbroker belt house in Surrey and his boring wife, not to mention her boring friends. It was not that he didn't love his wife, he did, but somehow the relationship had gone flat and he found more and more reasons to stay up in town.

As Chairman and Chief Executive of Amalgamated Products PLC he needed an apartment in town and had frequent need to use it. In any event his wife, Sarah, had neither the interest in his job nor the curiosity to question it, or so he fondly imagined.

A smart, tooled leather briefcase stood by the side of his chair. He glanced down at it. There was a pile of briefing papers he had to read before the morning. He was not one of those people who could concentrate in any environment and reluctantly he concluded that it was time to push Angela out of the door.

'Get some proper clothes on, Angela; time to go.'

Angela pouted. She didn't want to go. She liked the luxury of the Eaton Square apartment, much better than her small Fulham flat. Besides, she rather liked Martin too. The thought rather surprised her. She had had many liaisons during the last five years or so: pop stars, stockbrokers, industrialists, any one in fact who had money or access to the things that money could buy. Some were fun, some were generous, most she could tolerate but very few could she, with her hand on her heart, actually say she liked for what they were themselves rather than for what they gave her in entertainment or monetary reward.

'Do I have to Martin?'

She had learned very early on in their relationship not to 'darling' him. Almost immediately she regretted asking. She saw the now familiar little pantomime he went through when he was angry. A slight intake of breath, not sufficiently loud to be described as a sigh but audible nevertheless, accompanied by the deliberate removal of his spectacles which he then folded with equal deliberation. She didn't wait for the process to be completed. She was a successful courtesan (as she liked to think of herself) because she was not simply a beautiful woman who was good in bed, but also reasonably intelligent and, above all else, was very sensitive to the moods of her men.

'I'll get a cab; do you want anything to eat before I go?'

'No thanks, I'll get Wilberts to send something round later.'

He was already swinging his briefcase up onto his knee. As far as he was concerned, Angela had already gone. She slipped quietly out of the room.

Martin flipped through the pile of papers. Mostly they were financial reports from the Divisions. These would not take him long. He was very practised at picking out the weak points. For a start the reports were in the form he dictated and accordingly he had no need to plough through the detail. The summaries would tell him most of what he wanted and needed to know. Secondly he had a nose for trouble. By and large he found that people tended to over justify themselves if they had something to hide.

He glanced down his schedule for the following day. Not too bad. He liked to keep Mondays relatively free of heavy internal meetings. It was important that Divisional Chairmen were in their Divisions on Mondays. After all they had businesses to run and Martin didn't believe that the best place for them to do this was from Amalgamated House. Two items on the schedule captured his attention. They were totally unconnected in terms of Monday but very much connected in terms of his and the company's future. It was 'the company' to him, he disliked the nickname 'Big Apple' although he knew he had to live with it. 9.30 Stephen Barber. 12.30 Lloyd, Meisson & Co. for lunch.

He had high hopes of Stephen Barber. A real high flier with an impressive track record. Martin had even broken one of his own rules to get him and paid him a 'Golden Hello'. The fact that this had become necessary was indicative of the problem. Amalgamated was no longer the darling of the City and really ambitious people no longer fell over themselves to become part of it. He was looking to Stephen Barber to play a major role in changing all this, and he had already set it up that this should happen as from day one.

Lloyd, Meisson & Co. were the company's merchant bankers. Martin wondered whether the time had come to change. They had always been Amalgamated's merchant bankers, at least for as long as it had been fashionable for companies to have merchant bankers in an almost permanent advisory role. They still had a high reputation in the City but somehow Martin felt uncomfortable about them. He could not quite pin it down. Maybe it was simply that somehow he always felt slightly inferior in the presence of James Markby Smythe whom he regarded as a typical merchant banking blue-blood. Markby Smythe was always supremely confident in his views and his whole demeanour almost defied anyone to question his advice.

Martin realised that most, if not all, of the rest of his Board would be appalled if he suggested changing them. If he was to suggest it he would have to put up a good case; the decline in Amalgamated's reputation in the City was a good starting point. Somehow the company had become dull in the eyes of the financial press and the City, despite the steady and unbroken rise in profits over the five years Martin had been Chairman. Those five years had been a period of consolidation following the rapid expansion by way of takeovers during the mid and late seventies. Clearly the financial world wanted a return to those heady days. Martin's own private view was that the company was large enough already. He saw no merit in size for the sake of size. Amalgamated was still in the top twenty in the United Kingdom on almost any financial measure one cared to choose. He viewed with some distaste the present scene where takeovers seemed more and more to be dictated by a desire to make a quick buck by taking advantage of a 'special situation', as the pundits liked to call it, than by any industrial logic. The darlings of the City were the financial operators, as Martin thought of them. The men who bought a company, slimmed it down by way of disposal and manpower reductions, cut back on capital investment and research, thus jeopardising the future, and in the short term squeezing more profit out of the company. The only problem was that to keep the show on the road it was necessary to acquire bigger and bigger companies to hide the fact that earlier acquisitions had, at best, plateaued in profit terms, and in many cases had already gone into decline.

Martin was nothing if not a realist. If that was the name of the game and the price of survival both personally and for the company, Martin would play it. Nowadays even companies like Amalgamated were starting to look vulnerable to the insatiable appetites of the present breed of corporate raiders. Indeed, the very technique they adopted made it inevitable that they would become vulnerable.

Enter Stephen Barber, thought Martin. A go-getter who would not only shake things up on the corporate planning side within Amalgamated but also, hopefully, would stimulate those blue-blooded merchant bankers down in

10

the City into some decisive action. Martin was getting slightly tired of the negative advice that seemed to flow from Lloyd, Meissen & Co. these days, much as he privately agreed with the philosophy behind it. Joining the Peter Bartons of this world was 'un-Amalgamated'. Barton Industries had grown from a small and very uninteresting engineering company in the Midlands ten years ago to such a size that they had joined Amalgamated in the top twenty British companies. Whatever you thought of Sir Peter Barton and his methods, you had to admire him. The City loved him.

Martin determined to give Lloyd, Meisson one last chance at the meeting arranged for the next day. It all depended upon their reaction to Project Jupiter and, in particular, their reaction to the fact that they had neither proposed it nor been involved in the preliminary feasibility study. Martin hoped they would react in the right way for, whatever his reservations about the stodgy nature of their advice in recent months, they were still the number one merchant bank for a hard fought takeover battle.

'Electronics Giant Makes Mega Bid For French Company.' The headline only evoked a modicum of disappointment in Stephen Barber's breast. True he had done all the detailed work leading up to the bid, and would miss the thrill of the chase, but Jeremy Sutton, his erstwhile boss, would no doubt have garnered all the credit and glory in his usual charming fashion had Stephen still been there.

As Stephen Barber stood on Millbank with his back to the Thames he was satisfied that he had made the right decision. Where he was going he would be but one step from the seat of power and not two. It was a beautiful autumn day and the sun mellowed the otherwise stark façade of the imposing building on the other side of the road that was the object of his attention. He smiled to himself. Tomorrow he would walk into the foyer of Amalgamated House and be treated almost as if he were a director of the 'Big Apple'. His smile was partly one of satisfaction that at the tender age of thirty-one he had landed one of the plum corporate planning jobs in British industry, and partly one of amusement at the recurring thought that, despite the senior status he would enjoy, he would still be merely a pip in the context of the size of Amalgamated Products PLC which was referred to as the 'Big Apple' by one and all.

In his happy and rather carefree frame of mind he visualised a huge neon apple emblazoning the front of the building, for the nickname 'Big Apple' was not just another example of the penchant of the City to coin names for companies from abbreviations of the corporate name, it also happened to indicate the origins of the company. The company had started just after the First World War when Fred and Arthur Walker had put their gratuities together and bought a small orchard. Through a combination of hard work, good fortune and flair they had built this into a major corporation with interests spreading right across the world.

Stephen laughed inwardly at himself for harbouring such an irreverent thought. The company had long ago passed through the ostentatious phase that almost invariably seemed to afflict companies as they grew in size and influence. The only remaining suggestion of their origins was a discreet stylised corporate logo which, if one already knew the origins of the company, could be seen to incorporate an apple.

It was three o'clock on a Sunday afternoon but Stephen Barber was not surprised to see two people carrying briefcases entering the building. He would no doubt be doing a fair amount of weekend working himself. A brisk fifteen minute walk from his apartment in Pimlico would see him to the portals of Amalgamated House.

He turned his back on the building and scanned the sluggish progress of the Thames. Hardly a reflection of the go-go atmosphere of the Big Apple, he mused, but then, like the Thames, the Big Apple showed every sign of going on for ever; and he would not only be part of it, but would play a significant role in its development.

The meritocracy had clearly arrived. Far from being Eton, Oxford and MBA Harvard, he was Selly Oak Comprehensive, Leeds and MBA Bradford. Not that his accent or anything about him would indicate his background. His accent was classless, his clothes understated; casual when off duty and smart, but not over-expensive, suits when on duty.

He wondered what his reception would be in the Corporate Planning Department. He had, of course, met them all before he had accepted the job, but there was all the difference in the world between the politeness and pleasantries of such meetings and the reality of being boss of a group of people who were all older than him, many of whom had been with the company all their working lives and some of whom were indeed Eton, Oxford and MBA Harvard.

Whatever his initial reception, it was unlikely to be indicative of the view many would have of him in a relatively short time.

He walked slowly along Millbank enjoying the fresh autumn air that had a slight nip in it now that the sun was beginning to drop behind the London skyline. Yes, he thought, he would have little difficulty in manipulating Martin Chandler. For all his outward show of power and decisiveness he had marked him down as an insecure man who was uncertain of himself. The judgment was intuitive rather than based upon any particular evidence. He usually summed people up pretty quickly, and he was seldom wrong. He would soon put it to the test. The one thing he had not been able to squeeze out of Martin Chandler as a condition of his joining Amalgamated was a seat on the Board. He did not intend to let that worry him; he was confident that he would be able to persuade Martin Chandler to let him sit in on most of the Board's deliberations. After all, he had been hired specifically to come up with ideas and action fundamental to the company's future, and he could hardly do that if he was denied access to the collective mind of the Board.

Stephen Barber's real motive for wanting to sit in on Board Meetings was quite different. He could quite easily do his job by making presentations to the Board and then withdrawing once they had got what they wanted from him by way of information and opinion. No, his real motive was to observe the Directors at close quarters, identify their strengths and weaknesses, assess who liked whom, spot the cabals, get a feel for who appeared to wield power and who was listened to. This was all essential information to him in building his power base in the company.

Yes, he was looking forward to nine thirty the next morning. He would arrive at nine twenty-five and go straight to Martin Chandler's suite. It would make a much greater impression for him to arrive in his Department on his first morning hot foot from the Chairman. Indeed, he fully intended to make it clear at the very earliest opportunity that not only did he have the ear of the Chairman but that he was indispensible to him. The latter process would not exactly be conducive to the good of the family lives of his staff. Stephen Barber would get Martin Chandler used to a very rapid turn-around of work which would necessarily involve much burning of the midnight oil.

Oh yes. He mustn't forget to report to his boss! Theoretically this was Howard Irwin, the Finance Director. Stephen had no intention, however, of allowing theory to get in the way of practice. He had little or no regard for Howard Irwin. Irish and a windbag he had decided, rather more quickly than he had decided that Martin Chandler was insecure. Nevertheless, he must not alienate the man; enemies in high places were not a good idea however ineffectual one might think them. Stephen Barber laughed to himself. Whoever had heard of an Irish Finance Director; surely they were all Scots!

Sarah Chandler shut the fridge door with sufficient force to make the bottles inside rattle. Yet another weekend would pass without seeing Martin. Despite everything she still loved him. What still surprised her was not that she continued to love him despite his unfaithfulness, but that at the same time she could actually hate him. She had discovered his infidelity over three years before. The truth of the matter was that it was not the infidelity itself that angered her, and had eventually produced the hate, but the fact that he had not told her. She marvelled at the power of sex; not simply its physical power, but its power to cause even highly intelligent men like Martin to act in such a stupid manner. How could he believe that he could carry on his affairs without her getting to know? For God's sake, he not only entertained them at the company apartment, he actually took them out to dine at well known restaurants! More than one little bird had trilled in her ear.

He must think she was stupid. Whatever else Sarah Chandler might be, she was not stupid. If she was honest with herself she was not exactly a sex symbol. However, her homely appearance, even though she was twelve years younger, masked a very determined and intelligent woman.

She calmed herself down. She didn't want Martin to divine her anger when she spoke to him on the phone. She picked the telephone up and dialled the apartment in Eaton Square. As she waited she wondered whether a 'secretary' would answer. That was Martin's transparent little ruse. At least, she thought, he was not completely stupid. The girls always answered with the words 'Amalgamated-Chairman's apartment'; and Martin always made a point of answering the telephone himself after nine pm.

Martin answered. He must be alone as it was only seven o'clock.

'Hello darling, had a busy day?'

She tried to keep out any tone of irony in her voice.

'Will you be home tomorrow night?'

'No, sorry, Board meeting on Wednesday and I have meetings tomorrow night and Tuesday night as well. I may be home Wednesday if all goes well.'

Sarah knew perfectly well that this would be the answer, it was the usual pattern. She also knew that he would not be home before Friday night at the earliest. He never was in a Board week.

She twittered on, she knew she was twittering but could not stop herself. She needed the stimulation his warm brown voice gave her. All she got was a series of monosyllabic responses which did nothing to disguise his boredom and impatience.

'Look dear,' (he rarely 'darlinged' his wife when he was busy and wanted to get on) 'I've got a lot of work to do still. Can't this wait until I get home?'

She accepted defeat. She was angry with herself. She

hadn't meant to irritate him. Why it should worry her that he was irritated she could not imagine. He treated her as if she didn't exist more often than not. The hate started to overcome the love and need for him. She knew that at the right time and in the right circumstances she would get her own back for all the misery he had caused her.

2

Stephen Barber strolled into Amalgamated House on the dot of nine twenty-five am and asked for Martin Chandler at reception. He did not ask for 'the Chairman' or even for 'Mr Chandler'. He intended to make his mark from the start, and at all levels. As part of this he would make it abundantly clear to all and sundry that there was some special relationship between him and the Chairman of the company.

Reception at Amalgamated was not manned by attractive young women, but by smartly dressed men in black suits who were still called porters. Fred Gill picked up the phone and was through to Ann Gordon, the Chairman's Secretary, at the press of a switch.

'Mr Barber is in reception for the Chairman, Ann.'

Stephen Barber heard the muffled response from the other end.

'Miss Gordon will be right down, Mr Barber.'

Fred Gill knew precisely who Stephen Barber was, hence the use of 'Mr Barber' rather than 'Sir'. 'Sir' was reserved for visitors and, somewhat peculiarly, Non-Executive Directors. Amalgamated was full of traditions and strange little conventions.

Ann Gordon stepped out of the lift. Stephen Barber gave her an admiring glance. He had been impressed the first time he had met her when he had come for interview. The admiration was in no way physical; which was not to say she was not an attractive woman, she clearly was. Ann was a tall, well groomed woman, probably in her early forties he thought, although she looked less, but, most impressively, she exuded competence. Martin Chandler was not one to surround himself with attractive young things of doubtful

17

competence at work whatever he might do in his private life. Stephen had resolved to make an ally of Ann Gordon.

'Hello Ann, nice to see you again.'

'Good morning Mr Barber and welcome to Amalgamated,' she responded as they walked towards the lift.

'Oh I think we can dispense with the Mr Barber bit Ann, certainly when we are not in a formal situation.' She smiled in response.

The lift came smoothly to a halt on the fifth floor which housed the Chairman's suite, the Company Secretary's Department, the Board Room, two Committee rooms and various offices for the use of visiting directors from the Divisions. The journey up had been uninterrupted. This was not by chance. Martin Chandler hated to waste time and accordingly he and Ann Gordon had a special key to one of the lifts which ensured that it went straight to the fifth floor. The lift was not for the exclusive use of the Chairman, anyone could use it. Indeed anyone could travel up in it with the Chairman provided they didn't mind going up in order to come down.

'Mr Barber is here to see you Mr Chandler.'

'Send him in,' came the jovial reply over the intercom. He really was in a good mood today thought Ann. Stephen Barber stepped into the room. Martin Chandler was already rising from behind his large partner's desk. That desk must be worth a fortune he thought.

'Welcome, welcome Stephen.'

Martin motioned to his casual sitting area furnished with exquisite antiques. The room was vast and split into three quite separate areas. There was a desk area which Martin Chandler used for most of his paperwork, telephoning and occasions when, for one reason or another, he wished to create a formal atmosphere; a small meeting area which consisted of an oval table at comfortable working height and six chairs; and a casual sitting area. Everything immediately visible in the room was high quality antique, right down to the pen stand on Martin Chandler's desk.

As Stephen sat down he reflected that the cost of furnishing the room, excluding the pictures which clearly were worth many thousands, would probably buy a very reasonable semi-detached in a provincial town and, what was more, the sheer size of the room was such that it could readily be converted into a comfortable apartment with separate bedroom, living room, kitchen and bathroom.

Martin Chandler was sorting out some papers on his desk giving Stephen time to note and wonder at the number of doors there seemed to be in the room. In all he counted six but could not quite believe that they were all genuine doors, despite being identical in design. He was soon to learn that indeed two of them were dummies leading to the drinks cupboard and what Martin referred to as his 'Communications System'. This was somewhat of a misnomer since the equipment in the cupboard did not enable him to communicate with anybody. It was simply two television screens plus various other bits of hardware adding up in toto to a perfectly ordinary television and a computer monitor from which he could page up almost any piece of financial information about the company in almost any form he chose.

Martin Chandler came across the room and eased himself into the comfortable armchair opposite Stephen. He handed him a plastic folder with some papers inside. He was clearly not going to waste time upon pleasantries.

'Have a look through these and let me know what you think.'

Stephen glanced at the top piece of paper, noticed the classification 'Secret' and the heading 'Project Jupiter'. This was clearly something of importance. What he had been handed was doubtless the tip of an iceberg and he decided to master the information as soon as possible and have a paper in Chandler's hands by the next evening at latest. He was soon to find out that he had roughly two hours to gain a working knowledge of the folder and until the morning to produce a paper.

Martin Chandler had a second folder in his hands.

'This is the specification of my communications system. Have a look at it and let me know whether there are any improvements you could suggest.'

He got up out of his chair and motioned to Stephen to follow him.

'Come and have a look at it.'

He was slightly puzzled. Martin Chandler had gone

across the room and was sitting down at his desk. His hand went out to what appeared to be a slim but slightly larger than normal calculator. He did not quite know where to look, let alone sit. He didn't have to wonder for long. Martin pressed one of the buttons on the pad and there was a slight whirring noise behind his right ear. He turned towards the noise and saw one of the six doors sliding effortlessly open to reveal, apparently, two television screens. He chuckled but said nothing. He clearly got a childish pleasure out of playing with gadgetry and surprising people with it. He pressed another button and one of the screens burst into life. A menu appeared.

'What would you like to see?'

Before he could answer Martin pressed another button and another menu flashed up on the screen. A few more rapid button depressions and there on the screen was a month by month record of sales of tinned goods through the Northern Division Supermarkets.

'Impressive isn't it? I can even get that information up on the screen week by week and store by store.'

Stephen did not consider it was impressive. He thought it was ludicrous. The man hours involved in producing such nitpicking information for the Chairman's delectation must have been enormous.

'You certainly have access to detailed information,' he replied diplomatically whilst at the same time resolving to change the system entirely so that it cgncantraled on the things wpicp he wished Marlin Chandler to concentrate upon.

The door to Ann Gordon's room opened and she came in carrying a tray containing two delicate china cups and a silver coffee pot, cream jug and sugar bowl. She put it down on the low table between them and poured out the coffee as Martin and Stephen settled into the easy chairs. She handed the first cup to Stephen, inviting him to help himself to cream and sugar. Interesting, he thought, I wonder if she always does that or is it because she still classifies me as a visitor. He was to discover that it was all part of Martin Chandler's natural good manners which were not to be confused with a quiet but formidable determination in business matters.

Ann turned to leave the room.

'Hang on a minute Ann.'

Martin turned to Stephen.

'Are you free for lunch?'

The question was almost rhetorical as Martin Chandler turned immediately back to her.

'Give Markby Smythe's secretary a call at Lloyd, Meisson to let her know that Mr Barber will be joining us for lunch.'

This was going to be easy, he would not have to work too hard at gaining Martin Chandler's confidence and thereby influence over him. Little did he realise that his attendance at the lunch had been fixed ten days previously.

'Who else will be with us?' he asked, rather expecting that Howard Irwin the Finance Director would be part of the party.

'Oh, just you and me from this end.'

Better and better, he thought.

'I want you to get a feel for where we are going on the acquisition front. Lunch with our merchant bankers is as good a starting place as any. A quick glance at the Project Jupiter file before we go would be a good idea. We leave here at twelve.'

He would have to do a rapid rethink. He had planned to go straight from the Chairman's office to his department, spend most of the morning meeting everyone, and then on to Howard Irwin. Martin Chandler broke his thoughts.

'They will give you a buzz from the front door when it is time to go.'

He was already up from his seat and moving back to his desk. Stephen realised this was the signal to leave.

He picked up the pile of papers he had been given and left via Ann Gordon's office. She smiled up at him from her desk.

'Do you mind if I use your phone?' He wanted Ann to hear what he had to say.

'Not at all. Internal or external?'

'Howard Irwin please.'

She pressed out two digits and handed him the telephone. He was faintly surprised to hear Howard Irwin's melodious voice on the other end. He had expected to have to go through the secretarial barrier.

'Stephen Barber, Howard. I'm afraid I won't be able to make our meeting at twelve thirty. Martin has set up a meeting for me at lunch time and I need to have time to read the papers.'

He was giving several thinly disguised messages with this statement. Item one, he was already on Christian name terms with the Chairman. Item two, the Chairman was wasting no time in involving him in important matters. Item three, Howard Irwin could wait. He half expected some form of protest but none came, nor did any inquiry as to whom the meeting was with.

'No matter, old boy, how about four o'clock?'

'Fine.' He handed the telephone back to Ann and wondered at the lack of curiosity and the laid back reaction to the broken appointment.

He went quickly down the stairs to his office on the fourth floor making a mental note on the way to get himself an office on the fifth floor with the minimum of delay. In less than an hour he had been round the whole department, met the twenty members of it and managed to leave most of them with the feeling that here was a man who was interested in them and likely to further their interests.

He settled down to read the Jupiter file. Very quickly certain things began to become clearer. For a start, none of the memoranda had been prepared in-house. As far as could be ascertained from the file none of its contents had been copied to anyone else at Amalgamated House, not even to Howard Irwin who was the Board member with responsibility for corporate development. Most surprising of all, none of the memoranda or correspondence had come from or been sent to Lloyd, Meisson & Co. Indeed, the generators of the memoranda and correspondence were Jacob Wildstein & Co., a prominent New York investment bank, and Randles, Milne & Co., a Chicago based firm of business consultants. The proposals in the file were dynamite, suggesting as they did a complete change of direction for Amalgamated and giving it a much more aggressive image. He realised he would have to tread very carefully at the meeting and take his cue from Martin Chandler who would presumably give him some sort of briefing in the car on the way to the meeting.

He was impressed with and excited by what he read. He was clearly in at the start of something big. He closed the folder and leant back in his chair intertwining his hands at the back of his head, a posture he usually adopted when he wanted to think things through. Suddenly he picked the folder up again. Yes, his subconscious had registered something very odd. The last communication on the file was dated some three months previously and was a letter from Jacob Wildstein & Co. suggesting a round table meeting with Randles, Milne & Co., whichever English merchant bank Martin Chandler chose to use and an inner group of Amalgamated directors. The letter had not even been acknowledged. Why the delay and why resurrect it now, and with Lloyd, Meisson? He allowed himself the indulgence of assuming that the delay was to accommodate his arrival. The Lloyd, Meisson angle was, however, more puzzling, but no doubt all would become clear at the lunch meeting.

'You won't need that,' Martin Chandler remarked as Stephen made to sink down into the plush seat of the Rolls. He handed his briefcase to Fred Gill who was holding the door of the car open for him. Fred took it and unobtrusively, but sufficiently obviously for him to see, spun the combination locks on each handle.

'I will ensure that your secretary gets this safely, Mr Barber.'

He mentally kicked himself and hoped that Martin Chandler had not noticed the incident.

Peter Barton, or Sir Peter Barton as he preferred to be described in the media, stroked his putt across the carpet toward the gadget which simulated the hole. It stood no more than ten feet away but, as was more often the case than not, the ball missed the hole comfortably, being deficient in both weight and direction. He swore, using a word that would not have been understood by the average Englishman, examined his putter and angrily threw it onto the couch resolving to purchase yet another to add to his already substantial collection. Failure was not an experience to which he was used, and when it occurred, the cause was invariably attributed to another agency, human or otherwise. He stabbed at the intercom button that connected him directly with his secretary.

'Come,' he growled, immediately pressing the button again to cut off the contact.

Pru Wetherby sighed. He was in one of those moods again, but she had not survived eight years as his secretary without knowing how to cope with him in all his variety of moods. She suppressed a little giggle as she played over in her mind yet again what reply she would like to give to his peremptory command. The currently favoured response was, 'Certainly Sir Peter but I regret that I cannot do so without some form of acceptable physical stimulation.' She picked up her notepad and went into his room. He was seated behind a vast desk with virtually nothing on it apart from two telephones, the intercom and a gold pen stand. He did not even look up.

'Tell Walters to come up, and get rid of that,' he said pointing to the guilty putter, 'and bring me the Robot file.'

His hand was reaching towards the telephone. Before he had lifted it she had already turned and was on her way to retrieve the putter and make her exit. She knew when her presence was no longer required.

She rang Charles Walters to pass on the message and to warn him of Sir Peter Barton's mood. Walters knew all about the moods, he had been with him ever since the early days in Birmingham when shortly after the war Peter Barton had bought a very run down and old fashioned small engineering company. At the time Peter Barton had had virtually no money and a peculiarly mixed accent; New York Lower East Side with a trace of something else not easily identifiable. The accent had long since been ironed out. Quite how he had persuaded the bank to loan him £200,000 to buy a business apparently upon the verge of bankruptcy was still a source of wonder to Walters, despite the benefit of having seen him build up one of the largest and most successful conglomerates in the country. At the time, Peter Barton had no track record and a decidedly misty background. He was, however, a most persuasive and determined man.

Charles Walters knocked and walked into the office. Sir Peter Barton did not believe in any unnecessary formality such as having his close and trusted colleagues announced by his secretary when he had summoned them.

'Where are we with Robot, their share price is going up out of line with the market — I trust there hasn't been a leak?'

'We haven't got the full analysis from Leroy Viner yet Peter.'

'Well get it,' he growled, 'these Yanks seem to think they are doing us a favour rather than the other way round. Who is paying the money for Chrissake?'

Charles Walters knew better than to give a direct answer, and concentrated on giving the positive progress rather than trying to explain the reasons for the negative.

'Robot is shaping up well, there is good evidence that we will be able to rationalise the UK business by way of disposals at prices which will enhance the return on our investment significantly. Furthermore, there is considerable scope for pruning costs on the businesses we keep.'

'Good, what's the time scale then?'

'That rather depends upon our share price. It is somewhat depressed, as you know, because the market hasn't yet fully digested all the paper we issued to buy Rayboulds. Mather Richards believe that we should give it at least another six months. They also consider the time is approaching when we should make a quantum leap in our acquisition strategy — go for something really big rather than a series of medium sized companies. Robot is a good prospect, but the benefits relative to our size may not appear all that exciting to the professional investors and commentators. It seems to me that Mather Richards have a good point. In my view we need either to run another acquisition in tandem with Robot, and of similar size, or make a much larger single acquisition. If we follow the larger acquisition route then I think it should be outside the traditional field — possibly consumer goods is the area to go for.'

Sir Peter had listened with growing enthusiasm. His anger had long ago disappeared. He never allowed his notorious temper to get in the way of what really mattered

— making money. The thought of swallowing one of the big consumer goods companies excited him. Some of them, in his view, tended to be run by less than competent products of nepotism. Furthermore they did not accept him socially, despite his knighthood. It would give him a lot of pleasure to have some of them dependant upon him for their future.

'I like the sound of that, Charles. It is worth exploring. Fix a meeting with Mather Richards.'

As Martin and Stephen were getting out of their Rolls at Lloyd, Meisson, not a quarter of a mile away Sir Peter and Charles Walters were sipping their gin and tonics in the plush ante room to the even plusher dining room of Mather Richards.

3

Martin Chandler had thoroughly enjoyed himself at Lloyd, Meisson. The look on James Markby Smythe's face when he had cut him off in full flow to announce that his analysis of where Amalgamated stood and where it should go was all very interesting, and no doubt accurate, but boring and irrelevant, was a memory Martin Chandler would cherish for a long time. For the first time he had not felt intimidated by Markby Smythe. Fair play to Markby Smythe, he had recovered quickly and rapidly adapted to the new situation outlined. This factor had saved the Amalgamated business for Lloyd, Meisson. Martin was in no mood for anything less than enthusiastic support from his merchant bankers.

Stephen outlined the Jupiter project and, before Markby Smythe had any opportunity to raise any questions either on the project itself or on its genesis, Martin briskly revealed the birth place of Jupiter to be Jacob Wildstein in New York, ably assisted by Randles, Milne of Chicago. Markby Smythe had not batted an eyelid. He calmly enquired who was handling the matter at Jacob Wildstein and, when informed that it was Saul Arnoff, had simply intimated that he knew him well and was sure that they would be able to work well together. He professed not to know Randles, Milne other than by reputation, but felt sure that a productive working relationship would rapidly be established.

Martin quite admired the manner in which Markby Smythe had handled what must have been quite a bombshell. It smacked a little bit of a patrician assumption that the handling of the deal would stay with Lloyd, Meisson in the UK, but on the other hand there had been no attempt to elbow out the Americans. Nor had an eyebrow been raised when he had revealed that Stephen Barber would be the primary contact at Amalgamated on the project, and not Howard Irwin. Martin had had the grace to nominate Howard Irwin as the man with overall responsibility for the project, but he had left Markby Smythe in no doubt that Howard Irwin was merely a figurehead in this respect. The set up would suit Howard down to the ground. If the project turned out to be a success he could bask in the glory, and if it was a dismal failure he had a ready made scapegoat in Stephen. Martin smiled to himself. Howard, the great survivor, would survive whatever the outcome.

Martin left Lloyd, Meisson's having enjoyed the excellent lunch and claret more than he had done for many a month. He left Stephen behind to begin setting up the super-structure of the teams which would be necessary for such a major project. He felt very pleased with himself as he drove back to Amalgamated House. The adrenalin was pumping away, and he recognised the familiar, but latterly rare, urge which that engendered. First, however, he must put Howard Irwin in the picture, then Angela.

He quickly briefed Howard Irwin and asked Ann to call his wife to tell her that he had business meetings at Eaton Square that evening and was not to be disturbed. Then he rang Angela. Unlike some industrialists who, in his view, inexplicably arranged their extra-marital affairs through their secretaries, and thereby ensured that there would almost certainly be embarrassing entries in their diaries and telephone books, Martin always fixed his via his ex-directory private line which was the only telephone in the building which did not feature on the monthly print out of calls made from the building.

Angela was already waiting for him at the Eaton Square apartment. Not only was she already waiting, she was already sexually aroused. Angela enjoyed Martin Chandler's company, no more so than when it involved sex, and she knew from past experience that a summons at four o'clock in the afternoon meant sex. Angela heard the scrape of the key in the door and arranged herself in a provocative pose on the couch showing plenty of her dramatic legs. As Martin Chandler entered the room she did not rise and throw her arms around his neck. She knew that he would regard it as a false show of affection even though from her side it would be quite genuine.

'Hello Angela, nice to see you.'

Angela had hardly time to return the greeting before Martin was through the sitting room and into the bedroom having thrown his briefcase on a chair. Angela stayed where she was. She had guessed the scenario he wanted since he had given no signal for her to follow him into the bedroom. She moved over to the CD player and selected a nice sensuous piece of music and put it on, selecting automatic repeat. It would be disastrous if she had to stop to restart the music in the middle of her performance. She returned to the couch. Her pulse was beginning to race. There was nothing which gave her more excitement than stimulating a man to the point of ecstasy. It was sublime if the man chose or was able to reach his orgasm by way of normal sexual intercourse with her, but it was only marginally less stimulating for her whatever his choice of method. She was equally expert and enthusiastic at a wide variety of methods.

The bedroom door opened and Martin entered wearing his silk dressing gown. He said nothing to Angela as he walked over to his chair un-knotting the cord of his dressing gown and letting it fall open. Angela waited until he had sat down and had wriggled himself into a sprawling position of comfort. Then she rose slowly from the couch, her body moving sinuously in time with the music. Her hands moved erotically up and down her body. Slowly she unzipped the back of her dress, but she did not let it fall immediately. The tease was the thing that he enjoyed. One part of him could not wait for all to be revealed, the other part of him craved the heightening of the tension. Angela knew his needs precisely. The dress dropped and Angela quickened the sinuous movements of her body in time with the quickening pace of the music. She could see already that he was aroused, indeed it would have been difficult not to have noticed. She did not rush things and continued at her own sensuous pace. Slowly she removed her bra, again teasing and disguising the moment when she would let it drop revealing her full, pert, beautiful breasts.

Martin Chandler by this time was starting to breathe in a somewhat laboured manner as the stimulation of Angela's performance had an ever increasing effect upon him. Next went the panties in the same, slow, teasing rhythm. She always wore a suspender belt for Martin, and as the music slowed, so did her sensuous gyrations no more than two feet in front of him until she stood there quite still, her black-stockinged legs slightly apart and her tongue slowly circling her lips. He was almost screaming with desire. She took one pace forward and, looking him straight in the eye, slowly sank to her knees placing one hand on each of his thighs. Martin Chandler did not have to wait long for heaven.

Stephen meanwhile was enjoying a very different form of ecstasy. In his wildest dreams he had not expected to be pitched into something quite so big and exciting so early. After Martin had departed he had settled down with James Markby Smythe to sketch out the logistics of mounting what would be a major takeover: not the largest takeover ever seen in the UK maybe, but nevertheless one of the most significant. Meetings were set up with Saul Arnoff of Jacob Wildstein. Henry Robirch of Miller Michaels, generally regarded in the City as the top corporate lawyer, was retained; as were tax and company law counsel. By six o'clock he was satisfied that he had tied up all the experts he was likely to need and hopefully had ensured that the target company had been deprived of advisers they would have liked to use. The first meeting of what he proposed to name the 'Battle Committee' had been fixed for the following afternoon. There was just one more thing to do. He must put Howard Irwin in the picture.

'Damn,' he thought, 'I forgot to call him to cancel the four o'clock meeting.' Howard would, in theory at least, chair the Battle Committee as director responsible for corporate planning. Martin would chair the 'Strategic Committee' which would decide on bid tactics.

Stephen got back to Amalgamated House at six thirty

and went straight to Howard Irwin's office. He could hardly believe it. The office was in darkness, the desk tidy and showed every sign that Howard had gone for the day. Stephen pressed the intercom button which would put him straight through to Howard Irwin's secretary. Immediately Helen Tutton responded with a slightly puzzled sounding 'Yes?'

'Is Howard around?' And then he remembered that she was unlikely to recognise his voice, having only met him once and that briefly. 'This is Stephen Barber, I need to see him urgently.'

'I am afraid he has gone Mr Barber. He had an urgent appointment in the City. He won't be back until the morning.'

He was soon to learn that Howard Irwin's 'urgent appointments in the City' usually meant he had sloped off to one of the three squash clubs to which he belonged. One might accuse Howard of indolence in connection with his work, but no-one could accuse him of indolence in connection with his own physical well being and enjoyment.

'Can I contact him at home?' Stephen asked, expecting an affirmative reply.

'Well I don't know, he doesn't like to be disturbed at home.'

He gave up. Helen Tutton was clearly a loyal and protective secretary and he was not going to make any headway there. He had Howard Irwin's home number in the back of the company filofax he had been given. Status in the company was very much reflected in which inserts one was or was not given. Stephen Barber had the home number of all the directors in his.

He want back to his office. He had a long night in front of him as he wished to present Martin Chandler with a complete outline of what was involved in the takeover bid, how he saw it being organised within Amalgamated and how Amalgamated would interface with the outside advisers. He called in his secretary Sheila Birch and outlined what was going on and much to her surprise suggested she go home. The sting was in the tail, however, as he asked her to report at seven in the morning. Sheila would soon learn that he was more than competent on the word processor, indeed he had already requested one for his own personal use, and that often her role would simply be to tidy up what he had already created and then come up with the necessary number of copies.

He found that for complex matters he could think and create better by using the word processor himself. He could see and revise what he had written as he went along, rather than having it read back to him or have to wait for it to be typed up.

He rapidly sketched out his plan of campaign for the evening. First the paper for Martin Chandler, then some more research into the target. He smiled quietly to himself. He was about to take his first decision within the company which, whilst not earth shattering, would at least leave its mark within Amalgamated whatever happened. He would change the codename. Jupiter was a typically American piece of fancy thinking resonant of reaching for the sky and all that. No, something more pithy and direct seemed appropriate. Stephen turned over a few possibilities in his mind.

'Got it,' he said out loud, 'TAG.' Take Axehouse General. It was nice, it worked on more than one level. He headed his paper 'SECRET-OPERATION TAG'.

It had just gone midnight when Stephen Barber put the finishing touch to his paper ready for Sheila Birch to tidy up in the morning. He printed it out and then locked the floppy disc away in the double locked security safe. He thought he would try out the apartment on the top of the Amalgamated building. The key came with his filofax, yet another little unspoken indication of his status. A quiet drink before he walked home to his flat was just what he needed to stop his mind racing; besides he was curious to see what it was like. The apartment was mainly intended for out of town senior executives and top level meetings. It was luxurious with three double bedrooms, a magnificent sitting room furnished with antique furniture and some very expensive pictures. The dining room was only marginally less impressive than the sitting room. It was all very much in keeping with the period of the building. Amalgamated House had an air of solidity and permanence, unlike many of the modern excrescences it viewed from its windows. The apartment had been designed so that it could with equal facility house a smart dinner party or a small conference.

He turned the key in the door and gently pushed the door open. He was in a smallish lobby lit by low intensity hidden lighting. Opposite was a set of double doors with a table just to the left of them bearing a beautiful flower arrangement and a small pile of business magazines. As he put his hand on the door knob to enter the next room his eye caught the message emblazoned across the front of the top magazine. 'Is Sir Peter Barton Losing His Golden Touch?' Stephen picked up the magazine and started to flick through it to find the article. Then the light went out. It was obviously on a time delay of some sort. He turned the knob and entered the sitting room. It was in total darkness. He fumbled around for the light switch, eventually made contact with one and depressed it. The result was somewhat astonishing. A gentle swishing noise came from across the room and gradually the room filled with moonlight. The effect was quite beautiful, he thought as he cast his eyes around. The moonlight, augmented as he now recognised by the lights of London coming across from south of the river, was sufficient to enable him to study the array of gadgets close by what he had thought to be the light switch. The only conventional switch was indeed the one which had slowly opened the curtains with such breathtaking effect. Next to this switch was a series of what looked like tuning knobs on a modern Hi-Fi system. He tried turning each in turn. Nothing. There must be some switches elsewhere, these were obviously dimmers. In the muted light he cast his eye further along the wall beyond the dimmers and then along the wall on the other side of the doorway. Nothing.

'Come on,' he said to himself, 'you may be tired, but you are not stupid – think, dunderhead.'

With this he leant back against the wall. The room filled with brilliant light giving him a considerable fright. Then he laughed out loud. It was like the third degree, he thought to himself. Any minute someone would ask him in a sinister voice to reveal the secret. He stepped away from the wall and immediately realised what had happened. The dimmer switches were dual purpose, initially he had simply turned them up to full intensity and had only activated them when he had inadvertently depressed them.

He adjusted the lights to a more tolerable level and sought out the drinks which he eventually found in a black and gold lacquered cabinet (Queen Anne he decided) which stood near a display cabinet containing expensive looking crystal glass. He poured himself a generous measure of Glenmourangie malt whisky and thought back over the day. He could hardly believe how momentous it had been for him. To get involved in a key position on such a major acquisition on his first day almost beggared belief. The more he thought about it, the throwaway manner in which Martin Chandler had asked him if he was free for lunch, and the suggestion that he have a glance at the Jupiter file, was not indicative of impulse. It had been planned all along. If this was a correct analysis then the long period of apparent inactivity on Jupiter began to make sense. Martin Chandler was waiting for him to arrive to take effective charge of the acquisition, and in the meantime had not wanted Lloyd, Meisson to be in the picture as they would simply have run rings around Howard Irwin and organised things to suit them, and not Martin Chandler and Amalgamated. Similarly, Martin Chandler had not wanted to involve any of the other directors before he arrived in order to avoid giving the opportunity for opposition to fester. Boards of directors of large public companies tended not to be cohesive units all pulling in one direction, but either dictatorships dominated by the chairman or a series of cabals which the chairman had to try and manipulate in order to achieve a common purpose. Amalgamated, Stephen decided, was clearly on the latter pattern. Martin Chandler was no domineering dictator.

Stephen Barber's analysis of the situation had, unbeknown to him, been amply confirmed during the evening. Martin Chandler, in his brief meeting with Howard Irwin before seeking the comforts of Angela French, had asked him to set up two meetings for him that evening. One with the

34

non-executive directors at the Eaton Square apartment at seven o'clock, and a conference call with the chairmen of the Divisions of Amalgamated at nine o'clock. This left Howard Irwin himself, and Martin Chandler knew Howard Irwin would follow whatever he wanted him to do, Richard Gibbs the Personnel Director and Charles Lytton the Public Affairs Director. Martin Chandler calculated that both Gibbs and Lytton would follow his lead but he could not be absolutely certain of it. They could, however, wait until the morning as both were based in Amalgamated House and neither had a power base. Unlike the chairmen of the Divisions they did not generate profit, they were simply advisers. They nevertheless had a vote like all the other directors and could not be ignored, particularly if Martin Chandler's initial sounding of reaction indicated any pockets of resistance. He didn't want either of them to be recruited into any one else's camp.

The meeting with the non-executive directors had gone well. They all clearly had other things to do that evening and, apart from putting down markers such as wanting to know much more about Axehouse General and how it would fit in to Amalgamated, they had expressed enthusiasm for the concept and given a clear impression of wanting to get the meeting over with quickly. In his view the non-executives were not, for the most part, the influential men his predecessor fondly thought them to be. At best they were reactive. Martin Chandler could not recall any initiative of any importance emanating from any of them. He was under no illusions, however, that he was dependant upon their goodwill. They were four in number and it only needed two from the executive directors to form a majority on the Board if anything ever came to a vote. Nor did Martin underestimate the chairmen of the three Divisions. Their reaction would be somewhat uncertain as Axehouse General would be bigger than any of their individual Divisions, and each of them would feel somewhat threatened. They could be expected, therefore, to bend the ear of the non-executives. A collective approach was unlikely in his opinion as the three men involved had only one thing in common – rivalry. However, the threat to them was so great that a collective approach could not be entirely ruled out.

He mentally reviewed his non-executives to try and identify which of them, if any, might be susceptible to pressure from the Divisional chairmen. They had all been appointed by his predecessor for what he thought were shallow and unconvincing reasons. First Lord Leven-Sumpter, a former minister of the Crown who had been invited to join the Board shortly after his elevation to the peerage. As the Chairman at the time had explained to his Board, he was a man whose influence with the Government would be invaluable. Rubbish, Martin Chandler had thought at the time. He had been Postmaster General, and had been kicked upstairs to make way for a more able young man. Next Sir Ralph Hartlebury, former Permanent Secretary at the Ministry of Agriculture, Fisheries and Food. The theory here was that he would be invaluable not only because he knew his way around the Ministry, which was Amalgamated's sponsoring Ministry, but would actually be able to influence the Ministry to Amalgamated's advantage because of his former influence and continuing contacts. The first part was true, the second part was not. Sir Ralph was in the best tradition of British civil servants. It would not even cross his mind to use his former position to advantage Amalgamated, or any one else for that matter. Martin Chandler had great respect for Sir Ralph as a person, but at the time of his appointment had been absolutely certain that Sir Ralph would never use whatever influence he continued to have at the Ministry for the benefit of Amalgamated. He was nevertheless the most useful of the non-executives and chaired the various non-executive committees, such as the senior executives salary committee which, amongst other things, fixed the Chairman's salary. At least Sir Ralph read briefing papers before Board meetings, which was more than could be said for most members of the Board.

Next Humphrey Lester, former Chief Executive of Lloyd, Meisson. He was on so many boards that Martin wondered how he possibly found time to attend all the meetings, let alone understand the businesses he was meant to be giving the benefit of his experience. Furthermore, he could not quite see the point of having him on the Board at all. It was the up to date advice of Lloyd, Meisson that was needed, not that of eight years' ago. He also seemed to have the effect of inhibiting Lloyd, Meisson personnel in meetings. They tended to look to him to see his reaction rather than give the advice straight.

Finally, Joyce Bennett. 'God help us all,' Martin said aloud. His predecessor had appointed her on the basis that, as a great majority of Amalgamated's customers were women, Amalgamated should have a woman on the Board. Martin Chandler had never followed that logic. The Board dealt with the strategic management of the business, not the design of packaging and where to put the bread on the supermarket shelves. Joyce Bennett was a journalist by trade, and a very good one. Her speciality was consumer affairs, and this had been another part of the rationale of her appointment. Martin Chandler, however, had never been over impressed with her contributions to Board Meetings.

Martin sipped his whisky and turned his mind to the conference call with his Divisional chairmen. On reflection he decided to call them individually, he would retain better control that way as it avoided any cross chat which cut him out.

He called James Walker first, he usually did. It had more to do with the subconscious feeling he had that the Agricultural Division was the senior Division than any tactical or other reason. Amalgamated had, after all, had its roots in agriculture, having started in a very modest way with a fruit growing business. The Division had of course developed much wider interests over the years. The retail side had been spun off into a separate Division as had the frozen food interests. The Agricultural Division still had major food growing interests all over the world and had a sizeable agricultural chemicals business as well. James Walker was in point of fact a distant relation of Martin Chandler, both being descended from the founding Walker brothers. The family relationship benefitted neither man. Martin had only ever known James in the business environment and treated him on his merits as he would anyone else. James slighly resented Martin as he regarded himself as representing a more senior line of the Walker family, and as such should be the boss. However, he considered his time would come as he was ten years younger than Martin and, as the chairman of the senior Divison and a member of the founding family, he was the obvious choice as his successor. James Walker accordingly did not go out of his way to create waves. Nor, on the other hand, did he give anyone reason to believe that he was Martin Chandler's poodle.

James Walker had been non-commital. Yes he saw the need for Amalgamated to make a big acquisition, but was it wise to move right outside what they knew? Martin Chandler had expected a reaction of this nature. He was aware of his expectations and ambitions and clearly the addition of an entirely new Division bigger than any of the three existing Divisions would not exactly enhance James Walker's chances of becoming Chairman when he retired. He would have to tread carefully with James Walker. He would be a potentially powerful nucleus for opposition.

He called Robert Brodie next. He liked Robert Brodie and got on with him well. The two men were as different as chalk and cheese. Martin Chandler was the product of Public School and a moneyed background; Robert Brodie was a self made man who had built up his own food processing business, been taken over by Amalgamated and ultimately succeeded to the chairmanship of the Frozen Food Division. Brodie was blunt as always.

'About bloody time this company started to do something other than grow, shell and sell peas.'

An outrageous exaggeration but Martin Chandler knew what he meant. He logged him as a potential supporter but did not make the mistake of assuming him to be in the bag. Brodie would examine the proposal acquisition with a toothcomb and make his own mind up on a purely financial and strategic basis. At least he would not be drawn into alliances which had more to do with internal power and politics than what was best for the company.

Finally Terry King, chairman of the Retail Division. A highly competent professional manager who was a chartered accountant by training. Another non-commital response. Martin Chandler knew that as soon as he had put the telephone down Terry King would be on the telephone to James Walker. This owed nothing to any particular friendship between the two men but everything to ambition. Martin Chandler had long ago realised that, whilst Terry King fought James Walker hard and strong where inter-divisional matters were concerned, King had ambitions to be Chief Executive to James Walker's Chairmanship once he had gone. King had more than once suggested to him that the Chairmanship and Chief Executive roles should be split, and he had no doubt who King saw in the Chief Executive's chair once Martin Chandler was out of the way.

Martin knew life was not going to be easy, but he felt confident that if he was careful he would be able to carry a majority of the Board. It would need a fair degree of intrigue, however. Playing one man off against the other.

4

Nathan Sanson sat back, his tie was at half mast, his jacket on the back of the chair and his red patterned braces stood out boldly from his white buttoned down shirt. His accent reinforced the sartorial impression, American. At least first impressions suggested American but an acute ear would rapidly pick up inconsistencies and the vocabulary was more English than American most of the time. Mid-Atlantic did not quite describe it, two thirds of the way across maybe was nearer the mark. The impression was not entirely misleading. Mather Richards were an American investment bank and Nathan Sanson had not only worked for five years in their New York head office, but prior to that had been at Harvard doing his MBA. Sanson was English born and bred. None of this was of the slightest interest to Sir Peter Barton who stood by the ultra modern fireplace that somehow at the same time gave one the feeling of an inglenook.

'Consumer goods,' Sanson seemed almost to be savouring the taste. 'Consumer goods,' he rolled the words around in his mouth yet again. 'Yes, it might work. The profit margins and return on capital involved are much tighter than in engineering, but as against that the high turnover produces profits capable of making the earnings per share look good. That of course depends on how you finance the purchase, another large tranche of shares at this stage wouldn't exactly be hailed by the City as God's gift to capitalism. It would need to be a fairly highly leveraged bid.'

Sir Peter Barton punched the air with his cigar.

'Our balance sheet is very healthy. By the time we have

40

digested Rayboulds and sold off the bits we don't want we will have a substantial amount of cash. Increasing our borrowings will be no problem. We have an enviable track record of rapidly reducing borrowings raised to finance purchases. I don't see any great problem in financing any purchase primarily with debt. Some of the larger consumer goods outfits have massive stocks of real estate which is either under utilised, ill utilised or not utilised at all. Rationalisation of the businesses and the disposal of some of the real estate would rapidly bite into the debt taken on for the purchase. The consumer goods business is a dog eat dog affair. Everyone covets everyone else's brand names. We would be able to run an auction for even the less good ones.'

Sir Peter Barton was warming to his theme. He had not in fact had much time to get any in depth studies done either in general terms or in relation to a specific target. He was nevertheless pretty accurate in his assessment. Some of the biggest names in the consumer goods field were like Amalgamated. Profitable, yes, Well run, yes, provided you did not look too closely at the utilisation of their assets. This was particularly true of those with a manufacturing bias. Retailers were a bit more real estate conscious.

Sanson put the tips of his fingers together and made an arch.

'I agree with your general analysis, Sir Peter,' he had learned very early on not to call him Peter, 'do you have any particular target in mind?'

'Well, someone like Suttons or Makefield and Price or Amalgamated, it's your job to come up with the analysis and recommendation,'

He was not fazed in any way by the rather blunt response. That was Sir Peter Barton's style.

The three names Barton had mentioned represented three of the biggest in the consumer goods field. Each was an amalgam of manufacturing and retailing with their roots in manufacturing. Sanson quickly considered the three names.

'They are all a bit parochial, aren't they?'

'Parochial. What do you mean, Nathan?'

'Well, they all primarily operate in the UK. I think it's time you expanded your wings overseas a bit more. There are some great opportunities out there where your particular skills at making assets sweat would be well rewarded. It wouldn't do any harm to your Stock Market rating either if you were seen to be becoming more international.'

'Amalgamated has quite extensive overseas interests, Nathan. Wouldn't that be quite a good launching pad?'

'Not really, Sir Peter. They are mainly in primary producing countries. Yes, they probably have vast tracts of unused and under utilised land. The problem is that most of these primary producing countries tend also to be underdeveloped and not particularly ripe for sophisticated asset manipulation. The US of A is where you want to be. Not only are there plenty of opportunities for the application of your medicine, a US presence is essential to a growing company like yours. A quotation on the New York or American Stock Exchange would do wonders for the image of Barton Industries. This was partly the thinking behind the Robot project. Whilst it is a British company it has quite substantial US interests which would give you the kind of foothold you need. My reservations about Robot are purely doubts about whether it is big enough to keep your momentum going.'

Peter Barton chewed on the end of his cigar. He could see the logic and attractions of Sanson's argument but instinctively was unhappy with it. The idea of taking one of the large consumer goods companies appealed to him enormously. They were high profile but what was more important to Sir Peter Barton, many of them were still run by descendants of the founders. He had no high opinion of such people. In his view being born with a silver spoon in one's mouth did not necessarily impart business acumen. He would love to show some of these parasites, as he thought of them, how to really run a business. The fact that Suttons as well as Makefield and Price, which both still had a large family interest in their management, were both very profitable and highly thought of in the City did not alter his view of them. He felt the same about Amalgamated and Martin Chandler. In fact the more he thought about Amalgamated and Martin Chandler the more he liked the idea of swallowing the Big Apple and spitting out the pips. He had never forgotten how Chandler had snubbed him the first time they had met. It had been at the Annual Conference of the employers' organisation The Confederation of British Industry. Chandler had at the time been Chairman of the Marketing Committee and Peter Barton, as he then was, had been introduced to him as a potential member of the committee. Chandler had made it very clear that he did not think that someone from a tinpot little engineering firm had anything to offer to the world of marketing. Peter Barton had not only walked out of the conference, he had resigned from the CBI, regarding it as all part of the old boy network he despised.

Charles Walters could sense Sir Peter Barton's feelings, he had not worked for him all these years and survived without developing very sensitive antennae.

'Why not both?'

Sanson and Barton were temporarily nonplussed.

'Both?' they chorused almost in unison as the implications of the suggestion sunk in.

'Yes, why not?'

'At the same time?' queried Sir Peter Barton. 'Could we manage it?'

'I think not,' chipped in Sanson.

'If you are talking about physically managing it, Nathan, there is no doubt. You simply employ as many experts and journeymen as it takes. If you are talking about whether we can manage it financially, then obviously we have to take a close look at the likely cost and how we finance it. Robot we can probably get for £350 million. Let's take Amalgamated, for the sake of argument. That would cost us in the region of £1·5 billion. Are you saying that we couldn't finance a purchase of £1·85 billion, because that is what we are talking about.'

Sanson considered. The more he thought about it the more enthusiastic he became about the idea. He was cross with himself for jumping in and expressing doubts too quickly. He had been temporarily thrown by the idea of two big bids in tandem. Why should it not work?

'Yeah, it might just work and it would be a first if we announce both bids simultaneously. I had a brief chat with Leroy Viner last night. They have done some more work on the preliminary figures for Robot which they are in the process of building into a report for you. Taken together with the figures we have for the UK end, I think you should make the deal self financing within eighteen months with disposals and rationalisation. Yeah, it can work. We shall have a difficult task with the City and Institutions, however. Despite your reputation, Sir Peter, for making assets sweat and deals finance themselves, this is in a different ballpark.'

'Right,' said Sir Peter Barton. 'Work on it. I don't want to hang about. Let me have a recommendation on the targets by the end of the week. I assume it is still Robot, so you can concentrate on the consumer goods target.'

☆ ☆ ☆

Sarah Chandler put the phone down ever so gently, getting great satisfaction out of conquering her urge to slam it down. Martin's call had ruined her evening yet again. It was the anniversary of the day upon which he had proposed to her, and she had prepared a very special meal with all Martin's favourite dishes and wines; scallops in a white wine sauce accompanied by a bottle of Vouvray, then pheasant with a bottle of Gevrey Chambertin, then creme brulée and finally Roquefort cheese. Martin could select his port from the wide selection he kept in his cellar. Sarah did not expect Martin to remember what the anniversary was, he never did until she reminded him, but once they had gone through the little charade of his guessing, he always responded affectionately and entered into the spirit of the evening with enthusiasm. After such good food and wine in a relaxed and happy atmosphere he was invariably a gentle and loving bedmate. Such occasions were rare these days and becoming ever more infrequent. Sarah savoured them for Martin was a good lover.

Sarah had not told Martin what she had planned, or what the day was, when he had rung to say that he would

44

not be home that evening. She saw no point in doing so. It would not alter his plans and would simply enhance her own desperate disappointment. Her emotions were all mixed up. She suffered the loss of a loving evening and strengthened her resolve one day to get her own back for all the suffering he had caused her over the last three years or so. She knew that she would not leave him nor take a lover herself.

Stephen was enjoying his stroll along the Embankment at six-thirty in the morning. It was a beautiful, crisp, early autumn morning and there was little traffic on the roads and even less pedestrian traffic on the footpath to disturb his thoughts. He pondered how he could get to know the directors in the time that was available. The bid for Axehouse General would take some weeks to organise, but he would be heavily involved in the process and would be unlikely to have the time to visit the Divisional directors. The Head Office directors were no problem, since he would see them most days over lunch. The non-executive directors were a greater problem, as they rarely came into Amalgamated House, and he had little excuse to visit them elsewhere. Stephen Barber considered it vital that somehow he did get to know the directors, and quickly. He realised that the Axehouse bid would not necessarily be a foregone conclusion as far as acceptance within Amalgamated was concerned.

The capture of Axehouse General, or Tag as he already thought of it, must succeed. He realised that his star would be firmly associated with Tag. Succeed and his future was made, fail and he could forget any great future in Amalgamated The committed support of the great majority of the directors was essential. The Battle Committee was likely to consist of Howard Irwin in the chair, Philip Renton from the corporate department at Lloyd, Meisson, Henry Robirch from Miller Michaels, Amalgamated's solicitors, Charles Lytton the Public Affairs director and Richard Hinton the company's Group Chief Accountant. Not a terribly influential bunch, he thought, in terms of his future with Amalgamated. Furthermore, the role of the Committee, in his view, would be primarily technical and of little influence on the real management of the takeover bid except where technical considerations dictated. He knew from past experience that such Committees ran the risk of becoming less than popular with Boards of Directors when legal and extra-legal requirements, such as the City Takeover Code, prevented them from doing what they wanted in the management of a bid. The Strategic Committee was far more important, and was likely to consist of Martin Chandler, all three Divisional directors, Howard Irwin, Humphrey Lester the former Merchant Banker as representative of the non-executive directors, and James Markby Smythe. Yes, he thought, I must persuade Martin Chandler to co-opt me onto the Strategic Committee in some way. There are probably status problems in making me a full member, but being there and having day to day contact with the senior directors is vital if I am to make any impression. He decided that a two pronged attack was most likely to succeed. He would point out to Martin that a permanent link between the Strategic Committee and the Battle Committee was essential, and that this was probably better provided by Stephen than Howard Irwin who would thus be freed to concentrate on his major role in organising the finance for the takeover and massaging the City to ensure their support. Secondly, the Strategic Committee would need a Secretary and that, whilst a senior member of his Department would normally fill this role, for a project as important as Tag it would be more appropriate and efficient if he himself filled the role.

By the time he was walking up the front steps of Amalgamaged House, Stephen had sorted out his strategy in his mind and felt fully confident that it would succeed. He doubted that Howard Irwin would insist on being the link between the two committees. Howard Irwin enjoyed the quiet life and being the link between the two committees would be an arduous job. It would be of no consequence from his point of view if Howard neverthe-less was a member of the Strategic Committee. Once he was present at meetings of the Strategic Committee as of

46

right rather than as an adviser from time to time, the fact of technically not being a full member of the Committee became immaterial. He would be a major contributor both as the liaison link with the Battle Committee and as the de facto manager of the project. Yes, he thought, such an arrangement could work out well for me. I will get direct contact with all the directors who matter, and it should not be difficult to persuade Humphrey Lester that briefing meetings for his fellow non-executive directors, carried out by me of course, would be both welcome and beneficial. The strategy would also have the beneficial side effect of cementing a close relationship with Martin Chandler and also the opportunity to influence his views. In short he planned to make himself indispensible to Martin Chandler. Following a successful takeover of Axehouse General, Stephen saw himself being appointed Corporate Affairs Director. Howard was, and would be seen to be, no competition in this respect.

By eight o'clock Stephen had got the plan committed to paper. He had headed it 'Outline Plan For Management Of Tag Acquisition'. He had used the word 'Outline' because he knew that the actual paper would go to those concerned as from the Chairman. He knew from experience that if one presented someone in authority, like Martin Chandler, with what appeared to be a *fait accompli* the chances of it being changed in a fundamental respect were fairly high. If, on the other hand, one presented it as a draft and encouraged discussion on some relatively unimportant aspect and gracefully gave way to the views of superior experience and authority, then there was a very good prospect of achieving the main objectives. In pursuit of this tactic he had not detailed in his paper the proposed names for the Strategic Committee and Battle Committee. He had set them out on two pieces of paper which he would produce once the main paper had been agreed. His paper in this respect concentrated upon the duties of the two Committees and their relationship. Once he had got Martin Chandler's agreement on these aspects he anticipated no great problem in getting his proposed membership of the two Committees accepted. He was confident of steering the meeting, and its outcome, in this direction. He had already noted Martin's penchant for immersing himself in detail from their first meeting when he had been shown the incredibly detailed computerised information system.

He came out of the Chairman's office breathing a sigh of relief. His plan had succeeded, but only just. There had been two close shaves. Right at the beginning Martin had said 'we had better get Howard Irwin in on this'. His hand indeed had been about to press the remote control button to summon Ann. Fortunately for Stephen he was quick enough to stop him, and without appearing rude.

'Just a moment Chairman,' he had said, 'don't you think it might be better to get him in when you have crystallised your views. It should save time spent on unnecessary discussion.'

Martin Chandler had readily agreed. Whilst he found Howard Irwin useful in many ways he could be an exceedingly irritating nit picker. The second worrying moment had come when Martin Chandler had wanted to discuss the composition of the two Committees before going through the detailed proposals concerning their roles and relationship to each other. Stephen had been able to persuade Martin however that this would be putting the cart before the horse on the basis that, until one had a clear idea what the Committees' respective responsibilities were, it was not possible to select the appropriate composition of their members.

Howard Irwin passed Stephen on his way to the Chairman's office and stopped briefly to enquire how things were going. Stephen replied that the Chairman seemed to have everything under control and well planned.

5

Sir Peter Barton was feeling frustrated and angry but for the time being, at least, was hiding it. Later someone would suffer but not anyone of any importance. The source of his frustration and anger was the slow progress in his planned twin takeover strategy of Maxpoint Industries, codenamed 'Robot', and of Amalgamated, codenamed 'Castor'. Sir Peter Barton had suggested that the codename for Maxpoint Industries be changed to Pollux. He was rather pleased with the imagery of the classical mythological twins. The idea had been knocked on the head by Nathan Sanson who had pointed out that newspapers often got hold of the codenames of bids, and there was plenty of mileage in headlines such as 'Are Barton Industries making a Bollocks of Pollux?' Sir Peter Barton had insisted upon keeping Castor as a codename, being quite adamant that none of the financial journalists had the intelligence and education to associate Castor with Pollux.

This little debate had not put Sir Peter Barton in the best of moods for the rest of the meeting. When Sanson had revealed that it would take four to six weeks to get to the stage of even announcing the bids, Sir Peter Barton had had great difficulty in keeping his temper. Sanson tried to explain that they were not dealing with a straightforward bid for a single company well within the financial compass of Barton Industries, but with a complex twin bid that would not only stretch Barton Industries financially, but would require a considerable effort to persuade the City and the Institutional Investors that the bids were a viable proposition for Barton Industries. There was little or nothing to be gained by rushing matters. Both Maxpoint

Industries and Amalgamated would still be there in six weeks' time.

Sir Peter Barton reluctantly accepted the advice, but when Sanson had gone he asked Charles Walters to stay behind.

'Charles, I do not want these smart-assed Investment Bankers justifying their enormous fees by spinning this out, and nor do I want the lawyers justifying their large fees by raising all sorts of piddling legal obstacles. They only raise them usually to show how clever they are in getting round them. If it is possible to get round them they are not problems in the first place in my book.'

Walters thought rapidly. He knew that there were some very complex issues. For starters, the structures adopted for the deals were critical from a tax point of view. The deals would also inevitably need substantial borrowing to finance them. This would necessitate not only going to the Trustees of their existing Loan Stocks to get dispensations from the borrowing limits imposed by the Trust Deeds, but also going to the Barton Industries shareholders to increase the borrowing limits enshrined in the company's Articles of Association. The latter aspect of borrowing limits was no real problem as it could be put to the shareholders at the same time as approval was sought for the two bids as the City Takeover Code required. The Trustees of the Loan Stocks were a different kettle of fish. They were obliged in law to protect the interests of the Loan Stockholders. In effect Barton Industries would have to persuade the Trustees that the two bids were a viable proposition. This was no mean feat in a short span of time. Charles decided to face the wrath of Sir Peter sooner rather than later. This way the markers were down if the going got sticky later.

'I quite agree with you, Sir Peter. However, I don't think we should underestimate the complexity of what we are undertaking. There are certain aspects which are totally outside our control, like getting dispensations from the Trustees of our Loan Stocks to enable us to increase our borrowing powers. This is not just a formality. We have to persuade them that the bids are viable, and also try to avoid their seeking to increase the interest rates on the Loan

Stocks as a quid pro quo for their consent. All this takes time.'

'I hear you, Charles, but I rely on you to keep things moving as quickly as possible.'

Barton's hand was already reaching for the telephone and Walters knew he was dismissed. He noticed it was the direct outside line Sir Peter was reaching for and gave an inward sigh. He knew the signs.

The girl thudded back against the wall, sliding down into a sitting position. Her eyes showed a combination of disbelief and fear. She had been a high class call girl long enough to have come across some pretty odd behaviour and requests but never anything quite like this. The man had sounded perfectly normal on the telephone. Although she knew this was no guarantee of normal behaviour she had never before experienced such instantaneous and cold blooded violence.

The door bell of her very smart apartment had rung within half an hour of the telephone call. She had looked through the spy hole and seen a smartly dressed, well built man. She judged him to be in his late fifties, but she was wrong. Satisfied, she had opened the door and before she had had even time to say 'hello' a hand had come out, grabbed her blouse ripping it down the front, whilst the other hand gave her a forcible shove backwards against the wall.

'Get up.'

Emily Wishart stayed where she was, breathing hard, her ample breasts heaving inside her wispy black bra.

'Get up.'

This time Emily got up. She pressed herself against the wall as if somehow this would keep him away from her. Sir Peter Barton stepped forward, his face quite expressionless. His hand came out and took hold of her bra between her breasts. His grip tightened and with a twisting pull he tore off her bra. Her magnificent breasts bounced free. He looked at them briefly and quickly switched his gaze to her face. What next, wondered Emily.

Two hands came out, this time grabbing her skirt at the bottom and lifting it. He showed no curiosity as to what was underneath. His eyes continued to bore into hers. The skirt ripped from hem to waist, revealing Emily's long, shapely legs sheathed in white stockings held up by the minutest suspender belt and superimposed with brief black and red panties with two little bows at each side.

'Take it off.'

Emily assumed he meant what remained of the skirt and promptly unbuckled the belt and let the skirt fall to the floor. Emily, with a detachment that surprised her, wondered when the direct violence on her body would start.

Sir Peter Barton stepped back a pace and this time studied her now very provocative body. He took another pace forward, his eyes again fixed on her face. The hands came forward again, this time towards her hips. Emily braced herself. The hands touched her hips but instead of grabbing her panties they started slowly to work their way up her body. Please God, thought Emily, don't let him hurt me too much. The hands reached her breasts. Emily closed her eyes. A thumb slid under each breast with the fingers cupping the sides. Slowly the thumbs slid up each breast and the fingers moved round towards her nipples. Then they met and each nipple was gripped between a thumb and forefinger. Gradually the pressure increased. Emily gasped involuntarily and quickly suppressed it. She was determined not to scream but wondered how much she could take before she did. She kept the palms of her hands firmly pressed against the wall, resisting the temptation to try and tear his hands away.

Suddenly he let go. Emily opened her eyes. He was smiling.

'Get me a whisky.' Emily needed no second invitation to move away from the wall. She stepped over her torn clothing, turned and walked into her sitting room. Sir Peter Barton followed her.

'You're an intelligent, clever girl.'

Emily did not reply. She knew now that she had been right not to resist. She had disarmed him with her passivity.

Peter Barton sat down in one of the two comfortable looking armchairs. Emily was surprised to see this as she turned from the side table where she kept the drinks. She had expected him to have sat on the sofa, most clients did, obviously regarding it as a better venue for the business in hand than an armchair. She handed him his drink, hesitated briefly to see whether he would indicate where he wanted her to be and, in the absence of any indication, fetched herself a drink and sat down in the other armchair.

An hour later Emily let him out. In bed he had been gentle and almost loving. Emily had set out to meet his every wish, as she still felt an undercurrent of violence which she had no wish to provoke. In the event, his needs had been simple and conventional. She had almost enjoyed it. She certainly enjoyed the size of the present he had given her, but she was under no illusion that had she resisted the initial onslaught or become hysterical, she would now be black and blue.

The chauffeur was waiting outside patiently. He was used to waiting without knowing how long. He also knew when Peter Barton was visiting a woman, not only from the addresses where he took him but also from his demeanour. He spoke hardly a word to his chauffeur on these occasions, either on the way or on the return journey. Normally he was very chatty.

Sir Peter Barton sat back in the rear seat of his Rolls Royce. He felt strangely calm and satisfied, despite not having cleansed himself of his inner anger by beating up and then having violent intercourse with a prostitute. He always chose prostitutes for this as they could always be bought off and comebacks were unlikely. Usually he needed the girl to fight to give him his release. He realised that once he had begun to look upon this one as a woman he had reacted to her as a normal male would react to a half naked beautiful woman. Although violence had hitherto given him a release from his inner anger, it usually left him with a sense of shame and a resolve not to indulge himself in this manner again. Maybe he had found a better, and more satisfying, way of gaining his release.

Stephen Barber looked around the Boardroom which was

53

dominated by a large oval mahogany table matching the mahogany panelling. Around the walls were portraits of all the former Chairmen, each with its small identifying brass plate. The chairs, too, were mahogany, with deep red leather seats and backs. The room exuded an aura of permanence and solidity. In front of each chair was a red leather writing case with a name embossed in gold and flanked by what looked like rolled gold biros and pencils. Charles Timpson, the Company Secretary, had explained that he would be sitting immediately to his right which in turn was to the right of the Chairman. The Chairman's place was precisely at the broadest part of the oval table and back to the window. It was marked not only by the high backed chair with arms, but also by what at first glance looked like a particularly elegant chess clock. There were two dials and on top of the casing two brass buttons. On closer examination one dial was a perfectly ordinary clock face and the other a rather sophisticated stop watch. The stop watch not only had a hand for counting off the time but also another hand, which could presumably be set for a predetermined time. Within the face of the stop watch there were two small lights, one green and one red. He guessed that these were in some way related to the hand that was capable of being preset.

Stephen walked round to his place and was pleasantly surprised to find that not only had he qualified for the red leather writing case with notepaper inside, but also merited his name being embossed on the front. He noted that he had a clear sight of the Chairman's clocks. The clocks could be a source of amusement, he thought, as the Chairman was clearly in the habit of giving those present a predetermined span of time in which to speak. His seat was just on the curve of the table, which would give him a clear view of all those around the table without his having to move his head. Very convenient, he thought, as a lot could be learnt about individuals from observing their reactions in group situations.

He opened his folder and inside found a notepad and a seating plan. On his right was Howard and then a blank space, intended no doubt for Markby Smythe when he joined the meeting. Next round was Robert Brodie, followed by Charles Lytton, Terry King, Humphrey Lester, James Walker, Lord Leven-Sumpter, Richard Gibbs, Joyce Bennett and, finally, immediately on the Chairman's left, Sir Ralph Hartlebury. Very cleverly organised, he thought. The chairmen of the Divisions were separated from each other, thus preventing any little alliances being formed during debate. To the left and right of the Chairman were the two people he would most likely want quiet words with during meetings. Charles Timpson, who was responsible for all the formalities and administration of the meetings, and Sir Ralph Hartlebury who, whilst not formally designated Deputy Chairman, clearly fulfilled that role. Those whose views mattered least, like Stephen himself and Joyce Bennett, were at such an angle to the Chairman that he would need physically to move his head for them to catch his eye. Martin had made little effort to disguise his poor opinion of Joyce Bennett when he had given Stephen a pen picture of the Board members. The remainder of the Board were all in direct eye contact with the Chairman without his having to swivel his head.

It was eight thirty in the morning and Stephen had already had a meeting with James Markby Smythe and the Chairman. Howard should have been at the meeting but had called him late the previous evening to ask him whether he was happy to handle it on his own. Stephen had been delighted and had rapidly set up a meeting with the Chairman for eight o'clock so that he and Markby Smythe could take him through the broad outline of how the bid for Axehouse would be handled.

Timpson came bustling into the Boardroom carrying a pile of Minute Books and small textbooks. Stephen immediately recognised the City Takeover Code, the Stock Exchange rule book known to all as the 'Yellow Book' from its colour, and books on secretarial practice and company law.

'Oh, aren't you going into the ante-room for coffee? You are invited you know.'

'Next time maybe. I think it better if the Chairman introduces me formally at the meeting rather than for me to go round introducing myself. I have only met Gibbs, Lytton and King so far.'

What Stephen did not tell Timpson was that he wanted to study the faces of the Directors when he was introduced in the remoter atmosphere of the Boardroom. He had no doubt that all of them would greet him with courtesy on a face to face introduction but doubted that he would get an equally responsive reception in the Boardroom.

The clock in front of the Chairman was showing a minute to a quarter to nine. The Directors drifted in from the ante-room. Within seconds the door at the opposite end of the Boardroom opened and Martin Chandler strode in. He went straight to his seat and sat down, smiling greetings to the members of the Board as they took their places and caught his eye.

At exactly eight forty-five Martin opened the meeting.

'Good morning lady and gentlemen. Thank you for making the effort to reorganize your busy schedules to attend this meeting. Before I deal with the formality of the Minutes of the last meeting and get down to real business I would like to introduce Stephen Barber to those of you who have not met him, although I think you all know the important role he has come to fulfil.'

During this brief introduction Stephen Barber studied the members of the Board. Joyce Bennett had not even bothered to stop bending the ear of Richard Gibbs next to her. Richard Gibbs in turn was clearly trying not to appear discourteous to Joyce Bennett whilst at the same time trying to direct his attention to what Martin was saying. Sir Richard Hartlebury nodded briefly in his direction at the mention of his name and smiled a welcome, as did Humphrey Lester and Terry King. Lord Leven-Sumpter seemed to be studying something above Stephen's head and did not even flicker. Brodie was scribbling something on his pad and did not raise his head. James Walker gave him a curt nod. The rest he did not take particular note of as he had met them on a number of occasions within the office before. Howard put his hand on Stephen's forearm and whispered, 'Welcome, old boy.'

Stephen smiled back for those who chose to acknowledge him, mentally noting that Brodie was probably the only one who mattered he would need to work on to gain acceptance. James Walker would need a little work, Joyce

Bennett only merited everyday courtesy and Lord Leven-Sumpter probably would react favourably to being treated as if he mattered.

The formality of the Minutes of the previous meeting was quickly dealt with and Martin Chandler turned his attention to the main business of the day. He made a little speech to the effect that the decision to be taken by the Board was crucial to the future of Amalgamated, whichever way it went. A vote against the proposed takeover of Axehouse General was a vote against Amalgamated spreading its wings and growing into a multi-faceted powerful company. Two options were left for the company's future. Either it could stay as it was or it could expand by buying related businesses. On either scenario Martin Chandler was of the view that Amalgamated would itself fall prey to a predator. Time was not on the company's side. The City had become disenchanted with its performance and as a result the shares were underperforming the market. If this was allowed to go on for much longer its capacity to mount a credible takeover bid of any significance would be severely prejudiced.

Stephen studied the faces of the Board members during this introduction. None of them showed a great deal of reaction except for Howard who, with great frequency, nodded his head in assent in a manner which he felt sure was meant to be sagacious. Joyce Bennett was fiddling in her handbag throughout Martin's assessment, giving every impression of not having heard a word of it.

'Before we go any further I would like, with your agreement, to ask James Markby Smythe to join us.'

Without waiting for any indication one way or the other whether the Board did or did not agree, Martin turned to Timpson and told him to go and fetch Markby Smythe.

James Markby Smythe entered the Boardroom and took his seat as if he belonged there. He exuded an air of languid ease which was often mistaken by those who did not know him very well for a lack of interest and competence. He was in fact a highly competent operator and a very tough nut in negotiations.

At Martin's request Markby Smythe gave a succinct analysis of the rationale for picking Axehouse General as a target, how the acquisition would be financed, and what was needed by way of lobbying in the City to get the large institutional shareholders on the company's side.

Martin thanked Markby Smythe and suggested that before questions were thrown at him it would be helpful for the Board to have a projection of how Axehouse would be assimilated into Amalgamated and what the financial benefits would be. Martin suggested that they would be wasting their time if, after assimilation and reorganisation, Axehouse did not make a significantly greater contribution to the profits of Amalgamated than the company presently made for their shareholders.

This was Stephen's cue. He asked Timpson to pass round the folders he had prepared and suggested to the Board that, rather than try and read them there and then, it would be better for them to be used as aide memoires for the subsequent discussion. All the information in the folders would be presented on screen and explained.

He got up from his chair and moved over to the series of flip charts that were already in place on an easel where each member of the Board could see it without too much trouble. He spent a few brief moments arranging his notes on the small table beside the easel and then pressed a small button on the wall; a projection screen slid silently down from the ceiling. He had spent some time before the meeting making quite sure that the slide projector was properly lined up to the screen and in sharp focus.

It took Stephen nearly forty minutes to get through the presentation. This was fifteen minutes longer than he had estimated and was largely due to Joyce Bennett and Lord Leven-Sumpter continually asking for clarification.

'Well, there you have it. Thank you Stephen. It is a lot of information to assimilate all at one go, but I think the summary slide which has been left up encapsulates the critical information. If all goes as projected we strengthen our Balance Sheet and very rapidly improve our earnings per share over current levels once the assimilation and rationalisation process has taken place. This in turn, as James pointed out, will improve our share price and give us a strong base for further acquisitions. There will, of course, be an initial drop in our earnings per share because of the new shares we shall be issuing to part finance the purchase. Can I have your views please?'

James Walker started off the debate.

'Chairman, we have seen a very professional and interesting presentation of all the financial information and how Axehouse General would be assimilated into Amalgamated from a purely financial and structural point of view. Nothing has been said about how it will relate to the existing Divisions.'

Martin realised immediately that what James Walker was really asking was which Divisional Chairman, if any, would have responsibility for Axehouse and thus the enormously increased power that would go with it.

'Well, as I think is obvious from the figures we have seen, Axehouse is considerably larger than any of the existing Divisions. It is also in a business that is totally different from any of our existing businesses. On both these counts it is clear that it will have to be a Division of its own and not an adjunct of any existing Division. As far as personalities are concerned it is far too soon to speculate. I intend to approach Sir Richard Brookes, the Chairman of Axehouse General, if of course the Board approves the proposal to make a bid for the company today, to see whether it can be done on a friendly basis with their Board recommending the bid to their shareholders. I think it highly unlikely that either Sir Richard or his Board would agree to this, but you never know. If they do, that is one scenario and consideration will have to be given as to how Sir Richard fits into the scheme of things if he personally wishes to join us. If, as I anticipate, the bid is strongly resisted, that is another kettle of fish.'

James Walker was not particularly happy with this reply. Nor were Brodie or King. Each could see that his position of power might be eroded. James Walker decided not to pursue it further for the present. He also decided that he would back the proposed takeover. It made good commercial sense. The presentations by James Markby Smythe and Stephen Barber had been superb. Indeed, the only real argument was the philosophical one of whether or not a consumer goods business like Amalgamated should be venturing into financial services. James Walker was confident one of the non-executive Directors would raise this, probably Sir Richard Hartlebury.

Joyce Bennett raised it and it became clear that her worry was not so much a philosophical as a practical one. What did Amalgamated know about financial services, she asked. Wouldn't Amalgamated be dabbling in something they knew nothing about with all the risks that that entailed?

Martin pointed out that Axehouse would be coming along with a highly talented and experienced team and there were plenty of very competent people who would jump at the chance to head up a business as large as Axehouse General within Amalgamated.

The discussion went on for an hour. It was obvious to Stephen that there was a clear consensus in favour of making the bid. Brodie and King both in their own way put down markers to indicate that how Axehouse would fit into Amalgamated was still very much a matter for debate. Sir Ralph Hartlebury had demonstrated an awesome capacity for taking complex detail on board and ferreting out the weaknesses. Stephen was both impressed and in no short measure relieved that he and James Markby Smythe had been able to satisfy Sir Ralph on all the points he had raised. Humphrey Lester had addressed most of his questions to Markby Smythe and it was apparent that he found the experience an uncomfortable one. He was clearly still in some awe of Humphrey Lester. The rest of the Board contributed very little.

'I think the consensus is that we proceed with the bid,' Martin said more as a statement of fact than as a question. He quickly looked to each member of the Board. No-one contradicted him.

6

Sarah Chandler sat back in the large armchair in Miles Wartnaby's Park Lane penthouse. Miles Wartnaby, her father, was nearer seventy than sixty but did not look it. His hair was still thick and, despite the fact that it was now silver, it tended to flatter his age rather than exaggerate it. The overall impression was one of power and indeed, most people were afraid of him despite his legendary charm. BCI had been a very successful conglomerate when he had taken over the chairmanship eight years before. He had privately set himself the target of doubling the size of the company within five years and trebling it within ten. Not only had he achieved his targets with ease, he had comfortably exceeded them. BCI was now four times the size, and one of the top five UK companies.

'Well, Sarah, how are things? I haven't seen much of you for a few months.'

Sarah immediately felt guilty. She rarely came up to town these days now her mother was no longer around.

'Pretty boring by and large,' replied Sarah. 'Martin seems to be home less and less these days.'

'You ought to stay up in London with him more often. You of all people ought to know the demands that are placed upon the time of men in Martin's position.'

'Oh, I've tried. I used to finish up lying on the bed and watching television on my own. I can do that at home. As for having any of my friends around, that was out of the question as well, even during the day. When he wants peace and quiet or maximum secrecy for a meeting he uses Eaton Square and he expects it to be available at the drop of a hat.'

Miles knew his daughter well and realised there was

more to it than she was letting on.

'What is Martin up to these days?'

Sarah for a brief moment thought her father was talking about Martin's personal life but quickly decided that it was his business life that interested her father. BCI was a notorious wheeling dealing company under Wartnaby's stewardship and often took significant positions in the shares of other companies. These were almost invariably short term operations but just occasionally they blossomed into full blown takeovers. Sarah felt very tempted to tell her father that she suspected something big was in the offing as Martin had spent little time at home in recent weeks. However, her loyalty to Martin overcame her desire to hurt him. She knew from the past that when he was under pressure of work he needed sex to relax. She certainly had not been providing it recently, so who was?

'Oh, he never tells me what he is up to at work. In any case, even if he did, you know I couldn't tell you; particularly you. I may not be the most knowledgeable person on what is going on in the world of high finance, but I am fully aware of your reputation, papa!'

Miles smiled and indulged himself in one of his deep-throated chuckles. 'You may fool others, but you don't fool me. I know how astute you are and that you take quite a considerable interest in what's going on at both Amalgamated and BCI. You have large stakes in both companies. If you want help you know you can always come to me.'

'Thank you daddy, I have always known that I could.'

Sarah wondered what he had meant by his offer of help but felt it best not to pursue the point.

Miles had sensed Sarah's slight bewilderment at his offer and correctly concluded from her answer that now was not the time to elaborate upon what he meant. He knew his daughter well enough to realise that she would go away and analyse his remarks, almost certainly come to the right conclusion as to what he was getting at, and store the information away for future action if the situation demanded.

He changed the subject in his usual smooth manner and thoroughly enjoyed the half hour Sarah stayed. They both had a great passion for the theatre and music and got almost as much joy out of discussing them as they did out of the performances they had seen or heard.

Sarah sat back in the taxi turning over in her mind what had passed between her father and herself. She decided to try and find out what Martin was up to at Amalgamated. It wouldn't be difficult, he always brought his briefcase home and she knew the combination which would open it.

Martin put the telephone back on its cradle. There had been no reply. He wondered where Sarah was. He must remember to call again after the party. He thought of it as a party although it was only him, Angela and a friend of hers Martin had not met. Martin had been exhausted after the day's events. The Board meeting had been a success, with no opposition to the Tag proposal. It had been very clear that Martin would have a major job keeping his Divisional chairmen happy, however. He made a mental note to have a word with Stephen in the morning to get him to propose a scheme of things to keep the Divisional chairmen on the rails.

The Board meeting had not been the end of it. A succession of meetings had followed with the Strategic Committee, Lloyd, Meisson and Miller Michaels. Martin always found meetings with outside professionals a strain. For a reason he had never been able to define he always felt intimidated in the presence of lawyers. In the event it had not been as bad as he had feared. Stephen Barber had been magnificent. He not only had a complete grasp of all the commercial and financial implications of the bid, but appeared to have an immediate understanding of the subtle legal points that were raised and discussed. What a contrast to Howard Irwin, thought Martin. If Howard had been in the meeting on his own with Martin he would have been of little or no help to Martin except on the purely financial side. He would have bumbled along giving a very good impression of understanding what was going on but in practice contributing nothing original.

By six thirty, however, Martin had had enough. He was

meeting Stephen again at nine thirty to go through the timetable he would have prepared by then, and meanwhile he had two important things to do. Ring Angela and get her to come round to the Eaton Square apartment to relax him; and ring Sarah to let her know he would not be home that night. He had dialled Angela first as soon as he had got into the apartment. On his way to the apartment anticipation of Angela had aroused an expectant feeling in his groin. Maybe something a little different this time, he thought. Two girls together would be something new and exciting for him. He had always had a latent voyeuristic desire of watching two girls make love to each other as a prelude to making love to him, but had never had the courage to arrange it. He had wondered how Angela would react to the suggestion, and indeed whether she would be able to arrange a partner at short notice, even if she was willing. He need not have worried. Angela had accepted the suggestion as if it was the most natural request in the world. What Martin did not know was that Angela, like many of her kind, had a series of relationships with other high class call girls. The relationship served a dual purpose. A business one to meet requests such as Martin's, and, in some cases, a purely personal one when a genuine loving relationship developed. This had happened between Angela and Fiona. Indeed, it had been Fiona who had got Angela into the call girl business. They had been lovers on and off since school days where the repressions of boarding school had led initially to tentative sexual fumblings which had grown in to a full blown love affair. This had survived school days and continued on a more intermittent basis into adulthood.

Fiona had become a call girl within twelve months of leaving school and had got Angela into it two years later. It had started when Fiona had suggested that Angela accompany her on a threesome date on the basis that the man only wanted to watch, and Angela need neither fear being molested by the man whilst she and Fiona made love, nor look to see what he was up to whilst they did. After all, Fiona had argued, why not get well paid for doing something one enjoyed? Angela had needed a lot of persuading and a lot of gin to give her courage to go through with it when the time came. In the event she had found that her enjoyment was enhanced by making love with Fiona in front of a man, and what was more found she positively wanted to make love with the man afterwards and was very disappointed when he had made it clear this was not on the agenda.

Martin looked at his watch. The girls ought to be here soon, he thought. Outside two taxis were proceeding around Eaton Square towards the entrance to Martin Chandler's apartment. As the first one drew up, and two very attractive young women got out, the occupant of the second taxi quickly ordered the driver to drive past the first taxi and pull up two doors along. Sarah looked back through the window of the taxi. The taller of the two girls pressed the button of Martin's entrance phone.

'Victoria Station, driver.'

Martin looked at his watch. Christ, he thought, it's gone ten and I haven't rung Sarah. The evening had been such a fantastic experience that all other thoughts had gone out of his head. He had never before experienced such an acute sense of sexual arousal without actually being touched as he had when watching Angela and Fiona performing. Looking back upon it, Martin was sure they must be lovers and not merely two attractive girls who put on a show for money. The way they had slowly undressed each other, gently caressing and kissing every erogenous part as it was exposed could, of course, have been purely mechanical. The heavier, shorter breaths and little moans could easily have been counterfeit, but the looks of sheer devotion in their eyes and the screaming, uninhibited climax of orgasm told another story. They had not sought mutual orgasm, but each had quite obviously got great satisfaction from bringing the other gently and lovingly to an almost un-bearable pitch of enjoyment. Watching, Martin had found it necessary to exercise great control to prevent himself from reaching a spontaneous orgasm. It was the most erotic thing he had ever seen. When they had switched their attentions to him, it had been almost unbearable. His sensations had been so heightened that he had got to the stage where he found it difficult to identify exactly where the hands and lips were caressing his body. His whole body seemed to be alive with tingling arousal. Eventually, when they had both switched the attentions of their mouths and hands to his groin, he had had to call a halt, the exquisite pain had become unbearable.

By the time they had left it had gone past nine thirty and Martin was in a state of pleasurable exhaustion, all worries and stress excised. Until he remembered Sarah. Surely she must be home as she would be expecting him? He was about to put the telephone down when she answered.

'Rayworth two double seven seven.' The voice was without expression.

'Hello darling, sorry I could not ring before. We have got something big on, and I have been stuck in meetings until now.'

He knew it was weak. Even under the most extreme pressure he had always found time to ring Sarah or, at the very least, get a message to her.

Sarah resisted the temptation to observe that she had assumed that he had had something big on which was by now presumably no longer tumescent.

'Are you coming home tonight?'

There was no invitation or interest in the voice. She might just as well have been asking the time of the next train. Martin's heart sank. There was no point in going home now. It would be well past eleven by the time he got there and he had meetings from eight thirty in the morning.

'I'm sorry darling, there is no way I can make it. I have to be back in the office by eight thirty tomorrow morning.'

Hmph, thought Sarah, the time was when he used to get home past midnight, give her an athletic and enjoyable tumble in bed and get up at six o'clock next morning to make an eight o'clock meeting in town. Sarah did not reply. She put the telephone down with controlled anger, fighting back the tears.

Martin sighed. The telephone call had taken the gloss off the evening. He made a note for the next day; get a nice present for Sarah. He knew it would not in itself mend the fences, but it might help a little. He resolved that after Axehouse General was safely in the bag he would take at least three weeks off and take Sarah wherever she wanted to go in the world, regardless of expense. It would be a second honeymoon.

Sarah's mind wandered back to her meeting with her father earlier that day. Although Sarah knew Martin had been lying on the telephone when trying to excuse his absence and lack of communication, she was also certain that something big was in the offing. Martin had spent far more nights than usual in town recently and had far more calls at home late into the night when he had been at home. Yes, something big was on. She would find out what it was and have a quiet chat with her father. He would know how best to take advantage of both the situation and of Martin.

Stephen sank down into his armchair and took a considerable swig from his whisky and water. The day had worked out very well. He was more than satisfied that the bonding between him and Martin was now firmly in place. He had steered him through a potentially difficult meeting with the lawyers and merchant bankers. Martin had had the grace to thank him for holding his hand during the meeting. His opinion of Martin Chandler grew. Few men in his position were, in Stephen's experience, big enough even tacitly to admit to a subordinate that they were dependant upon them in certain circumstances.

Stephen thought back over the incredibly action-packed three weeks he had been with Amalgamated. Almost his entire waking hours had been spent on Tag. Jacob Wildenstein & Co must be kept on board. He had not spoken to Saul Arnoff for over two weeks. There was little for them to do at this stage, but they would be needed to help with things like Securities Exchange Commission and Federal Trade Commission filings in due course. Furthermore, they had done all the initial analysis of Axehouse General and recommended them as a bid target to Amalgamated. Stephen realised that Martin had used Amalgamated's New York investment bankers primarily as a means of geeing up Lloyd, Meisson into a more aggressive posture, but it was important not to alienate them at this stage by giving them the impression that they had been dropped. He doubted that James Markby Smythe had been keeping Jacob Wildenstein in the picture. He looked at his watch. Ten forty-five. Four forty-five in New York. He picked up his telephone and dialled the Jacob Wildenstein number.

'Saul Arnoff please.'

'One moment please, sir.'

'Hello Stephen,' came the friendly voice at the other end. 'How are things at Amalgamated and on Jupiter?'

Stephen Barber never ceased to be impressed by the way in which most Americans in business seemed to have the knack of putting you at your ease and giving the impression that you were their most important client. He had fully expected to be brushed off initially. Instead Saul Arnoff had greeted him as if he was a friend of long standing.

'Fine thanks, Saul, and so are Amalgamated and Jupiter; although it's now Tag.' Stephen quickly explained the change of codename and brought Saul Arnoff up to date with where matters stood.

'That sounds great, Stephen, keep me in the picture, I am sure we can help considerably in seeing this baby put safely to bed. We can organise all the pain in the arse bureaucracy for you and, if you need any help in the market during the bid, we can help you there. We would, of course, work in close liaison with your UK brokers. I know Chris Beaumont of Hawkesmeres very well. I'll get Dick Rensberg, our filings expert, to contact you to set up a procedure for collating all the information necessary for the Securities Exchange Commission, and any others we need to do.'

Stephen agreed and said that he would be putting Alan Packman in his Department in charge of all the statutory filings that needed to be made.

A thought occurred to Stephen as he was speaking. Jacob Wildenstein & Co. were not Amalgamated's regular American investment bankers, Evans Kramer were. If it was not general knowledge that Wildenstein were acting for Amalgamated there might be circumstances where this could be put to advantage.

'Saul, before I ring off there is just one point of detail I would like to check. Does anyone else know that you are advising us in this matter?'

'Not to my knowledge, Stephen. Why do you ask?'

'Well, it occurs to me that there might be circumstances where it could be to our advantage for it not to be known that you are advising us.'

'OK I get your message but there is one small problem. We have only been hired on a one-off basis for this transaction. We would need some sort of retainer for the future if we were to act in your interests in a way which might involve turning other potential business away.'

'No problem. Shall we say a rolling yearly retainer determinable by either side by six months' notice?'

'Fine by me. I will talk with my partners to confirm and also come up with a fee structure.'

Stephen smiled to himself. Typically American, he thought. No suggestion of a suggested fee structure for discussion. It would be a take it or leave it fee and that would depend on their assessment of future business prospects generated by Amalgamated.

'Thanks Saul. I look forward to hearing from you. I'm sure we will be doing a lot of business together in the future. Bye.'

Stephen put the telephone down well satisfied with his call. He had established a good rapport with Saul Arnoff and felt sure he would come in useful at some stage. He made a mental note to talk to Martin Chandler about their American investment bank representation. He was firmly of the view that Wildenstein would be a far more dynamic outfit than Evans Kramer. He picked up the telephone again and began dialling Alan Packman's number, but changed his mind. After eleven was somewhat uncivilised and there was nothing Alan Packman could do before morning in any event.

7

James Walker moved away from the display cabinet with a large Waterford cut glass tumbler in his hand and wandered over to the Sheraton sideboard where drinks stood on a silver tray. He poured himself a generous measure of Bell's whisky and added as much Malvern water. He said nothing as he moved around the room bent on his purpose, but his eyes and ears missed nothing. Robert Brodie and Terry King were sitting in armchairs cradling their drinks, avoiding each other's eyes. James Walker smiled inwardly to himself. He had gained the initiative. Immediately after the Board meeting he had suggested to the other two that they meet in the company flat to mull over the events of the day. Brodie and King had both obviously thought that he was suggesting an impersonal discussion of the implications of the Axehouse General bid. Instead James Walker had come straight to the point. How would the advent of Axehouse General within Amalgamated affect their own positions? He had expressed the view that acquiring Axehouse General would be good for Amalgamated. The other two had nodded their assent. He had then grasped the real nettle, pointing out that each of them had aspirations to step into Martin Chandler's shoes one day, and that where and how Axehouse General fitted into Amalgamated would have a critical influence upon this. At this point James Walker had left them to fetch his drink. He had deliberately let the other two fix their drinks and sit down whilst he had remained standing to deliver his little time-bomb, thus giving him the opportunity to move away from them and observe their reaction at a distance. Critically he wanted to see if there were any signs of closing the ranks between them. James was pleased to see that there were not.

'I think it is unlikely that Sir Richard Brookes will agree to a friendly takeover and accordingly the chances of his joining the Board are almost certainly remote. If he did, of course, it would seriously prejudice each of our individual positions. He is only in his early fifties and would demand the Deputy Chairmanship with a clear view to becoming Chairman when Martin goes. Bearing in mind our own ages, we would all wave farewell to any chance of further advancement. What we have to do, on the assumption that he will not join the Board, is agree a common approach that causes the least prejudice to each of us. Maintain the status quo in fact, and ensure that whoever joins the Board to represent the Axehouse General viewpoint does so in a capacity that has as little influence as possible.'

James turned to Robert Brodie, inviting his opinion. Brodie hesitated. In common with both of the others his initial private thoughts had been along the lines of how best to go about getting Axehouse General under his control.

'I don't disagree with you in general terms James, but I doubt if any one of us would voluntarily give up the opportunity of getting Axehouse General under our wing if we could.'

Terry King nodded in agreement. James remained impassive.

'If we squabble amongst ourselves, I agree we could all miss out with some outside party coming in and upstaging us.'

Brodie had noticed King's nod of assent and turned to him for support. King had his own ideas of how best to turn the advent of Axehouse General to his own advantage. He firmly believed that Amalgamated needed a Chief Executive to run the day to day business of Amalgamated, and the Chief Executive in this plan was naturally to be himself. He saw Axehouse as a stepping stone toward this goal. He had, in fact, already started to lobby the non-executive Directors on the idea of splitting the Chairmanship into separate Chairman and Chief Executive roles.

'I agree, Robert. We are all in danger of losing out if we fight each other. What I suggest is that we agree to take a

71

neutral stance in relation to each other.'

'I'm not quite sure what you mean,' James chipped in, beginning to get the feeling that things were not quite going the way he had hoped.

'What I mean is that we do not vote against each other if Martin and the non-execs come up with a scheme that appears to advance one of us to the detriment of the other two.'

'Oh, come on Terry, be realistic. We all know that leaves each of us free to canvass Martin and the non-execs. It will be the free for all I think we should try to avoid. Voting won't come into it, you know these things invariably go through the Board on the nod. Everyone is squared beforehand. In any event I do not see Martin and the non-execs regarding any of us as having the right experience to take on responsibility for Axehouse General. Private canvassing on our part will be seen for what it is, power seeking.'

'What's wrong with that?' growled Brodie.

'Nothing in normal circumstances,' replied James, 'but in the context of a major deal such as this it will divert time and attention away from the primary goal of capturing Axehouse General in the first place, and we will be giving a very good impression of being more concerned with our own interests than those of Amalgamated. If one of us tries to advance his own interests, the other two are bound to follow to protect their own position.'

King thought for a moment. James was right. Now was not the time for jockeying for power. That could come later. What was needed was a solution which prejudiced none of them and left the field open for the future.

'We need a holding position that does not prejudice any of our prospects.'

This was what James wanted to hear.

'Any ideas, Terry?'

Brodie answered. 'I'm not going to prejudice my career prospects by going along with some compromise now that blocks me in the future. Holding positions have a nasty habit of growing into permanent power bases.'

James judged that the time was ripe to make his proposal. Brodie's retort had been typical, and could have been misunderstood by anyone who did not know him well. The message was that he agreed with the general proposition but the detailed solution had better be a good one.

'It seems to me that what we need is some figurehead representation on the Board for Axehouse General who poses no threat.'

A loud guffaw emanated from Brodie.

'Howard Irwin,' he shouted.

Terry King murmured, 'Beautiful, beautiful.'

James feigned surprise. 'What a great idea, Robert. Just the man.'

Inwardly he congratulated himself. It had worked out exactly as he had planned. If he had suggested Irwin straight away before laying the groundwork, King and Brodie would have laughed him out of court.

The more Brodie thought about it, the more he liked it. Howard Irwin was a threat to nobody. He could be moved aside whenever it became necessary. It would give time for Axehouse to be digested and meanwhile he could be quietly furthering his own plans. It would probably be necessary for an Axehouse General man to be on the Board as well, but he would clearly be subordinate to Howard Irwin and, almost by definition, powerless. King was having similar thoughts, and then a snag occurred to him. How on earth did one persuade Martin and the non-executive Directors to buy such a deal? Surely they recognised Irwin for what he was, a lightweight?

'How do we sell this?'

'How do you mean?' James replied.

'Well, let's not beat about the bush, Howard is useless. How can we expect Martin and the non-execs to take the suggestion seriously?'

'That's easy. Howard may appear useless to us, but we view him in a wider business context. He is first class at presenting a façade of competence and that includes the non-execs. Martin will understand the real reason behind the proposal. The last thing he needs during a hard-fought takeover bid is a set of Divisional chairmen all trying to cut each others throats.'

Robert Brodie indicated his agreement.

☆ ☆ ☆

Martin had decided to approach Sir Richard Brookes earlier rather than later. He took the view that the sooner he knew whether Sir Richard would bring Axehouse General along quietly, the better. If he said 'no', then Amalgamated would know where they stood and the bid could be planned accordingly. James Markby Smythe had counselled against such an early approach on the basis that it gave Axehouse more time to build their defences. In the end they had compromised and Martin had held back whilst a two per cent stake in Axehouse General had been built up in nominee names.

He had chosen the Connaught Hotel for the meeting. The telephone was too impersonal, and in any event not one hundred per cent secure, and his presence at the offices of Axehouse or Sir Richard Brookes' presence at Amalgamated would inevitably cause speculation. The Connaught had two other advantages. The lounge opened on to the foyer almost immediately to the left of the front door and was in effect a continuation of the foyer itself. Its design enabled one unobtrusively to observe who came in and out without being seen.

Even if someone coming into the hotel chose to approach the lounge immediately, they had to turn back on themselves, giving anyone in the lounge time to see them before they entered. The lounge also offered discretion. If you chose to sit in the far right corner nobody could see you without walking right up to your sitting area. The other advantage of the Connaught was that it was a mecca for well known and important people. The presence of Martin Chandler and Sir Richard Brookes in the hotel at the same time would not be a matter for comment.

Martin Chandler and Sir Richard Brookes were both members of the Council of the Confederation of British Industry and knew each other well. Martin used this as the excuse for the meeting and had suggested the Connaught as a civilised place to meet.

Martin watched Sir Richard turn into the lounge and quickly scan the small groups of people. Martin half rose from his position and Sir Richard spotted him immediately.

'Well, Martin, what is so important about the next CBI Council meeting that necessitates you and I having a clandestine meeting?' Sir Richard's tone was jovial and bantering. It was soon to change.

'Actually Richard, that was just an excuse to get you here. I have been thinking about our two companies. Whilst we are both large in our respective fields, in the overall picture we are getting relatively smaller. Our power bases and thus our influence are getting smaller. I think we would both be in some difficulty with the Monopolies Commission, not to mention Brussels, if we tried to make any significant expansion in our own fields. The solution to this would be a merger of our two companies.'

Sir Richard Brookes had followed the logic of Martin's argument until the last remark. He couldn't for the life of him see why merging Axehouse General and Amalgamated was an obvious solution to the state of affairs Martin had outlined. Axehouse and Amalgamated had nothing in common. There would be no synergy in their getting together and, what was more, there were plenty of opportunities for each of them to expand into fields related to their existing businesses which probably would not run into Monopolies Commission problems.

'Before we even start to consider whether there is any industrial logic in what you have just proposed, Martin, I think I need to know what you mean by our two companies merging.'

'What I have in mind is a total coming together of our two companies, Richard, to create a single powerful unit. We would be back in the top ten companies, where we both once were, and be much more strongly placed to expand further into other fields and to fight off predators, domestic or foreign.'

'What you really mean is that you want to take us over, isn't it?'

'No, no, I genuinely mean partnership. Obviously, for structural legal reasons there will have to be a single company for Stock Exchange quotation purposes and also to reflect the real strength of our merged companies, but within these constraints Axehouse General will continue to exist as will the operating companies within Amalgamated. From your own individual point of view, there is the potential for greatly increased power and influence.'

Sir Richard Brookes was not taken in and Martin hardly expected him to be.

'You are talking about taking us over, Martin, however you try to wrap it up. What you have just described implies that Axehouse General will become a subsidiary of Amalgamated along with all the other companies, big and small, which currently make up Amalgamated. I assume that you are not proposing to give up the Chairmanship of Amalgamated nor form a joint Board with equal Axehouse and Amalgamated representation?

'Amalgamated is bigger than Axehouse General, Richard. The City would expect Amalgamated to be seen as the continuing entity with me as Chairman. You would become Deputy Chairman. I am five years older and I give you my undertaking that I would retire no later than the age of sixty-three, giving you a potential run in the chair of twelve years if you decide to go on until seventy. As for other Axehouse representation on the Board of Amalgamated, we can of course discuss that once you have agreed to the principle of merger.'

'The answer is "no". I do not believe that it would be in the interests of Axehouse General or its shareholders to become part of Amalgamated. On a personal level I am quite happy with what I have. I can build on it without surrendering the autonomy of Axehouse or my own position. I am in no way tempted by your offer of the Deputy Chairmanship of the enlarged Amalgamated nor the prospect of the Chairmanship in a few years time. Whatever undertakings you may give me, the succession to the chair is not in your gift. A majority of the Directors at the time of succession will decide.'

Martin gave it one last try. 'I think you ought to put it to your Board. There is a lot to gain for both companies.'

'I will decide what I do or do not put to my Board. In any event it would be a waste of time. They have far more to lose than I do from a "merger" as you describe it.'

'So be it, Richard. I am truly sorry that you are not even prepared to explore the possibilities. There are many ways of skinning a rabbit. I am sure corporate structures could have been devised to overcome your fears. For example, we could reverse both our companies into a newly formed public company so that both Axehouse General and Amalgamated became subsidiaries. My Board and I are fully convinced that a merging of our two companies is the right way forward, and I do not think we will change our minds.'

Sir Richard Brookes did not respond to the thinly veiled threat. Chandler would not have approached him if Amalgamated had not already decided to make a takeover bid for Axehouse General. He had simply been trying to smooth the path for Amalgamated.

'I don't think we have anything else to discuss, Martin, and thank you for laying to rest a slight worry I had. As you have every reason to know, our share price has been creeping up for the last few days, bucking the market trend. I now know why and who.'

Martin stayed on after Sir Richard Brookes had left. He was looking forward to the fight. A friendly merger would have been simpler, but it did not have the excitement of the chase. He thought about Sarah. He wondered why she had come into his mind just then. Maybe it was the thought of the excitement of the chase. His peace offering for last week, a rather nice diamond brooch, had been accepted as if it were a packet of flour. No kiss, just a perfunctory 'thank you'. He wondered what was wrong. She had turned away from his advances in bed and generally gave the impression that he was no more than tolerated around the house on the few occasions he was there. Surely, he thought, she doesn't know about my little adventures on the side? They mean nothing. As he thought about it he realised he really loved her. He resolved to tell her about Axehouse and the proposed holiday once it was safely in the bag. She would understand then why he had been absent from home so often. He caught the eye of one of the waiters and mimed a telephone cradled to his ear. He would call Sarah now, tell her he was on his way home and ask her to book a table at that nice little French restaurant. He looked at his watch. Seven o'clock. He would be home by eight.

The evening had been a success, at least Martin considered

77

it to have been. He realised he had been calling Sarah 'darling' for the first time in ages. A pleasant meal at Bistro Larousse, where they had in the past spent many an enjoyable evening, had been followed by a tender, gentle lovemaking. Sarah had really responded. It was quite like old times. Martin had told her that there was a big acquisition brewing up and that was why he had spent so many nights in London recently and also why he had not always been free to call her if he was going to be late. She seemed to have understood and accepted the explanation and the apology that went with it. He had not of course told her the target.

Sarah, as she lay in bed physically contented, admitted to herself that she had enjoyed the evening, and her response to his lovemaking had been genuine, but she was still determined to get her own back for his infidelity. The information about the large acquisition that was brewing confirmed her suspicions that his nights in London had not all been in the arms of some tart or another. When he had told her she had feigned indifference. Although she was dying to know who was the target, she had resisted the urge to ask him. It would be simple finding out. He was bound to have papers in his briefcase. Her thoughts went back to her conversation with her father. She was sure he would be able to use the information in some way that would hurt Martin but not drive him away from her. She did not know quite how this would be done, but she did not doubt that it could be done.

Martin was lying on his back, snoring gently. Sarah was not able to suppress a feeling of affection, and smiled to herself. After lovemaking he almost invariably finished up this way within minutes. It was quite like old times. Her resolve, however, was not weakened. She slid quietly out of bed and crept downstairs. His briefcase was, as usual, standing in the foot well of his desk. Sarah lifted it up and, with a few quick spins of the combination wheels, soon had it open. The briefcase was full to the brim. She knew she had hit the jackpot straight away as the top piece of paper was marked 'Secret — Operation TAG — Timetable'. Quickly she rifled through the rest of the papers to see if she could find a name. 'Damn,' she muttered under her breath as she got to the bottom of the pile without finding anything to indicate the name of the company. She slammed the briefcase shut in frustration. As she turned to leave the study a thought came into her mind. There must be clues in the papers which would be sufficient for someone like her father to identify the company. She opened the briefcase again and slowly sifted through the papers. There were frequent references to financial services, that must narrow the field pretty drastically. Then she found what she was sure was the vital clue. 'TAG shareprice currently 232p.' She ripped a piece of paper from the pad on the desk and copied this down, adding the date which appeared at the end of the document. Sarah realised that her father would have no trouble in identifying the company from the information she had.

When Sarah spoke to her father on the telephone the next day her confidence in him had been fully justified.

'Financial services, you say — share price 232 — it has to be Axehouse General. Do you have a codename?'

Sarah told him. Miles laughed out loud. 'TAG, surely you see it Sarah. The "AG" stands for Axehouse General and the "T" probably for something like "Target". Really, I would have thought Martin would have been rather more imaginative than that. Leave it with me, my dear, I am sure I can arrange something to embarrass Martin.'

Later that day the shares of Axehouse shot up ten pence, comfortably outperforming the market. Stephen noticed it on the screen in his office and called James Markby Smythe.

'What's happening, James? I thought we agreed not to start our main buying programme of Axehouse General shares until Monday, and then only buy in parcels which would not create too much excitement in the market.'

'We haven't bought a single share recently, Stephen. Either there has been a leak or someone else is sniffing around Axehouse.'

'What do we do now?'

'Leave it for a couple of days. It might just be a rise caused by unfounded rumour. I have already got my contacts briefed to keep their ears to the ground. The rise might easily dissipate if it is only based on rumour, and if we go piling in we shall of course fuel the price rise.'

'O.K. James, keep me in touch. I hope you are right and the jump is only the result of an unsubstantiated rumour.'

During the next two days the price of Axehouse shares rose another fifteen pence and James Markby Smythe reported to Stephen that the word was that a big and persistent buyer had appeared in the market. Who it was had not been revealed.

Martin called a crisis meeting for Friday afternoon, thereby spoiling several arrangements for weekends in country homes.

Miles was feeling very pleased with himself. He would make a packet on Axehouse General shares, and he would have a nice little hold over Martin.

8

'Shit.'

Sir Peter Barton did not like being thwarted. It was something to which he was not accustomed. Charles Walters had just told him that Amalgamated Products had, ten minutes before, announced a takeover bid for Axehouse General.

'This screws up your plans good and proper, Charles.'

Charles had already thought the situation through in the few moments he had before bearing the bad news to Sir Peter Barton.

'I don't see why, Peter. As far as I am aware there is no law or requirement of the City Code which says you cannot bid for a company which is already bidding for another company.'

'That's as maybe, but is it a realistic proposition? If we bid for Amalgamated, how on earth do we value our bid? With Axehouse on board or without it? If we have to pitch our bid on the assumption that Amalgamated will be successful in their bid, won't it put Amalgamated out of our reach, and won't we be left with egg on our face if we bid successfully for Amalgamated and their bid fails?'

'Obviously we will have to talk to Nathan Sanson, but I do not think these problems are insurmountable. The position is complex and I think we shall probably have to wait for the detailed Offer Document Amalgamated put out before we can make a final decision. We shall also have to analyse what we know about their offer at this stage.'

'We don't know very much do we? They only announced the bid a few minutes ago.'

'Before the morning is out I shall have the outline details

of the structure of the bid. It would be a very big acquisition for Amalgamated and is very unlikely to be a straight cash bid. I expect there will be a variety of options involving shares for shares, loan stocks and cash. I will get onto Sanson straight away and get his assessment of the situation.'

☆ ☆ ☆

The weekend had been hell for the advisers of Amalgamated and at least some of its directors. The mysterious rise in the share price of Axehouse General had thrown a large spanner in the works. Opinion had been divided between those who wanted to wait a few days to see what would happen to the share price over the next week and those who advocated bringing forward the bid and preempting whatever someone else might be up to. In the end there had been a compromise of sorts. Although a lot of work had already been done getting together the structure of the bid and all the associated mechanics, Henry Robirch of Miller Michaels, Amalgamated's solicitors, had made it quite clear that there was at least four days solid work to be done to get to the state where the bid could be announced. James Markby Smythe had backed him up and, accordingly, Friday had been pencilled in as the announcement date.

This decision had been reached at lunch time on the Sunday. Most of the directors had disappeared to their weekend retreats in the early afternoon of Saturday and had been kept in touch by frequent conference calls. Typical, Stephen had thought, no matter how important the matter for Amalgamated, most of the directors had pushed off for the weekend, pleading unbreakable commitments. In the end, only Martin, Charles Lytton, the Public Affairs Director, and James had stayed the course. Howard Irwin had been one of those pleading unbreakable commitments and had left immediately after the last non-executive director had left. This had been Sir Ralph Hartlebury. His excuse had been that he was due at Chequers later that afternoon and for dinner. Amongst his many other commitments he was a member of the Prime

Minister's Think Tank. Irwin had obviously concluded that Sir Ralph would not be returning at any time during the weekend and accordingly his absence would not be noticed. Irwin did not really care what Martin Chandler thought of him, but he did care what Sir Ralph Hartlebury thought. His assessment was that Sir Ralph might be useful to him in the future but that Martin was unlikely to be.

Stephen and Richard Hinton, the company's Chief Accountant, had been left with the responsibilities that Irwin should have been fulfilling. As Irwin had put it to Martin Chandler as he was making his excuses to leave, 'It's nuts and bolts time and Stephen and Richard have their fingers on that particular pulse. I am, of course, available at any time of day or night on the telephone to advise you on the policy front.'

Martin had not been sorry to see Irwin go. He had a much greater respect for the commitment and competence of Stephen and Richard Hinton.

Irwin had been useful in his time. He had been Finance Director when Martin had succeeded to the chair. He had steered Martin through the first few months of his Chairmanship with a Machiavellian skill, ensuring, with a little word here and carefully placed rumour there that the Board of Directors, and in particular the executive directors, were neatly balanced against each other and not given the opportunity to unite against Martin. Martin had been a controversial choice, and it had only been the considerable power and influence of the outgoing Chairman that had seen through the appointment. Martin had known that he was very much on trial and needed all the help he could get. Howard Irwin had been superb in this role. His easy charm and scheming mind had been invaluable. As Finance Director in charge also of corporate development, he was not actually a disaster, he was too clever in the use of his subordinates for that, but he had the respect of neither Martin nor his fellow executive directors. Irwin knew this but was sufficiently thick-skinned for it not to bother him. He fondly believed, however, that he had the respect of the non-executive directors.

Both Stephen and Richard welcomed the absence of Irwin, who contributed little or nothing that was original and only slowed things up. When Sir Ralph Hartlebury had reappeared on the Sunday morning, as he had promised, he had endeared himself to both Stephen and Richard by remarking, 'Left holding the baby again I see, well I suppose it is better for the baby to be left in competent, professional hands rather than those of an uncaring mother.'

By lunchtime on the Sunday the outline of the bid had been agreed, right down to the offer price, the mix of shares, cash and loan stock to be offered in exchange for the Axehouse General shares; the programme for lobbying the large institutional shareholders of both Amalgamated and Axehouse; approaches to relevant government ministers to try and ward off any reference to the Monopolies and Mergers Commission and the public relations exercise to be pursued through the media. A vast amount of detail still needed to be added to the outline but all concerned were confident this could be achieved before the announcement deadline the following Friday.

It was also decided to start buying Axehouse shares in the market first thing Monday morning. It was accepted that this would both run the price up and also stimulate the rumour mongers, but it would be unlikely to push the price up to the figure agreed for the shares of Axehouse General when the bid was announced. In any case rumours had already started with the rise in the price of the shares the previous week. There might even be a bonus to be gained apart from the base stake that would be built up; the other major buyer might be frightened off.

Stephen had averaged four hours sleep each night during the following days. He had been in his element. Hard work and long hours were no chore to him when he was involved in something as big and complex as the Axehouse takeover bid. The excitement he got from it all was almost sexual. The bid had been announced at eight o'clock in the morning on the Friday and had created a sensation in the City and media. All week long there had been speculation that a bid was in the offing for Axehouse General and the share price had climbed relentlessly. Two weeks before it had stood at 232p; by Thursday evening it had soared to 260p. Half a dozen companies had been suggested as the predator, but nobody had even whispered the name of Amalgamated. Axehouse started to put out press announcements stating that they had had no approaches and were unaware of any potential bidders for the company.

By twelve o'clock Martin Chandler had already held a press conference and recorded interviews for radio and television. At twelve thirty he appeared on the Channel 4 Business Programme. Stephen was an unseen and unheard presence at all these interviews, feeding Martin with all the necessary facts and figures when needed. This was not often as he had a very good grip on his brief and was a smooth performer on radio and television.

The media were clearly excited by the coming battle, and intrigued by the identity of the bidder. They had a field day with their headlines. 'A Sleeping Giant Stirs' went one headline. 'Food Giant To Gobble Money Manipulators' shouted one of the tabloids, prejudging the outcome. 'Amalgamated Signal Change Of Direction' was the more sober message in the *Financial Times* which had two articles analysing the bid in addition to an editorial. The two articles were nicely balanced. One doubted the wisdom and commercial logic of the bid, whilst the other praised the breadth of vision demonstrated by Amalgamated in planning to move into a new field that promised much greater growth than food related business. Overall, Martin was delighted with the initial response. He was under no illusions, however, that Amalgamated faced an uphill struggle in persuading the large institutional shareholders that the acquisition was right for Amalgamated. The institutional holders were critical. They held in excess of forty per cent of both Amalgamated and Axehouse General and could easily block the bid either by voting against it at the Extraordinary General Meeting of Amalgamated that would be necessary both to approve the bid and the changes to the capital structure of Amalgamated, or by not accepting Amalgamated's offer for their shares. Whilst on the face of it it seemed illogical for an institution to approve the bid at the Amalgamated EGM and then not accept the offer of Amalgamated for the Axehouse General shares they held, James Markby Smythe had pointed out to Martin Chandler that the institutions were great last minute merchants. This way they kept all their options open.

James Markby Smythe had no great opinion of the institutional shareholders. His view was that they were almost invariably swayed by the prospect of making a quick buck when the bidder was an established and respected company like Amalgamated. The offer price was generous and intended to be a pre-emptive strike to discourage another bidder coming on the scene. In these circumstances he did not foresee any great problems in seeing the acquisition through. Martin was not so sanguine. There was no all cash option in the bid and any acceptor would have to take a large slice of Amalgamated shares or loan stock. If the institutions were not happy about the prospect they would kill the deal. He did not intend to take any chances and had already briefed Stephen to set up a series of meetings with the larger institutional shareholders in both Amalgamated and Axehouse General. This would be where Howard Irwin came into his element. He had maintained good relations with the institutional shareholders over the years and had their confidence. His charm and willingness to talk openly would stand him in good stead.

☆ ☆ ☆

Nathan Sanson arched his hands, pushing his fingertips together and then gently drumming them against each other whilst keeping the base of his palms pressed firmly together. Sir Peter Barton could not hide his growing impatience and flicked imaginary flecks of dust from his immaculate pinstripe blue suit with increasing irritation. Sanson decided to wait no longer. He had of course known the answer straight away, but it didn't do to give the client the impression that problems that were seemingly insoluble to the client were in fact straightforward procedural matters that had known and well tested solutions.

'I think I have it.'

Sir Peter Barton leaned forward in anticipation, all attention.

'We make our bid conditional upon the Amalgamated bid for Axehouse General failing.'

Charles Walters mentally kicked himself. It was so obvious and he had missed it. Instead Sanson had been given the chance to appear the genius in Sir Peter Barton's eyes.

'Brilliant.'

Walters groaned inwardly.

'I knew we would get a more innovative approach from an American investment bank than from a stuffy old British merchant bank.

'Yes,' Sanson replied, accepting both the compliment to his own skill and the superiority of American investment banks. 'It has a simple beauty.'

Walters hopes rose. With any luck Sanson would go right over the top.

'It puts a considerable spanner in the works of the Amalgamated bid without putting Barton Industries at risk. You pitch your bid on the basis that Axehouse General will not be part of Amalgamated and the institutional shareholders will have a straight choice between Amalgamated as part of Barton Industries or Axehouse General as part of Amalgamated. Pitch the price right and it is no contest. Barton Industries are the ones who have the reputation of making their acquisitions hum, not Amalgamated.'

Charles Walters thought it was about time he got in on the act again. He did not want Sanson hogging all the limelight. 'When do we announce our bid?' He didn't wait for an answer. 'I recommend we wait a couple of weeks. This will give us time to get ourselves thoroughly prepared and make it more likely that we dictate events rather than react to them. We will be able to assess the Amalgamated bid in detail and act accordingly.'

'No, no. We must get our bid in as soon as possible. We don't want to give Amalgamated time to build up a strong position in relation to Axehouse and have a free run to sweet talk the institutional shareholders. We must sieze the initiative straight away.'

Walters smiled inwardly, he knew this would be Sir Peter Barton's reaction. When he had the smell of the chase in his nostrils his impatience almost invariably outpaced mature thought. Walters always thought of him as the young bull, which, upon seeing the gate to an adjoining field of cows swinging open, says to the older bull, 'Let's rush down and screw a couple,' whereas the older bull insists that they walk down and screw the lot.

Sanson responded exactly as Walters hoped he would.

'No, I think Charles is right, Sir Peter. Amalgamated will not be putting their formal offer document out for a couple of weeks. In fact they do not need to do so for twenty-eight days. We would be well advised to await publication of their offer document. It will enable us to get a much clearer idea of their tactics and design ours in the most effective way.'

Walters now felt better. Sanson would appear in Sir Peter's eyes as having responded positively to his advice, accepting it as if it had been novel and not merely plain common sense, which was all that it was.

Sir Peter Barton had the business acumen to see when the advice he was receiving was sound, even if he found it unpalatable.

'All right, I seem to be outvoted but surely there is something we can do to strengthen our position before we actually make a bid for Amalgamated?'

'Well, Sir Peter, that is precisely what we will be doing by delaying our bid until we are in possession of more detail of the Amalgamated bid, and taking the time to get our bid properly structured.'

Sir Peter Barton was not listening. He already had an idea.

'I've got it. We start buying Amalgamated shares now.'

For a moment there was silence. Neither Sanson nor Walters had given any thought to this possibility. Sanson was the first to respond.

'I'm not sure that is a good idea, Sir Peter. If we start buying at this stage it will bolster their share price.'

'So what?'

'Well the Amalgamated share price has dropped ten pence since their bid was announced. This is a pretty clear indication that the market is unsure of the wisdom of their bid for Axehouse General. If we start buying on a large scale the price will recover and give the impression that the market, on second thoughts, thinks the bid is good news for Amalgamated and its shareholders. One should never underestimate the influence market sentiment can have on a bid.'

Sir Peter Barton was way ahead of Sanson.

'Yes, yes, I know all that,' he responded impatiently. 'But don't you see it puts us right in the driving seat? If we build up a sufficient stake, say ten to fifteen per cent, this gives us considerable clout. It might even be enough to block Amalgamated. For example, if we vote those shares against the bid for Axehouse when Amalgamated have their Extraordinary General Meeting to approve the bid, that could be an end to their aspirations there and then. A holding of that size could well carry the day on a card vote. Alternatively, if circumstances dictate, we can dump them on the market and cause a collapse of the Amalgamated share price, which will in turn hit the value of the Amalgamated bid for Axehouse and kill it that way.'

Sanson was quick to pick up the theme.

'Hey, I hadn't thought of it that way,' he enthused, always being careful to humour the client. 'It could work out. We would have to check it out with the City Code. There might be rules against our playing the market in such a fashion. Then there is the financial risk to consider. If we dumped the shares we might suffer a considerable loss.'

Sir Peter Barton thought nothing of the rules and regulations. They were there for the sole purpose of being circumvented.

'To hell with the City Code. Nobody need know it is us buying. We can do it in nominee names spread over a number of nominees seemingly unrelated. Better still, the nominees should all be overseas organisations spread around Europe and the USA. In any case, surely there are no rules which prevent your buying shares in the market if you are planning to bid for a company?'

'There are some quite strict rules on that subject, Sir Peter, but I think you are probably right that they would not stop you from buying shares at this stage, although there are limits to what you can buy.'

Walters could feel things slipping away from him again. 'Why not buy Axehouse as well?' He let the question hang without providing his rationale. He wanted Sanson to respond without the benefit of knowing the reasoning behind the suggestion. Preferably he wanted him to ask for an explanation of the reasoning, thus demonstrating his limited vision.

Sanson was too wily a bird to fall into that particular trap.

'Yes, why not. If we build up a substantial holding through the market we could be a thorn in the side of Amalgamated. It could start rumours of a counter bid, thus throwing doubt on the Amalgamated bid. It could be very disruptive. I think a more detailed rationale and a viability study, particularly regarding financing, would be very interesting, Charles. The financing would be a particularly interesting challenge.' Sanson kept his real views to himself. Privately he thought the suggestion a waste of time, money and effort. Barton Industries couldn't purchase sufficient Axehouse General shares to frighten Amalgamated off without actually having to make a bid themselves. Quite apart from this technical point, he doubted the financial ability of Barton Industries to make significant purchases of both Amalgamated and Axehouse shares.

Walters recognised immediately that Sanson had trumped his ace. He had accurately identified the rationale he had in mind and then dropped in a little time bomb. He had not thought through financing of such an exercise, nor the technicalities involved. He was determined, however, not to be upstaged over the matter.

Sir Peter Barton loved the idea, which made it the more important that Charles Walters found a way of implementing it. Sanson felt a little uneasy. The idea was a good one, he had to admit that, but implementing it would create horrendous problems, and he knew he would be expected to come up with the ideas for financing the massive purchases of Amalgamated and Axehouse General shares which the proposal envisaged. He quickly decided that the original plan of bidding in tandem for Amalgamated and Maxpoint Industries, or Robot as it was code named, was not a viable proposition in the new circumstances.

'We will have to drop Robot, Sir Peter.'

'What! Over my dead body. Robot is all part of the

strategy, we have gone over that ground already.'

'I'm sorry, Sir Peter, there is no way you will be able to finance the purchase of Robot at the same time as bidding for Amalgamated and building up a significant stake in Axehouse General. It will be difficult enough as it is, with Robot on top it would be impossible. I am not saying that you should drop the idea of Robot altogether, you can always return to it once Amalgamated is safely in the bag. You may, however, at that stage feel Robot is too small to fit the new image of Barton Industries.'

Sanson was no fool. He knew this last remark would appeal to Peter Barton.

'Hmph.' Barton was not going to give in easily, although he had already made up his mind that a larger acquisition than Robot sometime after Amalgamated was safely in the bag was the preferable option. 'I'll think about it.'

Nathan Sanson knew he had won his point.

The next morning the shares of Amalgamated shot up 15p, having dropped 10p on the announcement of their bid for Axehouse General. Martin Chandler was delighted. He was thoroughly convinced that the market, on more mature thought, had concluded that the bid for Axehouse was a good thing for Amalgamated. His delight was to be short lived.

9

Miles Wartnaby was enjoying himself hugely. He had a near two per cent stake in Amalgamated bought at an average price of 157 pence with the shares now standing at 172. He did a quick sum on his calculator. A profit already of £2·4 million give or take a few thousand for expenses. Axehouse was even better. His average purchase price was 245 pence and with the Amalgamated bid coming in at 280 pence, he was showing a profit of £3·3 million for his near three per cent stake. These figures were peanuts in the context of BCI, which on the current share price was capitalised at just over £14 billion with annual profits running at £2·4 billion. Nevertheless he was delighted with his investments.

He sat back in his chair and closed his eyes. He always found it easier to concentrate with his eyes closed, a quirk of behaviour which had misled many an opponent in tough negotiations. What to do next? The Amalgamated bid had a long way to run yet. Axehouse would not fall easily and Amalgamated would almost certainly have to increase their bid. Indeed Miles was slightly surprised that the market price of Axehouse was showing such a small premium over the bid price. Miles reckoned Amalgamated would need to go to 300 pence to win the day. There was an obvious case for buying even more shares. There were big profits to be made. What of his holding in Amalgamated itself? The current price slightly puzzled him. Only half his present holding was recent and he did not think his recent purchase of another one per cent stake justified a rise in price of some 15 pence. The advance in the price did not exactly mirror his buying pattern and furthermore the Amalgamated image was somewhat tarnished in the City. They were not regarded as astute predators. The general view was that they paid too much for their acquisitions and were not very good at making them justify the purchase price. The Axehouse General bid was by far their largest and totally outside the businesses they knew. All in all Miles reckoned the Amalgamated price should hardly have moved. His buying should have cancelled out the fall in price one would have anticipated upon the announcement of the bid. There must be someone else in the market. The question was who and why.

His musings were rudely interrupted by the noise of the telephone ringing.

'Hello Daddy, I was just calling to see if you were in. I'm in town and thought I might pop round for a drink with you before I go home if that's O.K. with you.'

'Delighted to see you Sarah. I have to go out around eight but I expect you will want to get a train home before then.'

'I'll be round in about half an hour.'

Miles replaced the telephone. Sarah's voice had jolted him. In the thrill of the chase he had completely forgotten why he had started building stakes in Amalgamated and Axehouse in the first place. He now remembered his promise to Sarah. Much as he loved his daughter he resolved not to let that love be an overriding consideration in extracting the maximum benefit for BCI and himself from the Amalgamated Axehouse General situation.

He turned a few ideas over in his head. If he could get ten per cent of Axehouse General that would put him in a strong position. It might be enough to frustrate the Amalgamated bid altogether if it was a close call, which it could well be, and even if this was not the case a 10 per cent holding would prevent Amalgamated from getting a compulsory buy out of shares not assented to the Amalgamated offer. Miles rather liked the latter scenario. Being a ten per cent minority shareholder did not worry him particularly. Companies disliked minority holdings of this nature and he was sure he could engineer a good deal for himself and BCI at a time of his choosing. If Martin became difficult over the buy out terms he would simply threaten to take Amalgamated over and break it up. The only slight problem was that when his holding got to five per cent he had, under the law, to inform Amalgamated of that fact. He always bought his stakes in other companies through offshore nominee companies whose ultimate ownership was virtually impossible to discover. If necessary he could simply ignore the five per cent rule. He had done so in the past and got away with it.

Ten per cent of Axehouse General would cost him, or more accurately BCI, a lot of money, about £168 million at a rough guess. Not an over large sum in the context of BCI, but nevertheless significant. It would probably be going a bit over the top to expect his fellow directors to agree to a large speculative investment in Amalgamated as well. He might invest a few million of his own money in Amalgamated he thought. There was something going on there which might turn out to be very interesting. His reverie was broken by the sound of the door of his apartment opening. Sarah had arrived.

He decided not to bother her with what had been going through his mind and merely assured her in a jovial way that he was cooking up a nasty surprise for Martin.

'Nothing too nasty, I hope Daddy. Just something to shake him a bit.'

'Never fear Sarah, I think his pride will suffer more than his pocket.'

Sarah knew her father well enough not to probe for more detail.

☆ ☆ ☆

Martin looked across the table at Stephen and James Markby Smythe. He still did not want to believe what he was being told.

'Surely, James, the rise in our share price could be due to the market taking a favourable view of our bid for Axehouse General.'

'I'm afraid not Martin. Amalgamated shares are now nearly ten per cent above their level prior to the bid. You don't get that sort of rise in the price of the shares of a predator following the announcement of a large bid even if you are one of the BCI's of this world. No, something is going on. Someone must be buying your shares in fairly large quantities. There has been a sudden surge in the turnover of your shares on the market, quite out of line with the normal level of business. I doubt very much that this is a mass of speculative buyers. It is far more likely to be someone building a stake in Amalgamated for some reason.'

'Be that as it may, James, it still helps us surely. Amalgamated's price goes up and consequently the share element of our offer for Axehouse becomes more attractive to their shareholders. If someone does have their eye on us we are well ahead of the game. The Axehouse General bid must complicate matters for anyone looking to make a bid for Amalgamated.'

'I don't disagree Martin, but the word is complicate and not kill.'

Martin looked over at James Markby Smythe. He really did not like the man. He was probably right, but it was the supercilious manner in which he delivered his views that stuck in his throat.

Stephen sensed the air of hostility that was building up and wanted to get the discussion back upon a positive track.

'Let us assume, James, that someone is building up a stake in Amalgamated, and let us further assume that the stake building is with a view to making a bid for Amalgamated. What steps do you suggest we now take to give us the best chance of fighting off a predator?'

Markby Smythe winced inwardly at being addressed by his Christian name by Stephen. He recognised that Stephen Barber was highly competent but he did not recognise that his background or the length of their acquaintance gave him the right to address him in such a manner. He let none of this show and certainly would not stoop to the pomposity of requiring Stephen to address him by his surname.

'Well, Mr Barber,' he said, clearly but obliquely making his point about the use of Christian names, 'we have already generated most of the information necessary to mount a defence as part of our bid package. Primarily it is simply a matter of recasting it in a manner suitable for the purpose. Other strategies must await the identity of the bidder; if there is such a creature.'

Martin had regained his poise. He had rather enjoyed Markby Smythe's obvious distaste at being addressed by his Christian name by Stephen and his manner of conveying this distaste.

'Will you see to that then Stephen? I suggest you get together a small team to help you. Charles Lytton will be helpful from a PR angle and I am sure James here will have some helpful input from his perspective.'

Martin was enjoying himself now. Suggesting that Markby Smythe be part of a team headed by Stephen tickled his sense of humour.

Markby Smythe was not so easily put out of his stride.

'Splendid idea, Martin, I will arrange for Philip Renton from our Corporate Affairs Department to contact Mr Barber. Philip is highly experienced in defence tactics. I will see that he keeps me fully in the picture.'

Stephen wasted no time in getting in touch with Philip Renton. He really did not care if Marky Smythe snubbed him. The bid for Axehouse General was what mattered most. A successful outcome would enhance his position with Martin Chandler and Amalgamated enormously. He had already decided that Markby Smythe and Lloyd, Meisson had no long term future with Amalgamated.

Renton however was a different kettle of fish. He was much more in Stephen Barber's own image. Stephen knew him well from the time he was with a rival merchant bank, and he had a high opinion of him. Stephen doubted that he would stay with Lloyd, Meisson very long, he was much too ambitious for that.

He went down his check list with Philip Renton. The Office of Fair Trading was the first item. He did not anticipate any problems there.

'How about the OFT Philip? Have you had any response yet?'

'Yes. I sent the dossier round a couple of days ago outlining the rationale behind the bid and setting out our views as to why the bid was not a candidate for a referral to the Monopolies and Mergers Commission. I had a chat with them on the telephone this morning. They seem very relaxed, but I really did not expect any other reaction. There is little to excite their interest. Government policy, as you know, is very much geared toward a *laissez faire* approach. I am confident we have a clear run.'

'Good. Howard Irwin and I have seen the four largest institutional investors in Amalgamated and Axehouse General. They were fairly receptive but gave no clear indication which way they will jump. Their major concern seemed not to be the level at which the bid is pitched, but how we would integrate and manage Axehouse if we were successful in our bid. In their own inimitable way they implied that they had doubts, based on our track record, of our ability to justify such a large and unrelated acquisition in the long run. I have to admit Howard Irwin was magnificent. He obviously has more than a dash of Celtic religious fervour in him. His description of how we had seen the light would have done justice to an old style non-conformist preacher. 'Follow me and you will see the light as well!'

Stephen chuckled at the memory.

They agreed the plan of campaign for the next few days and set up a meeting with Charles Lytton for that afternoon.

The formal Amalgamated Offer Document contained little that was not already known and created little excitement; except, that is, in the breast of Sir Peter Barton. It was his green light. The past two weeks had been almost unbearable. He hated having to wait once he had made up his mind on a course of action. It was not as if there had been nothing to do. Far from it. The pace had been hectic, getting everything in place for his bid for Amalgamated. There were seemingly endless meetings with bankers, lawyers and God knows who else. He found it all very frustrating but now he only had the weekend to cope with. The Amalgamated Offer Document had come out on the Friday and, in his view, it would not take his advisers more than the weekend to suck the small print off it and firm up the final details of the Barton Industries bid for Amalgamated. Tuesday at the latest, he reckoned. Monday would see the Amalgamated share price settle to a level which reflected the considered views of the City to the Amalgamated bid for Axehouse General. He could then finally fix the level of his bid. He was going to enjoy this. He would give a lot to witness the consternation at Amalgamated House when his bid landed on the table; in particular the sight of Martin Chandler's face would have given him a great deal of pleasure. He hated the man and he hated his class and all that it represented. It almost hurt not being able to have the pleasure of witnessing his discomfort. Hey, he thought, I can enjoy the next best thing. I will ring him up an hour before the bid is announced to the Stock Market. He smiled at the thought. He would ask Chandler to endorse the bid. That would make him choke. He decided not to tell Nathan Sanson or Charles Walters of his intention. They would be bound to find some piffling reason why he should not do it and he was not going to be denied his pleasure.

What should he do for the weekend? He had to find something to take his mind off the impending bid for Amalgamated. If he didn't he knew that he would be at such a pitch of frustration by Monday that he would be in danger of making a bad decision. He pressed the intercom.

'Yes, Sir Peter?' Pru Wetherby said in her beautifully modulated voice.

'Have my plane ready to go to Nice by four this afternoon.' No please, no thank you, but then Pru Wetherby was used to that.

'Certainly, Sir Peter.'

He picked up his outside telephone.

'Oui,' Madame Celine replied. She wasn't noted for her loquacity.

'Ah, Sylvie. I'm coming over to the apartment for the weekend, get everything organised. I'll be there early this evening.'

'How many?'

Madame Celine's English was not particularly good but

she had sufficient command of the essentials of the language to cope with Barton's needs and desires. Perversely he spoke near perfect French but when speaking to Madame Celine on the telephone from England he almost invariably spoke in English, only slipping into French when in France.

'Two.'

Madame Celine did not need to ask two what. She seemed to have access to a seemingly unending supply of willing, attractive girls available at short notice to indulge Sir Peter's tastes. She knew that he rarely resorted to the same girl twice and accordingly did not need to ask him if he had any particular preference.

Sir Peter Barton put the telephone down. He was already filled with anticipation. He looked at his watch. Ten to twelve. He knew he would not settle to anything on his own. He picked up the internal telephone.

'Charles, I'm going out to lunch. Join me.'

It wasn't a question. It was an order.

'We can go over the details for next week. From the market reaction to the Amalgamated Offer Document it looks as if 185 pence a share is going to be enough for the initial offer although no doubt we may need to up that later.'

Charles Walters did not reply to the comment on the bid price. He knew that he would be going round the subject endlessly over lunch.

10

The intercom buzzed on Martin's desk.

'Yes, Ann.'

'I have Sir Peter Barton on the telephone, Mr Chandler. He says it is very urgent.'

Martin looked at his watch. Eight thirty. He had a meeting with Markby Smythe, Stephen and Howard at eight forty-five and a Board Meeting at nine. Nothing Sir Peter might have to say to him could be more urgent than these meetings.

'Tell him I will call him back around lunchtime.'

Martin Chandler flicked the switch on his intercom and picked up Stephen Barber's paper setting out the progress of the bid for Axehouse General and outlining the proposals for its conduct over the next week.

The buzzer went again. Martin Chandler ignored it. He must have a word with Ann Gordon. When he said he did not want to be disturbed, he meant he did not want to be disturbed. Once was just about forgivable. Twice in a few seconds he would not tolerate.

The buzzer went again. This time the tone was held for a fraction longer, taking on an insistent air.

Angrily Martin Chandler flicked his switch.

'Ann, I told you I did not wish to be disturbed.'

His hand was already on its way to flick the switch off again. He did not expect Ann Gordon to argue the toss with him. It was not in her nature.

'Martin.'

His hand stopped. Ann Gordon never, but never, called him Martin. The ploy worked. Ann Gordon had bought herself enough time to get her message across and she was quite certain it was vital that she did. She did not wait for him to speak.

'Mr Chandler,' she continued, 'Sir Peter Barton says you will regret it if you do not speak to him now. Those were his precise words.'

Martin Chandler looked at his watch. Eight thirty-two. He had already wasted two precious minutes. It would probably be quicker to speak to the wretched man and get rid of him fast than continue the pantomime of whether or not he would speak to him. Besides, the threat not only angered him, it intrigued him.

'OK put him on.'

'Good morning Martin, and it is a very good morning.'

Martin seethed inside. He did not have the time to indulge in debate upon the quality of the morning. His innate good manners, however, prevented him from demanding that Sir Peter Barton get on with it.

'Good morning Peter, what can I do for you? If it is likely to take any time, could I call you back later? I am just about to go into a meeting.'

'Oh, you can do an awful lot for me, Martin.'

Sir Peter Barton was enjoying himself. He could sense the pent up anger at the other end and he knew that Martin's upbringing would prevent him from giving vent to it.

'It is a very simple thing I want. Indeed, it is so simple that I believe one word from you over the telephone will resolve it immediately.'

Martin Chandler clenched his fists and took a deep breath. He did not have the time to play games but he was determined not to lose his temper.

'Fire away,' he said, doing his best to inject a jovial tone into his voice.

Sir Peter was disappointed. Chandler clearly was not going to lose his temper. Furthermore, he had time constraints as well. Indeed they were undoubtedly more pressing. The bid would be announced at nine.

'I am making a bid for Amalgamated, Martin. It will be announced in twenty-three minutes time. Your endorsement would, of course, be very welcome.'

Martin felt a hammer blow in his stomach. He bent

101

forward to compress the pain. It was the same sensation he used to experience as a child when, afraid of the dark, a movement of shadow in his bedroom convinced him there was someone in his room.

'Hello.'

No answer.

'Hello, are you there Martin?'

No answer. Sir Peter felt himself getting cross. The blasted telephone system was depriving him of his sport. Nobody would receive news of a bid for his company without making some sort of response. Curiosity alone would induce most people to at least ask the bid price, and more than one Chairman he knew would certainly tell him in very basic language where he could go.

Martin Chandler gently replaced the receiver in its cradle. He had no intention of giving Sir Peter Barton the satisfaction of experiencing his reaction to the bombshell that had just been delivered.

Sir Peter Barton held the receiver away from him and looked at it quizzically. The bloody man had hung up on him without giving him the satisfaction of experiencing any reaction whatsoever. He had hardly expected him to say, 'What a good idea, let's meet to discuss it,' but he had expected some sort of response that would have enabled him to have a few moments enjoying Chandler's discomfort. He banged the receiver down.

Martin looked at his watch yet again. James, Stephen and Howard would be with him in just four minutes. There was no point in trying to contact anyone or do anything. He sat back in his chair, closed his eyes and put his hands behind his head.

He did not even hear the door open as Ann Gordon came in.

'Are you all right, Mr Chandler?'

Martin opened his eyes with a start.

'Oh, yes – just relaxing before the meetings.'

Ann Gordon busied herself setting up the papers for the meeting. A neat folder for each participant. She debated whether or not to apologise to Martin for insisting on interrupting him. She stole a surreptitious look at him. He was still sitting there, leaning back in his chair, just as he had been when she had entered the room, except that his eyes were now open. He did not seem to be particularly preoccupied.

'I want to apologise . . .' she began, but got no further.

'No, no, you were right. Think no more of it.'

'Is there anything else before your meeting, Mr Chandler?'

'No, show Markby Smythe in as soon as he arrives and get Howard and Stephen in here now.'

'Mr Markby Smythe is in your waiting room now, working on some papers.

'Splendid, show him in.'

Martin felt strangely relaxed and unworried about the bombshell that had just fallen. He did not know quite why, for he realised that the Barton Industries bid created considerable problems in connection with their bid for Axehouse General.

There was a discreet knock on the door and James, Howard and Stephen came in together. Martin beckoned them to the table and, as each of them sat down, they automatically picked up their folders and began to extract the papers.

'We won't be needing those.' All three looked enquiringly at him. He paused briefly for effect. 'I have just had Barton Industries on the telephone.' He preferred not to refer specifically to Sir Peter Barton. 'In precisely thirteen minutes they will be announcing a bid for Amalgamated.'

James and Stephen started to speak together. Howard Irwin, in typical style, just sat there with an inscrutable look on his face. Martin smiled inwardly to himself. Good old true to form Howard. Keep your powder dry until you see in which direction the deer is running.

Stephen Barber deferred to James Markby Smythe.

'What price, what terms?'

'I have not the foggiest idea, James. I put the phone down on him before he could expand upon the subject. I did not wish to give him any glimmer of satisfaction by indicating in any way that I was remotely interested. We have only to wait eleven minutes to find out.'

'I suppose he rang you as a matter of courtesy.' James

103

always found it difficult to accept that others did not necessarily share his innate good manners.

'Oh no. The cheeky bugger wanted me to endorse the bid. At least that is what he said, but I am quite sure he rang just for effect and to gloat. I don't think he likes me. The feeling is mutual.'

Stephen rapidly homed in on the immediate practical considerations.

'I think we ought to postpone the Board Meeting for a quarter of an hour, Chairman. There is little point in your going in and announcing the bid to the Board before we know the terms. Better still, let them convene in the Boardroom, leave them for five minutes or so, and then Ann can go in and apologise for your late arrival. That way there is little danger of them becoming aware of the bid before you announce it. It will also give us a little more time to sort out what you are going to say and for James to marshal his thoughts on the implications for our bid.'

'Agreed, arrange it with Ann please Stephen, and ask her to make sure no-one contacts the Boardroom before I am ready to join them.'

☆ ☆ ☆

Lord Leven Sumpter drummed his fingers on the table and looked at his watch for at least the fifth time in five minutes and turned to Richard Gibbs on his right.

'It's too bad, Martin gets us here at this early hour of the morning at short notice and then does not have the courtesy to be on time himself.'

Diplomatic as ever, Richard Gibbs responded to the effect that there was sure to be a good reason and no slight was intended.

To the right of Richard Gibbs, Joyce Bennett was bending the ear of Sir Ralph Hartlebury, in all probability oblivious to the fact that the Board Meeting was already twelve minutes late in starting. Sir Ralph Hartlebury feigned polite interest and was much more interested in the note Ann Gordon had just passed him. Could he join Martin Chandler? It must be something vital. He excused himself, leaving Joyce Bennett in mid sentence.

Elsewhere around the Boardroom some were sat quickly flicking through their papers and others chatted in small groups. Robert Brodie saw Sir Ralph slip out of the room and, as soon as he was able, detached himself from James Walker and Terry King, and went over to Charles Timpson, the Company Secretary.

'What's up, Charles?'

'I really don't know, Mr Brodie.'

Charles Timpson felt he should be on Christian name terms with the executive directors at least, but had never had the confidence to take the plunge. After all, he had sat in on Board Meetings as Company Secretary for as long and longer than most of them.

'It is very strange, he invariably goes through the agenda with me before the meeting but this morning Ann headed me off.'

Robert Brodie wandered off in the direction of his seat and did not have to wait long. Martin Chandler entered the Boardroom in earnest conversation with Sir Ralph and closely followed by James Markby Smythe, Stephen Barber and Howard Irwin. Brodie had not even noticed that Irwin had been absent from the room, which said everything as far as his respect for him was concerned.

Martin walked briskly to his seat and sat down. Around the room there was an almost general move to take up places at the Board table, except for James Walker and Terry King who, although they must certainly have seen Martin Chandler come in as he had walked right by them, continued their conversation. Joyce Bennett carried on talking to Richard Gibbs.

'May we start please gentlemen?' This was directed at Terry King and James Walker who immediately made their way to their usual seats either side of Humphrey Lester. A general quiet fell on the room, all except for the twittering voice of Joyce Bennett who was still talking to Richard Gibbs as if she were at a social gathering, rather than a formal meeting.

'Joyce, please,' implored Martin Chandler. His anger was barely suppressed.

Joyce Bennett turned to him, giving him the benefit of her famous smile and crinkled eyes, both calculated to mollify him.

'Oh, sorry Chairman,' she purred. Martin did not even look at her. Out of habit more than anything else he started the second of the two clocks in front of him. As he was doing it he realised that time was the least important part of the meeting. He looked round the table. There was an air of expectancy. He didn't waste time on formalities.

'Twelve minutes ago, Barton Industries announced a bid for Amalgamated Products PLC.'

He didn't pause to give anyone time to jump in and start throwing questions, although many mouths and gestures signalled a move of that nature.

'I will ask James Markby Smythe to outline the implications.'

'Thank you, Chairman. The bid values Amalgamated at approximately 185 pence per share, although it is difficult to be specific since it is an all paper bid, and highly leveraged. No Barton Industries shares and no cash. We do not yet have full details of the bid, but it is bound to be conditional upon your bid for Axehouse General failing. As it is structured and priced at the moment I see little chance of the bid succeeding. On the valuation put on their bid by Barton Industries themselves they are offering only eight pence per share premium over the share price of Amalgamated prior to the announcement of the bid but, as we all know, there has been speculative buying of Amalgamated this last two or three weeks.'

Joyce Bennett interrupted James Markby Smythe in full flow.

'Has there!' she exclaimed.

James Markby Smythe ignored her and carried straight on. 'The bid as structured is distinctly fuzzy; a lot more detail is needed for a proper assessment to be made. I anticipate, however, that the structure of the bid will change after the first closing date for acceptances to include an element of cash and shares as well as an uplift in the value of the bid. At the end of the day, the institutions will decide the issue; which is better for them as investors. Axehouse General as part of Amalgamated, Amalgamated as part of Barton Industries or a maintenance of the status quo.'

106

Stephen mentally applauded James. He had summed up the situation in a few short sentences and pre-empted virtually all the intelligent questions that could be asked at this stage. This did not stop the questions coming and old ground was covered more than once before Martin put a halt to it.

'Lady, gentlemen. I am sure you all realise that the company's response to this turn of events is going to require a great deal of time and thought. We have no time to waste, and I am sure you will forgive me if I abandon the remainder of the agenda. You will all be kept fully in the picture. It will be necessary to call meetings at short notice and, whilst I appreciate that you all have other commitments, I hope you will make every effort to attend them. The future of Amalgamated is at stake. I think the conduct of the defence against the Barton Industries bid is best dealt with by the teams already established for the Axehouse General takeover. The two situations are closely allied and need co-ordination. I will, however, confirm the arrangements to you all before the end of the day. Thank you.'

A buzz immediately spread round the table. There was an air of excitement. To some there was the realisation that their careers were on the line. Sir Peter Barton was not noted for keeping senior management in place once he had acquired a company. Robert Brodie did not feel this threat as much as the other executive directors. He knew Sir Peter Barton rather well and indeed quite liked him. He admired his uncompromising style. For the non-executive directors the thrill was rather different. It was more of a game. Indeed, it was a battle with no real blood as far as they were concerned.

To Stephen the situation was critical. He had had no time to make his mark at Amalgamated and thus enhance his marketability. If he had anything to do with it, Barton Industries would not succeed in acquiring Amalgamated and he did not care too much how he went about achieving that end.

☆ ☆ ☆

Sarah Chandler pressed the remote control button and

turned the television off. She was puzzled. She had not really been paying full attention to the newsreader on the one o'clock news, but she could have sworn that he had said Barton Industries had made a takeover bid for Amalgamated Products. The problem was that her attention had not been fully attracted until she heard the name Amalgamated, and by that time the identity of the predator had been revealed and had not been repeated. It had been no more than a one-liner, tucked into the rest of the news. Barton Industries. Sir Peter Barton was an obnoxious individual if ever there was one. She had been seated next to him once at a Confederation of British Industry dinner and had spent most of the evening removing his hand from her thigh. Surely Daddy had no tie-up with Sir Peter Barton and Barton Industries? On the other hand, if one was trying to think of a way of hurting Martin, inflicting Sir Peter Barton upon him could hardly be bettered. She knew her father was devious, especially in business matters, but surely not that devious? She must ring him. Lunchtime. No point in trying to contact him now. He would be out and about cooking up some deal or other over a leisurely lunch somewhere. Best call him on his home number and leave a message for him to call her when he came in.

The Amalgamated bid for Axehouse General had further diminished the already, in her view, inadequate amount of time Martin spent with her. The Barton Industries bid for Amalgamated would almost certainly ensure that he hardly ever came home until everything was resolved. On the other hand, it served him right. He deserved Sir Peter Barton. What was more, if Barton Industries succeeded, Martin would be out of a job and she would see far more of him. On reflection she was rather pleased with the turn of events.

Miles Wartnaby called his daughter back at seven o'clock that evening.

'Hello darling, exciting day, what?'

'Hello Daddy. Thanks for calling back. What have you been up to? It all seems a bit devious to me.'

'Devious. What's devious?'

'Oh, come on, you know. The Barton Industries bid for Amalgamated. How are you involved? I didn't think you had any tie-ups with Peter Barton.'

'I don't and I am not involved in any way with the Barton Industries bid, but it's intriguing isn't it? There are definitely ways of making a bob or two out of this scenario. Martin must be devastated. What do you want? If you want Barton to succeed, I think that might be arranged. The present bid is a Mickey Mouse effort. It hasn't a hope in hell of succeeding. Peter Barton is no fool, however. This bid is just testing the water. The real bid has yet to come.'

'You know, Daddy. I want to to get Martin to realise that I am more important to him than Amalgamated. If a little pain and suffering brings him to that realisation, all well and good. I think Barton Industries might just be the catalyst to bring about what I was praying for.'

Sarah realised as she spoke that her love for Martin was the dominant emotion. When she had asked her father to get at Martin, revenge for his neglect and peccadillos had been uppermost in her mind. She knew now that, deep down, it was a desire to find a way to bring him back to her.

11

Sir Peter Barton threw the last of the morning papers onto his bedroom floor. For the first time in his business career the financial press were questioning not only his ability to succeed in a takeover, but also whether it was wise to launch it in the first place. They questioned whether, even if it did succeed, the level of borrowing needed to finance the deal would be such as to seriously undermine the whole Barton Industries empire. Whilst it was irritating to be doubted on either of these two points, particularly as he had, up to now, been treated as a bit of a favourite of the financial press, it did at least give him the ultimate satisfaction of the opportunity to prove them wrong. What really hurt and made him angry was the description of the bid in one of the tabloids as a 'Mickey Mouse' effort. To make it worse, most of the other papers, in rather more polite tones, seemed to agree. Even the *Financial Times* stated, 'We cannot believe that this bid, as presently structured, is intended to be taken seriously. No doubt the real bid will follow in the fullness of time.' At least the *Financial Times* had got it roughly right. It was intended to be a sighting shot.

He picked up the telephone, barely keeping a hold on his temper.

'Nathan, have you read the papers this morning?'

'Yes. Not very complimentary are they? They are demonstrating their usual lack of financial acumen.'

'Don't give me any shit, Nathan. The bid strategy and the structure of the opening shot were fixed on your advice. You have made me a laughing stock in the City. I won't have the paper I am offering described as junk.'

Nathan decided not to enter into detailed argument on

the telephone. The loan instruments were not junk bonds in the true American sense.

'Sir Peter, I do not need to remind you that we discussed and agreed the strategy at length with the whole bid team, including yourself. I venture to suggest that in the final analysis it will be you who is laughing at the financial press.'

'That does not alter the fact that the genesis of the whole strategy was yours. That's what I pay you enormous sums for, for Chrissake!' Sir Peter Barton was barely containing his temper.

'What the hell do I say on television at lunchtime? I will look an idiot.'

'Plenty of time to devise your tactics for *Business Daily*,' smoothed Nathan Sanson. 'If you recall, the whole basis of the strategy was to open up with a bid that signalled your intention to acquire, but keeping your powder dry as to where exactly you were really coming from. It will lull Amalgamated into a false sense of security. They will think you are struggling to put the deal together, whereas we know that everything is lined up and fully committed.'

He remained unconvinced. Quite apart from anything else he was cross for allowing himself to be talked into accepting Sanson's strategy. He preferred straightforward, simple tactics. They had always worked in the past.

'Look, Nathan, this had better work out.' The threat was left hanging.

'It will, Sir Peter, it will. See you at nine thirty as arranged.'

Nathan put the telephone down. He saw no point in continuing the debate in Barton's present frame of mind. He fully understood his reaction. Nathan had been surprised by the press reaction himself. Had he got it wrong? Had he badly misjudged the bid? He decided he had not. What he had misjudged, in his view, was the sagacity of the financial press. They were unable to cope with anything new or out of the ordinary. They had heard of junk bonds from the American scene and thought they understood them. In essence the loan element of the Barton Industries bid was good old fashioned loan stock jazzed up a bit. It wouldn't take much effort, he decided, to get a more rational and understanding view of the bid across to the Sunday papers.

Peter Barton was not mollified. The week had started out in fine fashion. The couple of days at his retreat in France had been a great success. Both girls had more than met his needs. They had complemented each other perfectly. One had fought back and the other had been submissive. The more he thought about it, the more he was coming round to the view that maybe he did not really need violence to get satisfaction from girls. Maybe the catharsis it afforded him could be achieved in somewhat gentler ways. He could not be certain, however, that the dark side of his nature did not demand the violence. Since his return things had not gone as he wished. First that snobbish wimp Chandler had not even had the balls to give any sort of response to his call to inform him that he was about to be taken over, and now the press had been far from complimentary about the bid. Damn them all. He would show them.

Stephen too had been surprised by the press reaction to the Barton Industries bid. They had clearly misunderstood its nature and, apart from a couple of the more sober and percipient, had not recognised it for what it was; a sighting shot. He wasn't fooled, however. The bid was deadly serious and could not be relied upon to burn itself out. Amalgamated would treat it with less than full seriousness at their peril. He took stock. There had been only a trickle of acceptance from Axehouse General shareholders, but that was par for the course for a bid at this stage. Amalgamated had picked up seven per cent of the Axe-house shares in the market. This had not been easy. The stock had stubbornly hovered around the bid price and there seemed to be a shortage of it in the market. The only conclusion he could draw from this was that there was another buyer in the market. Was it just a speculator or was it a potential counter bidder? There was no means of knowing. Maybe if he could find out who the buyer was he could have a better idea. This would be difficult to find out, predators and speculators were adept these days at hiding their identities, despite all the laws designed to flush them out. Some predators just ignored the law and others had a strictly economical understanding and interpretation of it.

As far as Barton Industries were concerned, Stephen had no doubt whatsoever that they would fight as dirty a campaign as was necessary to obtain their goal. He would have to persuade both Martin and Markby Smythe that this was no time for behaving like gentlemen. Amalgamated would have to fight dirt with dirt, and preferably strike first.

Sir Peter Barton and Barton Industries had not got to where they were so rapidly and effectively by following the path of righteousness. He would dig out dirt by whatever methods were necessary. He resolved not to ask Martin for permission to do this. He knew that there was a very good chance that the tactic would be killed at birth. He could almost hear the phrases that would be thrown back at him. 'No, Amalgamated has a clean reputation. We will not stoop to the low standards of others – we are more than capable of fighting off the likes of Barton Industries without sinking to their level,' and so on. Markby Smythe would be at Martin's shoulder endorsing every word. No, Stephen would find the dirt first and then present it to Martin. He would find it more difficult to reject a *fait accompli*, particularly as others on his Board would not hesitate to use any information that might be uncovered.

Stephen flicked to the back of his diary where he kept a variety of useful telephone numbers. Many he had never used. Throughout his career, however, he had followed a policy of garnering and recording any information that might be of some use later in life. The telephone number of Brabent Agency and the associated name of Trevor Jacques were two such pieces of information. He could not remember where he had got the names from, but he recalled very clearly being told that if he ever needed the service of someone to dig out information that was buried deep down, then the Brabent Agency, and more specifically Trevor Jacques of the agency, was his man.

The telephone was answered with a brisk, 'Brabent Agency'. The voice was well modulated and belied the down market reputation private investigation agencies enjoyed. 'Can I help you?'

'Trevor Jacques please.'

'I am afraid he is in a meeting at the moment. Can I let him know who is calling?'

Stephen Barber smiled to himself. He recognised the old 'he's in a meeting' ploy.

'Tell him I represent a major British company which needs his special services and give me the earliest time at which I can meet him.'

Well-modulated-voice was more than familiar with the desire of many of the clients of the Agency to maintain anonymity on the telephone. She was also a very good judge of when such enigmatic callers were worth humouring.

'Can you manage one o'clock?' It so happened that Trevor Jacques genuinely was in a meeting which had every likelihood of lasting until lunchtime.

'Fine. I'll be there.'

Rachel Masters put the telephone down and immediately typed a note to Trevor Jacques. 'You have a meeting at one o'clock. Identity not revealed. Claims to be major British company. I have a hunch this is something important.'

She knocked gently on Trevor Jacques' door and walked straight in. The knock was more of a gesture than a means of attracting attention to request entry. She walked over to his desk, not saying a word either to him or his client, and slipped the note onto the side of the desk so that he could look at it when he wished but without distracting his attention from his client. She did not wait for any response and left the room immediately. Trevor Jacques carried on as if nobody had entered the room, but by the time the client had returned his attention to him he had read the note.

Rachel Masters had hardly sat down at her desk when the telephone rang. It was Stephen Barber again. He neither introduced himself nor explained that he was the person who had called moments earlier. No problem, she had recognised his voice immediately. She had the auditory equivalent of a photographic memory. Even disguised voices did not deceive her ear. This facility had more than once been of crucial importance to an investigation.

114

'Do you have a television and video recorder in your office?'

'Yes we do, sir.'

'Tape the Channel Four *Business Daily* programme at twelve thirty and have it available for our meeting.'

'Certainly, sir.'

'Thank you.'

Stephen Barber put the telephone down, already impressed with the efficiency of the agency, but not half as impressed as he would have been had he been a fly on the wall in Rachel Masters' office over the next few minutes. As soon as Stephen had put the telephone down she had called a friend at Channel Four studios and found out which guests, if any, were appearing on the programme later that morning. Two, she had been told. The President of the CBI and Sir Peter Barton. She typed another note to Trevor Jacques. 'I think you will find that your client at one o'clock represents Amalgamated Products Plc and that he is interested in Barton Industries and Sir Peter Barton.'

She repeated her performance of earlier in delivering the note and returned to her office where she quickly assembled all the information the agency had on file regarding Barton Industries and Sir Peter Barton and added to it the press cuttings of the previous two days on the subject. She looked at her watch. Eleven fifteen. Time enough to précis the information for Trevor Jacques. A quick glance through the papers told her that Sir Peter Barton was a character of somewhat misty origins, and that Barton Industries was an aggressive predator. There was nothing, however, of real substance that might be useful to anyone interested in getting a hold over him or Barton Industries. Just the promise from the flavour of the collection of press cuttings that a bit of digging would produce something.

Stephen decided not to use the chauffeur-driven Bentley as he was fully entitled to do. He did not want anyone to know where he was going.

Fred Gill looked up from his post as Stephen stepped out

from the lift into the reception area of Amalgamated House and quickly checked his list of bookings for cars. Stephen Barber's name did not appear upon it. He stepped out from the small internal lodge that served both as his office and reception, and without appearing to be in any hurry moved to intercept Stephen Barber before he got to the door.

'Can I get you a car, Mr Barber? I can't see you on the list but I believe there is one available.'

Fred Gill knew perfectly well that there was a car available. It was twelve fifteen. One chauffeur always took his lunch break between twelve and twelve thirty in order to be available for the lunchtime rush for cars. It was a rule, however, that if the journey was important, the chauffeur gave up his lunchbreak and took it later whenever he could.

'No thank you, Fred, I am lunching in Westminster and the short walk will do me no harm.'

Stephen mentally kicked himself as he walked along Millbank towards the Houses of Parliament. He had no need to explain himself to Fred Gill. He could simply have said 'no thank you'. He had been careful to instruct Sheila Birch, his secretary, simply to say that he was not available if anyone asked for him, and if it was Martin or one of the other directors inquiring, to say that he had a meeting in town.

He looked at his watch. Twelve thirty. He must get a cab as soon as possible. The programme was starting. His luck was in. A cab pulled in just in front of him and disgorged its passengers. Stephen quickly climbed in before anyone else could beat him to it. Cabs were at a premium at lunchtime and it was every man for himself. The cabbie slid the partition back.

'Where to, guv?'

'Tothill Street, please.'

Stephen Barber calculated that even in the busy lunch period it would only take five or ten minutes at the outside to reach Tothill Street. He could then walk through to St James's Park. The interviews usually came on *Business Daily* in the second half of the programme. Plenty of time. Nevertheless, to be on the safe side he opened his briefcase and extracted his miniature television set, switched it on and plugged in the earphones. The picture did not appreciate the environment of the cab very much. Indeed, it was virtually impossible to make out what the picture was. This did not worry him, the sound reception was perfectly adequate. There was a brief mention of the Amalgamated/Axehouse/Barton Industries scenario which was really no more than a peg upon which to hang the announcement that Sir Peter Barton would be interviewed after the commercial break.

The cab drew into Tothill Street at twelve forty-two. Perfect, he thought. Time to walk through to St James's Park, find a seat and watch Sir Peter Barton perform before walking back to Tothill Street and his meeting with Trevor Jacques.

Sir Peter Barton had come over rather well, he thought as he walked briskly back towards Tothill Street. He had employed his usual bluff 'I'm a bit of a character' approach, but had nevertheless made a pretty good shot at repairing some of the damage the press had done to the credibility of his bid for Amalgamated.

A quick glance at his watch told Stephen that he had three minutes before his meeting. He hated being late. Seventeen Tothill Street had been the address he had garnered from the Yellow Pages directory. He could not see any sign of Brabent Agency amongst the small forest of brass plates fixed either side of the rather imposing entrance to the building. He was sure that seventeen was the correct number and walked in. On his right near the lifts was a directory of the occupants of the building. Sure enough, there was Brabent Agency listed as occupying offices on the fourth floor. Very discreet, he thought, no obvious sign of the existence of the Agency at street level.

As he stepped out of the lift he saw a small plate on the solid looking door immediately to his left. He decided to walk straight in and stepped into a small lobby with two doors leading off, one marked 'Waiting Room' and one marked 'Reception'. He moved towards the door marked Reception but before he reached it the door opened and a very smartly dressed lady greeted him.

'Good afternoon. May I help you?' Stephen Barber guessed that he was being appraised.

'Yes, I have an appointment with Mr Jacques. My name is Stephen Barber.'

'Mr Jacques is ready for you, Mr Barber. Would you like to follow me?'

Stephen Barber was impressed. This was quite obviously a professional, well-run outfit.

The office could have been that of a senior executive of Amalgamated. It was spacious and with good modern furniture. Trevor Jacques stood up as he entered and moved round the desk to greet him.

'Pleased to meet you, Mr Barber, and what can we do for you?'

As he shook Stephen's hand he gestured him towards a comfortable looking leather chair and sat down opposite. Stephen could not help noticing the folder of papers on the low mahogany table between them. There was no indication on the folder as to what it contained.

'I represent Amalgamated Products, Mr Jacques, but for reasons which I will explain in due course it is important that nobody at either Amalgamated or elsewhere knows that I have consulted you. It may help by way of introduction to indicate what you can do for Amalgamated if you have a look at the video recording of the *Business Daily* programme which I asked your secretary to record. It is the interview with Sir Peter Barton that I want you to see.'

'Certainly.'

Trevor Jacques picked up the small remote control unit from the table between them and pointed it at the television set across the room. The face of the presenter appeared and the tail end of a sentence came from the set '. . . interview with Sir Peter Barton.'

Stephen Barber looked sharply across at Trevor Jacques, who gave him a brief smile and turned his attention to the televison set. Stephen Barber was impressed. In the few minutes it had taken him to walk across from St James's Park they had correctly identified his interest and set the recording up to start at precisely the right point. He turned his attention back to the television and Sir Peter Barton.

The interview was only about five minutes long. Trevor Jacques switched the set off and turned to Stephen, giving him no time to explain his mission.

118

'I take it that we are concerned with the Barton Industries bid for Amalgamated and that you are looking for our help in thwarting it?' Trevor Jacques did not wait for confirmation and carried straight on. 'We have put together a file on both Barton Industries and Sir Peter Barton.' He picked up the folder on the table and as quickly put it down again, merely wishing to indicate its presence.

'Oh, and by the way, it wasn't difficult. When you asked for the *Business Daily* programme to be taped you could only have been interested in someone appearing on it. We did not think that the President of the CBI was likely to be the subject of your interest. Also, we read the financial press.'

'You're quite right, of course. If I may explain. I am here entirely upon my own initiative. I am the Corporate Planning Manager at Amalgamated with particular responsibility for both our bid for Axehouse General and, now, fighting off the bid from Barton Industries. If I had suggested to my Chairman that we should employ an agency with a view to finding out anything we could about Barton Industries and Sir Peter Barton in order to use it as one of the means of fighting off the bid, I believe he would have rejected the idea. Martin Chandler is of the old school, although I doubt he would either be flattered to be so described or accept the description. If you will forgive me, I believe he would probably regard your profession as somewhat shady and would oppose Amalgamated using its services. On the other hand, if I present him with a *fait accompli* and, hopefully, ammunition with which to defeat the bid and also present it at the right moment, I think he will accept it and act upon it. People change when their backs are to the wall.'

'So what precisely do you have in mind?'

'Well firstly, any information about the activities and methods of Barton Industries that may not be general knowledge, particularly in relation to its activities in the takeover field. Are you familiar with the rules by the way?'

Trevor Jacques gestured to his desk and the yellow and blue books sitting there. Stephen immediately recognised the Stock Exchange Listing Agreement, often ironically referred to as 'The Yellow Peril', and the City Code in its distinctive blue cover.

'Of course, and we have access to some useful and knowledgeable sources in the City itself.'

'You have just seen Sir Peter Barton on the box. You can see the kind of person he is. He has a reputation for getting what he wants and is not too fussy how he gets it. I must say straight away, however, that that is purely reputation. I have no knowledge or evidence that he has broken the rules or the law in any of his takeover bids, but it would not surprise me if he had. I want you to find out for me. Secondly, I want to know all there is to know about Sir Peter himself. Does he have any personal skeletons in his cupboard? Anything you come up with must be cast iron.'

'Mr Barber, if I am to work for you it is best we fully understand each other from the start. Firstly, I do not come cheap. Secondly, I will only ever report to you on information that I am personally satisfied is absolutely cast iron. You will realise, of course, that this means you may well pay me a lot of money for absolutely no result. I will not report rumour to you nor will I give you information of which I am reasonably, but not absolutely, certain. If you want that kind of service I can recommend a number of perfectly reputable agencies who are prepared to work on that basis, leaving it to your judgment whether to use the information or not. Thirdly, once I have given you any information it is entirely a matter for your discretion if and how you use it, and you will not disclose, in any circumstances, where it came from. You will be asked to sign a detailed contract before I start covering all these points in detail.'

Stephen Barber did not respond immediately. In a way he was disappointed. He had hoped to get details of everything Trevor Jacques found out, however insubstantial and unsubstantiated it might be. At least he then would be able to use it as a basis for further enquiries, if he thought it worthwhile, and depending upon his assessment of the validity of the information he could then decide to take the risk of using it. After all, a lot of harm could be done by judiciously dropping a few words here and there. Nobody needed to know where it came from. On reflection, however, he concluded that Trevor Jacques' terms were on balance better for him and Amalgamated. He would be guaranteed a thorough and efficient service. After all, there was no mileage in it for Trevor Jacques and the Brabent Agency if they got the reputation for charging high fees for little or no result. They would be motivated to find what there was to find. It also removed uncertainty from the scene. Any information was going to be accurate and fully reliable.

'Fine. I accept your terms. As you will appreciate, time is not on our side. Bids, by and large, work to a fairly predictable timetable. The bid was announced yesterday so the formal Offer Document will be sent within the next twenty-six days, the first closing date for acceptances will be twenty-one days after that, the last date for revising the offer is a further twenty-five days on and the last date for declaring the bid unconditional, unless of course there is a competing bid, is just fourteen days after that. It sounds a long time but, of course, it can be telescoped and I think it will be as Barton Industries may try to move fast to gain control and spike the Amalgamated bid for Axehouse General before it can become unconditional.'

Stephen Barber was really thinking aloud. He was fairly certain Trevor Jacques was more than familiar with the course of takeover bids.

'Be assured we will not drag our feet. Rachel will outline our fee structure for you and get you to sign the agreement. I take it you will be signing on behalf of Amalgamated and have the authority to do so, despite what you have told me regarding the secrecy of the investigation?'

'Oh yes, certainly. If you want to contact me at the office call me on my direct line; the number is on my card. If anyone else answers just say Mr Bennett called and would I call him back.'

As he left the offices of the Brabent Agency Stephen Barber had the feeling they would strike gold for him.

12

Miles Wartnaby decided it was getting more and more like a game of chess. Each move made the situation more involved, generating more complexities in the next and succeeding moves. The Barton Industries bid for Amalgamated had come in at 185 pence per share. The market had not been all that impressed. The shares had stood at 173 immediately before the bid, had briefly shot up to the bid price of 185 and then, within a couple of hours, settled back to 175. Nevertheless that two pence increase had boosted his profit by another £300,000 or so. Short term movements in share prices were not his immediate concern however. The more important issue was how did the Barton Industries bid affect his overall strategy in relation to Amalgamated and Axehouse, not forgetting his promise to his daughter Sarah. If the Barton Industries bid for Amalgamated succeeded, then, by definition the Amalgamated bid for Axehouse would have failed, as this event was a condition of the Barton Industries bid. This outcome would certainly be unwelcome to Martin who would be out of the door in no time. This would certainly wound him deeply. Amalgamated was his life and he always considered that he had an obligation to the founding fathers to ensure that Amalgamated prospered; preferably in the hands of someone connected with the family. Would Sarah wish the outcome to be so dire for Martin? From a purely financial viewpoint he stood to gain most by the Barton Industries bid succeeding. They would probably have to go to 200 pence per share to win. This, on his present shareholding, would give him a profit of £6·8 million. If the bid failed the Amalgamated share price would obviously fall back. In comparison if the Amalgamated bid for Axehouse General succeeded, and a price tag of 300 pence per share was a realistic figure for success in his opinion, he would show a profit of about £5·3 million on his present shareholding. This outcome was less attractive on two counts. Firstly he would make less money, and, secondly, Martin would have won and he would have failed to deliver his promise to Sarah. A triumphant Martin would spend even more time on the affairs of Amalgamated, and Sarah would see even less of him.

It all seemed fairly straightforward. He should do all he could to block the Amalgamated bid for Axehouse General and support the Barton Industries bid for Amalgamated. The Barton Industries however would be an uphill struggle. It had got off to a bad start and, furthermore, was second in line. The Amalgamated bid for Axehouse would come to the crunch first. He had no great opinion of the large investors; the insurance companies, the pension funds and the investment and unit trust companies, who, at the end of the day, effectively determined the outcome of virtually all bids for companies quoted on the Stock Exchange. Whatever they might say publicly, in his view, most of them would go for the bid which seemed most likely to show the best short term profit. Their protestations that they cast their votes in the best interests of the future of the company rang very hollow indeed. In present circumstances they would most likely use their power to support the bid which appeared to have the best chance of success. All the indications pointed toward this being Amalgamated at this stage. What was more, there was a considerable incentive for them to support the Amalgamated bid for Axehouse, for, if they killed it off by not assenting their shares, they could fall between two stools. The Barton Industries bid for Amalgamated might subsequently fail as well leaving them with nothing. What was nearer to Miles Wartnaby's heart, such an eventuality would leave him with little or no profit.

Miles Wartnaby took another sip of his whisky. Beethoven's Pastoral Symphony moved on its tranquil way in the background. He always found a whisky with just a dash of spring water, allied to a Beethoven Symphony, aided his thinking. The wind was now gently caressing the corn and he could see its ebb and flow in his mind's eye. The image was not inappropriate to his thoughts. The fortunes of companies ebbed and flowed. Some, like Amalgamated, had the small tidal range of the Mediterranean, others like BCI enjoyed the high spring tides of the North Atlantic but not, he fervently hoped, the associated extreme low tides; although there had been plenty of companies which, having reached the heights, had subsequently sunk to very low levels indeed. He drew himself back from his reverie. There was a lot to be considered. He did not yet have a solution in his grasp. The scene would change as the bids wound along their respective paths. Time was on his side. He had the luxury of being able to decide when to jump, and in which direction, much later on. The only decision now required was whether to buy more shares at this stage in Amalgamated, Axehouse General, both or neither.

If he bought more Axehouse he was betting upon an Amalgamated victory, or was he? If he bought enough of them he could probably block that victory, but at what a price? If on the other hand he bought more Amalgamated he would probably help support their price which, in turn, could strengthen their bid for Axehouse General, on the other. . . no, it could all wait a few days. It was approaching midnight and the whisky was no longer an aid to his contemplations; it was dulling his senses.

James Walker looked across the room to Robert Brodie and Terry King who were in deep conversation as he entered the apartment on the top of Amalgamated House.

'What are you two cooking up?' he enquired jovially as he crossed the room. They both turned their heads towards him, looking slightly startled. They had not heard him coming in. He laughed inwardly. Hole in one, he thought. He had only intended the remark as a bantering way of announcing his presence.

'Just chewing the fat over the Barton Industries bid,' growled Brodie, irritated with himself for having reacted as he had to the arrival of James Walker. This was nothing less than the truth, as far as it went. What he did not say was that he had been sounding out Terry King to gauge his reaction to a proposition that could turn to the advantage of Robert Brodie, and to the detriment of Martin Chandler and James Walker. He had a strong suspicion that, whatever the merits of other candidates, James Walker was earmarked as Martin Chandler's successor. Blood was thicker than water.

Brodie's irritation was increased by having been cut off in mid stream before he could judge Terry King's reaction. He had been careful to broach the subject in a way which King could not take as a clear indication that he was proposing something disloyal to Chandler and Amalgamated. He had been careful to express it in a way that suggested that if Barton Industries should win, which heaven forbid, how best could the new situation be turned to advantage. Now thanks to James Walker's untimely arrival, King might get the precise impression that he had been so careful to avoid.

Brodie was quite correct. The unexpected break in the conversation, and his reaction to the arrival of James Walker, had caused Terry King to stop and think; and his thoughts were not travelling down a path which Brodie would have wished them to be travelling. It had dawned on Terry that Brodie was not simply speculating upon the situation that might obtain if Barton Industries were successful in their bid; he was considering whether a successful Barton Industries bid might not be turned to his own advantage. Terry King wanted none of this. Whilst he had no family connections with Amalgamated, unlike Chandler and Walker, he nevertheless felt a strong loyalty to the company. He could think of nothing worse than being part of Barton Industries, and subordinate to Sir Peter Barton. What was more, if Brodie really did have in mind in some way assisting Barton Industries from within, he needed his head read. Peter Barton was not the man to worry too much about past favours if it did not suit him and, in Terry King's opinion, he would shoot the senior management of Amalgamated out of the door pretty damn quick. Terry mentally thanked James Walker for his timely arrival. A few moments more and he could have been enmeshed in a web from which he would have found it difficult to escape. A quiet word in Walker's ear would not come amiss.

Brodie regained his composure quickly. He realised he would have to tread very carefully.

'Yes, Terry and I were just speculating upon the scenario if, against all the odds, Barton Industries did succeed in taking Amalgamated.'

Terry King decided not to chip in and point out that it had been Brodie who had been speculating, and that he was the listener for the most part. A quiet word in Walker's ear was definitely the better way of dealing with the matter.

'It is a highly unlikely event, I know, but it could happen and I think we would be wise to give some thought as to how we cope with the situation in order to salvage what we could from the wreck. We have a responsibility to our employees to protect their interests as best we may.'

He is getting a bit pompous now, thought King. Brodie also realised he was in danger of over justifying himself and thereby certainly giving clues to his real thoughts.

'Just a few thoughts, James, and probably premature at that.'

James was slightly bemused. There was an odd atmosphere and Brodie was not his usual bluff self. He was coming across in an almost apologetic way. He decided not to comment. He would no doubt find out what was going on in the fullness of time.

'I'm glad I found you both together. I am worried about the Barton Industries bid. Despite the City and media reaction, we must take it seriously and I am not at all certain Lloyd, Meisson are the right merchant bank to act for us. They have a very good reputation in attack but in defence I am not so sure.'

Terry King saw an immediate opportunity to nail his colours to the right mast.

'I entirely agree, James, Lloyd, Meisson are very professional but they are also ultra correct. Life has changed in the City. There are a number of merchant banks now which can best be described as ruthless, and not averse to bending the rules a little if it is in the interest of their client and, not least, in their own interest in order to maintain their reputation as winners. I am not suggesting that they would knowingly do anything illegal; but so much of the regulation governing takeover bids is extra-statutory that it can be ignored if it is expedient.'

Terry King stopped. He had not quite expressed his thoughts as he had wished. What he had said was 'un-Amalgamated'. James Walker came to his rescue.

'You are right Terry: whether we like it or not others do not play the game as we would wish to play it. I am sure none of us would be party to anything that was illegal, or even in clear breach of the City Code or the Takeover Code. However neither code is definitive. and there are many areas of uncertainty. Some merchant banks, like Lloyd, Meisson, will stick to the spirit of the codes; others will turn uncertainty to their advantage. I think we need the latter kind of merchant bank to defend ourselves against Barton Industries. I certainly do not see Barton or his investment bankers, Mather Richards, fighting with the gloves on.'

What James Walker did not go on to say was that he had just come from a lengthy discussion with Stephen Barber who had been propounding just such thoughts as James Walker was now presenting as his own. The truth was that James Walker had not given the matter too much thought himself. He had been content to stick with Lloyd, Meisson. After all they were still regarded by many as the leading merchant bank in takeover matters. Once Stephen had got into his stride James had readily accepted his arguments for staying with Lloyd, Meisson on the Axehouse bid and switching to someone more aggressive to defend the Barton Industries bid. Sir Richard Brookes, Axehouse General and their merchant bankers, Threadgolds, were all likely to fight the battle the Lloyd, Meisson way. Sir Peter Barton, Barton Industries and Mather Richards were not.

Brodie, for his own reasons, would have preferred to stay with Lloyd, Meisson but felt he would be unwise to swim against the tide. Certainly at this moment to do so would call in question where his true loyalties lay.

'I couldn't agree more. We must meet fire with fire.'

It came across with conviction for such was Brodie's natural instinct. He was one of nature's fighters and he would just have to be careful not to let his real thoughts come too close to the surface. Barton Industries might well not succeed and he did not want to queer his pitch with Amalgamated.

☆ ☆ ☆

Stephen was confident that he had James Walker on his side and pondered whether he needed to canvass any of the other directors before approaching Martin. He decided not. James could be relied upon to raise the matter of merchant bankers for the defence with the other senior executive directors; Richard Gibbs would follow their line, and it was up to Martin to persuade the non-executive directors always provided he himself could be persuaded. Stephen also wanted to be the one to make the proposal to Martin. He did not want James or anyone else to appear to be the initiator of the idea. He had suffered enough during his career from those senior to him taking his ideas, selling them and then taking all the credit. He was fairly confident that James would not go direct to Martin with the idea. He would first clear the ground with his peers. He was not one to put himself out on a limb.

Stephen knew Martin was still in his office and decided to go straight up there rather than ask Ann if he was free. As he walked up the stairs to the fifth floor he reminded himself that he must get an office there. He would speak to Charles Timpson who organised these things. He would tell him Martin Chandler wanted him nearby. Stephen was confident Charles Timpson would not check. As he got to the top of the stairs the door opposite opened and Howard Irwin started to come out. Christ, Stephen Barber thought to himself, I've forgotten to ask him.

'Hello Howard, I was just coming to see you,' he lied.

Howard looked at his watch.

'Will it take long old boy? I have an appointment in

town in half an hour.'

At the squash courts no doubt, thought Stephen.

'No, no I don't think so. Just a couple of minutes.'

He did not want it to take any longer in any case. It suited him that Howard was in a hurry. He could be incredibly pedantic and long winded sometimes if he was not busy, and Stephen wanted to catch Martin before he left the building.

'Come in, come in.'

He turned on his heels and went back into his office, which was notable for its untidiness above all else. Piles of paper everywhere; they were on his desk, on his table, and even on the floor. Stephen doubted that he had read even a fraction of them, or indeed had any intention of so doing. Howard Irwin did not sit down but stood there and, with an almost imperceptible nod of the head, invited him to get on with whatever he had to say.

He briefly outlined what he was about to propose to Martin Chandler concerning a change of merchant bank for the defence against the Barton Industries bid. He added that James Walker was in agreement with the proposal. Howard gave every impression of listening closely to what he had to say.

'Splendid, splendid. I have been having the same thoughts myself actually.'

With that he turned on his heels and made his way from the room. Stephen stood there momentarily stunned. The man had not even bothered to ask if he had any particular merchant bank in mind. He shrugged his shoulders and followed Howard from the room and made his way along the corridor to Ann Gordon's office.

'Is he in?'

'Yes, Mr Barber, but I think it might be better not to disturb him. He's immersed in some papers and I know he wants to get through them before he leaves this evening. His car is already waiting at the front door.'

'Not to worry Ann, I'll say I pushed past you if he gets cross at being disturbed.'

He knocked lightly on the door and entered in the same motion. Martin looked up, a momentary expression of irritation crossing his face.

'Can it wait until morning?'

'I think not Chairman.'

'Oh alright make it quick.'

Stephen succinctly outlined his proposal for replacing Lloyd, Meisson on the defence. He could see Martin's interest quicken as he spoke.

'Have you anyone in mind, Stephen?'

'Yes, Greensmith Leonard.'

He saw Martin Chandler's expression cloud again.

'Do you really think Amalgamated Products should use a merchant bank of that reputation Stephen?'

'Yes I do. I know they have had their knuckles rapped once or twice by the Takeover Panel, but they have never been accused of doing anything illegal or in clear contravention of the codes. They sail close to the wind, but more often than not they win. I think such a move will earn us more respect in the City than opprobrium.'

'Isn't there anyone else, equally effective, but with a more reputable image? Harrison Prentice, for example.'

'I don't believe their reputation is generally regarded as disreputable in the City, Chairman. Just hard and effective. Yes, there are others rather more aggressive than Lloyd, Meisson but less aggressive than Greensmith Leonard, but if we are going to change horses why settle for less than the best?'

Stephen was confident that he had won the argument. The principle of changing merchant bankers had already been implicitly conceded. It would be difficult now for Martin to reject what he was being advised was the best.

Martin thought for a moment. He did not really like the idea of Greensmith Leonard, but he could not deny that they currently had the reputation of being the most effective merchant bankers in defending the targets of takeover bids. He decided his own personal distaste should not override the best interests of Amalgamated. If Greensmith Leonard gave Amalgamated the best chance of escaping the clutches of Barton Industries, so be it. He was not going to capitulate immediately however.

'OK, fix a meeting with them. I will see what they have to offer, and then decide what to recommend to the Board.'

He checked his diary.

'Anytime tomorrow afternoon will do, there is nothing I can't reschedule.'

Stephen left the office feeling more than satisfied. He had no doubt that Greensmith Leonard would be on board before the end of tomorrow and the credit would be his. James Walker would be unable to upstage him.

As soon as he got back to his office he rang Alan Mortimer at Greensmith Leonard. He had worked with him on a small takeover before he had joined Amalgamated. He had been suitably impressed with his style and efficiency. Anyone meeting him for the first time could easily be misled as to his true nature. His manner was mild and almost apologetic. This masked a very tough and determined character which was allied to a formidable intellect. Stephen was very pleased that he would be on their side. Had he been aware that Miles Wartnaby and BCI were interested in the web of bids involving Amalgamated, he would have been even more pleased for Greensmith Leonard were BCI's merchant bankers. Their appointment by Amalgamated would block them from acting for BCI.

It took Stephen an hour to get hold of Alan Mortimer. He had been in a meeting when he had first called and he had left a message for him to call back as soon as possible on his private line.

'Hello Stephen, long time no see. What can I do for you?'

Alan Mortimer never wasted too much time on casual chit chat. He preferred to get straight down to the business in hand.

'I want to fix a meeting for you with my Chairman, Alan. Tomorrow afternoon if it is possible. The matter is urgent.'

'Defence side I assume Stephen?'

Alan Mortimer, like any merchant banker worth his salt, kept abreast of everything that was going on in the takeover world. He considered it unlikely that Amalgamated would wish to bring them in on the bid for Axehouse General at this stage, although it was not entirely beyond the realms of possibility. It had happened before for a merchant bank to be brought into a bid in mid stream to work with the existing merchant bank.

'Yes, that's right. It might be helpful if you and I could meet this evening, so that I can put you in the picture before you meet Martin Chandler tomorrow.'

'Not so fast Stephen. I don't know whether I can act yet. Let me check my Bible.'

Everyone at Greensmith Leonard with authority to agree to act on behalf of a client had a loose leaf folder by his side which was kept up to date on a daily basis. It contained a record of every company Greensmith Leonard had acted for in a takeover as well as a list of companies whom Greensmith Leonard considered would regard them as their merchant bankers, even if they had not acted for them on a takeover. It might be that Greensmith Leonard had acted for a company on a financing deal. The final section of the folder listed all companies which had been advised by Greensmith Leonard in connection with any current or anticipated takeover, even if they were not active participators. Alan Mortimer scanned through the folder. No listing for either Axehouse General or Barton Industries. A scan through the final section of the folder revealed no entry for any client interested in any of the protagonists in the two bids. What Alan Mortimer did not know was that Miles Wartnaby had discussed the Amalgamated bid for Axehouse and the Barton Industries bid for Amal-gamated with his colleague Ray Schuster. Ray Schuster had meant to register the interest in the folder but failed to do so. He would later regret that omission. He should have been put on guard that the interest was more than theoretical by the fact that Miles Wartnaby had spoken to him twice on the subject, and had specifically sought his views on speculating in the shares of both Amalgamated and Axehouse.

'It looks clear Stephen,' Alan Mortimer confirmed. 'I don't see any problem in our acting for you. Let's see, I can manage three thirty tomorrow afternoon. Is that OK?'

'That's fine. What about this evening?'

'I won't be away from here before eight thirty. I'll meet you at the Grenadier in Molton Street. Know it?' Alan

132

Mortimer did not wait for an answer. 'I suggest we meet tomorrow at our Whitehall apartment. It's more anonymous. It is one thing for you to be seen walking into our offices but quite another for your Chairman. Some journalists almost make a career out of sitting outside the front doors of merchant bankers. Our Whitehall apartment is totally secure. It is not rented in the bank's name and there are over thirty apartments in the complex. I will tell you the address and how to get in when I see you this evening.'

'See you around nine Alan. Bye.'

Stephen put the telephone down with some satisfaction. He was starting to get his hands on the levers at Amalgamated. This was the first major initiative accomplished. He had no intention of letting the fact of Greensmith Leonard being brought on board on his initiative go unnoticed. Unless, of course, Barton Industries should win; in that case it would be irrelevant.

13

Nathan Sanson was worried. There was no doubt that the bid tactics had misfired. To start out with a package containing such a high proportion of debt that looked suspiciously like junk bonds had not been a good idea. The financial press had misunderstood the nature of the securities being offered. They were not the high interest, high risk animals so beloved of the American corporate raiders. They were half way between this and good old fashioned British unsecured loan stock. He had to admit that Sir Peter Barton had done a very good job on the Channel Four *Business Daily* programme to retrieve the situation. He also had to admit that he was not exactly flavour of the month in Barton's eyes. He would have to do some pretty nifty footwork to retrieve the situation. A takeover bid tended to develop a life and style of its own, and once it had got into a particular rut it was often very difficult to shift it. The idea at the outset had been to start with a package that whetted the appetite but was essentially a sighting shot. To create interest, and then follow up with something even more interesting and attractive had been the plan. The timing on this had been to see what level of acceptance the starting package received, assess its reception generally and then come in with a revised bid two or three days before acceptors could withdraw if the bid had not gone unconditional. This would have to change now. Judging the timing was both difficult and crucial. Too early and it would smell of panic, and give a downward twist to the spiral of the fortunes of the bid. Too late and the bid would have lost such a degree of credibility as to be incapable of being given the kiss of life. The formal Offer

Document setting out all the minute details of the bid would clearly have to be rushed out as soon as possible to start the clock ticking on the bid timetable. The revised offer, and it was clear there would have to be a revised offer, could then follow almost immediately on the expiry of the first closing date for acceptance of the bid which followed twenty-one days later.

What form should the revised offer take? Nathan Sanson turned the options over in his mind. All cash was out of the question. Barton Industries quite simply did not have the capacity to raise such a huge sum. A combination of cash, with a loan note alternative for those with a Capital Gains Tax problem, Barton Industries equity, and unsecured loan stock with an attractive interest rate was probably the answer. Boring and unadventurous, but then that was what would appeal most to the Amalgamated shareholders, and would be understood by the press. The big risk was the Barton Industries equity part of the package. This would have to be greater than originally planned. It had two drawbacks. Firstly, it would inevitably dilute the interests of the existing Barton Industries shareholders to a greater extent, and thus might make it more difficult to get the bid approved by them. Secondly, it meant that the Barton Industries share price during the bid would be crucial. If it fell much below the price upon which the package was structured, this would inevitably reduce the value of the package and undermine the prospects of the bid succeeding. The Barton Industries share price would have to be closely monitored and, Sanson decided, a programme must be mapped out to help maintain the share price of Barton Industries if it showed signs of flagging.

He called Peter Barton and outlined his plan for the future conduct of the bid.

'That's more like it,' he growled, conveniently overlooking the fact that he had endorsed the structure of the original bid.

'I don't understand why we could not have gone down that path at the outset. All we would have had to do then was sweeten the bid a little at the appropriate moment without having completely to rebuild it.'

Sanson saw no profit in passing comment on the outburst.

'I'll get to work on it straight away, Sir Peter, and let you have a detailed structure and timetable before the close of business tomorrow.'

Sir Peter Barton put the phone down. He needed to release his anger otherwise it would cloud his judgment. He pressed the intercom.

'I'm going out, Pru. Get my car to the front door in twenty minutes.'

Pru Wetherby knew better than to ask him where he was going. She had worked for him long enough to know when not to ask such questions.

'Certainly, Sir Peter. I'll send any important messages round to your apartment later.'

The lack of response indicated agreement, and Pru had found out without having to ask that he was not planning to return to the office that day.

Peter Barton picked up the handset of his direct outside line and dialled a number he knew from heart. An upper class female voice answered.

'Clarissa Morton.'

'Ah, Clarissa, Peter Barton here.'

Clarissa Morton was about the only person in business, and she was in business, with whom he did not use his title when introducing himself.

'I need a nice, discreet little number who will keep her mouth shut. Someone new.'

Clarissa Morton sighed. It was becoming increasingly difficult to get Sir Peter Barton fixed up. His reputation had spread amongst her girls. Whilst there were some who were prepared to indulge his taste for violence, indeed one or two even seemed to enjoy it, and they all enjoyed the substantial present that accompanied it, finding new girls prepared to endure it was a different matter. It was the more difficult because he insisted that they were not warned in advance.

'I will do my best, Sir Peter.'

She knew he liked to be addressed by his title and, however much she despised a good client, she stroked his ego.

'Half an hour, then.'

'I doubt that I will be able to fix anyone up in such a short time, Sir Peter, especially as you want someone new.'

'Not to worry, I will let myself in and wait for her.'

Sir Peter, as a regular and valued client, had a key to the luxurious apartment Clarissa Morton kept for the sole purpose of providing a place in which her clients could be entertained. He put the phone down. This could be quite entertaining. The more he thought about it, the more entertaining he concluded it would be. Previously the girl had always been there first and the drama had followed a predictable course. This time he would be sitting there sipping a glass of Clarissa Morton's excellent single malt whisky when the girl came in. He would be exuding an air of calm innocence and the girl would be oblivious of what was in store for her. Yes, the scenario had definite possibilities. Very entertaining.

Sir Peter Barton considered himself to be very lucky to have come across Clarissa Morton. She catered for his needs in such style, and with the utmost discretion. He thought back to the times when he had needed to resort to seedy hotel rooms, or even worse, less than desirable bedsitters. The girls had been less than choice and he had needed to be very careful what he did. He had had one very nasty confrontation with the pimp, and only the very rapid production of two hundred and fifty pounds, a lot of money fifteen years ago, had saved him from a vicious beating which would have put what he had just done to the girl very much in the shade.

Clarissa Morton had found him rather than the other way round. He had been at a smart cocktail party on his own when he had spotted a very attractive blonde across the room. She was tall and slim and was dressed in a manner that made it less than difficult to form a judgment as to whether she was in perfect proportion or not. He had been unable to take his eyes off her. Unfortunately, she was very securely attached to another man who clearly had no intention of letting anyone get near her. Most of the time his right hand was gently stroking her bottom.

'Nice, isn't she?' A very upper class voice purred into his ear. He had turned round startled at the intrusion into the fantasies that were by now occupying his mind. What he saw was an elegantly dressed, good looking woman of about forty.

'Er, yes,' he had stammered. 'Very nice. Peter Barton,' he offered, for once in his life not using his title.

'I know. Sir Peter Barton. Clarissa Morton.'

She smiled at him but only with her mouth. Her eyes remained expressionless. Sir Peter Barton felt uncomfortable. He did not quite know how to react. Flirtation was clearly not on the menu. She saved him.

'Would you like to meet her? Not now, you understand.'

She glanced across the room, his eyes needed no invitation to follow. 'She seems to be happily settled for the evening.' She did not wait for an answer. She already knew it. 'I have a nice little apartment which you can rent for a very modest fee. Lucinda can meet you there. I am sure you would be more than delighted to give her a little present in return for her company.'

Clarissa Morton reached into her handbag, took out a card, quickly wrote something on the back of it and passed it to him without comment. Before he could say anything she had slipped from his side and was greeting someone else. This time he noticed the eyes smiled as well as the mouth. He recognised that he was purely business. He glanced at the card. It simply gave a telephone number. He turned it over. On the back was written £250 + £250. The meaning was obvious.

On the first few occasions he had behaved himself and stifled the urge for violence. Then it had broken out. He had given the girl £500, but she had still complained to Clarissa Morton. She had not called him immediately but the next time he wanted a girl she rebuked him mildly. She merely indicated that if he wished to have a girl with whom to indulge his penchant for violence he was to let her know in advance. Almost anything could be arranged.

☆ ☆ ☆

A taxi had been sitting across the street from the offices of Barton Industries since Sir Peter Barton had arrived at eight thirty that morning. Indeed, it had followed him there from his apartment overlooking Hyde Park. It was not always the same taxi, but the man sitting in the back was always the same. From time to time the man would get out of the taxi and walk slowly away. The taxi would then leave its post and motor round the block and pick the man up again on its way back. About every second hour it was a different taxi that appeared to pick the man up. In the busy rush of London traffic nobody noticed this little panto-mime; certainly no-one at Barton Industries noticed.

Unsurprisingly, Sir Peter Barton did not pay any special attention to the taxi across the street when he emerged and stepped into his chauffeur-driven Rolls Royce. Neither did he notice when the taxi pulled out smoothly into the traffic just two vehicles behind him. He sat back all anticipation. The late afternoon traffic was beginning to build up. The rush hour traffic gets earlier and earlier, he thought impatiently to himself. Clarissa Morton's apartment was normally only a ten minute ride from his office. He looked at his watch. Fifteen minutes already. He managed to resist the temptation to tell his chauffeur which traffic lane to get in. He also resisted the temptation to criticise him for the route he had chosen. He had stopped doing both of these things after Nathan Sanson had once sarcastically asked him if his chauffeur offered him suggestions on how to run Barton Industries after he had been giving his chauffeur a particularly hard time one day telling him how to drive.

At last the car pulled up outside Fairfield Mansions. Sir Peter Barton forced himself to get out in a leisurely manner as if he were in no particular hurry.

'You needn't wait, Bob. I'll make my own way home.'

He didn't bother to try and justify himself by suggesting he was going to a meeting which might run on for a long time. Bob Allcock had brought him to Fairfield Mansions many times, and Sir Peter Barton was quite sure he knew the purpose of these visits.

The taxi drew up fifty yards behind the Rolls Royce on the opposite side of the street. From this position its occupant could get a good view of the building Sir Peter Barton was about to enter. Neither he nor his chauffeur noticed the taxi.

He climbed the five steps up to the front door and fished in his jacket pocket for the key. The man in the taxi swore quietly to himself. He would be unable to see which apartment he was going to. As soon as Barton had disappeared from sight, and the Rolls Royce had glided smoothly round the corner, Harvey Cook stepped out of the taxi and sauntered across the road. He examined the entrance of Fairfield mansions. Just as he had expected it sported an entry phone system. He studied the names underneath the five buttons. There were only four names. He wondered whether that could be significant, or maybe the fifth apartment was simply empty. Unlikely, he thought. This was a fashionable and much sought after area. He studied the four names. Just initials and surnames. No indication of whether the occupants were male or female. Nothing unusual in that. Women in London, if they were wise, did not advertise the fact that they might be alone in a flat or apartment.

He crossed back over the road and sat down in the taxi again. He would just have to sit it out and see if anything happened which might indicate which apartment Peter Barton had entered. Two people approached the building and let themselves in with their own keys. Both were men. Next an attractive looking woman. Might be promising. She had her own key as well. No indication one way or the other, Harvey Cook thought to himself. He felt confident, however, that Barton was up to no good. He had a sixth sense about these things. Sir Peter was some way from his own apartment and this area was exclusively residential.

Now this was promising. A taxi pulled up outside Fairfield Mansions and another attractive woman got out. She was younger than the one who had entered the building five minutes earlier. She looked slightly flustered, as if she were late. She also seemed uncertain of her bearings. She stepped back from the building and peered at the stone inscription above the doorway which announced that it was Fairfield Mansions. She took some time over this, screwing her eyes up. She needs spectacles, Harvey Cook thought somewhat irrelevantly to himself. She eventually decided it was the right building and mounted the steps. She examined the buttons closely and pressed the button which had no indication of who the occupant was. Now that really was interesting. Harvey

Cook noted it was the third floor apartment. He glanced up. The curtains were closed and a chink of light showed through them. The girl pressed her ear to the loudspeaker and then spoke into it. The front door clicked open. She pushed it fully open and went in. She had clearly got the right apartment and was expected.

Harvey Cook waited five minutes and then crossed the road to Fairfield Mansions. He pressed the unidentified button and waited. No reply. He tried it again. Still no reply. He returned to the taxi and put his hand down to the driver's window.

'Go for a little ride, Bill; about ten minutes. I'll just wander about here for a bit. Oh, and call up Harry. I want to follow the girl as well when she comes out.'

Harvey Cook was pretty confident that Sir Peter Barton would not be coming out of Fairfield Mansions in the next ten minutes or so. He was also pretty confident that the girl would not be doing so either. He would put money on their being in the apartment together; but he had no actual proof. Trevor Jacques would want him to be absolutely certain. He looked up, the light was still on in the apartment. At that moment the curtains bulged, swung partly open and as quickly closed again. It was as if someone had fallen against them. Unfortunately, Harvey Cook had been unable to see who it was. He crossed the street again and pushed the unidentified button. He waited. No reply. Whoever was in the apartment obviulsy had no curiosity as to who was paging the apartment, or alternatively did not wish to acknowledge their presence.

Melanie Hunt had felt almost sick with apprehension sitting in the back of the taxi approaching Fairfield Mansions. If she was honest with herself it was fear. She had not worked for Clarissa Morton before, but she knew from her flatmate Helen Saunders that to be one of 'Clarissa's girls' was a passport to a very comfortable life, provided one kept quiet about it. Clarissa Morton did not like her girls talking about her business or her clients. Helen Saunders had put a word in for her with Clarissa

Morton some weeks before and had backed it up with a photograph. Melanie Hunt had heard nothing more – not, that is, until half an hour ago. The telephone had gone in the flat and a very upper class woman's voice had asked if she could speak to Melanie Hunt. Identity having been established, Clarissa Morton had asked her very briskly if she was free immediately 'to meet a friend', as she put it, and on receiving confirmation had spent a full two minutes making it very clear that under no circumstances was Melanie to talk about her association with her, nor say anything about any of the 'friends' she might meet. Last, but not least, she set out the introduction fee. Twenty-five per cent of the present. The friend was Sir Peter Barton; he would be at Fairfield Mansions. Melanie had hardly been able to contain her excitement and sense of elation. At last she was getting into the top end of the trade. She had bounced into Helen Saunders's room bubbling over with the good news. Helen Saunders had been excited for her.

'Who's the lucky man?'

Melanie Hunt peered down at the name she had scribbled on the telephone notepad.

'Oh, somebody called Sir Peter Barron, or maybe it's Barton, I can't quite read my scribble.'

She had seen the joy vanish from Helen Saunders's face as she bit her lower lip.

'What's wrong?' Melanie asked, puzzled by the sudden change in Helen Saunders's manner.

'Did Clarissa tell you anything about him?'

'No, why, is there anything to know? I don't suppose he is any different from most men. They all want roughly the same. OK, some are a little quirky. So what?'

'Oh, but he is different, very different. He gets his thrills by knocking you about first and taking you forcibly.'

Helen Saunders had made it very clear to Clarissa Morton that, whilst she would do most things in the line of duty, she was not interested in taking on a sadist on any terms. Clarissa Morton had respected this wish. Helen Saunders had found out about Sir Peter Barton by chance when she had noticed another of 'Clarissa's girls' sporting a very nasty black eye. On enquiry she had insisted that she had walked into a door but Helen sensed there was more to

142

it than that, and a bit of pressure had brought the whole story tumbling out. It was then that she had told Clarissa Morton she wanted nothing to do with any sadists.

Melanie Hunt did not know what to do. This was her big chance, but she was very afraid of violence and couldn't bear the thought of her looks being damaged.

'What do I do?' she wailed.

'Simple. You don't go. Call Clarissa and say you have changed your mind; but for God's sake don't tell her why or I will be off her list.'

Melanie was torn both ways. Maybe a little pain was worth it in the long run, but then it might be more than a little pain. Time was slipping past. She did not have the luxury of thinking it over at leisure.

'What shall I do?' she wailed again. 'I can't turn down this opportunity.'

Helen Saunders sensed that whilst Melanie was afraid, she would always regret passing up the chance of getting on Clarissa's net if she didn't go.

'Look Melanie, it won't be nice if you do go, but if you must, you must. I don't know in what manner he is violent, but whatever you do don't fight back. That is usually what they want. They want to humiliate and subjugate you. If you don't fight back it rather destroys the point for them. You will suffer a bit but probably not too much.'

Melanie made up her mind she would go.

As the taxi approached Fairfield Mansions she repeated to herself under her breath, 'Don't fight back, don't fight back.' The voice on the intercom had sounded quite pleasant. Maybe Helen had got it all wrong, she thought to herself as the lift rode smoothly up to the third floor. She pressed the bell of the apartment, her heart beating like a steam hammer in her chest. She resisted the temptation to run. A large but not unattractive man opened the door.

'Come in my dear, come in.'

This is going to be all right, Melanie thought. She shrugged off her coat, threw it on the small couch in the entrance lobby and followed him into the beautiful sitting room. Sir Peter Barton had sat down on the comfortable sofa.

'Come here.'

It was a warm and pleasant invitation. His hand was held out towards her. Melanie's confidence was growing now. She walked over to sit down beside him. Before she could sit down his hand shot out and grabbed her wrist, dragging her on top of him. She gasped in pain and surprise and forgot her instructions. As he adjusted his position to carry on what he had started, he slackened his grip on her wrist. Melanie snatched it away and ran towards the door. He was too quick for her. He caught her by the shoulders and threw her towards the easy chair between the door and the window. Instinctively she put her hands out to save herself and only succeeded in catapulting herself beyond the chair into the heavy brocade curtains. The curtain swung open under her momentum and then back again. Sir Peter Barton was momentarily off balance and Melanie had a couple of seconds grace. Then she remembered. Don't fight back. She stood absolutely still and dropped her hands to her sides. He came roaring over and grabbed her dress just above her breasts. She didn't move an inch. The next few moments were frightening but she didn't suffer too much. At least he had not damaged her face.

As abruptly as it had started it had stopped. He had stood back, appraised her voluptuous body, most of which was now exposed to his gaze, and without expression in his voice or face had told her to get him a whisky and put on some music. Melanie breathed a sigh of relief, poured his whisky and gave it to him and, in some trepidation, chose a compact disc and put it on. She held her breath. Was he going to explode again because she had chosen the wrong music? She chose Vivaldi's Four Seasons on the basis that it was soothing. Tchaikovsky's 1812 Overture she had immediately rejected on the basis that it might rekindle his aggression. She need not have worried. He neither commented on her choice nor showed any signs that he was aware that the music was playing. The rest of the proceedings had been ordinary in that the violence had clearly been dissipated; the need to subjugate and humiliate was still there, however, and Melanie had had to go through some odd little rituals, but nothing she had not done before and nothing she didn't regard as all being in a day's work. The present of £400, even after deducting Clarissa

Morton's twenty-five per cent, made it all worthwhile. She had made it to the top. She thought she could even cope with Sir Peter Barton again.

Harvey Cook was getting bored. He looked at his watch. It was nearly two hours since Sir Peter Barton had gone into Fairfield Mansions. Time for another stroll, he thought. He started to get out of the taxi but hesitated as another taxi drew up outside the building. The driver got out and mounted the steps and after a quick examination of the names under the buttons pressed that for the third floor apartment. He picked up the small two-way radio from the seat beside him and pressed the send button.

'Harry, I think they are coming out. If they don't leave together, you follow the girl and I will follow the man. Hang around until she does come out.'

Barton emerged from Fairfield Mansions and got into his taxi. It took him straight to his apartment overlooking Hyde Park. Harvey Cook looked at his watch. Eight thirty. He would give it half an hour. If he didn't come out in that time he was unlikely to do so, he thought. Nightshifts with nothing happening were for junior investigators, not Harvey Cook, he had decided long ago. He had done more than his fair share of night hours, often cold and wet, waiting in vain for something to happen. He dialled a number on the telephone discreetly fitted in the taxi.

'Hello Trevor. Harvey here. We've had a useful lead. The target is now back in his apartment. I don't think he will go out again tonight. Send young Gillings along to do the night shift. Harry is following a contact of our target.'

Trevor Jacques acknowledged the information and confirmed that Kevin Gillings was on his way. Harvey slumped back in his seat and closed his eyes, confident in the knowledge that his driver, Bill, would wake him if there was any action before Kevin Gillings arrived.

After Sir Peter had left, Melanie decided she would take

full advantage of the facilities of Clarissa Morton's apartment. She had never had the free run of such luxury before. Clarissa Morton could wait for the phone call to let her know the job was finished. She sank into the jacuzzi and luxuriated in the soothing streams of water. As she towelled herself down she wondered who cleaned the apartment and how Clarissa Morton ensured it was in pristine condition for each strictly temporary occupant. Obviously the phone call as she left was the system for ensuring that the apartment was free for the next arrivals. What she did not know was that the arrival and departure of all users of the apartment was observed on closed circuit television in the top floor apartment which was occupied by Clarissa Morton's housekeeper. The television only observed arrivals and departures. Clarissa was not interested in what people got up to in her apartment. That was their business. Melanie Hunt was also unaware that the phone call to Clarissa was automatically switched through to the housekeeper on the top floor.

Melanie Hunt got dressed in leisurely fashion, congratulating herself on having the good sense to bring a spare dress and underclothes in her small case that was really no more than a slightly oversized vanity case. The fact was that she never travelled without a change of clothes when she was on business. One never quite knew what might happen to one's clothes. This was the first time, however, she had needed them because her original clothes had been almost completely destroyed.

She called up a taxi which arrived within a quarter of an hour. Harry, who had been despairing of the girl coming out of the building, had seen the taxi arrive and its driver press the unmarked button. The light in the third floor apartment had gone out soon afterwards, and the blonde girl carrying a small blue case he had been briefed to follow had emerged from the building a few seconds later. He followed her taxi into Maida Vale and watched her get out in front of a rather unprepossessing block of flats. He had quickly entered the entrance to the flats as the girl was paying off her taxi. There was no porter, he was glad to see. Harry went over to the lifts and kept an eye on the doorway. As soon as he saw the girl coming in he pressed the button to call the lift.

The timing was perfect. She arrived just as the lift door slid open. He smiled at her and gestured for her to enter the lift. Melanie Hunt hesitated slightly. It wasn't the safest thing at nearly ten o'clock at night to step into a lift in Maida Vale with a strange man. Then she noticed his cabbie's badge, smiled at him and stepped into the lift. Harry followed after her.

'Which floor?' Harry enquired, his hand hovering over the control panel.

'Fourth please.' Harry pressed four and six, considering it very unlikely she would know anyone on the sixth floor.

'How many apartments are there on each floor?' he enquired, making a show of examining a grubby piece of paper he had fished out from his pocket.

'Four,' Melanie replied, 'A and B to your left and C and D to your right, if the pattern is the same as on our floor.'

'Thanks.'

The lift juddered to a halt on the fourth floor and Melanie stepped out. Harry noted that she turned left as she did so. A or B, it shouldn't be difficult to find out which. He travelled up to the sixth floor and immediately down to the fourth floor again. He stepped out of the lift and turned left. A neat little notice in the middle of the door to apartment A announced that a Mr and Mrs Constantcou lived there. A rather less neat little notice on the door of apartment B announced that H. Saunders and M. Hunt lived there. The nice looking blonde was clearly either H. Saunders or M. Hunt, Harry decided. It wouldn't take him long to find out which.

14

The journey from Millbank to Russell Court was quite
short. If Stephen had been on his own he would have
walked. He did not think, however, that it would be quite
the done thing for the Chairman of a major British
company to arrive at his merchant banker's on foot and,
possibly, slightly sweaty from his exertions. Number 15
was indistinguishable from the other buildings on the
river side of the street, a modest four stories high and
firmly attached to its neighbours on either side. The outer
door was open and they stepped into a rather narrow and
dark entrance hall. Stephen hesitated for a moment
looking for some sign to indicate where the Greensmith
Leonard apartment might be, or, to be more precise,
where Mr Williams's apartment might be. He had been
instructed by Alan Mortimer the previous evening to ask
for Mr Williams on arrival. He was slightly startled by the
voice coming from the far end of the hallway.
   'Can I help you gentlemen?' Following the directions of
the voice Stephen Barber then saw what was no more than
a small counter with a door leading off behind it. A man
in discreet porter's uniform was stood at the desk looking
towards them. He had obviously just emerged from the
room behind.
   'Mr Williams, please.'
   'Certainly sir.' The porter pressed a button on the panel
behind him. 'Follow me please gentlemen.' Stephen was
slightly surprised that the porter had not asked their
names. Clearly they were expected and the porter had
indicated their arrival when he pushed the button on the
panel.

The porter came out from behind the counter and moved over to a door opposite and swung it open. The door led on to quite a lengthy corridor with no obvious sign of any other doorways leading off, except at the far end. The porter opened the far door and they stepped into a replica of the hallway they had just left. He opened yet another door that looked identical to the other doorways leading off the hallway and revealed a small lift. He opened the door, ushered them in, pressed the button for the fourth floor, and sent them on their way with the enjoinder that they would be met at the other end.

Alan Mortimer was waiting for them as they stepped out of the lift. Stephen quickly effected the introductions. The apartment was magnificent. The large spacious rooms were beautifully furnished, the epitome of elegance and gracious living. Stephen realised immediately one of the reasons why Alan Mortimer had suggested they meet in the apartment. It would put Martin Chandler more at ease with the prospect of employing Greensmith Leonard as merchant bankers to fight the Barton Industries bid. The apartment oozed City establishment, tradition and stability, a far cry from the hard nosed, slightly disreputable reputation enjoyed by Greensmith Leonard in some parts of the City which were probably more renowned for clinging to the traditions of the past than for progressiveness. The irony was that Greensmith Leonard could trace their origins back every bit as far as the more blue-blooded and traditional style of merchant bankers such as Lloyd, Meisson. They had simply moved with the times and believed in hiring competence and hard headed business acumen ahead of pedigree and family.

'Coffee?'

Martin and Stephen indicated assent. Whilst Alan Mortimer was pouring it out from a beautiful Georgian coffee pot Stephen wandered over to the window. There was an uninterrupted view to the Thames. This place must cost them a fortune, he thought.

'Who is Mr Williams, Alan?'

Alan Mortimer laughed lightly.

'Oh, he doesn't exist. He is what you might call part of

149

our security system. There is nothing to connect Green-smith Leonard with this apartment. The lease is in the name of a nominee and each client has a code name to ask for. In your case it is Mr Williams. Even if you were followed here there is no way anyone interested could determine who you were meeting. This building is interconnected with the one next door; you may have realised that you are now in the building next door to the one you entered by. There are over thirty apartments between the two buildings. It is an extremely good venue for holding discreet meetings. More than one major deal between companies which are household names has been struck in this room. The beauty is that one party can enter by number 15, as you did, and the other can enter by number 17. Well to business Mr Chandler. Stephen has outlined to me what you have in mind. You fire away.'

Martin had already virtually made up his mind. He liked the style of Alan Mortimer. He felt comfortable with him. Maybe the reputation Greensmith Leonard enjoyed in some quarters was a myth.

'Thank you Mr Mortimer. As I am sure Stephen has explained to you, Amalgamated is a company with an enviable reputation for playing it straight. The reputation of your bank, if you will forgive me, is that it sails somewhat close to the wind. If we employ you to help us fight Barton Industries we shall not be party to anything shady.'

Shut up you pompous fool, Martin thought to himself. If you insult him and his bank any more he could well turn round and tell you to get lost. Stephen was having very similar thoughts. 'I am sure you would not do or suggest anything shady,' Martin finished rather lamely.

Alan Mortimer was not in the least put out. He did not really care too much what his clients thought of him or Greensmith Leonard. The important thing to him was to do his job to the best of his ability.

'You don't have to worry about that Mr Chandler. You are the client. We won't do anything you might disapprove of. What we will do is give you the best advice on how to defeat this bid. On occasion this may involve proposing a course of action that, shall we say, falls into a grey area of what is permissible under the rules. We may also suggest tactics that are somewhat original. We will never advise you to follow a course that is illegal or clearly in breach of the rules. At the end of the day you are in charge.'

Martin Chandler was cross with himself for being so clumsy. He really need not have said what he had, particularly as he had already resolved that there was little he would stop short of in order to save Amalgamated from the clutches of Barton Industries.

'Thank you. I am confident you will give us a high class service.'

By the end of the meeting Martin was thoroughly convinced that hiring Greensmith Leonard would be one of the better decisions of his life. The straightforward and confident advice he got from Alan Mortimer was in stark contrast to the rather laid back and almost supercilious approach of James Markby Smythe. Markby Smythe always left Martin with the feeling that he was being talked down to; as if he couldn't be expected to understand the mysteries of the City and how it worked. Alan Mortimer had given direct answers to direct questions and was forthright in his advice. Martin appointed Greensmith Leonard there and then. His board of directors could lump it if they did not like it. He left Stephen behind with Alan Mortimer to set up the team and procedures for handling the Barton Industries bid for Amalgamated.

Martin sat back in his car well pleased with the afternoon's work. Initially he had decided to ask Stephen to call James Markby Smythe to tell him that from now on Greensmith Leonard would be running the defence against the Barton Industries bid, and that he would have to work closely with them, in a subordinate role, to ensure that the tactics for the Amalgamated bid for Axehouse General did not clash with the tactics for the defence against the Barton Industries bid. On reflection he concluded that this would be discourteous. It would also deprive him of the satisfaction of being the bearer of the news.

He stretched forward and picked up the telephone situated between the front seats and dialled Markby Smythe's number. The conversation turned out to be an anti-climax for he had given no hint of being surprised, hurt or anything else for that matter. Nor did he in any way question whether it was the right thing to do. He had been immediately practical. He had suggested that there would need to be cross representation of the two merchant banks on the respective teams handling the two bids. He would arrange for Philip Renton to contact Alan Mortimer as soon as possible. Martin put the telephone down feeling slightly cheated, but on reflection concluded that, had he thought about it, James Markby Smythe had reacted exactly as one might have expected him to act. His breeding and background would not permit him to act in any other way. More is the pity Martin Chandler decided; a bit more fire in the belly would not come amiss. Had Martin been a fly on Markby Smythe's wall he would have not felt cheated. As soon as he had replaced the receiver in its cradle he had picked up the file on the desk in front of him and flung it at the wall.

'Christ, Greensmith Leonard and Alan Mortimer of all people,' he had exploded.

☆ ☆ ☆

Sarah Chandler put the *Financial Times* down beside her. She was quite enjoying seeing Martin on the receiving end of a bid for Amalgamated from someone like Peter Barton. The thought of Martin having to report to Sir Peter Barton was particularly entertaining. It would certainly pay him back for all the suffering he had caused her by chasing after younger women and spending most of the rest of his time at the office. She realised that there was no way Martin would work for or with Barton, but the thought was a pleasing one.

Sarah was following the progress of the two bids with avid interest, reading everything there was to be read about them, not only in the *Financial Times* and the heavy dailies, but also specialist publications like the *Investors Chronicle*. On present form, she concluded, it looked as if the Amalgamated bid for Axehouse General had a fifty fifty chance of success and the Barton Industries bid for Amalgamated, whilst not quite dead in the water, needed something fairly dramatic to turn it round and give it some chance. What could she do, she wondered. She had a personal holding in Amalgamated, but there was little or no influence she could exert with it. The more she thought about it, the less sure she was that she actually wanted Barton Industries to win. If Martin lost Amalgamated he might be so depressed that it could damage their marriage rather than revive it. Maybe if she could in some way help Martin to defeat the bid, and be seen to be so doing, then he would be in debt to her and might appreciate her more. She would have to talk to her father again. He might have an idea.

The telephone jangled, rudely breaking into her train of thought. It was Martin. She nearly dropped the receiver in her surprise. His rich brown voice exuded good humour and relaxation. She felt her usual little thrill of excitement course through her body.

'Hello darling, just thought I would check that you were in. I should be home in about twenty minutes if this traffic doesn't snarl up any more.'

'That's lovely darling.' Sarah looked at her watch; only five thirty. She resisted the temptation to enquire as to what she owed the honour of his presence in mid week, and at such an early hour.

'Do you want me to book a table for dinner somewhere?'

'No, a nice quiet meal at home will be much better. I expect you have got something in the freezer. See you.'

Sarah replaced the receiver. Her surprise grew the more she tried to divine why he was coming home and in such good humour. What was more he had called her darling, and he rarely did that these days. With two bids on his hands she had already resigned herself to seeing him only occasionally during the next few weeks and then almost certainly only at weekends. In any case his good humour was genuine, not put on for her benefit. She understood him well enough after all these years to determine when he was being genuine.

She heard the crunch of the car on the gravel. She decided not to rush to the front door to greet him. The front door clicked open.

'Hi darling, where are you?'

153

He didn't wait for an answer and was in the sitting room in almost the same breath. He bounded across the room and gave her a huge hug and then planted a smacking kiss on her lips. He is almost like a boy again, Sarah thought, and decided that the humour was so boundless that a bit of light banter would not be taken as sarcasm.

'To what do I owe this honour then, fine sir?'

He laughed good humouredly; not really knowing the answer to the question. Come to think of it, he thought to himself, why am I in such high spirits, and home at such an early hour in mid week, when I have two takeover bids on my hands? He decided honesty was the best policy.

'I don't really know. I just decided I needed to see you, so I came.'

Sarah did not pursue the point and took it at face value.

The evening was a great success. She had cooked him fillet steak and chips, his favourite meal, despite all the fancy dishes he favoured when out at a restaurant, and complemented it with a fine bottle of claret. After the meal they sat either side of the fireplace like thousands of other married couples. They were comfortable in each other's company, and did not need to carry on a continuous conversation. Sarah wished it could always be so, but realised it never would be. She would savour the experience.

Martin Chandler rose from his chair.

'Another port?'

Sarah declined and watched him walk across the room to the sideboard near the door where the decanter stood. She then noticed for the first time his briefcase stood beside the sideboard. He must have dropped it there when he had first come into the room. He poured himself another glass of port and then stretched down to pick up his briefcase. The spell was about to be broken. Sarah did not want him to disappear behind a pile of papers, but realised his mind was now back on business. There was no way she would be able to deflect him from it. There was only one way in which she might still be able to command his attention.

'How are the bids going?'

She had not seen him since the Barton Industries bid

had been announced. 'The Barton Industries bid must be a considerable irritation.'

'Yes it is an irritation, but I don't think it will be more than that. The whole thing is misconceived.'

Martin then realised why he was in such good humour. He felt utterly confident that he would defeat the Barton Industries bid. The bid itself had got off to a very bad start and now he had Alan Mortimer and Greensmith Leonard on his side, he didn't seriously consider he could lose. His good humour was still with him.

'I trust you are not contemplating accepting the Barton Industries bid?'

Sarah decided to tease him a little.

'Oh, I don't know. It depends what they finally decide to offer me. I could make a lot of money.' She said it with smiling eyes and a light tone of voice. Martin didn't rise.

'Well, I suppose every women has her price,' he countered. Sarah laughed.

'The price for this one is very high.'

Martin smiled and silently toasted her with his glass of port.

'Do you have any Barton Industries shares by the way?' Martin and Sarah had agreed at an early stage of their marriage to take separate advice on investment and, although in the early days Sarah had always discussed her investments with Martin, in recent years she had got out of the habit of doing so.

'Yes I do as a matter of fact. Simon Reynolds put me into them four or five years ago. I have made a packet. They must have increased threefold in that time? Why do you ask?'

'Oh, it just crossed my mind that it could prove useful if you had a holding of any significance.'

'I doubt that my holding is of sufficient significance to alter anything.' The turn of the conversation to a more serious level brought Sarah back to reality. The evening was in all probability only a small oasis in the expanding desert of their marriage. Martin Chandler only gave a small grunt by way of reply and buried himself in his papers.

I wonder, Sarah thought to herself, if my holding in

Barton Industries can be turned to advantage. Maybe there is some way I can use it and get Martin beholden to me in some way. She sighed to herself. Maybe it was better just to let life take its own course and not try to manipulate it.

☆ ☆ ☆

Sir Peter Barton had enjoyed his evening. The encounter at Clarissa Morton's apartment had been highly satisfactory. The reaction of the girl had been just right. Initial resistance followed by complete submission. He didn't feel the sense of guilt he often felt when the girl had resisted all along the line and his violence had as a result got out of hand. What had rounded the evening off had been the phone call from Robert Brodie. Although he knew Robert Brodie quite well it had not immediately registered who he was when he had called. The penny dropped pretty fast when he had started talking about Amalgamated. Brodie had been very careful to couch what he had to say in a manner that could not on the face of it be taken as being outright treachery. The meaning had been very clear nevertheless. He was offering help in return for a guarantee of power if Barton Industries succeeded in acquiring Amalgamated. He had not specified the nature of the help he could give, nor precisely what he wanted in return. He had simply said that one had to be realistic in the world of business, and that it would be in the interests of all concerned if there was a smooth transition in the event of Amalgamated being acquired by Barton Industries. He had added that in his opinion the best interests of Amalgamated would be served if Amalgamated remained independent and that he, Robert Brodie, would be devoting his energies in this direction. Peter Barton was not fooled by this. He was more than clear that what Brodie really meant was that Brodie's best interests would be served by Barton Industries winning and Brodie being suitably rewarded for helping bring this about.

Peter Barton had not responded immediately. He wanted to think it over. A mole inside Amalgamated

156

would be very useful, but it would be necessary to be very careful how one used him. His usefulness could well disappear if it became too obvious that Barton Industries had inside knowledge of what was happening at Amalgamated. Knowledge of the defence tactics of Amalgamated would be more than useful in developing responses to negate their effect before they even got off the ground, but probably the most useful information would be that relating to the conduct of the Amalgamated bid for Axehouse General, particularly the timing of critical events such as any improved offer, the level of acceptance at any given time, and when the bid was likely to be declared unconditional. Timing was everything. Barton Industries were behind in the race and the prize could be snatched from them almost purely for this reason. Knowledge of the Amalgamated timing on their bid for Axehouse would be of incalculable benefit. Barton Industries would know whether they had time to proceed at their own pace or whether they needed to speed things up. He looked at his watch. Eleven thirty, a bit late to call Nathan Sanson, but then he was paid to be available when he wanted him. He picked up the phone. Three rings and Sanson was on the line sounding as fresh as a daisy.

'Nathan, I have had an interesting call this evening.'

Barton proceeded to outline the nature of the call and his interpretation of it. He did not however disclose the identity of the potential mole. Sanson tried to extract the name from him, but without success, and he had to be satisfied with the assurance that he was a main board member with executive responsibility. Sanson quickly concluded that it could only be one of three people, and of those three one was an unlikely candidate. Charles Lytton, the Public Affairs Director and Richard Gibbs the Personnel Director, had nothing whatever to gain by Barton Industries acquiring Amalgamated. Howard Irwin could in theory have something to gain, but Sanson was quite confident that treachery was not in his nature. He was far too easy going and not at all ambitious, Sanson wondered how he had ever got to be Financial Director, he must be a good technician. This left James Walker, Terry King and Robert Brodie. James Walker was probably heir apparent. He was competent and he was family and was an unlikely candidate for the Brutus role. It must be Terry King or Robert Brodie then; it could be either.

'Well, if this mole is in the position you say he is, Sir Peter, he could be very useful indeed. You're sure he is privy to all the Amalgamated plans?'

'Oh yes. He is bound to be party to the tactics on both the Axehouse General bid and the defence against our bid.'

'What is his motivation then? I think it is vital to know this if we are to devise the best way of using him.'

'I've been thinking about that Nathan. He hasn't made any demands, and he is only talking in terms of ensuring a smooth transition if we succeed in acquiring Amalgamated. I don't believe that for a minute. I am confident he wants to do a deal whereby he is made Chairman of Amalgamated, and with a fair degree of autonomy. It wouldn't surprise me one little bit if he did not demand a place on the Barton Industries board as well.'

'It would help Sir Peter if you told me who he is. I can advise you far better if I know this. Is there any good reason why you should not tell me?' Nathan was somewhat puzzled why Barton was being so coy about the identity of the mole.

'I will tell you as soon as I can Nathan, but I want to be quite sure I have not misunderstood the man before I reveal his name to you. It would be quite unfair of me to name him now before I am absolutely sure.'

Sanson was amazed by this response. The last thing he would ever have accused Peter Barton of was being sensitive to the feelings of other people.

'As soon as I can flush him out into the open, I will give you his name. To get him to reveal his hand will require me to make him some sort of offer, and that is where I want your advice. How we use him comes later.'

Nathan gave up; Barton was not going to budge on the point.

'OK Sir Peter, I will have to make a few assumptions if I do not know who he is. You will no doubt put me right if I make wrong ones. If this guy is one of the top executive directors, which I assume he must be, he is not going to risk his present position without the promise of something pretty substantial and influential in the new set up if Amalgamated becomes part of Barton Industries. At a minimum I am sure you are right in thinking he will want the chairmanship of Amalgamated and with real power. This alone is unlikely to tempt him. Whatever assurances you may give to him now, he will realise that he is there only as long as it suits you and that, whilst he is there, you have complete control over him. An offer of a place on your Board as well might be enough to get him on our side, but I doubt it. He knows that you run Barton Industries as if it were your personal business. Your current directors, whilst useful in their way, are completely subordinate to you. This guy will want more than that. You will have to give him a title that puts him above the other directors and with pretty firm guarantees that the title invests him with real power. Deputy Chairman or Managing Director come to mind.'

There was a silence at the other end. Nathan decided not to break it. Best to let the thought sink in.

'I don't really think I need to offer all that, Nathan.'

'I think you do Sir Peter, and not simply for the purpose of getting this guy to help us from within. Our bid is not exactly romping home at the moment, and any help we can get will be more than acceptable.'

Nathan saw no point in glossing over the obvious.

'Just as important though is planning ahead how you are going to handle the absorption of Amalgamated into Barton Industries. A friendly, highly placed face at Amalgamated would be invaluable. Perhaps the most important factor however, is how you are going to manage Barton Industries into the future. It will more than double in size if Amalgamated becomes part of it. You cannot realistically expect to be able to run such a large company as you have run Barton Industries. You will certainly need to restructure your Board to free you to concentrate on strategic issues. Many a good company has come to grief because the Chairman has insisted on keeping the role of Managing Director well beyond the time when such an arrangement was practical. You must not let this happen to you whether or not your mole comes on board. He might be the right kind of person to undertake the role I am outlining; that is why I really need to know who he is so that I can give you an independent assessment. There are some considerable advantages in having this guy as your Managing Director or whatever. Leaving aside the help he may be able to give in acquiring Amalgamated, he will inevitably be beholden to you to a considerable degree and, accordingly, less likely to be a threat to you from within as a person head-hunted from outside might be. I take it that you have nobody currently on your Board who you would be happy to give the much wider responsibility I have just outlined.'

Barton wasn't ready to respond. He had considered these wider issues, realising that he would not be able to run Barton Industries as he had in the past if Amalgamated became part of it, but instinctively he was against what Nathan Sanson had just suggested.

'I'll think about it.'

He put the phone down realising he did not have the luxury of very much time to think about it. Robert Brodie; was he the sort of man he would like to have within Barton Industries wielding power? He would sleep on it. At least if it had to be anyone from within Amalgamated he could think of nobody other than Robert Brodie who would even get to the starting line. The man had at least built up a substantial and successful business from virtually nothing before Amalgamated had come along and swallowed it. In many ways, he thought he was a fellow spirit. Maybe it wasn't such a bad idea.

15

The Ballroom at the Dorchester Hotel in Park Lane had a mournful air. Row upon row of empty chairs facing a raised platform appeared more threatening from the platform than if they had been filled with people. Charles Timpson peered anxiously at his watch. Nine thirty. Was everything in place? He swept the room with his eyes. Yes, there were microphones strategically placed around the room. Did they work properly? Of course they did. He had arranged a full test of all the microphones over an hour ago when Martin Chandler had briefly appeared, as he always did before any General Meeting of the company, to familiarise himself with the set up and have a brief rehearsal. Charles Timpson nevertheless could not resist yet another test.

The platform was arranged with a table at the front with three chairs and then a row of seats behind which were slightly elevated so that the audience could get a clear view of the individals sitting there. The second row also was placed behind a table so that the directors had somewhere to put their papers. The arrangement also simplified the organisation of microphones as each place could have its own. The seats at the front table were for Martin Chandler, with Charles Timpson on his right and Howard Irwin on his left. Martin insisted on sticking to this arrangement as he disliked having a long row of directors stuck behind the front table. His reasons were both aesthetic and political. If he placed any more directors on the front table he would face endless argument as to who should sit there, and where they should sit in relation to himself. As he knew from bitter experience, directors of large public companies were no different to anyone else; not only was status important to them, but any outward manifestation of relative status, such as who sat where, was capable of producing as much heat as the liveliest boardroom debate on a matter of real importance to the company. As it was, he had no great difficulty in maintaining his preferred format. No-one could cavil at the presence of the Company Secretary next to the Chairman as he was responsible for the organisation of the meeting and an essential aid to the Chairman in running the meeting. Most General Meetings of companies revolved around financial matters of one kind or another and the presence of the Finance Director at the side of the Chairman could hardly be objected to. The fact that the Finance Director was Howard Irwin made the position the easier to maintain, since none of the other executive directors saw him as in any way a threat to their futures within the company, and accordingly felt no slight from his presence on the front table.

Charles Timpson self-consciously moved from one platform microphone to the next, flicking the 'on' switch, blowing gently into it and then counting one, two, three. He had carried out these operations numerous times. An Extraordinary General Meeting of the company was not essentially any different to the Annual General Meeting and Charles Timpson had a well oiled system and team to carry it out. He nevertheless still had a dread of overlooking something.

Upstairs, in one of the Dorchester's bigger suites, Martin Chandler was going through his speech for the third time. James Markby Smythe, Howard Irwin and Stephen Barber were with him. Each in his own way was trying to convince Martin that his speech was fine and would not improve by further change. Martin was unusually nervous. Normally he took General Meetings of Amalgamated in his stride. This was different. For at least the third time in the space of half an hour he asked Stephen to check the proxy situation. Patiently Stephen confirmed that it was little different from the figures as they stood the night before. The morning mail had done little to alter the situation significantly. Martin did a rapid sum on his note pad.

'If it comes to a poll I only hold proxies in favour of the

162

bid for Axehouse General representing twenty-five per cent of the voting equity. This could go badly wrong.'

James Markby Smythe, not for the first time that morning, patiently explained that very few of the large institutional investors had submitted proxies and that, in all probability, they would simply sit on the fence and not vote in order to keep their options open.

'You only have proxies against amounting to one per cent of the voting equity, Chairman. In any event I think you will find that the resolution will go through on a show of hands. I doubt that anybody will call for a proxy count if the sense of the meeting is in favour of the resolution.'

Stephen had always thought it odd that most company business at General Meetings went through on a very informal show of hands on the basis of one man one vote, with no heed being paid to the number of shares held unless someone called for a poll and got the necessary backing from the shareholders. There was no doubt, however, that the system made it much easier to get things past the shareholders.

Martin Chandler was still uneasy.

'What is the count on the institutional investors, Howard?' He knew the answer already, but he wanted reassurance.

'I have spoken to all the major holders, Martin. Whilst only a small minority have indicated clearly that they are in favour of the bid for Axehouse, not one has definitively come out against it. I am completely confident that you have nothing to worry about. The resolution will go through without difficulty.'

'I hope you're right.'

Martin knew he was right. He just needed the reinforcement to overcome his nervousness. He had this niggling fear that something would go wrong.

☆ ☆ ☆

Down in the lobby Charles Timpson was casually flicking through the registration slips. Quite a few of the institutional holders' representatives had already registered. Then his heart skipped a beat. He recognised a name he

163

would preferably not have wished to see. Charles Walters. It could be a coincidence of course. Neither Charles nor Walters were uncommon names and nor, probably, was the combination of names. Nevertheless, he was certain it was Peter Barton's right hand man. The shareholding was an individual holding of one thousand shares. The number didn't matter. One share was enough to have the right of entry and audience. He cast his eyes around the room which was now filling up with people. He was fairly confident he would recognise Charles Walters if he saw him, even though he had only met him once. He was proud of his memory for faces and names. Yes, there he was, standing alone near one of the entrances to the Ballroom. The small strawberry birthmark was on the right temple just as he had remembered it. Timpson moved rapidly to a telephone and called the suite. Stephen answered and took the news with equanimity, telling Timpson not to worry.

'Who was that,' enquired Martin, 'and what did he want?'

'Timpson. He has just spotted Charles Walters of Barton Industries signing in.'

Martin Chandler's nervousness came to the fore.

'He could be trouble. What do we do about him?'

'Nothing,' James Markby Smythe volunteered, picking up the question that had been directed to nobody in particular. 'We know that Barton Industries have been buying Amalgamated shares and if they are properly on the register they have every right to attend like any other shareholder.'

'Charles Walters has signed in as an individual shareholder, James.'

'That figures. He can put the Barton Industries case without formally having to be seen as representing them. By the way, do we know how many shares they hold in Amalgamated?'

'No,' Stephen Barber replied. 'There is no doubt that they have been buying but very little that is identifiable has filtered through to the share register as yet. I suspect a lot of it is in nominee names. We are using all the means we have at our disposal to try and identify the real holders of nominee shareholdings, but it is an almost impossible task.'

Martin Chandler was still twitchy.

164

'Can't we stop him speaking?'

He knew perfectly well he could not prevent Charles Walters addressing the meeting if he wished. The question was an expresion of desire rather than one calling for a response. He got a response, nevertheless, from Markby Smythe.

'If you try to suppress him, Martin, you will do more harm than if you give him a polite hearing. You simply provide good copy for the press. If he gets persistent the technique to shut him up is very simply . . .'

'Yes, yes I know,' Martin didn't want a lecture on how to run a company General Meeting, 'I suggest to the other shareholders that he has more than made his point, whatever it is, and that someone else be given a chance to speak and then I invite him to talk to me afterwards if he wishes to pursue the matter. I know, I know.' Martin Chandler was getting annoyed, but more with himself than with anyone else. He looked at his watch. Twenty minutes to go. He would be glad when the meeting started. He would be better then and fully in control of himself. He got up and left the room to go to the bathroom.

'He's a bit on edge today, isn't he?' James observed. 'He won't do anything silly in the meeting will he?'

'You don't have to worry about that,' Howard Irwin interjected, 'he is always nervous before a General Meeting. It's just that he doesn't normally show it. He'll be his normal self once the meeting gets under way.'

Downstairs in the Ballroom people were beginning to take their seats. Charles Timpson calculated there were already about one hundred and fifty seated, although in the vastness of the room and the sea of chairs it looked no more than a handful. He nodded in acknowledgement of recognition and welcome to a number of familiar faces. Most of them were representatives of the large institutional shareholders but there was also a hard core of individual shareholders who rarely missed a General Meeting. Some of them had shareholdings which were so small that Charles Timpson reckoned that their annual dividends did not even cover the cost of attending the Annual General Meeting of Amalgamated, let alone any extra meetings that might be held during the year. They were the salt of the earth as far as he was concerned.

Most of the directors were now in the room. Some were chatting amongst themselves whilst others made the effort to go and talk to those attending the meeting.

Stephen gently jogged Charles Timpson's elbow to attract his attention.

'I think it is just possible that Walters may demand a poll, Charles. Is everything set up to deal with one if he does?' Stephen was quite confident it would be, and was more interested in how it would be dealt with. He had been so busy on the two deals that he had not had time to go into such details.

'Oh, don't worry Stephen, we have our usual set up. We have a fully up to date copy of the register in an adjoining room. All the proxies that have been sent in have already been verified against the register and, judging from the numbers present at the moment, it will only take about fifteen to twenty minutes to verify and collate the card votes coming from those present in the room. Are we expecting a demand for a poll then?'

'It's possible that Charles Walters may call for one in order to get a better assessment of strength of support for the bid for Axehouse. That could help Barton Industries determine their tactics in their bid for us.'

'I'll just go and check that everything is in place. Our Articles of Association require five people to demand a poll. I can only recall one poll being carried out, and that was when the Chairman wanted one to emphasise the level of support he had. I think you will find that the resolutions will go through on a show of hands in the usual manner.'

Timpson did not feel as relaxed as his response to Stephen indicated. He had a horror of things going wrong and the more uncertainties fed into the equation, such as a demand for a poll, the more there was to go wrong. He fervently hoped there would not be a demand for a poll. Deciding matters on a show of hands was a much simpler exercise than having a card vote. There was little that could go wrong, particularly as the Chairman's decision on whether a resolution had been passed on a show of hands was for all intents and purposes final.

Three minutes to go. Martin slipped quietly into the

Ballroom from an entrance behind the podium. The last thing he wanted today was to be stopped on his way to the platform and have to indulge in polite conversation or, much worse, be collared by a member of the press looking for a good quote. All that could come later.

He sat down behind the lectern on the table in front of him and organised his papers. Howard Irwin was already in place and Charles Timpson was hovering nearby. He looked at his watch. One minute to go. He glanced behind him and saw that all the other directors were seated.

Martin called the meeting to order and moved smoothly into the business of the day. No-one would have guessed that he had been a bag of nerves. There were three resolutions to put to the meeting. The main one came first; the approval of the bid for Axehouse General. The next two were purely technical, necessary to enable the bid to go ahead, assuming that the meeting approved the major resolution authorising it. Martin delivered his presentation of the case for approving the takeover bid for Axehouse General with great skill. There were no hesitations, and all the likely objections to the bid were dealt with, thus pre-empting attacks from the floor. He quickly got a proposer and seconder for the resolution; all carefully arranged beforehand. Now came the crunch.

'Before I put the resolution to the vote, are there any questions?'

There was the usual pause before someone stood up to address a question. A steward swiftly provided a micro-phone and the ball was rolling. Martin Chandler fielded a succession of questions with ease. None were openly aggressive, although it was clear from the general tenor of the questions that there was an element that was not over enthusiastic at the proposal to acquire Axehouse General. Martin was inwardly relaxing when a shareholder got to his feet and asked a question that set the alarm bells ringing.

'Richard Evans,' he announced. 'Mr Chairman, we have had brief mention of the bid for our company by Barton Industries, but you have not addressed the question of whether it might not be in the best interests of the shareholders for that bid to be accepted. It is to my mind a generous bid and, from a shareholder's point of view, is a bird in the hand and not two dubious birds in the insurance bush. On what basis have you rejected that bid?'

Timpson unobtrusively passed a note to Martin informing him that the questioner was sitting immediately in front of Charles Walters of Barton Industries and was probably acting as his mouthpiece. Before the meeting had started he had noticed Walters leaning over the man's shoulder, engaging him in earnest conversation.

'We have, of course, thoroughly considered the Barton Industries bid, Mr Evans. It is our considered view that the best interests of the shareholders and employees of Amalgamated Products will be served by remaining independent and widening its spheres of activity to provide for future growth and prosperity.'

Martin, more in hope than expectation, shifted his gaze from the questioner to the other side of the room and gestured to another shareholder who was indicating that he wished to ask a question. The questioner holding the floor was having none of that. He still had the microphone and quickly responded to the Chairman's reply.

'That may be the view of you and your Board, Mr Chairman, but it is not my view nor, I suspect, the view of a good many other shareholders. Barton Industries is a very dynamic company with an excellent track record. It is my belief that Amalgamated Products would prosper to a far greater extent as part of Barton Industries than it would by remaining independent and saddled with Axehouse General at an exorbitant cost.'

'You are entitled to your view, Mr Evans, and no doubt you will cast your vote accordingly.'

Martin saw no profit in debating the issue. Again he gestured to another shareholder who wanted the floor. Richard Evans was not giving in.

'I think shareholders are entitled to a more considered answer than that, Mr Chairman. Have you discussed the matter with Sir Peter Barton to find out what his ideas are for integrating Amalgamated Products into Barton Industries?'

An unidentified voice from the centre of the room just loud enough to be heard by everyone else muttered, 'Sit down, you have had your answer.'

168

Richard Evans was not easily to be put down.

'With respect I do not consider I have had my answer. We should debate this issue. This is our only chance.'

Martin Chandler sensed the meeting was mostly on his side. A few more 'sit downs' had followed the first when Richard Evans had continued with his speech, for that was what it was. It was no longer a question.

'This isn't a debate, Mr Evans. You have had your say and I don't think anyone here can be in any doubt where your sympathies lie. I think someone else should have a chance.'

This was greeted with a few 'hear, hears' and a ripple of applause.

Richard Evans was not to be easily deterred.

'Mr Chairman . . .'

The rest disappeared in a chorus of 'sit downs'.

Martin felt quite pleased. The questioner had successfully shifted the sympathy of the meeting his way. He fielded a few more questions without difficulty, even though two of them clearly had sympathy with Richard Evans, and decided the time had come to put the matter to the vote.

'Well, ladies and gentlemen, time is moving on and I think we should put the matter to the vote. Would all those in favour please show in the usual manner.'

A forest of hands pointed to the ceiling.

'All those against.'

About thirty hands were raised aloft. Timpson was intrigued to see that they did not include the hand of Charles Walters. He had obviously decided to keep a low profile.

'I think that is pretty conclusive. I declare the resolution to be carried. Now we move on to the next resolution.'

Richard Evans was on his feet again. He did not wait for a microphone to be handed to him.

'I demand a poll.'

More mutters of 'sit down' greeted this interjection. Timpson slipped Martin a note which indicated the voting strength represented at the meeting compiled from the details given as shareholders registered before the meeting.

Martin Chandler groaned inwardly, but kept his outward composure.

'The gentleman is quite entitled to demand a poll under the provisions of the Articles of Association of the company. I will briefly outline the procedure and what is involved. A poll is, in effect, a count of the number of shares voted for and against the resolution represented by those present here and by the proxies which have been returned to the company. A demand for a poll requires the support of five members here present or, alternatively, shareholders representing one tenth of the voting rights in the company. I and my fellow directors hold between us proxies in favour of the resolution amounting to just over twenty-five per cent of the total voting rights. We have other proxies voting against, totalling some one per cent. I am informed that, on the basis of the information given on registration this morning, approximately twenty-one per cent of the voting strength of the company is represented here today. Even if all these shares are voted against the resolution I think it is fairly clear that the resolution will be carried. Would the proposer of the call for a poll like to reconsider?'

Richard Evans was quickly on his feet again.

'I think it is quite wrong, Mr Chairman, for you to try and pre-empt the outcome of a poll in this way. It is the right of the shareholders to have a poll if they wish and . . .' He felt a strong tug at his jacket from behind. Charles Walters already had the information he wanted from what Martin Chandler had just said. '. . . and, and . . . but in the circumstances I will not insist upon it.'

Much to Martin's relief Richard Evans subsided into his seat and angrily turned round to say something to Charles Walters.

The rest of the meeting passed off without further alarm. The first hurdle had been negotiated, but Martin Chandler was under no illusion that he was home and dry. The big shareholders such as the pension funds and insurance companies had kept their powder dry. Very few had put in proxies and a quick check round indicated that hardly any of their representatives had voted at the meeting.

☆ ☆ ☆

Two weeks later Sir Peter Barton and Barton Industries had had a much more difficult Extraordinary Meeting to approve the bid for Amalgamated. There had been a lot of hostility to the proposed bid. It had only barely scraped through on a show of hands and a poll had been demanded and insisted upon. The result had been reasonably comfortable but not overwhelming.

Afterwards, Sir Peter Barton had called Nathan Sanson and Charles Walters together for a crisis meeting. He was now even more conscious that the Barton Industries bid for Amalgamated Products was widely regarded as being misconceived. The initial press reaction to the structure of the bid was one thing; for his own shareholders publicly to voice similar sentiments was quite another. It was an entirely new experience for him. He had enjoyed ten or more years of unadulterated shareholder adulation. Now he bitterly regretted that he had allowed himself to be talked into structuring the opening shot on such a highly leveraged basis. It might be all the rage in the States, but shareholder and financial commentator conservatism was clearly much greater in the United Kingdom. It would have been far better to have structured the deal in a more conventional mode right from the beginning. Sanson had been very persuasive at the time. It would give Sir Peter a reputation for being innovative, he had said, and quite apart from this, it would give Barton Industries the opportunity to test the water without being committed to the straightjacket of a conventionally structured bid.

Barton's anger and frustration had been increased by Sanson and the lawyers being quite adamant that he could not outline to the Extraordinary General Meeting the already determined structure of the revised bid that would be made in the near future without formally announcing it. He had reluctantly bowed to the advice that there were good legal and procedural reasons why he could not do this. This was hardly designed to improve his temper. Sanson and Walters endured a very uncomfortable forty minutes.

16

Martin had had no problems in persuading his fellow Board members to accept the change of merchant bank. The reaction had not, however, been uniform. Ralph Hartlebury had immediately been in favour of a change, but spent some time cross questioning Martin to make quite sure he was satisfied that Greensmith Leonard were the right bank to switch to. Lord Leven-Sumpter had said 'fine' and put the telephone down almost immediately; clearly indicating he did not care one way or the other, and was not going to waste his time discussing it. Joyce Bennett had said that, whilst she did not disagree with the reasoning behind the change, she was not convinced it was the 'nice' thing to do. Martin had been very patient with her and used his charm to persuade her that niceness did not come into the equation. The executive directors, with the exception of Robert Brodie, had all agreed readily. Brodie had argued in favour of continuity and consistency by staying with Lloyd, Meisson for both bids. He had not pressed the argument, however, indicating that he would go along with the majority. This reaction had puzzled Martin as Brodie did not usually give way without a fight. The potentially difficult member of the board was Humphrey Lester because of his association with Lloyd, Meisson. Martin Chandler hardly expected the former Chief Executive of Lloyd, Meisson to support a proposal to drop the bank. In the event it had been very easy. Humphrey Lester, in true patrician fashion, had immediately said that it would be entirely inappropriate for him to play any part in the appointment of merchant bankers to fight the Barton Industries bid.

The Board meeting to review the progress of the two bids had accordingly not been the difficult session Martin had thought it might be. Alan Mortimer had been invited to join them as soon as Martin had gone through the formality of announcing the appointment. For practical purposes, more than anything else, Mortimer had been seated next to James Markby Smythe. There were bound to be occasions when this would smooth the progress of meetings as they would be able to confer before speaking. Nevertheless, the thought of James Markby Smythe having to sit next to the man who had just displaced him appealed to Martin Chandler's slightly puckish sense of humour.

The Barton Industries Formal Offer Document had come out that morning and Stephen and Alan Mortimer had spent the morning analysing the document with a view to making a presentation to the Board that afternoon. Markby Smythe had been invited to join the session but had politely declined, pleading other engagements. Instead he had sent Philip Renton along. He had arrived some thirty minutes after the agreed time for the meeting. Stephen was quite sure that a point was being made, and none too subtley at that.

Martin invited Alan Mortimer to take the Board through the Barton Industries Offer Document. He wasted no time on preliminaries and went straight to the heart of the matter.

'Gentlemen,' Alan Mortimer ignored the presence of a lady, 'I suggest we do not waste any time considering this document in any detail. There is some useful technical detail about Barton Industries, and we shall of course be examining this to determine how best to use it in our defence, but I suggest we do not waste our ammunition at this stage. Their bid got off to a very poor start and it is obvious that the real bid will come very shortly. Barton Industries have clearly rushed the document out more quickly than would have been the case had you not been bidding for Axehouse General. They have time to catch up. If I was advising Barton Industries, my advice to them would be to revise their offer sooner rather than later. The longer the present offer stays on the table, the less credible it becomes. I think we shall have a revised offer within the week. In other words, they won't wait for the first closing date for acceptances to pass before revising the offer. The new offer will almost certainly have a significant element of Barton Industries shares in the package. This means that the Barton Industries share price is going to be one of the pivotal determinants of the outcome of the bid.'

Alan Mortimer could see Joyce Bennett looking somewhat puzzled and her hand made a small upwards movement suggesting she was about to speak. He decided to explain the significance of the Barton Industries share price before she interrupted him.

'Clearly, if the Barton Industries share price falls, the value of what they are offering the shareholders of Amalgamated falls with it, and accordingly the chances of the bid succeeding diminish. Our task in this context is obvious. Do all we can to keep the Barton Industries share price down. They will, of course, be doing all they can to keep it up. On the question of timing, as I have already indicated, they are speeding things up and I think we can take it that they will do all they can to keep pace with our bid for Axehouse. James will no doubt be advising you on the implications for the timing of our bid.'

There was a lively discussion following Mortimer's analysis of the situation, focusing for the most part on the Barton Industries share price and how it could be depressed. He ducked giving any specific nostrums. He did not want to get tied down to any particular course of action. It could be both restricting and dangerous from his point of view. He contented himself with generalities, indicating that a close analysis of the effect upon Barton Industries itself of acquiring Amalgamated would be one of the crucial areas, but that this could not really be undertaken until the terms of the revised bid were known. Markby Smythe supported him in this, and emphasised the need to keep the Amalgamated share price up in order that the bid for Axehouse succeeded. He was unable to resist a small dig at Alan Mortimer and Greensmith Leonard by pointing out that the successful acquisition of Axehouse General would render the Barton Industries bid for Amalgamated a nullity, as it was conditional upon the Amalgamated bid for Axehouse failing, and would remain so whatever new terms Barton Industires might come up with. His motivation was to emphasise that the role of Lloyd, Meisson was pivotal. If they succeeded in steering Axehouse General into the Amalgamated Products fold, there would be no need for the services of Greensmith Leonard. Barton Industries would automatically go away. He had, however, overlooked one obvious situation where this would not hold true but, then, so had everybody else around the table.

Martin Chandler sensed that the discussion was starting to go round in circles and become theoretical.

'Well, lady and gentlemen, I think we have covered the ground as far as we can at this stage. As you know, we have two committees in place to deal with the conduct of both our bid for Axehouse General and the Barton Industries bid for us. On reflection I think two committees, one dealing with strategy and one with day to day detail, are unnecessarily cumbersome. On occasion we shall need to move with great speed. With your approval, therefore, I propose to amalgamate the two committees into one, giving it power to act on behalf of the Board and set up such sub-committees as it thinks necessary. You will all, of course, be kept fully in the picture and the really major decisions will come to the full Board for approval.'

He omitted to point out that the resolution gave the committee virtually unfettered power to act on behalf of the Board in relation to the two bids.

'The new committee will be a straight amalgamation of the members of the present two committees with, of course, the addition of Alan. The terms of the formal resolution setting all this up are before you; could I please have a proposer and a seconder.'

Martin Chandler deliberately omitted to invite discussion. He neither wanted to waste time nor, more importantly, run any risk of the powers of the committee being watered down. He need not have worried on this count as the three main players – James Walker, King and Brodie – were members and Sir Ralph Hartlebury had given it his blessing before the meeting. The only danger was that one of the other non-executive directors might query the sweeping powers proposed for the committee. None of them raised any objection. Indeed, Stephen

Barber noted, none of them made any noticeable effort to read the resolution. It was passed without comment. Stephen was delighted. It had been his brainchild and, whilst the rationale behind it had been to streamline the system both by having one committee, and giving it very wide devolved powers from the Board of Directors, it also served to strengthen his own position as he was now a member of the decision making body and not simply its secretary.

☆ ☆ ☆

Miles Wartnaby could hardly contain his anger. He had just heard the news that Amalgamated had appointed Greensmith Leonard as their merchant bankers to defend the Barton Industies bid. He had immediately picked up the telephone and called Ray Schuster at Greensmith Leonard.

'Ray, what the hell is going on?' Miles Wartnaby almost shouted down the phone. 'I was under the distinct impression that Greensmith Leonard were my merchant bankers.'

Ray Schuster knew what was coming. He realised he was in a tight corner. As soon as the note had come round announcing that Amalgamated had appointed Greensmith Leonard to act on the Barton Industries bid he knew he had slipped up. He should have registered a BCI interest in the bid in the bank's register as soon as Miles Wartnaby had shown an interest in what was happening at Amalgamated. He could hardly blame Alan Mortimer for accepting the appointment. He would have checked the register and seen that it was clear for Greensmith Leonard to act for Amalgamated as there were no entries to indicate that any client of the bank had an interest in the bid. He knew Miles Wartnaby well enough to know that he was quite likely to dabble in other people's bids, and he should have been put on enquiry when Miles Wartnaby had mentioned Amalgamated and the two bids in which it was involved. He decided to try and brazen it out.

'Of course we are your merchant bankers, Miles. I'm not aware of anything to have changed that.'

'You damn well ought to be. What are you doing acting for Amalgamated against Barton Industries?'

176

'But you're not involved in that bid, Miles, nor the Amalgamated bid for Axehouse General for that matter. We can't turn business away on the off chance that one of our clients might become interested in some bid or other that's going on.'

Miles Wartnaby did his best to keep cool.

'Ray, I have had two chats with you on the telephone about Amalgamated and the Barton Industries and Axehouse General bids. You cannot claim to have been ignorant of my interest in them.'

'But Miles, those chats were no different to hundreds of other chats we have had over the years concerning what was going on in the takeover market. You gave no indication whatsoever that you were, or were contemplating, becoming involved in those bids. They were just general chats.'

'Well I am interested,' Miles exploded, 'and if you want to keep my business you will resign your appointment as bankers to Amalgamated for the Barton Industries bid immediately.'

'I can't do that, Miles. You know I can't do that. We would be in breach of contract, and would doubtless face a nasty court action.'

'That's your problem, Ray. What about your breach of contract with me?'

Ray Schuster could see no benefit in pursuing this particular line of debate.

'Miles, I am deeply sorry that I did not realise you were interested in the Amalgamated bids. I accept that I should not have taken your chats with me as being no more than academic interest. You have every right to be upset, and I fully realise that if you do get involved in these bids and necessarily go to another merchant bank for advice, you may stay with them. I sincerely hope not, but I totally accept that you are quite free to do so. All I can say is that we have, I believe, given you an excellent service in the past and would continue to do so in the future if you chose to stay with us.'

Miles Wartnaby was not exactly mollified, but he couldn't deny that Greensmith Leonard had given him excellent service in the past. Indeed, it was that very fact that made him so cross. He was firmly convinced they were the best, and he tolerated nothing less than the best.

'That's as may be, but it doesn't exactly put things right, does it? If you cannot or won't act for me, so be it. I will have to go elsewhere. I may stay there.'

Miles knew he was unlikely to abandon Greensmith Leonard in the future, but there was no harm in making Ray Schuster sweat a little.

'What I do require from you now is that you keep my interest in the Amalgamated bids absolutely secret. I don't want Alan Mortimer finding out from you that I am interested and putting Amalgamated on notice.'

Ray Schuster was more than happy to agree. The last thing he wanted to do was publicise within Greensmith Leonard the fact that he might have lost the BCI business through a combination of not being sufficiently percipient and carelessness in not registering an interest in the client interest book. He would not make the same mistake again if Miles Wartnaby and BCI stayed with him.

Stephen Barber called Trevor Jacques at the Brabent Agency.

'Any news on our target, Trevor?'

'We have a confirmed sighting of him at an apartment where we are almost certain he was entertaining a young lady. We have subsequently established that the young lady in question is a call girl.'

Harry had had little difficulty in establishing that the H. Saunders and M. Hunt who occupied flat B in the block of flats in Maida Vale were call girls. All that had been necessary was a few minutes with the London telephone directory, which soon gave up the name of H. Saunders at the appropriate address, followed by a telephone call. He had toyed with the idea of pretending to be Sir Peter Barton but had dropped it on the basis that it might cause the girl to clam up rather than confirm what business she was in. The girl answering the phone had not given a name, so he had asked for it. When Helen Saunders had identified herself he simply asked for Miss Hunt, saying that a friend had recommended her as being good fun. Melanie Hunt was out and Helen Saunders was never one to miss a bit of business. In no time at all Harry had established that they were call girls. If Melanie had been any indication of what Helen was like, then Harry was decidedly sorry that he would not be turning up for the threesome he had arranged with them.

'I don't think that is anything more than just interesting, Trevor. A lot of top businessmen seem to have girlfriends of one sort or another these days. Besides, I don't think our target is married.'

'He isn't, and I quite agree with you. We need something specific and more reprehensible. I do have some interesting leads on the business side, however. He has never been particularly fussy what methods he uses to get his own way in business and I do not think it will be long before we turn up something interesting we may be able to use.'

'OK Trevor, keep me in the picture. We don't have much time.'

What next? He had not given much thought to the bid for Axehouse General these past few days; he had been too busy with Barton Industries. He checked the figures his department had prepared for him. Acceptances of the bid were a miserly two per cent. Still, this was not untypical for the stage of the bid. The first closing date for acceptances had not arrived yet. Things really started to hum after that. A quick look at his timetable told him there were only four days to this milestone. Tomorrow morning's meeting of the 'Battle Committee' would need to address the Axehouse bid in detail and thrash out the tactics for the days after the first closing date for acceptances. It looked as if an increased offer would be necessary. This was no surprise. It had already been assumed that this would be the case. It was simply a matter of assessing the size and nature of any increased offer. Stephen was of the view that the structure of the bid was probably right and, if this was the general view of the Battle Committee, then the only matters for debate were the level of the increased offer and the timing.

He had not told Martin yet that he had a private detective on the tail of Peter Barton. Now might be the right moment. It was possible that his reaction would be unfavourable. In extremis, however, it would probably be a different story. Whilst Martin Chandler might not be in favour of prying into the private life of Peter Barton, he might not be against making efforts to find out if he was lilywhite in his business dealings. Stephen thought it might be prudent to float the idea and see what reaction he got. He had been persuaded easily enough to employ an aggressive merchant bank to advise on the defence against the Barton Industries bid, so he should not be too unresponsive. No harm would be done if he got a negative response. Indeed, unless Trevor Jacques turned up something which would be really effective he would simply keep quiet and say nothing. Before he approached Martin he decided to have a word with Alan Mortimer. He picked up the telephone and dialled his direct line number.

'Hello, Alan. Stephen Barber. I just want to bounce something off you.'

'Fire away.'

'I've got a private detective on the trail of Peter Barton. Martin Chandler doesn't know about it at the moment and I would like your thoughts on whether it would be wise to tell him at this stage.'

Alan Mortimer laughed by way of response.

'I'm not sure I see what is funny about the idea.'

'Oh, nothing is funny about the idea of employing a detective agency. It is just that you have confirmed a suspicion I have been harbouring for the last couple of hours. It wouldn't be Trevor Jacques and the Brabent Agency which you have employed, would it?'

'Well, yes it would actually.'

Stephen was both puzzled and angry. He thought that Trevor Jacques was the epitome of discretion.

'How did you know?'

'Oh, don't worry, I didn't. Not for sure, that is. I was simply putting two and two together and making four for once. I use Trevor Jacques quite a lot; he is very good. I rang him with a view to getting him to do some digging for me on Barton Industries and Sir Peter Barton. I got a polite refusal. Somebody had obviously got there first. I thought it might be you.'

Stephen Barber was considerably relieved. Trevor

Jacques had not broken a confidence.

'Well, that answers at least part of my question. You obviously believe in using people like him. As a matter of interest, what would have been your instructions to him?'

'Oh, it would have been confined to the purely business side. If he has any peccadillos or peculiarities in his personal life, that is of no interest to me. This is not to say that such information might not be very useful in discrediting him, and thereby undermining his bid to some extent, but it would be entirely up to you whether and how you used such information. On an entirely unofficial basis I could give you some ideas how best to use it, but you would have to understand that it was unofficial and that I would deny any involvement. I would not put the reputation of my bank in jeopardy by getting involved in character assassination.'

'How about telling Martin Chandler?'

'You know him better than I, Stephen, but subject to that I can see no harm in telling him. I have no doubt that Sir Peter Barton would use any disreputable information he dug out concerning Amalgamated and Martin Chandler if he thought it would help his cause.'

'Can I quote you on that, Alan?'

'By all means. As you will appreciate, I was in the process of setting up an investigation myself. You must make it quite clear, however, that I am not interested in, nor would I use, any dirt that might surface concerning Barton's personal life.'

'Understood, Alan.'

Seven pm. Martin Chandler might still be in his office. Stephen had achieved his objective of getting an office on the fifth floor and was now only three doors away from Martin's small suite. He walked down the corridor, past the door that led directly on to the corridor, and put his head round the door of Ann Gordon's office. Empty. Her desk was clear and the filing cabinets firmly locked. She had obviously gone home, which meant Martin probably had done so as well. He knocked and turned the handle of the connecting door into Martin Chandler's office. Locked. He had gone home, too. A slight noise behind him caused him to turn back toward the door of Ann's office. Robert Brodie stood there. Stephen got the impression he had been there a few moments and had been watching him as he tried the door of Martin Chandler's office. He wondered why.

'The bird has flown by the look of it, Stephen. It wasn't important. I will speak to him tomorrow.'

Brodie turned on his heels and set off down the corridor towards his office. Stephen had the distinct feeling that there was something odd, but he could not quite put his finger on it. There was something in the circumstances of the encounter and Brodie's demeanour that was not quite right. He shrugged his shoulders. Probably nothing to do with him, whatever it was.

He decided not to call Martin at his apartment in Eaton Square. Better, he thought on reflection, to raise the question of private detectives as an aside in general discussion rather than make it a major issue.

Brodie did not close his door when he returned to his office. Instead he hovered just inside; waiting for the sound of a door shutting just two down from him on the opposite side. He only had to wait a few moments. A door was pulled shut and the scrape of a key in a lock followed soon after. He waited a few seconds and then peered surreptitiously round his door and saw what he had hoped to see: the figure of Stephen Barber, briefcase in hand and overcoat over his arm, retreating in the direction of the lifts. A few more seconds and he heard the lift doors open and close. He walked briskly down the corridor and into Ann Gordon's office, produced a key from his pocket, and silently let himself into Martin Chandler's office.

17

'I think it might be advantageous all round if we met.'

Robert Brodie's heart skipped a beat. He recognised the voice immediately even though the caller had not announced who he was. Sir Peter Barton.

'Certainly. Where, when?'

Brodie adopted the rather cloak and dagger atmosphere without being aware that he had done so.

'The sooner the better. How are you fixed this evening?'

Brodie thought quickly. He had promised to take his wife out for dinner as a peace offering. He had been up in London all week and she had been less than ecstatic when he had called her the night before at six o'clock to say he would not be able to make it to the dinner party she had arranged for that night. It had been too late to cancel the party and she had had to act as both host and hostess. He sighed inwardly. This was too important to defer. Molly would have to wait. He would make it up another time. At least when she calmed down she would understand. Six years as his secretary before she married him, following his divorce from Jean, had given her the training to understand that there were occasions when business came before everything else. Something Jean had never understood.

'Fine. It won't take me long to get up to town from Abingdon on a Saturday night.'

'No. I think it better we meet out of town. There is always the off chance that someone will recognise us, and the cat would really be out of the bag. I have a cottage near Aylesbury. It is quite remote, and the chances of our being seen together there are infinitesimal. I will see you

183

there in an hour.'

Barton gave Brodie instructions how to find the cottage and rang off.

Robert Brodie braced himself to break the news to Molly. She was already upstairs preparing herself for the evening out. As he entered the bedroom she was sat at her dressing table with her back to the door. Although she had turned forty he still regarded her as a very handsome woman. Sitting there in her bra, panties, suspender belt and black stockings she presented a highly stimulating sight. The effect was heightened by the reflection of her face and bosom in the mirror.

Molly caught sight of him in the mirror and gave a little wave of her hand without turning around. She smiled at him through the mirror.

'Hello darling. We've got plenty of time haven't we?'

Robert Brodie felt a real heel and, quite apart from anything else, he was about to deprive himself of what had promised to be a thoroughly enjoyable evening. Molly was fabulous in bed, or anywhere else for that matter.

'I've got to go out Molly. It's these wretched takeover bids again.'

He watched her face crumble in disappointment. The knuckles of her hand went white gripping her hairbrush tightly as she fought for control. He knew she would win her private little battle, but that in no way assuaged his sense of guilt.

'I promise I will make it up darling.'

He knew how weak this must have sounded. He had said exactly the same thing the previous evening, and not twenty four hours later was having to repeat himself. He would have quite understood if Molly had completely lost her temper and accused him of not caring. She put her hairbrush down and lifted her arms up wide in a gesture of despair. The action was highly erotic as her breasts rose in her wispy bra in sympathy with the motion of her arms. Robert Brodie took an involuntary step forward, instinctively wishing to take her in his arms. With difficulty he stopped himself. He didn't have time to start something which he knew neither of them would be able to stop until they were both sated.

'I really will.'

He dropped his arms helplessly to his side. Molly laughed. It was both a way of releasing her tension and a response to what she saw as a very funny sight.

'You look just like a naughty little boy standing in the headmaster's study awaiting his punishment, Robert.'

He grinned sheepishly.

'Maybe I deserve it.'

'Yes you do. Bend over.'

Robert realised he had to stop this quickly or he would never get to his meeting with Sir Peter Barton.

'Another time darling. I really do have to rush, and it really is very important.'

He gave her a brief hug and kiss on the cheek. He looked at his watch. Six thirty.

'I shall probably not be back much before eleven.'

Oh, you are coming back then. I thought I had lost you until at least next Saturday. I shall have to change my plans, or maybe I won't change my plans.'

She was teasing him now. He knew she would not go out and would probably sit in front of the television feeling miserable.

'Bye, darling.'

He reluctantly left the room. He cursed his overpowering ambition, but knew he would never be able to suppress it. It was part of him and no doubt was in some way part of his attraction for her.

☆ ☆ ☆

Harvey Cook was just about to call it a day and get Kevin Gillings to take over for the night shift when a blue Jaguar XJS drew up outside Sir Peter Barton's apartment. Whilst the suit the driver was wearing could not be classed as uniform, to the practised eye of Harvey Cook it shouted out that it was some form of standard dress. The car hire business seemed to specialise in a line of slate grey bordering on black suits for their staff. Chauffeurs on semi-formal duty also seemed to favour this particular sartorial genre.

There were a number of apartments in the building and

the man could have been calling at any of them. Harvey decided to wait and see who came out to the car. He very nearly missed him. The man who emerged in casual slacks and a floppy sweater, and went over to the car, would not have been immediately recognised as Sir Peter Barton by someone who did not know him fairly well. His public image was of an elegant and well dressed man. Casual clothes did not feature. It must have been the man's walk that had triggered recognition.

'Quick, Harry. Follow the Jag.'

The black cab pulled out behind the Jaguar and Harvey noted the number.

Harry had no problem following the car to start with. The Saturday evening traffic was sufficiently busy not to make it obvious that he was following the Jaguar; nor was it so busy that there was a danger of losing him. Harvey started to get a bit concerned when Sir Peter Barton sailed through Maida Vale into Kilburn High Road and on to Cricklewood. He clearly was not making a little visit to Melanie Hunt in Maida Vale as had seemed likely when he had headed for Marble Arch and turned into the Edgware Road. When he hit the North Circular and turned towards the M1, Harvey Cook's heart sank. There was no way a London cab was going to be able to keep up with a Jag on the motorway and, even if it could, it would be pretty obvious that it was being followed. The Jag duly indicated to turn onto the motorway and reluctantly Harvey Cook told Harry not to bother trying to follow.

Sir Peter Barton was quite oblivious to the anguish he had caused behind him. He had already decided on his tactics for dealing with Robert Brodie, and he mulled over them as he drove along. He would offer him the chairmanship of Amalgamated within Barton Industries and a seat on the Barton Industries Board as openers, but he did not expect that this would be sufficient to land his fish. Before upping his offer he would put Brodie on the line and get him to show how he could justify a better position. Nathan Sanson was quite right he had decided. If Barton Industries were successful in acquiring Amalgamated Products he would have to alter the manner in which he managed Barton Industries. It would be far too big to run in the way he had in the past. He would need a Chief Executive to run the day to day affairs of the expanded group, whilst he concentrated on the strategic thrust of the company. He would still have virtually absolute control over affairs. The Chief Executive would report direct to him and his influence over the remainder of the Board would ensure that the Chief Executive did not become a threat to his power. He wanted to be quite sure however that Brodie was the right man before offering him the Chief Executive post. It would be very short sighted to offer him the post in return for any help he might be able to give in acquiring Amalgamated if he was not the right man. A mole in Amalgamated was better than not having a mole, but the chances of his being able to achieve anything decisive to ensure the success of the bid were small. At best all he could hope for was that Robert Brodie would be able to forewarn him of Amalgamated's tactics both in their bid for Axehouse General and in their defence against the Barton Industries bid. This would enable him to develop better tactics to enhance the prospects of Barton Industries. Peter Barton was sufficient of a realist, however, to appreciate that at the end of the day the bid would succeed or fail on its own merits. Somehow he had to get a bandwaggon rolling. Robert Brodie would not be able to do that for him.

Brodie took a little time to find the cottage. Peter Barton had not been exaggerating when he said it was remote. Eventually he spotted the gateway. He had passed it twice already without noticing it. He had expected a smart entrance even though Sir Peter Barton had made it clear the cottage was quite small. The five barred farm gate looked just like any other farm gate in the dark, and it was only because he had decided to stop at every gateway he passed on his left that he took any notice of this one. In the reflected light from his car headlights he was just able to make out the name Mulberry Cottage on the gate and, looking up, saw the cottage some twenty yards or so from the roadway. A light was on downstairs and a low sleek car stood outside. Sir Peter Barton had arrived ahead of him as he had expected.

The front door opened as he drew up alongside the Jaguar and Sir Peter stood silhouetted in the light. They shook hands briefly and went into the room which led straight off the front door.

'This is a nice little place you have got here,' Brodie observed as he took in the low timbered ceiling, the comfortable looking furniture and the welcoming log fire that was already beginning to take a good hold in the fireplace.

'Do you use it much?'

'Not as much as I would like. It is my private hideaway for when I want to relax thoroughly or have total peace and quiet to think things over. Only my secretary knows of its existence, and I would appreciate it if you kept the confidence.'

'No problem there Peter, bearing in mind the reason I am here in the first place.'

Brodie had decided to go on to first name terms straight away. He felt it would help to set the right tone for what he hoped was to be a mutually beneficial future.

'Help yourself to a drink, Robert.'

Peter Barton accepted the intimate form of address and gestured towards the table which carried a variety of drinks. Robert helped himself to a whisky and water and settled himself down opposite.

'Well what can you offer me?' Barton enquired.

Robert parried the question. He didn't wish to commit himself until he was confident there would be something worthwhile in return. What he had to offer also very much depended upon his being in a position of some influence within the enlarged Barton Industries that would follow the successful acquisition of Amalgamated.

'I think that depends upon what you can offer me Peter. I am the one who will be taking the major risk.'

Barton sat back in his chair cradling his glass. He didn't speak for a few moments. He decided to change tack and approach the matter from another angle.

'Tell me, how do you rate the chances of Barton Industries succeeding in acquiring Amalgamated?'

Robert knew this was the crunch question and he had to be careful how he answered it.

'I am taking a considerable risk in meeting you in the present circumstances Peter. I would hardly be taking that risk if I thought Barton Industries had no chance of success. I don't think it needs me to tell you that the bid which is on the table at the moment stands no chance whatsoever. I recognise it for what it is. A sighting shot. It is a pity from your point of view that it has gone down so badly, it makes it that much more difficult to gain credibility for the real bid when it comes. I have followed your progress from way back and two things stand out a mile. First your determination and, second, the fact that you have never yet failed to acquire any company for which you made a bid. On the assumption that your next shot is a knockout blow, my money is on you, and that is why I am here. I am sure you will not make the mistake of pitching your next offer at a level where minor movements in your own share price effectively kill the bid. You also have to overcome the timing problem. If Amalgamated succeed in their bid for Axehouse I believe that effectively sinks your bid.'

'Well that summarises the situation fairly neatly. If we succeed I think it is pretty obvious that I shall have to rethink how I organise and run the company. It will be of such a size that it would be a grave error for me to try and run it the way I have run Barton Industries up to now. Much as I hate the thought of having to share power, I doubt that I can continue to run the business as if it were my own.'

Robert Brodie lifted his eyebrows in surprise at this last remark. Barton smiled.

'Oh, I might be a dictator, Robert, but I am not a blind dictator. I have no intention of finishing up against the wall because I fail to see the need for change and a degree of power sharing.'

Brodie recognised his cue.

'As you know Peter, I have run my own not insubstantial business. I have the same entrepreneurial spirit as you. I am not the product of a corporate bureaucracy where a modicum of ability combined with a highly developed political skill spiced with a sense of knowing which backs to scratch, smooths the path to the top. That is not my style, nor in my view is it the way in which to ensure that a business performs to its maximum. I offer you two things. I know the ins and outs of Amalgamated intimately. I can save you a lot of time and expense in identifying and correcting its weaknesses, and I can help you avoid making mistakes in staffing key posts. I know how to make that business hum. Secondly, and far more important in my view, I have the experience and skills to take a significant role in the management of Barton Industries itself. I am just the sort of man headhunters would be recommending to you if you went outside for someone to fill a key management role in Barton Industries. I would come doubly qualified.'

He had been careful not to mention any particular role. Far better to let Peter Barton open the batting on this.

'Don't you think we are jumping a step?'

'I'm not quite sure what you mean.'

'I haven't got Amalgamated Products yet. All you have just said is supremely irrelevant if I fail. What can you do to help me succeed? Once we have determined that, then, it might be appropriate to discuss where you fit into the new structure.'

Robert Brodie knew this was coming. He would have dealt with this first himself if the roles had been reversed.

'I do not think it would be helpful at this stage for me to come out into the open and endorse your bid. All this would do would be to cut me off from access to potentially useful information. For the present I believe I can be most useful by feeding to you details of the Amalgamated tactics in relation to their bid for Axehouse General, and in defence of your bid for them. It would be absolutely essential that you used this information with great circumspection. Under no circumstances must it be obvious that there was a leak from within Amalgamated. This would not only put me at risk but could very well harm you as well.'

'I don't disagree with that, but there comes a point when your open and active support might be crucial. Are there any circumstances in which you see yourself being able to come out into the open and recommend the bid?'

'Yes, Peter. I do not think it is possible to define them exactly now — but, yes I anticipate the right circumstances could arise.'

'I don't think that is good enough. If I am to offer you something worthwhile I want a stronger commitment than that.'

Brodie thought for a moment. He did not want to give a categorical undertaking that he would come out in open support at any given moment. On the other hand he appreciated Barton's desire for a firmer commitment.

'I don't think either of us has anything to gain by my giving you a firm undertaking now that in circumstances abc I will come out in public support of your bid. It must be a matter of judgement at the time. I lose everything if I come out in support when it adds little or nothing to your chances of success; and you gain little or nothing. The best I can offer is that, if in my judgement, my public support would tip the scales in your favour when otherwise you might lose out for lack of one final push, then, I would come out and recommend the bid. In such circumstances I think I might be able to bring one and possibly two other directors along with me. You have to trust me on this. If you find yourself unable to do so I may as well leave now. If you cannot accept my word in this respect I doubt that I am the right man for you.'

Barton did not need to pursue the point any further. He entirely accepted what Brodie had said. If he couldn't trust the man to give his open support at a crucial moment when there was a realistic prospect of this tipping the balance, then he certainly was not the man to take a leading role in Barton Industries.

'I accept what you say entirely, Robert. If we are unable to deal with each other on a basis of mutual trust, then there is no point in our continuing this conversation. The coin has two sides of course and you have to trust me to honour whatever we agree as to your future role in Barton Industries if the bid succeeds. I am certainly not putting anything down on paper.'

Brodie nodded his assent.

'What I am prepared to offer you is the chairmanship

of Amalgamated, which will retain its corporate identity within Barton Industries, and a seat on the main Barton Industries Board. It would be my intention to establish an inner core of the directors to form a Chairman's Policy Group to advise me on both the strategic development of the company and the short to medium term management and planning of the company. You would be a member of the Chairman's Policy Group.'

Robert Brodie decided to take the bull by the horns. Such an arrangement was neither attractive to him personally nor did he think it to be a sensible arrangement from the point of view of Barton Industries.

'I will be quite blunt Peter. That proposal does not attract me and I don't consider it would be in the long term interests of Barton Industries. You would be creating just the sort of stultifying bureaucracy that Amalgamated suffers from. You would find yourself cluttered up with endless committee work and no freedom to stand back and busy yourself with the wider strategic picture. You would be quite unable to resist keeping your finger on every detail of the business. What you need is a Chief Executive with real power and authority to deal with the day to day running of the business. He would obviously be set defined targets and manage the business within clear guidelines determined by the Board.'

Brodie smiled as he said this, confident that the implication of the continued domination of the Barton Industries Board by Sir Peter Barton would not be missed. What he saw, for the second time that evening, was white knuckles as Barton gripped his glass ferociously as he fought for control. Brodie ploughed on. He had to win this battle. If he lost there would be no point in joining Barton Industries. Whatever title he was given, he would simply be a cipher.

'Whether I am the right man for the job is for you to decide. What is clear is that you need someone to fill this role. If you offer it to me I do not want you to be under any illusion. I will stand up to you and will not allow myself to be pushed around.'

Sir Peter got up from his chair and went to the back of the small room. He was boiling inside. How dare this man

192

come into his home and not only tell him how to run his business but demand a leading role for himself. Robert Brodie knew when to keep quiet. Sir Peter went to the door and threw it open to the night air. He stood there motionless for what seemed an eternity to Robert Brodie. Order was beginning to return to his thoughts. He could not say Nathan Sanson had not warned him. He had also recommended that he should adopt a structure whereby significant power was given to a Chief Executive and, as he calmed down, he accepted that there was no point in having a Chief Executive if he were to be that in name only, whilst in practice being totally subservient. Brodie was right and what was more he was probably the right man. He would stand up to him. Life would not be comfortable, but then business was not about comfort. He turned on his heels and faced back into the room.

'Right.'

Robert Brodie waited for more looking enquiringly at him.

'Right,' he repeated. 'I think we have a basis for discussion.'

Brodie thought that was what they had been doing, but thought it better not to say so.

'I take it, Peter, that we are agreed in principle?'

'Yes I suppose so.'

Sir Peter Barton realised he was at risk of sounding indecisive.

'Yes, if Barton Industries succeeds in acquiring Amalgamated you will join my board as Chief Executive with effective day to day control over the running of the business within parameters which will be clearly defined.'

Robert Brodie decided not to pursue the detail of the role. It was far too premature. The principle had been established. The detail could come later.

'There is just one more matter Peter. The chairmanship of Amalgamated.'

'Oh, you can have that. There is no problem there.'

'You misunderstand me Peter. I am not asking for the chairmanship, at least not on an ongoing basis. I consider it would not be compatible with my role as Chief Executive of Barton Industries. On an interim basis I would be quite happy to accept it, on a sort of non-executive basis to help smooth the process of integration, but with a Managing Director responsible for the day to day running of the business. At the appropriate moment I would give up this post so that Amalgamated would be in the same position as all the other elements of the Barton Industries Group. The Chairman would report and be responsible to me.'

Peter Barton felt his anger rising again. The wretched man was talking as if he owned the business. He quickly controlled himself. What Robert Brodie was saying was only the logical consequence of what he had already agreed to. He would retain his power by ensuring that the responsibilities of the Chief Executive were closely and clearly defined.

'Fine, fine. Do you have anyone in mind?'

Brodie very much had someone in mind. Terry King. He was not letting on at this stage, however, as he yet had to land that particular fish.

'I have some ideas, Peter, but a lot depends on how things work out.'

He glanced at his watch. A quarter to nine. Things had not taken as long as he had expected. Maybe he could still get home in time to take Molly out to dinner. He looked around the room.

'Do you have a phone? I would like to call my wife. I take it there is little more for us to discuss this evening?'

'No, I don't have a telephone in the cottage as a matter of fact. I like to keep this place as private as possible.'

He paused briefly and noted the look of disappointment on Brodie's face and decided to relent.

'You can use my car phone though if you wish. We will have to set up a system of communication so that we can contact each other at short notice with the minimum of risk. I will give it some thought and get in touch with you.'

Molly had answered the telephone almost immediately. Robert Brodie could hear the low murmur of the television in the background and pictured Molly sitting on the couch with her feet curled up under her, watching television.

'Hi darling, have you eaten yet? I can be home by half nine. It's not too late to go out and get a meal.'

Molly had eaten but she was not going to admit it, in any case it had only been a minor nibble. He sounded in good spirits. The meeting must have gone well and she was not going to deprive herself of an enjoyable evening by punishing him for letting her down in the first place.

'No darling, not yet. I will ring around and see if we can get in somewhere.'

'See you soon.'

He passed the telephone back to Peter Barton and thanked him. He took it back to his car, envying Brodie his obviously happy relationship with his wife. A succession of young and willing girls had its excitement, but it did not have the contentment Robert Brodie obviously enjoyed.

18

Miles Wartnaby decided that the phoney war was about to end. The first closing date for acceptance of the Amalgamated bid for Axehouse General would come the next day, and the likelihood was that an increased offer would rapidly be winging its way to shareholders. Barton Industries were behind in the game, and Miles Wartnaby thought it unlikely that they would wait for their first closing date for acceptance to arrive before revising their offer for Amalgamated. Not only had they got off to a bad start with a misjudged opening shot, but they were behind the race on time. They had to get their bid running at least parallel with the Amalgamated bid for Axehouse. Miles checked his figures again. He was doing very nicely on both bids. The trick was to ensure that he jumped the right way at the right time. If the Amalgamated bid for Axehouse failed, the price of Axehouse shares would drop significantly and he would lose a large chunk of his paper profit. If the Amalgamated bid for Axehouse succeeded, the Barton Industries bid for Amalgamated failed by definition. The Amalgamated share price would drop somewhat, but probably not as much as the Axehouse General shares would if the Amalgamated bid for them failed. Then there was his promise to Sarah. That complicated the equation. Giving Martin a bad time might not be consistent with maximising his own personal profit. No decisions were necessary immediately, but he must think things through so that he was ready to move fast if it became necessary. He picked up his phone and dialled Sarah.

'Hello Sarah, how are things?'

'Oh, much the same as usual.'

Her voice sounded flat and, to her father's sensitive ear, gave a clear message of boredom.

'How's Martin?' The question was not a tender enquiry after the state of her husband's health. It was designed to elicit from Sarah what her current feelings were for him. Her response was an important element in determining which way Miles would jump in the takeover battles.

'Oh, all right I think. I don't see much of him these days. These wretched bids consume most of his time, and when he is not working on them he is no doubt scr. . .' Sarah stopped herself from completing the word that had leapt into her mind and rapidly changed it. 'Scr. . . scratching around for some other business deal to occupy his mind and time.'

Miles Wartnaby was not fooled. He knew what his daughter had been about to say. She had no inhibitions about using a word like screwing to her father. What intrigued him was why she had switched in mid stream.

'Come on Sarah. I know what you were about to say. Is it still going on?'

'Well, short of standing at the end of his bed in Eaton Square and watching, I am about as certain as I can be. I know him. He needs sex. On the rare occasions he is home these days that side of it is as good as it ever was, provided I don't mess it up by coming the injured wife bit. That doesn't make it any easier to bear, of course. I find myself swinging rapidly from one extreme to the other when I think about Martin. One moment I hate him, the next minute . . .'

'Do you still want me to give him a jolt of some sort, Sarah?'

'Sarah . . .'

Sarah hesitated.

'Yes, I'm still here, Daddy. I just wanted to think a bit before I gave you a reply. What I really want is to have Martin back.'

Miles thought it was a great help. It gave him almost carte blanche to do what he thought best for his own financial health. If the aim was actively to hurt Martin, he might have had to pursue a course which was not consistent with his own interests. As it was, events might turn in a direction that harmed Martin, but if so, then so be it.

'I get the picture, Sarah.'

The conversation switched to the current state of play on the takeover front and, not for the first time, Miles regretted that Sarah was not a boy. She had a real feel for business.

☆ ☆ ☆

The debate was lively and by no means a foregone conclusion. There was no disagreement on the principle of increasing the bid. It had been accepted all along that this would almost certainly be necessary. The two main questions were at what level to pitch the increased offer and whether to make it a final offer, or leave the door open for another increase. The two questions were inter-related. If it was to be the final offer then it had to be pitched at an attractive level, but not so high as to call into question whether Amalgamated were offering too much for Axehouse General, and thus making it very difficult to justify the acquisition in terms of its contribution to their profits. If it was not necessarily to be the final offer, then a more modest increase was called for to leave leeway for a further increase later, if that became necessary. To complicate things even further there was the almost random factor of Amalgamated's own share price. The offer package included Amalgamated shares as well as cash and loan stock. The movements in the price of Amalgamated shares obviously affected the value of the offer being made to Axehouse General shareholders. The random factor came in because of the Barton Industries bid for Amalgamated. Even though the City was not over impressed with the structure of the bid, it had nevertheless had the effect of bolstering the Amalgamated share price, and thereby increasing the value of the Amalgamated bid for Axehouse. If it was perceived that the Barton Industries bid was likely to fail, the Amalgamated share price would drop and so would the value of the Amalgamated bid for Axehouse, and this in turn could scupper the bid.

The Battle Committee had wrestled with this apparently

198

insoluble conundrum until Stephen suggested they take a simplistic line. The effect of the Barton Industries bid should be ignored in determining where to pitch the increased offer. The Amalgamated share price would inevitably slip back somewhat, but the sophisticated professionals would already have taken this into account if they decided to accept the Amalgamated offer for their shares in Axehouse. Since it had already been decided that the increase in the bid terms would be a mixture of more cash and loan stock, the share price should be ignored in determining where to pitch the increase.

Martin sat back in his chair and breathed a sigh of relief. The meeting had been in danger of getting bogged down in an 'ah, but what if' debate. He was not entirely sure he had completely followed Stephen's analysis but he could see that Markby Smythe and Alan Mortimer were nodding assent as Stephen developed his thesis. This was good enough for him.

'Well, gentlemen, we seem to have solved that little problem. The question now is how much more we offer by way of cash and loan stock, and whether we make this our final shot.'

Markby Smythe took up the cue.

'I think you all have before you the analysis of how far we can go in increasing our offer, and have a realistic chance of achieving the targets we have set ourselves in terms of the profit contribution, having made full allowance for the financing costs of acquiring the company and the savings by way of rationalisation. This target also inter-relates with our other targets, such as earnings per share growth and share price. The absolute ceiling, in my judgement, if we are to have any chance of meeting these targets following the acquisition of Axehouse is another twenty-five pence. I would not be particularly comfortable with such an increase, as I consider that at that level your prospects of being able to show that you have made the acquisition pay are no more than fifty-fifty.'

Martin looked towards Alan Mortimer for comment. He decided to hold his counsel. He considered Markby Smythe was being unduly pessimistic, but then this was to be expected from a representative of a somewhat stuffy merchant bank. He would have taken a much more robust line. There were ways and means of making acquisitions earn their corn. Uncomfortable ones for many of those involved maybe, but nevertheless they were available. It just needed the will and determination to use them.

'I doubt that I am sufficiently familiar with your plans for Axehouse General to comment on what you can afford by way of an increase in your offer, Mr Chairman. On the other aspect I would be a strong supporter of making your next shot your final shot, and making this quite clear. I consider it is in your interest to bring matters to a head as soon as you can, as this will make it that much more difficult for Barton Industries. They have timing problems already. If you can increase them that will be all to the good.'

Martin decided to let this thread of the debate continue and come back to the question of the level of increased offer later. He had no pre-determined views on whether to make the increase a final offer. He wanted to hear the arguments. The discussion ebbed and flowed, and it was becoming clear that opinion was divided. He disliked putting issues to a formal vote at meetings. He much preferred consensus. It did not help that he saw merit in both arguments. He was all in favour of paying less if he could, and there was the chance that a lower increase might succeed. He realised he would have to come off the fence and indicate a firm preference if he was to have any chance of avoiding a formal vote, and the likelihood of a fairly even split.

'Well, Joyce, gentlemen. I think we have covered the ground pretty comprehensively. There are good arguments on both sides and, in terms of the bid for Axehouse General alone, I consider they are fairly evenly balanced. However, I think we have to look at the wider picture and include the Barton Industries bid in our deliberations. I think that gives a firm push toward the option of making the increased offer a final offer. I accept Alan's view on this. Do we all agree?'

Martin looked round the table. He could see from the expressions on some faces that there were still doubts in the minds of some of them. He mentally crossed his fingers that no-one would come in with the alternative view. Such

200

an intervention could rally support and force him to take a formal vote. His heart sank. Robert Brodie took the floor.

'My view is that we should keep our options open. I believe we should make our decisions in relation to our bid for Axehouse in terms of what is the best way of conducting that bid, and not let it be fogged by extraneous considerations such as the Barton Industries bid for Amalgamated. That will take care of itself on its own merits and I do not believe that by making a knockout blow for Axehouse now that we in any way hinder the Barton Industries bid for us.'

Martin was blissfully unaware that, quite contrary to what he had said, Robert Brodie was very concerned that the strategy suggested by Martin Chandler would indeed make it more difficult for Barton Industries.

'I take it, Robert, that you are against making a knockout blow at this stage. Does anyone else strongly support that view?'

Alan Mortimer came to Martin's rescue.

'If I may, Mr Chairman,' he interjected in his somewhat diffident manner, 'I don't think the issue is quite as Mr Brodie has expressed it.'

Brodie gave him a very dirty look and muttered something to Terry King who was sitting beside him. Mortimer took no notice and carried straight on.

'The Amalgamated bid for Axehouse General and the Barton Industries bid for Amalgamated are inextricably intertwined. They cannot be dealt with in isolation.' He chose not to develop the theme any further. He sensed he had made his point; further elaboration would only give the opportunity for Brodie and any supporters to pick on a detail to continue pressing their view.

'Thank you, Alan.'

He looked round the table again trying to gauge the reaction to the interchange between Brodie and Mortimer. No-one showed any immediate inclination to come out in open support of the former. Stephen was itching to chip in with his view, which strongly supported Alan Mortimer, but decided that discretion was the better part of valour. He sensed an undercurrent that was best left to run its own course. Furthermore, he began to wonder about Brodie. He had behaved rather oddly the other evening when he had encountered him outside Martin's office, and now he was making an issue of a tactical matter and clearly showing his displeasure when a professional adviser recommended a contrary course to the one Brodie wanted. Stephen decided to keep an eye on him.

Martin Chandler decided not to encourage any further contributions on the matter.

'Right, there is clearly an overwhelming majority in favour of making our next offer our final offer.' No one dissented. 'The only question left now is by what amount we increase our offer. James?'

James Markby Smythe leant back in his chair and slowly brought the tips of his fingers together to form an inverted cradle just below his chin. The gesture had an almost mesmeric effect on the others around the table. It drew their attention unerringly to his face which exuded an air of deep concentration as if he were wrestling for the first time with a weighty and difficult problem.

'Silly bastard,' thought Alan Mortimer. He knew perfectly well what Markby Smythe was going to say. They had discussed it before the meeting, both agreeing the tactic of making a knockout final offer, and the amount and nature of the offer. Nevertheless, he could not help admiring the performance. It was no doubt repeated in many a Boardroom around the City, and probably earned many an unspoken plaudit for his perspicacity and wisdom. Mortimer knew what was coming next – about five minutes of analysis painting a picture of the difficulties inherent in pitching the increase at just the right level to achieve its purpose without overdoing it, and being at risk of being accused of panicking and paying well above the odds. He was not disappointed. He entertained himself by studying the faces and demeanour of the other Committee members and trying to read their thoughts. The tone of Markby Smythe's voice changed, drawing his attention back to what he was saying.

'. . . and so, Mr Chairman, our original offer was pitched at 280 pence per share on the basis of our share price as it then stood. As I have explained, we should ignore our current share price in making the calculation as it is falsely enhanced by the Barton Industries bid. I recommend we increase the bid to an equivalent of 300 pence per share by offering another 10 pence in cash and 10 pence in unsecured loan stock, with an option to take it all in loan stock for those wishing to do so for Capital Gains Tax purposes. This, of course, means that, as our share price stands today, the total offer is theoretically worth 323 pence.'

Martin sent a private little prayer heavenwards thanking God that the Battle Committee did not contain Joyce Bennett and Lord Leven-Sumpter. He could imagine it taking at least ten minutes to explain the difference between, and the significance of, the theoretical value of the proposed increased offer and its real value. He knew that he would have to call them after the meeting to get their consent to the increased offer, but at least he would be able to do this without befogging their brains with all the niceties and technicalities involved. Brodie was the first to comment.

'You all know my view on making this the final offer, but I do not think that debars me from having an opinion on the level of the final offer. I consider it is too high. I believe we could succeed by offering up to 10 pence a share less. Although I accept that we should not pay too much attention to our present share price in pitching our increased bid, it still remains a fact that the offer will apparently be worth well in excess of 300 pence per share if we pare the offer down by 10 pence. In my view, 300 pence per share is the psychological barrier we have to jump to succeed. Why clear the barrier by more than we need?'

The argument had a superficial attraction and gained some initial support. Terry King and Charles Lytton both expressed the view that maybe the committee should consider pitching the offer at a lower level. Lytton was particularly worried that the media would not understand the full ramifications of the complex situation created by the Barton Industries bid for Amalgamated, and would characterise the level of the increased offer as being excessive. Markby Smythe and Alan Mortimer both held their counsel. Their role was to remain silent until invited by the Chairman to summarise their advice in the light of the debate.

In the event, it was Howard Irwin who made the telling contribution.

'I believe that there is a lot in what Robert, Terry and Charles are saying, but in the final analysis it will not be the media or the small investors who will determine the outcome of this bid. It will be the large professional investors. They will already be valuing the share element of our bid on the basis of the likely price of our shares if our bid succeeds. They will already have stripped out the premium in our share price represented by the Barton Industries bid for Amalgamated. They will see very clearly that if our bid succeeds the Barton Industries fails, and that the premium in our share price vanishes.'

Martin noted the slight nods of agreement from King and Lytton.

'Well, gentlemen, I think we are agreed on 20 pence.'

He moved from face to face inviting disagreement, confident that there would be none. Brodie knew when to withdraw gracefully.

'Thank you.' He looked across to Henry Robirch from Miller Michaels, the company solicitors. 'Do we have to put this to the full Board, Henry?'

'No, no. The delegated authority the full Board has given this committee is quite wide enough to encompass an increase in the offer. I think, however, that it would be wise to get the verbal agreement of those directors not here present and, at your next Board Meeting, get them to ratify the increase. Belt and braces.'

Typical solicitor, thought Martin, always suggesting a further prop even when the structure was firmly based on the ground.

'Thank you, Henry. I shall call the other directors immediately after this meeting.'

☆ ☆ ☆

The announcement of the increased offer had much the reception that had been anticipated. The media response was varied in style, but virtually unanimous in its conclusion. Amalgamated were likely to succeed in their bid for Axehouse General and Barton Industries would there-

204

by inevitably fail in their bid for Amalgamated. The stockmarket thought so as well. The Amalgamated share price fell back to 170 pence, a full 15 pence below the price being offered by Barton Industries for the shares. Sir Peter Barton was less than happy when Brodie had contacted him to give him advance notice of the increased Amalgamated offer for Axehouse General. He had been able to maintain sufficient composure to thank Brodie for the advance notice, but it did not really give him any great advantage. His reaction was much the same as the papers' reaction some twenty-four hours later. He would have a very steep mountain to climb to succeed in taking over Amalgamated Products. He telephoned Nathan Sanson immediately after he had finished talking to Brodie.

Sanson listened to him in silence. He did not bother to ask him where he had got the information from. He had clearly got his mole on board. Sanson briefly wondered who it was. It could only be King or Brodie, he decided.

'Well, Nathan, what is our next step?'

'Well the first thing is not to panic.' He regretted the choice of phrase as soon as he had uttered it.

'I am not in the habit of panicking.'

Nathan Sanson considered it best not to try and explain himself. His remark had simply been an unthinking generality.

'I don't think either of us is surprised that they have increased their offer. I think the fact that it is clearly going to be expressed as a final offer works to our advantage. We now know exactly where they are coming from.'

'I'm not so sure about that, Nathan. It might encourage people to make their minds up quicker and take that particular bird in the hand rather than our bird in the bush.'

'I am sure that is the thinking behind their tactics. What we have to do is pursue our bid with vigour and try, as they say, to win the hearts and minds. The strength of our bid is not so much the immediate financial advantage but our track record in making acquisitions pay. We have to achieve the balance between making the bid attractive financially without undermining our ability to convince the Amalgamated shareholders that the future is rosier with us than with Amalgamated. There is no point whatsoever in paying so much to achieve victory that the prospects of making the acquisition pay are remote. Far better to swallow our disappointment and move on to the next piece of action.'

Barton did not disagree, but he was not satisfied.

'I am looking for something more positive than that.'

'I'll work on it and come back to you. We are already agreed upon the nature of our next offer. I think we ought to bring it forward. There is no legal or other regulatory reason why we have to wait for our first closing date for acceptance to arrive.'

'We shall have to make our next offer our final offer, so that the punters can compare the two bids and decide which one to go for.'

'I don't think that is necessarily the case. Although their offer is a final one, it is unlikely that they will declare it to be unconditional for quite some time yet. They will want to be sure of success before they do that. If our next offer is not made a final one, those shareholders with holdings in both Axehouse General and Amalgamated, and that includes the majority of the large institutional shareholders, will more than likely hold on and not commit themselves until they know what our final offer is. That gives us more time to develop our case and set about persuading those shareholders who really matter that their best interests lie with supporting our bid.'

Peter Barton was not convinced. He had an instinctive feeling that something dramatic was necessary to revive the Barton Industries bid for Amalgamated.

'I take it that the increased Amalgamated offer will be announced first thing tomorrow. I want to agree our response tonight and we will meet tomorrow afternoon to thrash out what our tactics will be. We have got to come up with something that will catch the attention and move the initiative our way.'

'OK Sir Peter. I will get in touch with Walters and thrash out a statement for tomorrow morning and fix a meeting for the afternoon.'

☆ ☆ ☆

Charles Walters left Sir Peter Barton's office in contemplative mood. He knew his man, and it was clear that Barton would not be satisfied with straightforward run of the mill bid tactics. He wanted something that would make the City sit up a bit. The stakes were high but he saw a golden opportunity to steal a march over Nathan Sanson and build an unassailable position for himself with Peter Barton. It was the more important that he do this now as he had also just been told about Robert Brodie. If the bid succeeded and Brodie joined Barton Industries in the role of Chief Executive, he wanted to be quite sure that he had built himself into such a position of strength with Peter Barton that it would be impossible for Brodie to sweep him aside.

Walters returned to his office. He was due at Covent Garden at eight. Opera was his consuming passion, only surpassed by the passion he felt for the lady he would be meeting there. That passion was the more enjoyable for the fact that the lady in question was his wife, and had been for fifteen years. He did not have much time. He must be ready to leave no later than seven thirty. That gave him twenty minutes or so to thrash out with Nathan Sanson the statement for the next morning, and forty minutes to get ready and give some serious thought to how he was going to seize the initiative for both himself and Barton Industries.

In the event, Sanson had only taken him fifteen minutes to sort out. The statement was to be anodyne, leaving all options open. This suited both Sanson and Walters; it left each of them free to develop a strategy that would both please Sir Peter Barton and enhance the chances of success. He left it to Sanson to contact Peter Barton to get his agreement to the wording of the statement. He could have done it himself but he wanted time to think.

The idea came to him in the car on the way to Covent Garden. He had no clue as to what had triggered the thought. His time in the office had been frustrating. The more he had wrestled with the problem, the less likely it seemed that a solution was in sight. In Trafalgar Square Walters's thoughts were no longer on Barton Industries and Amalgamated Products. He had already transported himself into the world of opera and, more specifically *Aida*. His eyes were closed and he was humming the tune of *The*

Grand March, visualising as he did the spectacle of the mass of people and their rich attire. Then, out of the blue, it came to him. Just a single word, but a word that was the key to solving his problem and, given a reasonable amount of luck, the problem of Barton Industries. He opened his eyes, startled. It could work. It was high risk, very high risk, but it could work. What was more it would very likely appeal to Sir Peter Barton. At heart he was a gambler. He would not have got where he was, and Barton Industries along with him, had he not been. Walters would really enjoy the opera now. He mentally hugged himself. Sanson would be non-plussed and would almost certainly oppose the idea, but he would lose the argument. Charles Walters was quite certain of that.

19

Trevor Jacques looked steadily across his desk at Stephen, idly flipping his way through an impressively fat file.

'He's a naughty man, your Sir Peter Barton. A very naughty man.'

Stephen pushed his hand forward as if to take the piece of paper Trevor Jacques had selected from the file. Seeing the gesture, Trevor Jacques returned the piece of paper to the file.

'We are not quite ready to let you have a written report – we need some more substantiation on some points.'

'Time is running out, Mr Jacques. Isn't there anything you can let me have at this stage?'

'Yes and no. The main reason for asking you to come in and see me was to acquaint you with something we have found, but have so far been unable to substantiate, and also to give you a progress report on the concrete information. Which do you want first?' Trevor Jacques did not wait for a reply. 'The concrete information is titillating, but probably of no great use to you at this stage; the other information is potentially much more exciting and has promise of being of considerable utility, not only for what it may tell us about his past but also as an indicator of how he might act in present circumstances.'

Stephen decided to opt for the titillating information first. Not that he had any prurient interest in the sexual habits of Sir Peter Barton, but because it could be dealt with quickly.

'Let's have the naughty bits first. What's new? You have already told me about his predilection for call girls.'

'I am confident we shall be able to prove that he is a sadist or, to be more accurate, he gets his sexual gratification out of beating up women before having sex with them. We only need one more piece of the jigsaw to complete the picture to my satisfaction.'

Stephen was not particularly interested in the details, nor how the Brabent Agency had got hold of the information, which was just as well, for whilst Trevor Jacques would have given him the details he most certainly would not have revealed how Harvey Cook had come by them.

'Hmm, I suppose there are circumstances in which that information might be useful. Let's get on to the more immediately useful stuff.'

'Before we do that, I think I ought to repeat what I have already said to you. Any disreputable information I give you about his private life is on the basis that the source is strictly not attributable to me or the Brabent Agency.'

'Yes, that is fully understood.'

'Good. Now to the really interesting stuff. We have carried out a very detailed investigation into each of the last three major acquisitions made by Barton Industries. The structure of each bid was similar in that it contained an element of Barton Industries shares as part of the consideration for the shares of the target company. Nothing unusual in that. In fact, we were just about to abandon that line of enquiry when one of my researchers came up with this.'

He passed Stephen a photocopy of a press cutting from one of the tabloid papers. It was no more than three lines of print. All it said was, 'Barton Industries share price is showing an unexpected resilience in the face of its current bid. Sir Peter Barton must be a considerable advocate of his cause – or is he?'

'I'm not entirely clear where that gets us. It's somewhat enigmatic.'

'Precisely, that is what intrigued us. We traced the journalist who wrote that piece and asked him what it meant. At first he was very reluctant to say, but a modest honorarium, accompanied by a promise not to use his name, soon overcame that little problem. It turns out that a colleague on the continent had been discussing the Barton Industries bid for Halbard Wrightson with him, and had remarked how clever they were in keeping their share price buoyant in order to underpin the bid. The response he got intrigued him. The continental guy had said that was as may be, but there were other ways of ensuring that one's share price did not drop during a bid. Press as he might, the guy would not elaborate; except to suggest that he considered for a moment what were the major factors which made shares go up and down. There are a myriad of factors that affect share price, but he decided only one was likely to be relevant. The weight of buy orders. He dug around for a bit but came up with nothing, and he decided he was wasting his time. His last shot was this rather enigmatic piece. He hoped it would intrigue someone else, and possibly open the door.'

Stephen turned over in his mind what Trevor Jacques had just said. He rapidly grasped the implication of the story.

'It sounds to me as if Barton Industries were in some way buying their own shares to prop up the price. Strictly illegal, unless they had shareholder approval to do so.'

'Precisely. There wasn't any shareholder approval to for Barton Industries to buy their own shares. So we began to do some digging of our own. Look at these.'

Trevor Jacques produced three pieces of graph paper from his file. Each piece of paper had an acetate attached which was folded underneath and out of sight. Each was headed with the name of a company acquired by Barton Industries in recent years, and each was a graphical representation of the movement of the Barton Industries share price during the course of the bid. Each showed a remarkably similar pattern. A slight but insignificant drop in share price immediately following the bid, followed by a fairly quick recovery to the starting price, and then followed by a small but steady downward drift that had all the characteristics of a trend downward. Only the trend did not continue. In each case there was a rapid recovery to the price level ruling at the start of the bid.

'Now look at this.'

Jacques picked up each graph and folded the acetates back over the graphical representation of the movement in share price. Another graph line was superimposed over the share price lines.

'These lines represent the volume of shares traded on matching days to those shown for the share price movement. Anything strike you?'

Stephen noticed immediately that there was a significant jump just where the share price line reached its bottom point. This was repeated on each of the three graphs.

'Well, yes, it's obvious isn't it? I don't quite see how that helps us, though. One would expect an increase in the volume of business where there was a significant move in the share price, assuming all other factors were equal.'

'I agree, Stephen, but we have dug a bit further. The bulk of the buying in the relevant periods came from the continent and the Cayman Islands. The buyers were buying in nominee names. Oh, and incidentally, the share price movements have been adjusted to reflect the overall movement of the market. We have a rather sophisticated computer programme for doing that. It is very good at showing up trends that might be masked by the manner in which the market as a whole had moved. Unfortunately, we have been unable to link the buyers with Barton or Barton Industries. Given time, I think we could, but the trail had gone cold and I have little doubt there is a web of companies involved; quite apart from which it is not the easiest thing to get information out of Switzerland, Liechtenstein and the Cayman Islands.'

'Where does this get us then?'

'Where it gets us is that we know what to look for if Barton Industries come up with a revised bid that includes a significant element of their own shares in exchange for Amalgamated shares.'

'How do you propose to proceed?'

'I have already started. Our computer is already programmed to track the Barton Industries share price and the volume of shares traded. I have a nice little tame journalist in Fleet Street who will be more than happy to pose a few awkward questions in his column if the computer throws up a similar pattern, and I have colleagues on the continent ready to start digging as soon as I press the button. All this will be very expensive and I need your approval, Stephen.'

'You've got it, Trevor. I take it you have no objection if I bring Alan Mortimer of Greensmith Leonard in on this?'

'None at all. That's your privilege. I believe, however, that he would already be in on it if you had not hired my services first.'

Stephen had forgotten that Mortimer had told him he had tried to engage the services of Trevor Jacques but had failed because of the potential conflict of interest created by his prior instructions.

'We will need to give some more thought as to how we use any information we get. Preferably I would like to be in a position of sufficient information to go to the regulatory authorities.'

'I don't disagree with that, but we must be realistic. We shall have a very short time span in which to work, and we will need an enormous slice of luck to nip the Barton Industries bid in the bud. I'll keep in touch.'

Stephen left the office in a buoyant mood. Things were going well. He didn't underestimate the difficulties but he was, however, an optimist.

Sarah was feeling unusually cheerful, but couldn't think quite why. She had seen virtually nothing of Martin during the last week, and this usually depressed her. She hummed to herself as she reached forward and extracted yet another tiny weed from a pristine flower bed. She loved her garden and in particular she loved her flowers. The autumn evenings were drawing in but even this did not depress her. She looked forward to next spring and the reawakening. Meanwhile, there were still enough late flowering varieties to enjoy, and even when they were gone her shrubs and perennials remained.

Her thoughts ambled back to her last meeting with her father. Maybe that was the source of her present content-ment. She always enjoyed his company but there was more to it than that. Was it something he had said? She played back what they had talked about. Much of it had been about the various bids, and then she remembered. Her father had put her on the spot. Did she really want to hurt Martin? She had decided she didn't, although if the outcome of the various bids meant that he had more time for her, then she would not cavil at a little pain.

Yes, that was it. She was no longer letting a gnawing hate ferment inside her. The increased bid for Axehouse had been announced that morning. She recalled from past occasions that, after the usual flurry of press conferences and interviews for radio and television, this usually heralded a short period of respite from the grinding demands of the takeover trail. Her reverie was interrupted by the strident jangle of the outside bell for the telephone. She got to the telephone before it stopped ringing, and wished she hadn't.

'Hello?'

She didn't give her name or number out of habit rather than for any positive reason. A voice she did not recognise replied.

'Is this Mrs Chandler? Mrs Martin Chandler?'

'Who is calling, please?'

The voice at the other end clearly decided it did have the attention of Mrs Chandler and ploughed on without responding to the enquiry.

'I think we ought to meet. We have a subject of common interest.'

Sarah did not like this at all.

'What do you want?'

'I want to save your husband considerable aggravation, Mrs Chandler.'

The tone of voice was in no way menacing, but Sarah nevertheless got a distinct whiff of menace. She felt frightened but managed to keep hold of herself and her voice.

'In that case I suggest you telephone my husband. I am sure you know where to find him.'

She put the telephone down firmly. She had no intention of waiting for a response. Many years ago Martin had warned her that, as the wife of a well known public figure, she might receive some menacing or otherwise strange calls, and had told her how to deal with them. She remembered. Don't let them get into conversation with you. Hang up.

Sarah Chandler took a deep breath and wiped her now clammy hands on her jeans. She was frightened. She must ring Martin. He would know what to do. As her hand moved toward the telephone the bell jangled again. She physically took a step backwards and her heart thumped. It rang again. Almost involuntarily she picked up the receiver.

'That was naughty of you, Mrs Chandler.'

She slammed the telephone receiver down again – waited for a few seconds and then lifted it off its hook. That would stop him for the time being, she thought to herself. With her heart still thumping, she went into Martin's study. Thank God Martin had his own ex-directory line in his study. That should be safe from the menacing caller, and she would not be cut off from the outside world. She picked the receiver up and dialled Martin's private number at the office, telling herself to keep calm. Ann Gordon answered. Sarah took a deep breath and swallowed hard in an effort to keep control of her voice.

'Oh, Ann, I must speak to Martin. It is very urgent.'

'I am afraid he is in a meeting, Mrs Chandler, and I have strict instructions not to disturb him.'

'I must speak to him.' Sarah was unable to keep the tone of desperation out of her voice. Ann knew Sarah well enough to realise that there was a real crisis of some kind. Sarah was not in the habit of ringing her husband at work and, on the few occasions when she did, she either left a message with her or asked her to get Martin to call back when it was convenient.

'Please hold on, Mrs Chandler, I will go in and see him.'

Ann quickly wrote a note saying that Mrs Chandler was on the telephone in a considerable state of distress and that she felt strongly that Martin should speak to her immediately.

She opened the door into Martin's office almost silently. Martin, James Walker, Robert Brodie and Terry King were sat around the circular table. They were so immersed in what they were discussing that none of them noticed she had come into the room until she was half way across it. Martin spotted her first as he was directly facing the connecting door to her office. His face clouded with irritation.

'What is it?' he demanded testily. 'I specifically asked that I not be disturbed.'

Ann ducked the invitation to justify her intrusion. Long experience had taught her that it was almost always counter-productive. She slipped her note in front of him. He quickly scanned the note and looked questioningly up at her.

'Do you really think it is something that cannot wait?'

He did not wait for or expect a reply. He knew she would not have ignored his instructions and broken into the meeting had it not been. As he spoke he got up from his chair, mumbled a brief apology and strode rapidly across the room to her office. Ann followed him and shut the door behind her. Martin picked up the receiver and gestured to her to stay in the room.

'Hello darling, what is it?'

The sound of his rich brown voice had an instant calming effect on Sarah.

I have just had two threatening calls, Martin. I don't know what to do.'

'Right. Stay where you are and leave the other phone off the hook. Call one of your friends and get her to come round to be with you. I will call the police. I will also send Arthur down with the car. He can stay in the house with you and drive you around, and don't worry. These calls are almost always hoaxes of some kind or another.

'But what is it about, Martin?' Curiosity was beginning to creep in now that Sarah had begun to feel more secure.

'I have no idea, darling. It could be someone from the past who believes that I, or the company, have harmed him. Don't worry. Even if the threat is genuine it is highly unlikely to be a physical threat.'

'Do you think it is connected with the takeovers?'

'No, no.' Martin could not imagine Sir Richard Brookes of Axehouse General being party to anything so crude and, whilst Peter Barton had a reputation for ruthlessness in business, he did not consider for one moment that he would descend to such depths to further his interests.

'Why do you think he rang me to make a threat against you?'

'I have no idea. He probably thought that the chances of getting through to me here were rather remote, and decided that contacting you was a more sure route.'

Martin did not believe this for a minute. He thought it very likely that the threat was one of substance and, what was more, that Sarah was just as much the object of the threat as he was. The man had almost certainly phoned Sarah as an oblique, but nevertheless effective, way of getting this message across.

'Look darling, I must get on and contact the police and get Arthur on his way down to you. Don't open the front door to anyone you don't know. I will come home this evening. It might be late, but I will be there.'

'Thank you, darling. I won't do anything stupid.'

'Hang on a minute.' He had just thought of a relevant bit of information he had not asked for. 'What was his voice like?'

'Well, ordinary I suppose. The menace was more in what he said then in the tone of voice.'

'No, that's not what I meant. What sort of accent did he have?'

'None really. He spoke standard Queen's English. I suppose you would call it refined without being far back.'

'OK darling. Look after yourself. I will see you as soon as I can. Bye.' Martin wasn't sure whether the fact that the voice had been a refined voice was an encouraging sign or not.

Ann had listened to Martin's end of the conversation with fascinated horror. Poor woman, she thought; but she hadn't lost her composure. Before Martin had put the telephone down she had already found the number of the local police station and dialled it when she sensed that he was bringing the conversation with his wife to an end.

'Fenbury Police Station, Mr Chandler.' She handed him the telephone. 'I'll ring down and make sure Arthur is free.'

He took the phone and offered up a small prayer for being blessed with an efficient secretary who kept her head and had the judgement to know when to disobey his orders. The desk at the police station quickly passed him on up the line when he revealed who he was and the nature of the problem. He put the phone down and dialled Sarah on the ex-directory number.

'Hello.' The voice was hesitant.

'It's all right darling, it's me. The police will be with you in five minutes or so. They will be in a marked car so you need not worry about a strange car driving in. If I can possibly rearrange my schedule I will come home at lunch time. The police want to speak to me and the telephone is not the best medium. I have told them all I know about the calls to you but they will want to hear it direct from you as well. Keep your pecker up. Bye darling.'

Martin knew he would be unable to give his full attention to anything until he had seen Sarah and satisfied himself that the arrangements were such as to ensure her safety. Funny, he thought to himself, you don't necessarily realise how important a person is to you and how much you love them until they are under some kind of threat. He resolved to make the effort to get home more, whatever the demands on his time in London might be.

'Are you all right, Mr Chandler?' Ann's voice broke into his thoughts and he realised he must have been standing there with his hand still on the telephone for some moments. He recovered his composure quickly.

'Yes, yes. I shall have to try and reorganise my day. What have we got on?'

Ann had already got his diary open on her desk. The afternoon was booked solid until six o'clock with meetings. He studied his commitments. They were all important, but only two had an immediate urgency and involved people coming into the office from outside.

'Rearrange all the meetings except for the one with Stephen, James and Alan Mortimer and the one with the non-executive directors. I will hold those on a conference call from home. Could you set them up please?'

Thank God for modern telephone facilities, he thought; without them much of the modern pace of business life would be impossible.

'Certainly, Mr Chandler. Any particular times?'

'Well, on the basis that they were all free to come here at the originally fixed times, I suggest we stick to those times.'

'Should I give any reason for cancelling the meetings?'

Martin gave this some thought. He did not want to

spread the news of the threats around Amalgamated. He would tell just a very limited circle who probably needed to know in any case.

'No. Don't give the real reason. For the purely internal meetings I am cancelling, just say that other more urgent matters have cropped up, and the meetings will be arranged for as soon as possible. For the two meetings which are to go ahead by conference call, tell them I will explain the reason for the change when I speak to them.'

He suddenly remembered that James Walker, Brodie and King were still in his room. It must have been at least fifteen minutes since he had left them.

'I must get on with my present meeting.'

He decided that they had to know what was going on. He outlined the events as briefly as he could, and what he was doing about it. Inevitably the three of them wanted to indulge in speculation but Martin neither felt in the mood nor had the time.

'We have a lot to do, gentlemen. Can we get on? If you have any ideas on what might be behind all this let me know when you have had time to think about it.'

They all nodded agreement and each had his own thoughts of what was behind the threatening telephone calls.

20

'That's brilliant Charles. Quite brilliant.'

Charles Walters accepted the praise modestly. He did not want Peter Barton to go completely over the top. He knew only too well that if the strategy went awry he would get the blame.

'It is just an idea, Sir Peter. I have not yet thought through all the ramifications. I shall be interested to get Sanson's reaction when we run it past him.'

'Well let's go over it again now and see if we can find any glaring holes. If I understand your proposal correctly, it is essentially very simple. Firstly, we make our revised offer before the first closing date for acceptance of our original offer arrives. There is no problem with that is there?'

'None at all. It might be a bit unusual, but there is nothing to stop us doing it. It has the great advantage of getting our bid on a similar timescale to that of the Amalgamated bid for Axehouse General. We have been over that ground already if you recall.'

'Yes, yes. I know that. I just want to through the whole picture in logical sequence.'

Charles Walters carried on without responding to the rebuke.

'As agreed, the revised offer will be a mixture of Barton Industries shares, unsecured loanstock and cash. No problems there. The authority we have from the Extraordinary General Meeting of the shareholders approving the bid gives us very wide powers to amend and increase the terms of our offer. In effect we can virtually do what we like. The offer will have one other major difference.

It will not be conditional upon the Amalgamated bid failing.'

He stopped. Peter Barton was deep in thought. Walters had learnt long ago that he was very astute and rapidly picked up and analysed complex matters.

'Right, let's just walk through that. A significant proportion of the shareholding of Amalgamated and Axehouse is held by shareholders who are common to both share registers. Do we have a precise figure?'

'Not exactly precise, Sir Peter, but accurate enough to justify reliance upon them for our present purpose. The large institutional investors constitute forty three per cent of the Amalgamated share register and forty five per cent of the Axehouse register. No less than seventy four per cent of these institutions have shareholdings in both companies. The common shareholding is almost certainly greater than this since a lot of shareholdings are in bank and other nominee names. I have excluded common shareholdings on this basis since nominees may not necessarily vote all their holdings the same way. The holdings will represent a wide range of interests with different investment aims. I think we can safely assume, however, that something approaching forty per cent of the shareholding of the two companies is in common hands.'

Walters paused to see if Barton was going to pick up the theme. He did.

'So the institutions will have to make their minds up which way to jump, and your plan is to encourage them to do this earlier than they might otherwise have done, and in our favour. Explain to me again why your plan will encourage them to do this. I want to see if I can find any holes the second time round.'

'Well, the rationale is, that by dropping from our bid for Amalgamated the condition that the Amalgamated bid for Axehouse must have first failed, the institutional investors cannot just sit back until the last minute and see which way the tide is flowing. They will be forced to make a decision rather than simply wait to see if the bid succeeds, in which event our bid would have automatically failed, and vice versa. The real twist to encourage them to vote our way is to exclude from our offer any share-holders of Amalgamated who are only shareholders as a result of having accepted the bid for Axehouse. So, we could have a scenario whereby their bid for Axehouse succeeds and our bid for Amalgamated also succeeds. In this event the former Axehouse shareholders simply become minority shareholders in Amalgamated with Barton Industries having a sufficient majority to do what it wants. I don't see the large institutional shareholders being very happy in a situation where they have a minority holding in a company with no effective power to influence what the majority shareholder does. There will be little or no market for such shares, and they would be at our mercy.'

'I see the main drift of the argument, Charles, but can't the institutional shareholders still just sit back and see which way the tide is flowing?'

'Theoretically they can, but if we track the timing of the Amalgamated bid we can manoeuvre them into a situation where they run the risk of finishing up as minority shareholders in Amalgamated if they accept the offer for their shares in Axehouse.'

'OK let's take that as read for the time being. What happens in the unlikely event of the bid for Axehouse succeeding and our bid for Amalgamated also succeeding? Can we cope with the situation financially?'

'Absolutely no problem. I have calculated that, on the basis of the Amalgamated bid, which is now a final offer and cannot be amended, the percentage minority share-holding in Amalgamated, once we gain control of them, will only be thirteen per cent. We can let that sit there as long as we want. It will cost us little or nothing. Our bid does not have to be made any bigger because of the Amalgamated/Axehouse situation, and we can easily cope with the cash and loanstock liabilities assumed by our new acquisition. We shall have two companies instead of one to rationalise. This situation is probably purely theoretical. I can't see the large institutional shareholders allowing themselves to finish up as minority shareholders in Amalgamated with Barton Industries being the majority shareholder. The risk free options for them are either to accept our offer for Amalgamated or to accept neither option.'

Barton liked the idea; in fact he liked it a lot. He nevertheless spent another hour probing and questioning to see where the weaknesses and dangers of the proposal lay.

'OK Charles, get on to Sanson and see what is his reaction. We need to move fast if we are going to seize the initiative.'

☆ ☆ ☆

Sanson listened to Walters in silence, waiting for him to paint the complete picture before commenting. He couldn't make up his mind as to whether it was a clever idea or not. It certainly had a superficial attraction and there was a good chance it might work, but somewhere he was convinced there was a flaw in the scenario being painted. He wished he could put his finger on it. Something Charles Walters had said did not ring quite right. Much as he probed he was unable to rekindle the thought.

'I don't want to say yes immediately, Charles. I must examine this from every angle.'

'You have not got much time Nathan. Peter is sold on it and will want to spend the time at our meeting with him this afternoon putting the details on the scheme, not trying to pull holes in it. If you think there is a fundamental flaw in the proposal you will need to be quite specific and certain.'

The process of putting Nathan Sanson on the rack was a pleasurable sensation. Sanson however ignored the ultimatum. He must keep a clear head and not allow himself to be rattled by Charles Walters.

'Just explain to me again Charles why these tactics will encourage the large institutional shareholders to favour your bid for Amalgamated rather than the Amalgamated bid for Axehouse.'

Nathan felt sure the flaw lay somewhere in the argument as to why this should happen. Walters sighed. He was getting rather bored at having to go over it again and again. This was the fifth time that morning. He made little attempt to disguise his feelings.

'If you wish, but haven't we covered this ground twice already?' He did not wait for an answer. 'It is quite simple, they will not want to get caught in the trap of finishing up as minority shareholders in Amalgamated with Barton Industries as the majority shareholder.'

Nathan Sanson turned this over in his mind.

'Yes, but won't they simply wait to see what is the outcome of your bid before deciding whether to accept theirs for Axehouse?'

'Precisely, Nathan. It puts us right in the driving seat. At the risk of being boring, we become the bird in the hand.'

He gave up. There was a flaw somewhere, but it was irritatingly elusive. Maybe he would be able to nail it if he had peace and quiet.

'OK Charles. See you this afternoon. Three thirty wasn't it? I will put some flesh on the bones of the revised bid in the light of this new approach. Incidentally, I have gone over the sums again. The only way in which the bid can be financed on a basis that is likely to be acceptable to the City, is by using some of Amalgamated's assets to underpin the level of Barton Industries borrowing implicit in the offer package. I will call you immediately if I find any major problems.'

Sanson was not about to concede that the scheme might not be flawed.

Charles Walters and Sir Peter Barton had always anticipated using Amalgamated's own assets to help finance the purchase of Amalgamated, and Sanson's little exercise with his calculator was no news.

☆ ☆ ☆

The next approach came through the letterbox. It was addressed to Sarah Chandler and simply said: 'Tell your husband that it would be very unfortunate if Amalgamated Products acquired Axehouse General.'

She had rung Martin immediately and he had contacted the police.

Inspector Rawlings examined the note, which was by now safely encased in a transparent bag. He had no great hope that the note would reveal any useful fingerprints, but you never knew and there was no point in complicating any possible identification by covering the note with a whole mass of other fingerprints. He held it up to the light and grunted.

'Anything useful, Inspector?' Martin equired.

'Not really. It is on good writing paper with a nice watermark which we will be able to identify, but there are no doubt millions of sheets of identical paper in circulation. It has been typed on a word processor. We shall probably be able to identify the make of printer – a laser printer if I am not much mistaken – but I don't think that is going to get us much further.' He picked up the bag containing the envelope. 'Matches the note paper, posted in Central London yesterday; same printer. Nothing much there. Can you tell me anything about the message Mr Chandler? I am of course aware that your company is currently making a bid for Axehouse General, but what does our friend mean by it being unfortunate if your bid succeeded?'

'I have no idea Inspector. It would no doubt be unfortunate for a whole host of other people, but I have no idea why it should be unfortunate for me.'

'Who would suffer if you succeeded? There may be someone out there who in some ways stand to lose, and is sufficiently concerned about the prospect that he has chosen to resort to this crude threat.'

'Well the list is almost endless. The Board and some of the employees of Axehouse General. There are bound to be job losses in the rationalisation following a successful acquisition.'

'Anybody else?'

'Well Sir Peter Barton and Barton Industries, I suppose. If Amalgamated succeed in acquiring Axehouse then their bid for Amalgamated automatically fails.'

'Anyone else?'

'Look Inspector, takeover battles are pretty tough uncompromising affairs, but nobody would indulge in these threatening tactics.'

'Somebody seems to think it might be worthwhile Mr Chandler.'

Inspector Rawlings looked quizzically at him, wanting him to volunteer thoughts on the subject rather than responding to direct questioning.

'Well I can tell you that there is nobody on the Board of Axehouse who would dream of resorting to these tactics. Sir Richard Brookes is not simply a business rival, he is a friend. I can vouch for him with absolute certainty and for his Board with almost equal certainty. Such ideas would not even enter their heads.'

Martin paused.

'Yes, Mr Chandler?'

Yes what.'

'Well, carry on. You mentioned some other parties I believe.'

Martin gathered his thoughts. He had been about to put Barton in the same category as Sir Richard Brookes, but had stopped. Sir Peter Barton was not a friend, indeed their dislike for each other was mutual. Nor did Martin have the same opinion of Barton's business ethics as he did of those of Richard Brookes. But surely he wouldn't stoop to these tactics?

'Sir Peter Barton has the reputation of being tough, Inspector, I have little doubt that he would not be too fussy in what tactics he adopted to achieve his ends, but I am sure that he would not stoop to anything criminal.'

'Criminal?' Inspector Rawlings was intrigued.

'How knowledgeable are you Inspector on the ins and outs of takeover bids?'

'Not very, Mr Chandler. Good old fashioned crime is more my line.'

'Well, there is a mass of rules and regulations surrounding what one may and may not do in the context of a takeover bid. Breaches of some of them are, I suppose, criminal offences; but not quite of the same nature as this threat. Peter Barton will sail as close to the wind as he considers necessary to achieve his objectives and I would not put it past him to overstep the line if he thought he could get away with it. However I consider it highly unlikely that he would even contemplate making threats

226

of this nature.'

Inspector Rawlings made a mental note to find out a bit more about Sir Peter Barton.

'I am sure you are right, Mr Chandler. Any more thoughts?'

Martin saw the opportunity to alter the course of the conversation. He did not enjoy being put on the spot and being asked to cast suspicion on people he knew, however much he might dislike them.

'Yes, Inspector. Why does this man keep contacting my wife and not me?'

'We can only speculate, Mr Chandler, but I suppose he thinks you are more likely to take notice if your wife is involved. He has made no threat against her, but you are only human and must be worried that the threat may be directed at her. It is quite a common tactic to get at someone through a weaker party. I don't think you need to worry. We will keep an eye on your wife. My gut feeling is that the threat is not a physical threat, but I am unable to fathom at the moment what its precise nature is. At present we have no means of contacting him, and, presumably, he will contact you or your wife again if he is serious. Unless of course you announce that you are dropping your bid. Presumably he would then be satisfied; but I take it that there is no possibility of your dropping it?'

'Of course not, Inspector. It isn't my own personal bid in any case. It is Amalgamated Products bid, and I do not own Amalgamated Products.'

Inspector Rawlings saw no mileage in suggesting that Amalgamated Products would presumably take notice of its Chairman if he proposed that the bid be dropped. He did not really understand the world of big business and high finance, and he did not want to demonstrate his ignorance.

'We will keep in touch with you Mr Chandler. Let me know if you have any ideas or further approaches.'

'Certainly Inspector.'

After he had gone Martin thought again about Peter Barton. He shook his head. Surely not.

☆ ☆ ☆

Miles Wartnaby mentally congratulated Sir Peter Barton, or whichever of his advisers had come up with the scheme. It was simple and it was clever. The stock market obviously thought so as well. The Amalgamated share price jumped not only in response to the improved offer for its shares but the discount in the market price as compared to the offer price had narrowed, clearly indicating that the market was now uprating the chances of success for Barton Industries. The message was reinforced by the drop in the Axehouse General share price. Neither movement was sufficient to indicate who would be the winner, but the race was now a much closer affair.

He jotted some figures on his note pad. They revealed a very warming picture. He was showing a very tidy profit on his investments in both Axehouse and Amalgamated. His investment in the former was showing a profit of £7·125 million and his investment in Amalgamated was showing a profit of £5·28 million. His instinct told him that he should take one or both profits, as clearly both share prices were unlikely to stay at their present levels. He drummed his fingers on the arm of his leather chair, deep in thought. There was another possibility he now had to consider. Both bids could succeed now that the Barton Industries bid for Amalgamated was no longer dependent upon its bid for Axehouse failing. He thought this an unlikely outcome; the large institutional investors wouldn't let it happen. Nevertheless he had to take the possibility into account. Ignoring the unlikely, but possible, was like leaving the farm gate open with the bull tethered. It was unlikely that the bull would escape from the field, but it could happen.

Miles took another sheet of paper from his pad. He always found it easier to analyse a complex situation if he jotted down the key issues on a piece of paper. He concluded that a decision tree, or at least his own individual version of a decision tree, was the ideal technique for the current situation. Twenty minutes and two false starts later, he had his decision tree. He had needed to resort to a horizontal pattern, as the paper in vertical mode had proved to be impractical. He had also had to tape a continuation sheet on the bottom of the first sheet. He got up and poured himself a whisky and returned to his chair feeling quite pleased with himself. The decision tree had demonstrated that the situation was even more complex than he had first thought. Without it he would certainly have made his decision on an inadequate analysis of the situation. He took another piece of paper.

The decision tree was giving him a very clear message; sell Axehouse. They were showing a larger overall profit both in pure money terms and percentage increase terms. More critically continuing to hold them was the greater risk. There was double jeopardy. The Amalgamated bid might fail, in which event the Axehouse General share price would fall back to around its pre-bid value; or the Amalgamated bid might succeed as well as the Barton Industries bid in which event he would finish up with a large chunk of Amalgamated shares locked up in a minority situation with Barton Industries calling the shots. If, on the other hand, he kept his Amalgamated shares the worst that could happen was that the Barton Industries bid would fail and the Amalgamated share price would fall back. He considered that if this did happen the price would not fall all the way back. The clinching factor was that he had a gut feeling that the Barton Industries bid had not only been given the kiss of life, it showed every sign of prospering. It might still be considered as being second in the race, but it was a close second and gaining. He made his decision. Sell Axehouse. He hated to have large piles of money hanging around however not earning their keep. His thoughts wandered onto the subject of capital gains tax and the conversation he had had with Roger Harris that morning. Try as he may he had been quite unable to persuade the man that it was nearly always a mistake to allow an investment decision to be swayed by capital gains tax considerations. The right time to sell was when it was the right time to sell; capital gains tax only arose if there was a capital gain to be taxed. Miles shook his head. Roger Harris could not be persuaded and would no doubt miss the opportunity of maximising his profit. He dragged himself back to his own immediate problem of what to do with the money.

He remembered his promise to Sarah; although it now seemed that she had come to terms with Martin's peccadillos, he still might be able to help her. He did a few quick sums. If he recycled the proceeds of the sale of his Axehouse General shares into Amalgamated it would lift his holding up to about three and three quarters per cent, another ten million pounds would lift him to just below five per cent of Amalgamated. Common sense told him that this was not a very good investment. He would be buying near the top of the market and with a significant risk that the price of the shares would plummet on the failure of the Barton Industries bid. No, not a good investment. The risks were too great, but the gut feeling was still there. His gut feelings rarely let him down, and had enabled him to make some considerable coups in the past. He looked at the numbers again. The Barton Industries revised offer had not been put forward as a final offer. They were leaving the door open. This was a plus factor, there could be profit in buying more Amalgamated shares. The gut feeling, however, told him that a near five per cent stake in Amalgamated would give him a powerful lever that he would be able to wield to his own considerable advantage.

Miles picked up his telephone and dialled his stockbroker.

☆ ☆ ☆

Stephen put the phone down. He did not really believe what Trevor Jacques had just told him, but he had been quite confident that the information was accurate. He only wished it had been more specific. Even the source of the information might have helped him identify the traitor, but all Trevor Jacques had said was that there was a mole in their midst and at very senior level. When pressed he had refused to reveal the source of his information. He had also refused to explain how he could be so certain there was a mole when he had been unable to identify the individual concerned. What was even more frustrating was that Jacques had made it clear that his information had come from a one off source that could not be tapped again.

He cast his mind back. Were there any indicators from anything that had happened to suggest leaks of confidential information? Nothing came to mind immediately. Certainly Barton Industries had used nothing in their campaign that they would not have been able to find out from information that was already in the public domain. He thumped his desk in frustration. There must be something. Trevor Jacques presumably would not have been able to detect the presence of a mole if the mole had not contacted Barton Industries in the first place, and a mole was unlikely to approach Barton Industries unless he had something to sell.

Sell? Stephen's line of thought came to a juddering halt. If the mole was at very senior level power was likely to be the motivation. That narrowed the field. What would help Barton Industries most, and yet could be used without necessarily revealing that there had been a leak? Financial information that was secret and unpublished could not be used without immediately signifying that there had been a leak. Such information might have been passed, and would undoubtedly be of some use to Barton Industries in developing their bid tactics, but he felt this was probably a blind alley in terms of trying to identify the mole. What else? Amalgamated's tactics both in relation to their bid for Axehouse and in their defence of the bid from Barton Industries. Now that information would be of real value to Barton Industries, and they would be able to use it without revealing that they had knowledge of it. It would enable them to develop their own strategies and counter strategies on the basis of prior knowledge. They would know not just the publicly stated elements of Amalgamated's strategies before their publication, but also the unstated rationale behind them. Such knowledge and its timing would be of considerable value.

Stephen assembled the three pointers in his mind. The mole was in a very senior position; the information he was passing probably included knowledge of Amalgamated's bid tactics; power was probably the motivation rather than money. So what did that tell him? The person involved must either be a member of the Board of Directors or of

231

the committee delegated to deal with the bids on behalf of the Board. It must be someone who considered he would gain from Barton Industries acquiring Amalgamated. Now that really did narrow the field. It ruled out all the non-executive directors; it almost certainly ruled out people like Irwin, Gibbs, and Lytton none of whom could realistically consider they had anything to gain. It did not rule out Walker, King and Brodie. Stephen smiled to himself. It did not rule him out or Richard Hinton, the group chief accountant, for that matter. Both of them theoretically might be in a position to do a deal with Peter Barton that would further their careers in return for help in acquiring Amalgamated. He quickly dismissed the thought of Hinton. He felt sure it was a bigger fish. Walker, King or Brodie. Which one?

He jotted their initials down on his pad and looked at them. RB, TK, JW. He had not consciously ordered them in that way, but the more he thought about it the more he considered that he had them ordered in descending order of possibility. James Walker was the least likely. He had every prospect of being Martin Chandler's successor when he retired, he also was younger than the other two. He probably stood to lose more than he might gain by clandestinely joining the Barton Industries camp. Terry King, yes quite a possibility. Ambitious and he probably saw Walker as a block in his path to the top. Robert Brodie, yes he had much the same potential motive as King, and he was a much more forceful character. He would concentrate on these two he decided, whilst not forgetting Walker and some of the less likely candidates.

He sat back and put his feet up on the desk. How on earth did he flush the mole out? Whoever it was would be unlikely to give any clues in public. All they had to do was act absolutely normally, and be very careful how they contacted Barton Industries. Face to face meetings were unlikely – too much risk of being seen. Letters were also unlikely – slow, and they left evidence. The telephone? Stephen Barber sighed in despair. He could hardly go around bugging the telephones of three senior directors. Indeed if he was to cover the field properly he had to bug the telephones of half a dozen other people, and surely the mole would not be stupid enough to use the office telephones. He dismissed the thought. Even if the mole did telephone from the office, he could hardly stand outside the offices of the various possible suspects and listen in the hope he might catch them out. He felt he was stymied.

He was so deep in thought that he did not immediately register that his intercom had buzzed. It buzzed again, more insistently this time. He glanced at the console as his hand stretched out to pick up the handset. The light was on above Martin Chandler's initials.

'Yes, Chairman?'

'Could you come along straight away please Stephen?'

'Certainly, Chairman. On my way.'

Stephen cursed under his breath. He could hardly not tell Martin of the suspicion that there was probably a traitor in the camp and, in so doing, it would be difficult not to reveal that he had been employing the Brabent Agency and Trevor Jacques. He would have to be diplomatic how he went about it.

Martin waved him to one of the easy chairs and rose from his desk to join him.

'Thank you for coming along Stephen.'

Not for the first time Stephen marvelled how he was unfailingly polite to people whatever their place in the pecking order at Amalgamated.

'I want to go over the ground to make sure we are doing everything we should be doing. I sense that the Barton Industries revised offer has gained credibility for their bid. I think we have a fight on our hands.'

Stephen sensed he would be able to engineer the revelation of the presence of the Brabent Agency on the payroll without creating too many waves.

'I wouldn't disagree with you, Chairman. The bid for Axehouse is progressing as smoothly as one would expect at this stage. I don't think we need to alter our tactics there too much. I believe the key to success is how we deal with the Barton Industries bid. They are wily operators and we will need to watch them like hawks. Now that they have injected an equity element into their offer, the performance of their share price is going to be a critical factor.

If we can talk it down, that devalues their bid, and its chances of success diminish. I have already got Alan Mortimer at Greensmith Leonard working on this. He has some good ideas. He is confident he will be able to show that the performance of some of their previous acquisitions is not all it has been cracked up to be. In his view there has been a good deal of highly creative accounting. Barton Industries are past masters at hiding the performance of acquisitions in their accounts. We should have something ready for you and the committee to look at the day after tomorrow.'

'Good. Anything else?'

Stephen saw his opportunity.

'Yes. In researching previous Barton Industries acquisitions Greensmith Leonard have identified just a whiff of their share price being supported in a manner which might not have been above board. We have already put some enquiries in hand to see whether we can prove it. Trevor Jacques of the Brabent Agency is handling the enquiries.'

He knew he was being somewhat economical with the truth. It was only a little white lie and who had first come up with the suggestion was irrelevant to Martin Chandler.

'I'm not sure where that gets us exactly Stephen.'

Stephen detected just a slight note of disapproval in Martin's voice.

'Well it's indicative, Chairman. If they have done it in the past they are doubtless prepared to do it in their bid for Amalgamated. As you are aware it is strictly illegal for an English company to buy its own shares. I think it is not only our duty in relation to Amalgamated and its shareholders to flush out this kind of behaviour, if it exists, but our duty as citizens.'

Stephen mentally kicked himself. He must have sounded terribly pompous. He need not have worried. Martin was far more likely to respond to that kind of appeal than one that every tactic was justified in a takeover bid.

'Keep me in the picture, Stephen. I want you to be quite clear, however, that no such information is used without my approval, and that of the Board.' Martin paused. 'How would we use it as a matter of interest?'

Stephen knew he had got acceptance not only for continuing the investigation but also for the principle that what came out of it, if anything, would probably be used if it was sufficiently soundly based.

'I don't think it would be up to us to blow the whistle and call in the police off our own bat. I believe the right way would be to inform the Takeover Panel. It would be up to them to decide what they did with the information.'

'What happens if we get evidence that they have bought their own shares in the past but do not come up with any evidence that they are doing so now? Surely it doesn't help us much?'

Stephen sensed that now was the moment to push the frontiers forward a little bit.

'I consider it would still help us to report the matter to the Takeover Panel, quite apart from the fact that I think it would be our duty to do so. The fact that we might not be able to prove that they were buying their own shares now is not evidence that they are not. The Takeover Panel would be put on notice that it was a distinct possibility. The enquiries that would inevitably ensue would do our prospects of seeing the bid off no harm at all.'

Martin merely grunted by way of response. Stephen took this to be acquiescence. He decided to push his luck a little further.

'It may well be, Chairman, that in the course of these investigations we may find out other things about Barton Industries or Sir Peter Barton.'

Martin snapped out of the contemplative mood that had overcome him as he digested what Stephen was suggesting.

'What do you mean by that?' he demanded sharply.

'Nothing specific, Chairman. I just wanted to indicate that what comes out of the woodwork is not necessarily predictable. We shall need to be flexible to take advantage of what information comes our way.'

Martin studied Stephen for a moment and decided not to delve too deeply. Theoretical debates had a habit of generating attitudes and passions that achieved nothing. Stephen was unable to read what was going through his mind, but he had not forgotten that he had still to deliver the bombshell that Trevor Jacques had dropped on his desk some twenty minutes previously.

'I said nothing specific, Chairman, and that is the case as far as disreputable conduct on the Barton Industries side alone is concerned. I am sorry to say however that just before you buzzed for me I had a telephone call from Trevor Jacques. He is convinced that Barton Industries have got a mole in our midst, and at very senior level.'

'For Chrissake, why didn't you tell me that straight away. Who is he?'

Martin Chandler looked completely stunned.

'We don't know. . .'

'Don't know?' he shouted. 'Don't know, what is the good of a detective agency that makes wild accusations like that?'

Stephen said a silent prayer thanking God for his decision not to mention the problem at the start of the meeting. if he had done so he would have had a very difficult job getting Martin's agreement to the involvement of Trevor Jacques.

'They are highly reputable, Chairman, and they are completely confident that their information is correct.'

'Then why don't they know who it is?'

He patiently went through what Trevor Jacques had told him. He could see that Martin was calming down. The shock of the revelation that there was a traitor in their midst had clearly unbalanced his usual equable temperament.

'OK Stephen, let's be constructive about this. How do we flush him out?'

Stephen Barber explained his analysis of who it might be and what was the likely channel of communication. Martin found it impossible to hide his disbelief.

'Oh no, Stephen. It can't be James, Terry or Robert. It can't be.'

'I'm sorry Chairman, but they must be the main candidates. Maybe not so much James Walker, but definitely the other two. We mustn't of course close our eyes to other possibilities.'

Chandler regained his composure.

'I shall tell Sir Ralph Hartlebury in his capacity as senior non-executive director, but I think it best we tell nobody else at this stage. I want you to do everything you can to flush this man out. I leave it to your judgement how you go about it. Have you any ideas on that score?'

'Well, as I said, whoever it is must communicate by telephone. This is probably from home but it could be from here on a direct line. Unfortunately we have no way of checking.'

'Oh but we do.'

He pulled out the top left hand drawer of his desk and produced what was very obviously a computer printout and passed it across the desk.

'With our telephone system every outgoing call is logged, and the computer produces a printout once a week showing from what extension each call was made, to what number it was made and how long it took.'

Stephen took the printout and glanced briefly at it.

'Does it also record calls made on direct outside lines as well as those made through our exchange?'

'Oh yes, except those made on my direct outside line of course.'

21

There was a decided air of stalemate. The Financial Editor of *The Clarion* summed it up as well as anyone. 'Barton/ Amalgamated Bore Draw.' Neither Barton Industries nor Amalgamated had been able to seize any decisive initiative in their respective bids.

Martin Chandler was feeling depressed. The meeting of the Battle Committee was not going well. Nothing really constructive had come out of it, and a good deal of the time had been taken up pursuing essentially negative lines of argument. They had returned time and again to the question of whether it had been wise to make their improved offer a final one. Terry King in particular had kept plugging this particular line, conveniently over-looking the fact that he had been party to the decision and had not opposed it in any serious manner at the time. The only plus, if one could call it a plus, was that James Markby Smythe had defended the tactic with resolution. This had, at least, deflected some of the flak from Martin. His defence had been utterly logical. He had pointed out that the level of the bid was already such that any increase would be difficult to justify. There was no point in paying over the odds simply in order to acquire Axehouse. That would achieve nothing but headaches down the road, and would make any future acquisitions the more difficult to justify. Amalgamated's reputation as an astute acquirer was already hardly inspiring.

King would still not let it go.

'That's as it may be, but I still consider that our bid would be in better health had we made a smaller initial increased offer, and left ourselves scope to come in with another increase at the psychological moment.'

'Please, gentlemen. We are wasting time. We are where we are. Let us concentrate on where we go from here.'

Stephen had kept his head down during this particular phase of the debate.

He could recognise when people were jockeying for position and putting markers down. He did not wish to get mixed up in any power struggles, but wanted to keep all his options open. He caught Martin's eye.

'If I may, Chairman? I think we are in danger of getting too worried about the level of acceptance of our offer at this stage. We know that the institutional investors leave their decisions to the last moment. The media are getting bored so they jazz up headlines by being negative. I believe the true position is that a lot of people are waiting to see which of us is going to emerge as the likely winner. Then a bandwagon effect is likely. I suggest we should concentrate just as much on our efforts to stop Barton Industries seizing the initiative as we do on trying to persuade Axehouse shareholders.'

Stephen stopped and looked across to Martin, hoping that he would take the opening offered to mention the suspicions about the tactics Barton Industries might well employ to bolster their share price. He was to be disappointed. Martin recognised the cue but had decided before the meeting, after having discussed the matter with Sir Ralph Hartlebury, that it would be a mistake to publicise the suspicions when one of those present at the meeting was very likely a Barton Industries mole. Sir Peter Barton would be tipped off immediately and take any necessary steps to cover his tracks.

'Thank you, Stephen. I agree, the two bids are inextricably intertwined. Alan, would you like to give us your ideas on how we should progress with our defence against Barton Industries?'

'I have done some more work on the revised Barton Industries offer, Mr Chairman. Despite the injection of a share element into the package, it is still crystal clear that they will need to use Amalgamated assets to finance the deal. The media have not picked this point up yet. I have arranged for our advertising agency to prepare some ads addressed to Amalgamated shareholders on the theme of "Do you realise that Barton Industries propose to use your own money to buy your shares in Amalgamated?" This is one prong of the attack. The other is aimed at talking their share price down.'

Alan Mortimer passed proofs of the ads around the table. The discussion immediately took on a more lively and positive air. Everybody liked the theme of the campaign and thoroughly enjoyed themselves trying out their skills as copywriters. He smiled quietly to himself. If only the great British public could see them. They were just like a bunch of schoolboys trying to outdo each other in coming up with the most telling slogans. Perhaps, he mused, it was a good thing that Joe Public could not see them. These particular directors of a large public company were not essentially very different from hundreds of others. The mystique of big business might be destroyed. He made a pretence of jotting down some of the slogans that were being bandied around.

'Thank you. I will pass these on to the agency. I am sure they will find some of them very useful.'

He thought they might well find them useful because they gave a good indication of the way in which they were thinking. It always helped a copywriter if he had some idea of what the client wanted and what style he found acceptable. He picked up another sheaf of papers from the floor besides him.

'These are just a few ideas indicating how we might go about talking down the Barton Industries share price.'

Stephen took them and handed them round the table. Martin had not seen either the ads or the other paper before the meeting. Normally this would have irritated him as he usually liked to be one step ahead of any meeting he conducted. This time his relief at having got the meeting onto a constructive course outweighed any other feelings. He closed the meeting feeling much happier than he had been some forty minutes earlier. It had proved to be highly worthwhile, having adopted a positive and aggressive line of attack on Barton Industries. He was more than glad that he had been persuaded to bring in Alan Mortimer to handle the defence against the Barton Industries bid.

As the others left the room Martin motioned to Stephen and Alan to stay behind.

'Any progress on finding out whether Barton Industries have been up to any dirty work?'

Stephen was relieved that Martin had not pushed this possible line of attack into the background.

'We are working closely with Trevor Jacques on this. We have some very promising leads on their past activities which might enable us to present a prima facie case to the Takeover Panel in the near future. What I think will be much more interesting and potentially useful are the results of our monitoring their share price, the volume of their shares traded, and who is buying them. Their share price has just started to drift down a little. If they are going to indulge in anything naughty I would expect them to start doing so very soon.'

'How firm are the leads you have on their past activities, Alan?'

'We have established a clear pattern of buying in critical periods of previous Barton Industries bids, and we have tracked them down to a small Swiss bank, a Liechtenstein nominee company and a Cayman Island nominee company. We are fairly confident that in two previous bids these companies have been used to buy shares on behalf of Barton Industries. The Swiss bank is common to both bids and the other two have each appeared in one bid. The pattern is significant. The buying takes place just at the moment the Barton Industries share price starts to falter, and continues until it has stablilised at an acceptable level. Once the bids have succeeded, these shareholders disappear rapidly from the Barton Industries share register. We believe that the Swiss bank is the key, and that it acts as co-ordinator for the buying of the other two companies. We have also established a link between the Swiss bank and Barton Industries going back for nearly ten years. The circumstantial evidence is pretty strong, but I do not consider it is sufficient to take to the Takeover Panel. We need something concrete. Trevor Jacques is working hard on this.'

Martin was intrigued. Swiss banks were notorious for being almost paranoid about keeping secret any information about their customers, and normally would not even confirm that any particular person was a customer.

'How on earth did the Brabent Agency establish a link between Barton Industries and the Swiss bank?'

Alan Mortimer laughed.

'Oh, that was easy. They went back over all the published documents put out by Barton Industries over the last fifteen years, as well as the press cuttings. They paid particular attention to anything concerned with financing and, bingo, the Swiss bank turned up no less than four times over the years as participants in syndicated loan arrangements for Barton Industries. A bit more digging established that for at least some of the period Barton Industries had an account at the bank. I suspect they have had one during the whole period and still have it. If they turn up on the share register of Barton Industries we shall know we are in business.'

'Good, I hope we shall not need to rely on that particular line of defence, but I am quite prepared to use it if it becomes necessary.'

Stephen had hoped for a stronger commitment than this. He considered the information should be used irrespective of the bid situation. The principle had been accepted, however, and for the time being was the important issue.

Sir Peter Barton could not relax. Every nerve seemed to be twanging and his concentration span was becoming sadly deficient. Pru Wetherby and Charles Walters had felt the sharp side of his tongue more than once during the day. He pushed the pile of papers in front of him aside in frustration. It was no good. He had read through the figures twice already and still they had not registered properly. He picked up the telephone and dialled Clarissa Morton.

'Certainly, Sir Peter. Usual style?'

He hesitated. He was not really sure whether he needed what Clarissa Morton had delicately described as his 'usual style' or not. Recently he had been able to get his satisfaction and relaxation without resorting to too much violence and, on occasion, without indulging in violence at all.

'Maybe,' he growled.

'When would you like to meet your friend, Sir Peter?'

He was beginning to find Clarissa Morton's cool, dispassionate voice irritating. He felt far from cool and dispassionate. He looked at his watch automatically, although the time was of supreme irrelevance. He needed a girl as soon as possible.

'Half an hour.'

'Oh, that is just not possible, Sir Peter. The apartment is being used this afternoon and the gentleman concerned rarely leaves before six. Can you leave me a telephone number? I will call you just as soon as the apartment is free, and your friend is there to entertain you.'

The anger was really beginning to boil up now. He hated to be thwarted at the best of times, but being thwarted when he desperately needed sex was almost unbearable.

'That's no good. Get the man out. I don't care what it costs.'

Clarissa Morton was tempted. Money could buy almost anything as far as she was concerned. She could probably sting him for a couple of thousand pounds with no trouble at all.

'Are you there?' he shouted down the phone.

'Yes, yes.' Clarissa Morton for once was slightly flustered, but she had made her mind up. This man was trouble. She thought it unlikely that she would want to keep him as a client for much longer. Very few girls were prepared to run the risk of being injured, however good the money might be.

'I'm sorry, Sir Peter. I cannot do that. The gentleman concerned is a very good client of long standing.'

Peter Barton could feel himself losing control. He clenched his fists tight and took a deep breath, held it against pressure and expelled it with a short explosive burst. It worked. He kept his control.

'What other arrangements can you make?'

Clarissa Morton was taken aback at the swift change in demeanour. It might almost be a different man. She thought for a moment. She never used hotels, and not all the girls on her list liked to use their own flats. Indeed, some of them were apparently happily married women and home was definitely not a possibility.

'I could arrange for someone to come to your apartment, Sir Peter.'

He hesitated. He did not like bringing girls of this sort to his apartment. There were too many knowing eyes, not least amongst whom was the porter to the apartment block. The girl would need to get past him. The strength of his need overcame his caution.

'Tell the girl to be there in one hour. She will have to check in with the porter. Tell her to carry a folder of some sort and say she is from Barton Industries.'

Clarissa Morton confirmed the arrangement and the address and number of his apartment.

As Sir Peter left his office building his faithful shadow, across the street in the black taxi, folded his evening paper in leisurely fashion and started his engine.

'I'm following our friend. It looks as if he is going home.'

Harvey Cook back at base at the Brabent Agency thought for a moment. This sounded pretty routine but it was unusual for Sir Peter Barton to go home so early. It might be worth his while to spend a little time outside the apartment.

'OK Harry, stick outside. I will join you as soon as I can.'

Peter Barton entered the apartment block and the porter looked up in slight surprise. He rarely came home as early as four thirty on a weekday.

'Good evening, Sir Peter.'

Arthur had learned many years before not to pass comment on the arrivals and departures of his tenants. Sir Peter Barton equally felt under no constraint to explain his early return.

'A young lady from the office will be arriving with some papers in about half and hour. Send her up when she arrives please, Arthur.'

Outside, Harvey Cook was beginning to think he was wasting his time. It was now forty minutes since Barton had entered the building and no-one of any obvious interest had entered since. Maybe he had gone home early for some thoroughly mundane reason, such as not feeling well. Then a taxi drew up outside the building and a smartly dressed young woman got out clutching a small handcase in one hand and what looked like a file folder in the other. Harvey Cook recognised her almost immediately. Melanie Hunt. Little doubt to which apartment she was going.

☆ ☆ ☆

'I'm sorry, I'm sorry. Oh Christ.'

Peter Barton looked down on the pathetic little figure cowering on the floor.

'Oh God.'

He didn't know what to do. He had beaten girls up before, but never as badly as this. Melanie Hunt's face was a mask of blood and looked in a bad way. Sir Peter Barton muttered to himself again. He could not remember precisely what he had done to the girl. He knew he had completely lost control.

Melanie was sore, but noted with some surprise that she did not hurt as much as she thought she would. She felt her eyebrow gingerly. The cut was in the eyebrow itself, and was producing dramatic quantities of blood. Thank God, she thought, it would soon heal and would not spoil her beauty. She spread her fingers open just enough to peep up at Sir Peter Barton and suppressed an urge to giggle. There he stood with blood, her blood, all over his white shirt; his trousers and pants were round his ankles and his prick dangled sad and unfulfilled. His hand was at his mouth and he seemed unable to stop muttering to himself. She could not make out what he was saying; it sounded very strange. He looked a pathetic figure. Melanie had been scared out of her wits when he had started. He had been like an animal, but now he was more like a pathetic little schoolboy who knew he had done wrong. She realised there was money in this. What had started out as a giggle turned into a heartrending moan. She moaned again, and curled herself more firmly into the foetal position. Peter Barton bent down, all tenderness now. His hand stretched out tentatively towards her. Melanie Hunt shrank away from him, timing it to perfection. He crouched there next to her, not knowing what to do. She gave another little moan. He stood up again.

245

'Please get up.' He walked towards the couch and picked up what remained of her dress. 'Please get up.'

He dropped the dress down beside her. She grabbed it and wrapped it round herself as best she could. Without looking directly at him she enquired where the bathroom was, managing a very effective little quaver in her voice.

'The guest bathroom is the second on the left through there.'

He motioned to the door to his left. Melanie nearly giggled again. Guest bathroom, indeed. He spoke as if he were responding to a polite enquiry as to the whereabouts of the loo at a smart cocktail party. Melanie glanced around the room for her handcase.

'Pass me my case, please.'

She was enjoying herself now. The man was craven. The case was only two steps away from her, but he nevertheless crossed the room and stooped to pick it up for her.

She took her time in the bathroom. A languid soak in the bath eased her aches and pains, and a thorough inspection of her body revealed surprisingly few bruises of any consequence, and none that could not easily be concealed. The cut in her eyebrow was not very large and would soon heal. The rest of her face appeared to be unmarked. She scrabbled through the drawers of the vanity unit searching for a sticking plaster of appropriately dramatic size to put above her eye. A bit of skilful make-up work with mascara, rouge and face cream soon produced a very impressive bruise on her right cheekbone. Forty minutes later she emerged from the bathroom in her spare dress, having practised a suitably cowed demeanour.

Peter Barton was fully dressed and sitting in an armchair sipping a glass of whisky. He had obviously recovered most of his composure.

'Help yourself to a drink and sit down, my dear.'

Melanie refused both invitations.

'I want to leave this place. You are not safe to be with.' She was quite sure he was now safe to be with, but it did not suit her purpose to give him any indication that she thought so.

'As you wish. Er, payment.'

Somehow he always felt embarrassed talking about money with a prostitute. Melanie did not feel disposed to help him in his difficulty.

'Well, I will make the usual arrangements with Clarissa Morton.'

He was at a loss knowing how to proceed. He took his cheque book from the table beside him and looked up at her.

'Five hundred?'

She shook her head.

'Seven fifty?'

She shook her head again. She saw him bite his bottom lip. She decided she ought to say something.

'Look at me. I won't be able to work for at least a week. I could lose a couple of thousand.'

She wondered if she had overdone it. The best she had ever done in a week had been marginally over a thousand and some weeks she only managed two fifty.

'Twelve fifty.'

Melanie kept her composure even though she would gladly have settled at that figure a few moments before.

'No. Quite apart from what I might lose, what about what I have suffered?'

She saw his fist clench and was afraid she had pushed too far. She held her breath. The silence seemed endless, then his fist relaxed and he picked up his gold pen and wrote out a cheque. He tore the cheque from the book and held it towards her. Melanie recognised when to capitulate. She wouldn't try to make him get up and bring the cheque over to her. She stepped forward and took the cheque and studied it. One thousand, four hundred and fifty pounds. She put it in her handcase without a word. She was not going to thank him for the privilege of having been beaten up.

'Will you let me out now, please?' She picked up her case and moved towards the door.

'You will forget this afternoon, won't you?'

It was a command, not a question. Melanie did not reply. She knew what he meant, but saw no point in saying what she thought. She had been aware of his propensity for violence from her previous encounter with him and she had been warned. She had accepted the business with her eyes open. It was one of the risks of the business. Besides, she would not have the first idea how to go about turning what had happened to her to further advantage. She would simply refuse to accept Sir Peter Barton as a client if he wanted her services in the future. She considered that possibility as extremely remote.

☆ ☆ ☆

Harvey Cook watched Melanie Cook as she emerged from the building and as soon as she came into the brighter light of the street lighting he saw the sticking plaster over her eye.

'Quick, Harry. Out.'

Harry Smart did not waste time asking questions and slipped quickly out from the driving seat of the cab, passing over his cabbie's badge to Harvey as he took his place. Harvey started the engine and switched on the light to indicate he was free and prayed that no other free cab would come along before he could pick up Melanie Hunt. He drove forward a few yards and did a quick U-turn. Melanie saw him and lifted her arm to hail him. He hardly needed to listen to the address. He knew perfectly well what it was.

'Certainly, Miss Hunt.' He waited for it to sink in as he slipped smoothly into the traffic. It didn't take long.

'How the hell do you know my name?'

'Not only your name, Melanie,' he decided a bit more familiarity would do no harm to his cause, 'I know who you've been entertaining, although from the look of it I doubt that it was particularly entertaining for you. Sir Peter Barton can be a nasty piece of work, can't he?'

Melanie Hunt was getting frightened. How did the cab driver know who she was and where she had been, and why was he interested in her?

'Let me out.'

'Don't worry, Melanie. I am not the slightest bit interested in you. It's Sir Peter Barton who interests me.'

She was not reassured.

'Let me out.'

'Certainly, but I think you might find it in your financial interests just to listen to what I have to say before you get

248

out.'

Harvey took a chance. He wanted to get her confidence and decided the best way to do so was to pull into the curb and let her get out if she wished. He held his breath as he watched her in his driving mirror. She slid across the seat and put her hand on the door catch. Then she hesitated. Harvey knew he had got her. He waited for her to speak.

'What do you mean by that?'

'It's quite simple, Melanie. I pay for information.'

She was interested now.

'How much?'

'It depends upon the information, Melanie. I know who you are and I know what you are. I know you have been with Sir Peter Brton and it is pretty obvious he has not exactly been gentle. How much did he pay you?'

'What has that got to do with it?'

'Everything, Melanie. Did he pay you by cheque?'

'Well, yes.'

'If you'll give me that cheque I will give you one in its place worth two hundred and fifty pounds more.'

Melanie was very interested now but she was also suspicious. She suspected this might be a massive con, but did not quite see how it worked.

'If I do that, how do I know your cheque won't bounce?'

'You don't. I will give you cash if you like.'

Melanie Hunt decided whatever it might be, it wasn't a con. What had she to lose? Nothing as far as she could see. The man had not asked for anything in return that he did not already know, as far as she could tell.

'Have you got the cash on you?'

'No, but I can get it within twenty minutes if you'll bear with me. We will just have to take a short detour on the way to your flat. You haven't yet told me how much Sir Peter Barton's cheque was for.'

'Fourteen fifty.'

'Right. Seventeen hundred pounds coming up in cash.'

Harvey silently congratulated himself. One thousand, seven hundred pounds for a cheque made out to Melanie Hunt in Sir Peter Barton's own fair hand, and bearing his signature, might prove to be worth many times that sum.

22

Stephen Barber was beginning to believe he had been wasting a lot of time. The pile of computer print-outs on his desk contained details of all the telephone calls made from Amalgamated House for the last four weeks. He had just finished ploughing through the latest batch of numbers hot off the computer. There was not one call to any number connected with Barton Industries or Sir Peter Barton, including those ex-directory numbers which Trevor Jacques had obtained for him in under an hour. He had concentrated on calls made by Brodie and King to start with, as they seemed the most likely candidates. When he had drawn a blank on these he had methodically worked through the numbers of anyone connected with the bids from directors right down to secretaries; nothing. As a final check he worked back the other way to see if any of the relevant numbers appeared; it was quite possible that the mole had used a telephone other than his own. Again, nothing.

He pushed the computer print-outs away from him, satisfied that he had been on a wild goose chase. He leant back in his chair and, clasping his hands behind his head, stared at the ceiling. He would have to find another way of identifying the mole; and he was now thoroughly convinced there was one. The Barton Industries response to each twist in the bid strategies of Amalgamated had been just that bit too quick and well informed. How would one go about transmitting information to a third party without actually meeting them? It must either be a personal delivery, delivery via a third party/dead letter box or the telephone. Idiot! Stephen Barber chastised himself for

250

being so stupid. Of course it wasn't the telephone, or at least not in its speaking mode. The information to be passed would be detailed. Verbal communication would be inadequate and, apart from anything else, would take too long. He pressed the intercom.

'Yes, Stephen.'

Sheila Birch had soon got used to calling Stephen by his Christian name. He was a hard taskmaster but, nevertheless, it had seemed quite natural to call him by his first name when they were alone.

'Do you keep a fax directory in your office, Sheila?'

'Yes. I will bring it in.'

It took him no longer than thirty seconds to find the fax number of Barton Industries. Another five minutes with the computer print-outs revealed that over the previous four weeks no less than twenty fax messages had been sent from Amalgamated House to Barton Industries. To be more precise, it was probably only ten messages as all the communications had been made in pairs. The first, and shorter one, no doubt being to warn that a high security message was coming through. This was followed two or three minutes later by an incoming fax, no doubt from Barton Industries, to give the go-ahead to proceed, and finally a further fax to Barton Industries of varying duration. He was elated; at long last he had cracked it. True, he still did not have the name of the mole, but he knew how to catch him now. He did not doubt for one minute that when he checked the fax room he would find that standard procedure had not been followed, and that the sender of the fax messages had not recorded his name in the record book. This hardly mattered. All he had to do was to arrange for the fax room to be watched by a member of his staff and sooner rather than later he would have his man.

Henry Robirch sighed inwardly. The client always wanted the impossible at some stage or other of a takeover bid. He supposed he ought to be flattered that Martin Chandler had faith in his skill to make the impossible possible. Martin

Chandler was not only the client but an old friend, and Henry Robirch understood his frustration.

'I'm sorry, Martin. If some of the Axehouse shareholders wish to make their acceptance of your offer for their shares conditional upon the Barton Industries bid failing, they are quite entitled to do so.'

'Henry, it is not just some shareholders, it is the large shareholders. The ones who are going to decide whether this bid succeeds or not. Surely our Offer Document makes no provision for acceptances to be made conditional in this manner?'

'That is quite correct, Martin, it doesn't. But I am afraid that does not make any difference.'

'Well if it doesn't make any provision for acceptances of our offer to be made conditional, surely that invalidates such acceptances.'

Martin was scarcely able to keep the sense of deep frustration out of his voice. They had five days to go before they reached the closing date for acceptance of their bid. If they were not in a position to declare the offer unconditional at that point the bid would fail and, if that happened, it would enhance the likelihood that the Barton Industries bid would succeed. What added to the frustration was the fact that, if the conditional acceptances were added to the unconditional ones and also added to the shares Amalgamated had bought in the market, some seventy-eight per cent of the Axehouse shares had been voted in favour of Amalgamated's offer. As it was, some thirty-seven per cent of the acceptances had been declared to be conditional, leaving Amalgamated with firm acceptances of just over forty per cent. In other circumstances that would have been regarded as highly encouraging.

Henry Robirch kept his own sense of frustration firmly under control. They were wasting time on a point which was so clear cut that there was no profit whatsoever in continuing the debate. There were plenty of other urgent matters that needed to be discussed and resolved.

'I think you have answered your own question, Martin.'

'How do you mean?'

'The fact is that such conditional acceptances are perfectly legitimate and you at least have the prospect that they may become unconditional if the Barton Industries bid fails.'

Markby Smythe thought it was time he entered the debate. He considered that Martin was unduly depressed by the situation as it stood.

'I think we are in danger of putting the wrong interpretation on these conditional acceptances. Over the last three weeks I believe that we have been gaining ground with the large shareholders in both companies. Our respective campaigns for the Axehouse bid, and the defence against Barton Industries have both been very positive and increasingly effective.'

He nodded almost imperceptibly in the direction of Alan Mortimer in acknowledgement of his contribution to the conduct of the defence.

'The tone of the media is at least now more balanced and, generally, they now seem to accept that our bid makes sense both from a commercial and financial angle. As for the institutional shareholders, I consider their conditional acceptances to be an encouraging sign.'

'I am not quite sure I follow the logic of that, James. I would have thought it was a sign that they were uncertain.'

'No, I am convinced it is an encouraging sign. In the normal course of events they would wait until the very last moment before revealing their hand. I believe they are signalling which bid they favour, but placing an each way bet so that if events go contrary to the direction in which they want and expect them to go, they still have the option of accepting the Barton Industries bid without risking having to swallow the poison pill.'

Martin Chandler was momentarily puzzled by this remark.

'Poison pill?'

'Yes, the provision of their offer for the shares of Amalgamated that excludes any Amalgamated shares issued to shareholders of Axehouse General in part exchange for their Axehouse shares.'

Martin had quite forgotten this little ploy of Barton Industries. It was quite clever, he had thought. It encouraged Axehouse shareholders not to accept the Amalgamated bid as, if they did, they ran the risk of finishing up as minority shareholders in an Amalgamated Products controlled by Barton Industries.

'By making their acceptances of your offer conditional upon the Barton Industries bid failing, the institutional shareholders effectively trump that little card. I don't think they would have bothered to do that if they intended to accept the Barton Industries bid for your shares, rather than your bid for their Axehouse General shares.'

He had not looked at it in this light and felt somewhat encouraged. He was not entirely convinced, however.

'Do we know what the situation is with Barton Industries?' Martin had addressed the question to James Markby Smythe but Alan Mortimer fielded it.

'They have been buying heavily in the market and the last figure I had was that they now own some thirty-three per cent of Amalgamated and have acceptances which bring them up to thirty-nine per cent.'

'I thought there were restrictions on buying that much in the market, Alan?'

'Yes there are, Mr Chairman, but only until the last date has passed for them to revise their offer. This has now gone and they can buy as much as they wish in the market. I am somewhat surprised, incidentally, that they have not improved their offer. They must be very confident.'

'Do we know whether they've got conditional acceptances too?'

'As far as we have been able to determine, Mr Chairman, they have not had any conditional acceptances of any significance. I think that supports James's theory. If it looks as if their bid for us is not going to succeed, they will simply make their acceptance of the Amalgamated offer for Axehouse unconditional, and not accept the Barton Industries bid for us. If, on the other hand, it looks as if the Barton Industries bid for Amalgamated is going to be the winner, they will accept that bid and their conditional acceptances of our bid for Axehouse will automatically become nullified. I believe the fact that they have put in conditional acceptances for the Amalgamated bid, and not the other way round, indicates where their preferences lie.'

'I am still not very happy about the situation. It could go

254

either way. Presumably if they can pick up another eleven per cent or so of our shares and get over the fifty per cent mark they will declare their offer unconditional and it will be all over. Can't they just carry on buying in the market until they hit this level?'

'Eleven per cent of our shares in issue is a lot of shares. I doubt if such a large number will become available in the market as the bulk of those which have not passed through the market already are probably held by the institutional investors. I doubt that they will jump in as sellers until they see which way things are going. I expect they are watching each other like cats watching mice. Quite apart from that, Barton Industries would need to borrow a lot of cash to make such a purchase.'

Martin was not content to sit back and hope for the best, however confident Markby Smythe and Mortimer were. There was still the matter of the mole unresolved. At least that should not be long now that Stephen had identified the method of communication. He still had a nasty feeling that the mole could somehow tip the scales the wrong way. He did not know quite how he would do this, but that did not take away the anxiety. Martin was finding the presence of the mole intolerable. He somehow felt disloyal having to confine meetings to the outside advisers and Stephen whenever possible. The only consolation was that it would not be necessary to do this for much longer. Stephen's plan to set the mole up with some convincing, but false, information should work.

'Have we any progress on our investigations into Barton Industries activities, Alan?'

'Stephen is more up to date on that, Chairman, I believe he was in touch with Trevor Jacques this morning.'

Stephen took his cue.

'We are as certain as we can be that Barton Industries have been indirectly buying their own shares to keep the price up, and thus keep the value of their offer for our shares up. The problem is that the evidence is almost entirely circumstantial. All three overseas buyers we identified as being active in purchasing Barton Industries shares in previous takeovers at critical times have appeared as buyers again this time, and at crucial moments. We can demonstrate a clear correlation between the appearance of these buyers and the Barton Industries share price stabilising and, indeed, moving up, when the trend had started to move the other way. We have also been able to establish a continuing business relationship between Barton Industries and the Swiss bank. Unfortunately we have not been able to link the Cayman Islands and Liechtenstein buyers to Barton Industries yet. Given time I am sure we will, but I do not think we shall be able to do so in time for it to be of use in the present situation.'

'I don't see why we should not go to the Takeover Panel with what we have got. There is strong circumstantial evidence. Surely that is enough for them to start asking Barton Industries some awkward questions? What do you think, Henry?'

'I don't disagree with that, Martin, but I always find it useful to look at these things as if I were the lawyer advising the other side. I know Tony Kingdom very well. He is smart and ruthless, but he is absolutely straight. We can take it, therefore, that if Barton Industries are indirectly buying their own shares contrary to the law, he is not privy to these arrangements. I think we can also take it that Sir Peter Barton and Barton Industries are unlikely to admit to him that they have been breaking the law in this respect. On these assumptions, if I were Tony Kingdom I would advise Barton Industries to adopt a line of attack as being the best course of defence. I would suggest to the Takeover Panel that there was not a shred of evidence that Barton Industries had been doing anything illegal, and that the whole thing was the product of Amalgamated's fevered imagination, induced by an increasing desperation brought about by the realisation they were going to lose the battle. I would also immediately issue writs for defamation against Amalgamated Products, all the directors of Amalgamated Products, and against such of their professional advisers who could be in any way connected to the approach to the Takeover Panel.'

Henry Robirch's little dissertation produced a deathly hush.

'That's it, then,' Martin Chandler said eventually.

'Oh, no. Not at all. I have merely told you how I would

256

defend the allegation if I were Barton Industries. That is a quite different matter from whether or not you should make the allegation. Their reaction is only relevant in the sense that it is one factor you should take into account in making your decision. Clearly, you do not approach the Takeover Panel unless you are absolutely confident that you will be able to substantiate your allegations. If, on the other hand, it looks as if an approach is likely to be the only way of avoiding being taken over by Barton Industries, then you might conclude it was worth all the risks involved.'

Alan Mortimer caught Martin Chandler's eye and got the nod to continue.

'In the light of that advice, Mr Chairman, and our overall assessment of the current state of play, I suggest we do not approach the Takeover Panel immediately. We still have a few days. Let's see if we can come up with something a little more concrete.'

The proposal got general approval with very little discussion.

Whilst the discussion was proceeding Alan passed a note to Stephen enquiring whether he had told Martin about the latest developments in the investigations into Barton's private life, and the incontrovertible evidence they now had as to its sordid nature. Stephen scribbled one word on the note and passed it back.

'No.'

☆ ☆ ☆

Peter Barton had come to much the same conclusion that Markby Smythe and Mortimer had come to; the balance seemed to be tipping in favour of Amalgamated. He read the conditional acceptances of the Amalgamated offer for the Axehouse General shares in much the same way as they had done. He turned to Charles Walters.

'The institutional shareholders seem to have trumped our ace, Charles. Any other bright ideas?'

The question was delivered with hardly concealed sarcasm. Nathan Sanson felt rather pleased with himself. He had known all along that there was a flaw in Walters's scheme. His only regret was that he had not been able to put his finger on it when it had been proposed.

'I do not consider that they have necessarily trumped our ace, Peter.' He was not about meekly to accept that his scheme had been stillborn. 'We have quite a nice level of acceptances for our offer for the present stage of the bid, and I am sure quite a significant proportion of that has come along because of the way in which we restructured our bid for Amalgamated.'

Barton had noticed the look of satisfaction on Sanson's face when he had made his remark to Walters, and equally had not missed the nuances in the response. The 'we' was clearly intended to bind Sanson into the decision that had been made. If the tactic had been a roaring success he had little doubt that Charles would have claimed all the credit. He had no time for these petty little rivalries. They distracted attention from the main business in hand – acquiring Amalgamated Products.

'What is the latest position on our market purchases of Amalgamated shares, Nathan?'

'We are up to thirty-three point seven per cent, Sir Peter. I really believe we should stop buying in the market. As I have already advised you, we are taking a risk in buying Amalgamated shares in such large quantities. If the bid fails we will be left with a major financial problem. We shall have to sell them at a considerable loss. There is no way we can keep them as the finance for acquiring them is planned to come from realising Amalgamated assets. The purchases we have made in the market up to this point have already disturbed the balance of our bid, any more could create real problems. The bid was dependent upon our issuing a significant proportion of new Barton Industries shares which effectively cost us nothing. Our current borrowing to finance the purchases is strictly short term, and win or lose we will need to reschedule this borrowing fairly soon.'

'The bid is not going to fail. The more shares we buy in the market, the more certain it is that the bid is not going to fail.'

Peter Barton did not go on to acquaint Sanson of the other pressing financial reason why it was critical that the bid did not fail. He did not mention the guarantees he had given to the Swiss bank and its two associates in respect of the Barton Industries shares they had bought at his behest in order to keep the share price healthy; they were a potential timebomb. If the bid failed the Barton Industries share price would drop dramatically because the City would soon realise that the large holding they would be left with in Amalgamated had been financed on a wing and a prayer. In this event, Barton Industries would need to find a considerable sum of money to make up the losses suffered by the Swiss bank and its associates. Charles Walters shared the worries that Sanson had expressed. Indeed, his worries were greater. He knew about the potential liabilities under the guarantees.

'I think Nathan is right, Sir Peter. I recommend that we should stop buying Amalgamated shares. As a matter of interest, I think there is another fairly substantial buyer in the market. I have not been able to identify who it is yet, but there is a larger turnover in the shares in Amalgamated than we would expect at this stage bearing in mind our own substantial purchases.'

Sir Peter Barton was not impressed by the arguments. He did not entertain the possibility that he might not succeed in acquiring Amalgamated. He had never failed before, and saw no reason why he should now. Once he had Amalgamated, all these worries about how the deal was being financed would disappear. There were plenty of realisable assets within Amalgamated, more than enough to meet any liabilities Barton Industries might be saddled with as a consequence of the way in which the bid was structured. The problems to him were theoretical.

'We are going to acquire this company, gentlemen, so let's not waste time worrying about what might happen if we don't.'

Martin Chandler was feeling the strain. This time next week he would know whether he was Chairman of a much larger company than he was now, or whether he would be looking for a new job. As each day passed the tension increased. He needed to relax; if he went on like this he would crack and probably make a poor decision or, possibly worse, not make a decision when he should. There was only one thing which was going to take his mind off all his worries and make him relax. Sex. He stretched out his hand towards the telephone on his desk giving him a direct outside line. He was about to call Angela, but he hesitated. Did he really need Angela? Things between him and Sarah had improved lately, despite the limited time they had had together. Sarah would give him the comfort and relaxation he so desperately needed, and with love as well. He sighed and picked up the telephone. He didn't have time to go home to Sarah and he needed the relaxation.

Angela answered the phone almost instantaneously. Thank God, he thought to himself. His need was now nearly at desperation level. Once he had thought about it, the need to assuage the demands of his body had to be met as soon as possible. He arranged to meet her at the Eaton Square apartment half an hour later. He glanced at his desk diary. Blast. He had forgotten about the meeting with Irwin and Barber to bring him up to date on the latest contacts with the large institutional investors. He decided that could wait until next morning. There was unlikely to be anything they could tell him which would make any difference, or require any action before tomorrow morning.

'I am going home now, Ann. Could you please get in touch with Howard and Stephen and reschedule our meeting for eight o'clock tomorrow morning? Oh, and get my car to the front door.'

'Certainly, Mr Chandler. Eaton Square I presume?'

'Yes, Eaton Square.' He flicked the switch off. Deep down he still wished it had not been Eaton Square but Haslemere.

☆ ☆ ☆

Angela was there waiting for him. He had noticed the letter on the side table as he walked into the room. Angela must have picked it up when she had come in. It was typed and addressed to him personally. He turned it over. There was no sign on the back to indicate from whom it had come. He put it back on the table. Plenty of time later to deal with the

260

letter. There were other more urgent, and certainly more entertaining and necessary, things to do first.

Angela had watched him pick up the letter and give it a very cursory examination. She knew him well enough to gauge his needs from his body language without his having to express them verbally. She recognised the insistence of his need. He had not spoken in the few seconds it had taken him to examine the letter, and he did not speak now. Instead he threw himself into his armchair and closed his eyes. Angela moved to his side and knelt beside him. Her long, sinuous fingers traced a path from his forehead round to the back of his neck and began gently to massage away the tension. He still did not open his eyes.

'Hello Angela.'

'Hello Martin.'

Her hands nimbly undid the buttons of his shirt and slid inside. Working, gently working. Martin could feel the tension starting to ooze out of his body and gradually to be replaced by another, and more desirable, tension. The hands expanded their area of exploration and the new tension became complete and vibrant. He needed her body now. Passive ecstasy was not enough. He took her hand and gently raised her to her feet and without a word led her to the bedroom.

The therapy was complete. He lay back on the bed, his hand idly coursing over Angela's magnificent body. Angela lay there enjoying the wanderings of his hand and waited for a signal from him. The fingers of his hand became intermittent in their journeys, and eventually ceased altogether. The hand relaxed in a dead weight on her thigh. He was asleep.

Angela gently extricated herself and left him sleeping. She stood at the end of the bed looking down at him. Not in bad shape for his age, she thought. She decided, not for the first time, that she was fond of him, and not for the first time she told herself not to allow herself to become involved. She was confident that he was fond of her as well, but knew that this was no indicator of any long term commitment. The relationship would last just as long as he wanted it to. That was the way of her particular style of life.

She showered and dressed, poured herself a gin and

tonic, and then looked at her watch. He had been asleep for forty minutes. She had better wake him. He would not be pleased if she let him sleep on. She returned to the bedroom and gently shook him awake.

'Eight ten, Martin.'

'What?'

He had been in deep sleep and took a few moments to orientate himself. He propped himself up on his elbow and smiled at Angela.

'I must have gone to sleep.'

She smiled back at him and he grinned back sheepishly, both recognising the rather foolish statement of the obvious.

'Can I get you anything, Martin?'

'No thanks, Angela. I will have a drink after I have showered.'

Angela turned to go out of the room.

'Er, Angela.'

She stopped and turned her head enquiringly toward him.

'Ring Wilberts and arrange for dinner to be sent round.' He hesitated, leaving a teasing little silence. 'For two.'

She smiled at him again. There was genuine affection in the smile.

'Anything particular?'

'No. You choose.'

☆ ☆ ☆

The dinner had been perfect. Angela had good taste in all things. He shuddered to think what the wine had cost. Pomerol was expensive at the best of times, but this particular vintage had to have been in the three figure class. Martin Chandler had resolved in the car on the way to the apartment that he would tell Angela that the relationship must end. The stronger pull was to Sarah, however much he enjoyed Angela and her company. It was not fair to Sarah for him to continue to enjoy the best of both worlds. But now he couldn't do it. The evening had been so perfect. He did not have the heart to ruin it for Angela by telling her it must all end. He determined to do it after the takeovers

262

had been resolved.

'Penny for your thoughts.'

'Oh, I was just thinking about the two takeover battles we are involved in. I won't bore you with all that.'

'That Sir Peter Barton is a nasty bit of work, isn't he?'

Martin was all attention now.

'Nasty bit of work? How do you mean?'

'Oh, he's notorious amongst the girls. He has a nice little habit of beating them up. It seems that is the way he gets his kicks.' Angela gave a dramatic little shudder. 'That's not for me.'

'Are you sure of this?'

'Oh, quite sure. I could find you at least three girls who have suffered at his hands.'

Angela was somewhat puzzled by the strength of his interest. His enquiry as to the veracity of her statement had not been just idle interest.

'Why do you want to know?'

He realised he had shown rather more than prurient interest in the revelation.

'Oh, no reason really. I was just surprised by what you said. He is a tough nut in business, but I would not have expected him to have such a dark side to his private life.'

Martin made a mental note. If the worst came to the worst he might be able to use that little bit of information. He pulled himself up, surprised at his line of thought. He had not realised just how desperate he was not to lose out to Sir Peter Barton. He was still digesting this piece of self revelation when the phone rang.

'Stephen. I hope I am not disturbing you?'

'Not at all,' Martin replied, whilst mentally adding that he would have been had he telephoned an hour or so earlier. 'What is it?'

'I've identified the mole. Brodie.'

Martin could not suppress a feeling of shock, despite the fact that he had already accepted that Brodie was one of the prime suspects.

'Are you absolutely sure?'

Absolutely. Half an hour ago he went to the fax machine. As soon as he left the room I put my secretary in the room to ensure that nobody else used the machine until I had had the time to check out whom he had been faxing by running a print-out of the outgoing calls. He had faxed Barton Industries. No doubt we shall see some evidence of our little bit of planted, but spurious, information surfacing very soon.'

'Right, don't tell anyone else.'

As he replaced the receiver he noticed the letter that had been sitting on the side table. He walked over to his desk and, extracting a paper knife from the drawer, slit it open. It was another threatening letter, but this time addressed to him and not Sarah. The message was short and simple. It read, 'I have warned you, Mr Chandler. You are getting too close. It would be in your best interests to drop your bid for Axehouse General.' It was unsigned. Angela had noticed the change in his expression as he read the letter.

'Nothing wrong I hope, Martin?'

He pulled himself together.

'Nothing that can't be dealt with, but I am afraid I will have to deal with it straight away.'

Angela was unsure whether this was a signal to go. Sometimes he would deal with business matters whilst she was still there.

'Do you want me to go?'

'I am afraid so, Angela. Someone is coming round for a meeting in about half an hour.'

As soon as Angela had gone he phoned Inspector Rawlings.

23

The telephone rang insistently. Robert Brodie tried to ignore it. Half past three on a Sunday afternoon was no time to ring somebody up. He gave up trying to ignore the disruption to one of the very few afternoons he had had at home with Molly for the last three months.

'Sorry, Molly. Whoever it is is not going to give up and go away. I had better answer it.'

Molly Brodie wriggled forward imperceptibly, taking her weight from his chest and enabling him to extricate his arm which had been cuddling her close to him. He did not hurry to leave the room; with any luck the phone would stop before he got to his study. No such luck. By the time he had settled himself in his swivel chair the only difference was that the noise was louder and seemingly more imperious. He sighed and picked up the receiver.

'Robert Brodie.'

'Ah, Robert, I was beginning to think you were not at home.'

It was not a voice he particularly wanted to hear at that moment, or at any time in the next few days for that matter.

'We must meet.'

'I don't think that would be a very good idea, Peter.'

Sir Peter Barton did not even bother to argue the point. 'Same place in about an hour and a half.'

'Hang on a minute, I really don't think it would be a good idea to meet at this stage. There is a real risk someone who knows us will see us.'

'This cannot wait, Robert, and it is not something I wish to discuss on the telephone. We are at D minus four on our bid, and you are at D minus three. See you in an hour and a

265

half.'

Brodie heard the click as the telephone went dead before he could even draw a breath to respond. He cursed. He knew he had no option. He was in too deep already. He had little doubt that if he did not do as Sir Peter Barton wished a means would be found of making him pay for it. He was beginning to regret his decision to throw his lot in with Barton Industries. Pull yourself together, he urged himself. Once this is all over, and Barton Industries are in the driving seat, I will be out in the open and in a much stronger position. Brodie was confident Barton Industries were going to win the battle. There were only four more days to go, possibly only three depending upon what happened to the Amalgamated bid for Axehouse General. All would then be resolved, and he would no longer need to play a double role. Either he would be on board with Barton Industries or, and less likely in his judgement, he would be resuming his career with Amalgamated with his brief flirtation with Barton Industries behind him, and soon to be forgotten. He looked at his watch. He would need to leave very soon to make the appointment. He went back to the sitting room.

Molly looked up at him enquiringly as he entered the room.

'Anybody I know?' she enquired lightly.

He did not answer the question. He had not told his wife what he was up to.

'I have to go out, darling.' He didn't say where or why. Molly knew there was only one thing that would draw him away from her.

'These wretched takeovers I suppose?'

He nodded.

'Will you be long?'

He looked at his watch and did a quick calculation. There and back was probably the best part of a two hour drive and, if it really was as urgent as Sir Peter Barton had suggested, there would be something like an hour of discussion. Three hours at a minimum, he concluded.

'Don't expect me back much before seven, darling. I will get away as soon as I can.' He gave her a warm kiss and reluctantly turned to leave the room.

As he drove through the Oxfordshire countryside and into Buckinghamshire, he sifted through the events of recent days in his mind. It always paid with Sir Peter Barton to be well prepared, and if he could identify what he wished to talk about, that would be a big advantage. There was no doubt both bids were in the balance. The bid for Axehouse was for the moment parked in a lay-by, and looked likely to stay there, unless the large institutional shareholders could be persuaded to drop the condition attached to their acceptances of the offer for their shares. It probably only needed one such large shareholder to drop the condition and most of the others would follow in short order. Amalgamated would then be home and dry. Barton Industries, on the other hand, had been buying Amalgamated shares heavily in the market. They must already own nearly forty per cent in their own right, and have unconditional acceptances for their offer for the Amalgamated shares amounting to another five per cent or so. Once they topped the fifty per cent mark there was nothing to stop them. They would no doubt make their offer unconditional, and the remainder of the shares would fall in very quickly. Brodie could not for the moment see what could stop them.

Admittedly the media had doubts about the financing of the offer, and he had seen the in-house Amalgamated projections which clearly demonstrated that Barton Industries would need to use a considerable chunk of Amalgamated assets to finance the takeover. He did not see this as a reason for the bid to fail. A high proportion of American takeovers worked this way, and UK takeovers would soon follow a similar course in his view. Brodie was confident that the odds were in favour of Barton Industries. What puzzled him was what Sir Peter Barton could possibly want from him which would make any significant difference.

The front door of the cottage opened as he drew up outside, the crunch of the gravel announcing his arrival.

'Thank you for coming over at such short notice, Robert.'

At least the greeting was a little more civil than the peremptory summons to attend.

'Come on in. Drink?'

'Not at the moment, thank you Peter.'

Brodie sat himself down without waiting for an invitation. Peter Barton refreshed the whisky glass that had been in his hand when he had first greeted him and came straight to the point. It was not in his nature to wrap things up or approach them from oblique angles.

'I want you to come out publicly in support of the Barton Industries bid for Amalgamated, Robert.' His eyes bored directly into Brodie's.

'What, when?'

He did not bother to repeat the nature of his request.

'First thing tomorrow morning.' He went over to his desk and picked up a piece of paper. 'Here.' He passed the paper over. 'I have saved you the trouble of drafting your statement. I don't think there is anything in there you can reasonably object to.'

Robert Brodie took the piece of paper, but not in any spirit of acceptance. He needed time to marshal his thoughts. Reading the statement at least would give him a small breathing space. Barton had no intention of letting him take his time in composing a response.

'I have my usual Monday morning press conference at nine thirty tomorrow. An ideal moment and venue for you to make your announcement.' He paused briefly but did not take his eyes off Brodie. 'There will be no problem in altering that statement to suit your own style, Robert, as long as the basic message remains the same of course.'

Brodie had not read a single word of the statement. He had simply used the pretence of reading to give him time to gather his wits. Barton had him over a barrel. If he refused he could no doubt wave goodbye to an influential position within Barton Industries. If he agreed publicly to announce his allegiance to Barton Industries he was sunk as far as any future with Amalagamated was concerned. What was more, he would not find it easy to get a new job. He would effectively carry the yoke of traitor around his neck. He decided his only line of approach was to try and persuade him that switching sides at this juncture would not achieve anything positive and could possibly have harmful side effects.

'Your bid is going very well at the moment, Peter. You no

doubt have the latest figures, but in broad terms I believe you have bought around forty per cent of Amalgamated in the market and have unconditional acceptances for roughly another five per cent. You are nearly there. I don't see how my publicly switching sides and endorsing your bid at this stage can make any difference. Indeed, I consider it would be a tactical mistake. My hidden presence within Amalgamated would be cut off immediately if I publicly supported your bid, and you would be cut off from the flow of information I have been able to feed you. I don't think you can deny that it has been helpful to you.'

'It would serve two purposes, Robert. It would demonstrate your commitment, and I believe it would play a significant part in persuading one or two of the institutional shareholders to come off the fence. You are highly respected in business circles and have the inestimable advantage of having an intimate knowledge of the financial health of Amalgamated from the inside. If you publicly support the Barton Industries bid, that will go a long way toward satisfying those large institutions who presently may be withholding their acceptance of our offer. It would be a clear signal that you considered that the fact we would need to use Amalgamated assets to finance the bid did not undermine the value of the bid and, more importantly, neither did it jeopardise the prospect of Barton Industries making the enlarged company a more valuable asset than the sum of the two separate parts.'

'My commitment is not in doubt, Peter. I do not need to demonstrate it in any public way to reinforce that commitment. As to your other justification for my publicly switching sides at this stage, I don't deny your logic, but I consider you overestimate my influence over the thinking of the institutional investors. You are doubtless lobbying the large shareholders on an almost daily basis. I have provided you with a lot of highly confidential information to enable you to do this with maximum effectiveness. I believe I can be more useful in this role than as a publicly exposed turncoat. The institutional shareholders are merely following their usual practice of leaving their decision to the last possible moment, and the fact that few, if any, have accepted the Barton Industries offer at this stage is not significant.'

Peter Barton twirled his glass between his fingers. What should he tell him? Brodie was obviously not going to cross the floor without a good deal more persuasion. The truth was likely to frighten him off rather than persuade him to agree to support the Barton Industries bid by publicly switching sides. The feedback from the large institutional shareholders was not good. There was clearly considerable scepticism. If the results of Charles Walters's survey of the key shareholders was right, the consensus was that Barton Industries had overstretched themselves this time, and would have considerable difficulty in making the deal tick. If the bid failed, Barton Industries faced a massive loss on the Amalgamated shares they had bought in the market. They could not afford simply to hang on to them and maybe relaunch the bid at a later date. Barton Industries had to win. He decided that telling Brodie how high the stakes were would not persuade him, indeed it might just have the opposite effect. He might conclude his best interests lay with keeping his head down and working to thwart the Barton Industries bid. He made one more try.

'At the end of the day, Robert, the institutional investors will jump in whichever direction they think profit lies without too large a degree of risk. Our track record stands us in good stead in that context. Unfortunately, I consider that, despite all our efforts, they have still not fully grasped the benefits of the manner in which we have structured this bid. Your public support could tip the balance. Where do your loyalties lie?'

Sir Peter Barton waited for his response. Brodie for his part needed time to think. If he turned him down flat now, that would be an end of it. He had little doubt that he would have made an enemy. But he was not ready to jump. He was far from convinced that the act of his changing sides would have any significant impact on the institutional share-holders and, if that was right, it would be a futile gesture with potentially disastrous results for him personally.

'I need more time to think, Peter. I think it is unfair of you to get me over here like this without any warning and expect me to make such a momentous decision on the spot.'

'We do not have time, Robert. I need an answer now.'

One last push might do it, he thought. The fact he had not said 'No' at least left open the possibility he might say 'Yes'.

'I'm sorry, Peter, I cannot give you an answer now.'

'Robert, there are three days until the Amalgamated bid for Axehouse reaches its crunch point. If our bid has not clearly demonstrated that it will succeed by then, it is likely to fail. We do not have time. Everything we can do to enhance our chances of success has to be done sooner rather than later.'

Brodie saw no point in disagreeing with Sir Peter Barton's assessment of the situation. It was not as black and white as he had painted it. He accepted, however, that he could not delay giving a straight reply for very long.

'I promise to let you have an answer by tomorrow night, Peter. In the meantime I will let you have any useful intelligence in the usual manner.'

Barton accepted he was not going to get an answer immediately. He was frustrated and angry but managed to keep himself under control. Losing his temper, or becoming openly threatening, would almost certainly provoke a refusal. As it was, his inclination was that Brodie would accept. He was not an indecisive man. If he had not refused outright now the odds were that he was going to agree. He merely wanted time to think through all the ramifications.

☆ ☆ ☆

Martin Chandler had spent most of the weekend at home. There was little he could do now to alter the course of events by staying up in London and endlessly treading over already well trodden land. Instead he needed the quiet of his own home, and the comfort of Sarah, to wrestle with his conscience. Was his need to win so all-embracing that he would stoop to tactics he would have dismissed out of hand a few weeks ago? He was confident he had in his grasp the means to stop Barton Industries in their tracks, and by stopping them the success of Amalgamated's bid for Axehouse became virtually automatic. If he followed this course, what were his real motives? If they were simply ones that were generated by concern for his own personal well being and power, then he would not be justified in using the information he had to spike Sir Peter Barton. If, on the other hand, there were wider and more reputable motives than these then the fact that incidentally his own well being and power were preserved was no reason for not using the weapons he had. Were there any such motives? Yes, he had concluded, there were. If Barton Industries acquired Amalgamated, not only would he be out of a job, but many other people would be too. Barton was not renowned for preserving jobs in any company he acquired, whatever soothing words might have appeared in the Offer Document on the subject. Quite apart from his effect on people, and their security of employment, there was the effect Barton Industries would have on the intangible, but nevertheless real, persona of Amalgamated Products itself. It had a style and personality of its own, a good style and personality, one that Martin was proud of, not just for his own contribution in maintaining and developing it, but one that was representative of generations of his own family and the thousands of people who over the years had been part of it. This style and personality would certainly not survive Barton Industries.

It was worth preserving. If using all the firepower he had at his disposal failed, he alone would take the blame. The risk was worthwhile. Profit was the aim and justification for the existence of a business, but it did not thereby justify the maximising of profit irrespective of the effect upon the people who were its lifeblood, be they employees, suppliers or customers. From time to time people were necessarily hurt as part of the process of running the business in the overall long term interests of a wider group of people. This was inevitable but nevertheless sad. Balance was the key, not only in measuring short against long term interest, but also in striking a fair resolution between the competing interests of a disparate collection of people. The shareholders risked their savings to finance the business – their interests needed to be protected. Employees gave their time, and often their whole working lives, playing their individually small but collectively essential role in ensuring the continued financial health of the business – their interests needed to be protected too. They had families who were dependent upon them. Maybe Amalgamated had in the past erred on the side of allowing compassion to override commercial prudence. Maybe it had been too soft and that was why a predator of the nature of Barton Industries had cast its eye upon the company. Tough decisions which would have been in the long term interest of the great majority of those whose lives were touched by Amalgamated had no doubt in the past been fudged or ignored. Maybe. Of one thing Martin Chandler was quite certain. The Barton Industries of this world were short term operators chasing the fastest buck, irrespective of who might be trampled underfoot on the way. Everything was justified in terms of maximising profit in the short term, whatever damage this might do to the business in the long term. That could take care of itself. Three years was a long time and five years was a millennium. The ravages of the ruthless pursuit of short term profit would long ago have been masked by the next, and bigger, acquisition – and so it would go on. It was crystal clear in his mind, virtually anything was justified to save Amalgamated from such a bleak future.

He paused in his musing. Should he not examine his own motives in seeking to acquire Axehouse? Was he not guilty of the very unworthy motives he attributed to Sir Peter Barton? He had genuinely not thought it through on this basis at the time of his decision to bid for Axehouse. What had been his real motives? Had they been the lure of increased personal power? Had they been a desire to join the Peter Bartons of this world? It was not always easy to be honest with yourself when examining your own motives.

Maybe there was a little of each of those motives, but the main impulse had been protection; protection against such as Barton Industries. Amalgamated had become a soft target and he had wanted to shore up the defences precisely in order to create a position where they would be safe from companies like Barton Industries. He wanted to preserve an environment in which the old traditions of Amalgamated could survive, albeit tempered by an approach more in tune with the demands of modern day business; but still with a human face.

Martin Chandler knew what he had to do, and he was satisfied that his motives were good motives. There was personal risk for him in pursuing the course he had decided upon, but what he might achieve for others made these risks pale into insignificance.

Miles Wartnaby had spent the afternoon indulging his favourite pastime; playing with numbers. On the face of it Barton Industries seemed to be in the driving seat. They had purchased nearly forty per cent of Amalgamated in the market and had other acceptances bringing them up to just under forty-six per cent and, as far as he knew, these acceptances had not been expressed to be conditional. It should be a formality from such a position of strength; but was it a position of strength? Such massive buying in the market masked a somewhat low level of acceptances of the offer at this stage of the proceedings. What was more, the share buying was a gamble on a massive scale. There was no way Barton Industries could finance it without first acquiring Amalgamated and using its financial strength. What about the large institutional shareholders in Amalgamated? They had yet to show their hand. What would he do in their shoes? They had three options. Do nothing – in which event the bid would almost certainly fail and Barton Industries would be left with a considerable financing problem. Accept the bid – this was a distinct possibility. Barton Industries had an enviable track record of being able to make their acquisitions perform and justify themselves. Miles considered they had a really uphill task this time if they were to emulate past successes. The structuring of the deal meant that a significant part of what Barton Industries bought would have to be realised to finance the deal. Would what was left then be of sufficient size and profitability to enhance the overall profitability of Barton Industries and key financial measures such as earnings per share and return on capital employed? On balance, he thought not. But it was not clear cut. Past reputation still carried a lot of weight with the institutions. Some might decide to accept the Barton Industries offer. The third possibility was that the large shareholders would sell in the market. This way they were assured of their profit. Some must undoubtedly have done so because of the large stake Barton Industries had already built up. Also, he himself had had little difficulty in making significant purchases in the market.

He turned the possibilities over in his mind. There was another factor. Many of the institutions might also be shareholders in Barton Industries. They had to feed this into the equation. All three scenarios suggested that Barton Industries' share price would suffer if his analysis was right. Indeed, as he thought about it he was somewhat surprised it had held up as well as it had. If they sold Amalgamated shares this would probably ensure victory for Barton Industries as effectively as if they accepted the Barton Industries offer, since Barton Industries were the only likely purchasers at this stage of the bid. The question was whether Barton Industries could afford to buy the shares. The purchases they had already made had already upset the balance of their bid. If, on the other hand, the institutions simply let the bid fail, Barton Industries would be left with a large minority stake in Amalgamated. They clearly could not afford to keep it and would have to place it in the market and take a substantial loss.

Miles smashed his fist into the palm of the other hand. Why had he not thought of it before? It was within his power to become the ringmaster. He could dictate events, make a very nice short term profit and achieve a long term objective. He leant over to his desk and pulled open the bottom drawer which held a number of neat folders in suspended filing. He extracted two files, shut the drawer and rose from his armchair, fixed himself a large whisky and soda and sat down at his desk.

Two hours later he flipped the two files shut. It would work.

24

Monday 8 a.m.

Martin got up from his desk as Stephen entered, walked round his desk and motioned him towards an easy chair placing himself in the chair opposite. He had rung Stephen at eleven thirty the previous evening to arrange the meeting. He had given no indication what it was about nor of who else would be there. It was now quite obvious that there would be nobody else.

He studied Stephen for a moment or two without saying anything. Was he doing the right thing? He had only known the man for a few months. Could he trust him? Was it fair to involve him? He had been turning these questions over in his mind most of the night. There was no reason why he should come to different conclusions now that he was sitting opposite him. Besides, he had little or no option if he was going to do anything positive. Alan Mortimer had been a possibility, but he might have got a blank refusal from that quarter. He undoubtedly had a reputation for being ruthless in the conduct of takeover battles, but Martin doubted that this extended as far as he was proposing to go.

Stephen sat silent, sensing that an inner struggle of some kind was taking place. Martin would say what he wanted to say in his own good time.

'Stephen, what I am about to tell you is for your ears only. I shall tell you as little as possible in order to involve you as little as possible. You may well draw some conclusions, but you must keep these to yourself. I want no advice from you, just information. Understood?'

He nodded his agreement, not entirely sure what he was

letting himself in for.

'I have received some information which I am quite sure is accurate but I want to be absolutely sure of it. I need to know the answer by lunchtime tomorrow at the very latest. After that it will probably be of no use. Indeed it may be of no use before the end of today. So the quicker you can get the information the better.'

Martin was fully aware he was skirting round the subject and putting off the moment when he had to come out in the open.

'You are quite free to refuse to do what I ask you, but if you do I want a telephone number from you.'

Stephen judged the moment to be right to precipitate matters.

'I fully understand. What can I do for you?'

'I have learnt something concerning the private life of Sir Peter Barton. It is irrelevant where I heard it, but I consider it highly likely that the information is accurate. I want, if at all possible to corroborate the information. That private detective you have been using might be able to help. I have been told that he has some rather peculiar personal habits. He beats up women or, more specifically, prostitutes. Do you think your detective agency would be able to find out if that is true?'

Stephen thought fast. Did he pretend that this was new information to him, or did he reveal straight away that he already knew and, what was more had incontrovertible evidence to prove it? There was only one reason Martin wanted to know; he wanted to use it in an effort to stave off the Barton Industries bid. He was not the sort of man to take a prurient interest in such information. He probably found it very difficult and deeply embarrassing even to mention it to him. Time was running out fast. There was no time to indulge in a little charade of pretending innocence and then miraculously coming up with the evidence in a very short span of time.

'As you know, I employed Trevor Jacques some time ago to investigate the activities of Barton Industries.'

Martin didn't know, he had thought that Alan Mortimer had brought them in. He let it pass. It wasn't important.

'In the course of their investigations they discovered

277

that he resorted to prostitutes. He isn't married.'

Martin failed to see the connection between the two pieces of information but said nothing.

'Last week one of Trevor Jacques's men came into possession of evidence that incontrovertibly links Sir Peter Barton with a prostitute he had just beaten up.'

Martin could not wait for Stephen to finish. The Gods must be on his side.

'What is it, what is it?'

'A cheque signed by Sir Peter Barton, and written in his own hand, made out to a prostitute.'

'That doesn't prove he beat her up.'

'Trevor Jacques's man spoke to her immediately after she had left Barton. He will be able to confirm the state she was in. The girl can also probably be persuaded to confirm what happened to her. She told Trevor Jacques's man.'

'Have you got this cheque?'

'No, but I have seen it. It is in Trevor Jacques's safe.'

'Get me a photocopy, fast.'

Stephen did not need to ask what he wanted it for. There was only one possible use.

'Would you also please let me have the dossier on the Barton Industries share buying, you know, the one showing how they have been buying their own shares illegally through foreign intermediaries.'

Stephen, guessing how all this information was almost certainly going to be used, decided he must emphasise the limitations of the Barton Industries share buying information.

'Certainly, but I think I ought to make it clear that the dossier contains nothing that actually proves Barton Industries have been indirectly buying their own shares, either in support of their bid for us or on previous occasions. The evidence is only circumstantial, admittedly very strong, but still only circumstantial.'

'Yes, yes I know that. Who else knows about this stuff on Barton?'

'Well, obviously Trevor Jacques and some of his staff, but apart from that only Alan Mortimer.'

'Anyone within Amalgamated?'

'No.'

'What about Brodie?'

'Only you and me.'

'Good, keep it that way. I haven't said anything to Brodie yet. That can wait. I doubt there is any more damage he can do at this stage. Nobody, and I mean nobody, must know what we have talked about this morning. Whatever happens you are to deny all knowledge of this meeting. That's for your own protection as much as anything.'

'Thank you Martin.' He felt the events of the last few minutes made it safe for him to be more familiar. 'I know what you are going to do with the information. I just want you to know that I would do the same in your position.'

In other circumstances Stephen knew that this would have sounded very pretentious and presumptuous; times were not normal, however, and he sensed that Martin was in need of moral support which he was unwilling to seek from anyone for fear of involving them in something that probably verged on blackmail.

'Thank you Stephen.'

Martin felt a genuine warmth towards him. He looked at his watch. Eight thirty. There was a full Board meeting at nine fifteen and a pre-meeting with Markby Smythe, Mortimer, Irwin and Stephen Barber at eight forty five.

'Stay with me Stephen. The others will be here shortly. I want to sort out what I say to the Board. I want to give an upbeat, confident assessment of the situation without revealing anything of what we have just been talking about. We are going to win.' He smiled for the first time that morning.

☆ ☆ ☆

Monday 9.45 a.m.

Sir Peter Barton, Charles Walters and Nathan Sanson went over the figures yet again. They were close, tantalisingly close. Sir Peter turned to Walters.

'Charles have you got that list of the ten largest shareholders in Amalgamated?'

He produced a piece of paper from his file and made to pass it over. He waved it away.

'Tell me, how many of those shareholders do we need to get us over the fifty per cent mark?'

'Just three, Sir Peter. In fact it doesn't even need to be the three biggest shareholders. Any combination of three of the top eight would be sufficient.'

He turned to Sanson.

'What efforts have you made to talk to these shareholders recently?'

'Charles and I between us have spoken to each of the top twenty within the last four days. I believe Charles has let you have our assessment of where they stand.'

Barton looked towards Charles Walters, giving every impression that he had not given him such information.

'I have it here Sir Peter.'

He extracted another document from his file and passed it across giving Sanson a venomous look as he did so. They had agreed over the weekend to do another trawl of the top ten shareholders that morning before presenting their assessment.

'It is not fully up to date. Nathan and I have already arranged to chase up the top ten again this morning. We will have a better picture by lunchtime.'

Sir Peter ignored the undercurrent of hostility between the two men.

'Take the half dozen which, on the basis of your previous contacts, seem the best prospects for coming down on our side. Concentrate your efforts on them. If enough of them come over to us to give us fifty per cent, the rest will follow in short order.'

Walters decided there was little point in raising hopes too high. The response the previous week from the large shareholders he and Nathan had approached was not encouraging. They had all questioned whether Barton Industries would be able to digest Amalgamated successfully on the basis the bid was now structured. They had not said 'no' but they had hardly been encouraging.

'I don't think we should be over optimistic that we shall be able to persuade them, Sir Peter. They are not convinced that we shall be able to make the acquisition pay. I don't think they are over enamoured of the extent to which we shall need to use Amalgamated's own assets in order to fund the acquisition.'

'We have been over all that a hundred times; it's yours and Nathan's job to persuade them. You can prove anything with figures, get on with it.'

Walters could see he was getting cross and there was nothing he could do to mollify him.

'What's the market like? How many more shares have we picked up today?'

Nathan Sanson responded, much to Charles Walters relief.

'It's very thin, Sir Peter. There is not much stock available. Most of what we do not already have is held by the institutions. I suppose some of them might sell. That gives them their profit without taking any of the risk implicit in accepting our offer. I strongly advise against buying any more shares. We are already seriously over-stretched and have altered the profile of our bid by buying to the extent we have already. It's a miracle our own share price has held up the way it has. If our share price begins to drop that could be the end of our bid in any case.'

Sir Peter was not about to enlighten Sanson how this had been achieved. Walters knew of the arrangements with the Swiss bank and its associates, but they had agreed long ago that it was best that their UK advisers knew nothing of it.

'Our share price holds up because the market recognises the deal is a good one for Barton Industries,' Barton growled.

He picked up the document analysing the reaction of the large shareholders and swiftly marked it.

'I'll take the ones marked with a 'B', you split the four marked with an 'X' between you. We shall meet again at two o'clock.'

☆ ☆ ☆

Monday 11.15 a.m.

The Board meeting had finished ten minutes before. Martin had given Ann Gordon strict instructions that he was not to be disturbed for any reason whatsoever, irrespective how urgent and important it might seem. He

281

finished jotting his aide memoire. It only covered one side of the piece of paper. He read it through and, satisfied that all the relevant points were covered, slipped it into the plastic folder that now contained a copy of Peter Barton's cheque in favour of Melanie Hunt and the dates of the purchases and sales of Barton Industries shares by the Swiss bank and the Cayman Island and Leichtenstein nominee companies. Pinned to this schedule was a series of graphs showing how the purchases neatly halted the trend of decline in the Barton Industries share price and returned it to a level that was healthy in the context of the respective bids by Barton Industries that were current at the time. The same presentation appeared for the Barton Industries share price and share purchases by the three overseas buyers in the context of the bid for Amalgamated Products. Martin picked up his phone and dialled Sir Peter Barton's ex-directory office number. Pru Wetherby answered.

'Sir Peter Barton's office. Can I help you?'

'I wish to speak to Sir Peter. This is Martin Chandler here.'

'One moment please.'

Martin was enjoying himself, and he was going to enjoy himself even further in the not very distant future. He was genuinely surprised to discover that he had a vengeful streak in him.

'I have Martin Chandler on the telephone, Sir Peter.'

'Put him through.'

Sir Peter Barton could hardly contain his excitement. There was only one reason why Martin Chandler should want to speak to him with only just over two days to go before the bid for Amalgamated was due to reach its climax. He was going to capitulate and wanted to sue for peace. No doubt he wanted to negotiate the best deal for himself.

'Hello Martin. It's a good day, isn't it?' Barton's voice was positively jovial. I will soon change that, Martin thought to himself.

'Yes, I suppose it is. I think we ought to meet.'

'Oh, I am sure we can do it over the telephone, Martin. A short little statement is all we need at this juncture. You know the sort of thing. Amalgamated recommend their shareholders to accept the Barton Industries bid blah, blah. . .'

Martin Chandler was not going to disabuse him over the telephone.

'No, we must meet. You must tell nobody. We don't want to risk any leak that might distort the market before the announcement is made.'

'Alright, if that is the way you want to play it. Where do you suggest?'

Barton didn't see the point of meeting, but he wasn't going to press the point. He had won and might as well humour the man. If that was the way he wanted it, then, that was the way he would get it.

'I have reserved a private room at the Waldorf Hotel. It is in the name of Henry Pensford. Give your name as Stephen Richards when you arrive at the desk. We don't want anyone to see us together, nor do we want to leave names around which can be connected. I shall be there in about twenty minutes. Get there as soon as you can.'

'OK, half an hour.'

He put the telephone down, clashed the heels of his hands together and, then, forming them into fists, thumped them on his desk. He could hardly contain his excitement. He didn't stop to think what had caused Martin Chandler to capitulate suddenly. He did not really care either, he had capitulated and that was all that mattered. He was sorely tempted to tell Charles Walters but decided to play the game and maintain secrecy as Chandler had asked. He pressed his intercom button.

'I have to go out Pru. I'm not sure when I shall be back.'

'Do you want your car Sir Peter?'

He paused for a moment. If he was to play the game it would hardly be wise to turn up at the front of the Waldorf in his easily identifiable chauffeur driven limousine. On the other hand he considered it beneath his dignity to walk out into the road in front of his offices and hail a taxi.

'Yes please, Pru.'

He would take his car as far as his club and then dismiss the chauffeur and get the doorman of the club to call him a taxi. Sir Peter Barton left his office at eleven twenty five. Nobody knew where he was going. Two minutes earlier Martin Chandler had left his office. Nobody knew where he was going either.

Monday 11.33 a.m.

Miles Wartnaby was enjoying himself hugely. As he watched the screen the Barton Industries share price started to fall. At first it had been almost imperceptible – just a penny. One penny became five pence and almost immediately five pence had become ten. By ten to twelve the Barton Industries share price had fallen a full seven per cent in value. As he watched the screen he listened on the open line to his broker reporting the prices he had obtained as Miles sold Barton Industries shares short. He did a quick calculation on his notepad as the final transaction in his planned series of sales was reported as completed by his stockbroker. His average sale price was 175 pence a share. They were already standing at 165 pence a share and by the time he had to go into the market to buy shares to meet his bargains he was confident they would have dropped at least another ten pence a share.

Miles switched his attention to what was going on in Amalgamated shares. They had dropped in sympathy with the Barton Industries shares. The fall in the value of the Barton Industries shares had automatically knocked the Amalgamated share price, reflecting the reduced value of the Barton Industries share element in their offer for the shares of Amalgamated. He did a quick calculation. The Amalgamated share price had dropped more than the strictly arithmetical drop that would have been consequential upon the fall in the Barton Industries share price.

Everything was going nicely to plan. Indeed everything was going even better than plan. He was blissfully unaware of the little drama that was unfolding not a mile away in a small room at the Waldorf Hotel.

☆ ☆ ☆

Martin rose to greet Peter Barton as he entered the room.

'Welcome Mr Richards. Welcome.' He did not offer his hand in greeting and sat down again at the head of the small rectangular table which, apart from the second chair at the other end, was the only furniture in the room. Barton removed his coat and looked around for somewhere to put it, finally deciding to fold it up and drop it in the corner of the room. He was puzzled. The jovial, verging on sarcastic, greeting was hardly that of a man about to offer surrender. He ignored the form of greeting, deciding that it was just Chandler's way of hiding his bitter disappointment.

'I am in no position to offer you any special terms Martin, at least none that would give you any long term role with any influence. A token deputy chairmanship maybe, on a strictly non-executive and short term basis of course.'

'I haven't come here to surrender. I thought it would be a courtesy on my part to give you the opportunity to withdraw your bid with as little loss of face and reputation as possible.'

Sir Peter Barton rose from his chair angrily.

'What the hell are you playing at? I am far too busy to come here on a wild goose chase and play silly cloak and dagger games for your amusement.'

Martin let him get as far as stooping down to pick up his coat.

'I would sit down and hear me out if I were you, Peter.'

'I doubt very much whether you have anything to say which could be of the slightest interest to me. Good morning.'

He strode towards the door.

'Melanie Hunt,' Martin said quietly, but just loud enough for Barton to hear. He swung round and realised immediately that his action confirmed that the name meant something to him.

'I see the name is not unfamiliar to you, but I think we will talk about other things first.'

If it could be avoided Martin did not want to have to make any threats in that context. Sir Peter still stood by the door, irresolute.

'I should sit down and hear me out if I were you.'

Sir Peter Barton seethed inside, but managed to keep a grip on his temper. He had to tread carefully. What did Chandler know? He turned and reluctantly took the seat opposite.

'I will deal with the more inconsequential first. I know about Brodie. Don't bother to deny it, that would be wasting both our time. You have no doubt offered him inducements, but we shall not need to go into that, provided, of course, you drop your bid. What is much more interesting is the Friedlander and Benesch Bank in Switzerland, and their associates in Leichtenstein and the Cayman Islands. I do of course have the names of these associates.'

Martin paused, Sir Peter neither said anything nor gave any indication that the names meant anything to him.

'Oh well, I suppose I am going to have to spell it out in words of single syllables.'

He did not flicker an eyelid as Martin took him step by step through the evidence that had been assembled. He did not even bother to glance at the schedules of purchases and sales pushed in front of him, let alone the damning graphs.

'Absolute rubbish. I have never even heard of these companies. I think it is probably my duty to report this matter to the Takeover Panel. It is intolerable.'

'Please do, that is exactly where I propose to go next if you do not announce the withdrawal of your bid by three thirty this afternoon. As for never having heard of the Friedlander and Benesch Bank, I suggest you have a look at some of your published documents, such as previous Offer Documents. That is not the only source. I can direct you to many others which prove the relationship between Barton Industries and the Friedlander and Benesch Bank.'

'Alright, maybe we have done business with them in the past. You can't expect me to carry round in my head the names of every tinpot little bank which might have been party to some syndicated loan we have raised, but I absolutely deny your libellous allegation that Barton Industries have been involved in anything illegal or contrary to the Takeover regulations. If you repeat them outside this room you will have a writ on your desk before the spittle is dry on your lips.'

Martin could not help but admire the man's aplomb. He had in no way been fazed by the allegations, or the evidence in support of them. Indeed, if he had not been thoroughly convinced of the evidence himself, he could easily have concluded that he had made a horrible mistake. Barton was a calculating bastard. He had listened, given nothing away and concluded, correctly, that the evidence whilst damning, was not conclusive. He was going to try and bluff it out. Martin sighed inwardly. He was going to have to resort to the tactic he had hoped to avoid.

'These papers will be in the hands of the Takeover Panel at exactly three thirty this afternoon unless I hear before then that your bid has been withdrawn. Think it over by all means, and whilst you are thinking spare a little thought for Melanie Hunt.'

He extracted the photocopy of the cheque from his folder and slid it along the table. He had struck home this time.

'Where. . .?' Barton stopped himself. The question was superfluous. Martin pressed home the advantage.

'You may or may not be able to bluff your way out of the hole you are in with regard to illegally buying your own shares, but you will not be able to bluff your way out of that. Three thirty this afternoon.'

Peter Barton realised he was probably beaten, but he was neither going to give this man the satisfaction of admitting it to his face, and nor was he going to capitulate until he had had time to think it through and see whether there might indeed be a way out of it. The girl no doubt had a price for her silence or, better still, her confirmation that nothing untoward had happened to her. As for the share dealing allegations – well they had to prove it, and that would be difficult. He got up and left the room without a word.

Martin Chandler stared after him, not quite sure whether he had won or not.

☆ ☆ ☆

Monday 12.35 p.m.

Sir Peter Barton walked into the foyer of Barton Industries offices and was immediately accosted by the receptionist.

'Ah, Sir Peter. Mr Walters has asked if you could please contact him as soon as you came in. He says it's very urgent.'

'Thank you Jane. Tell him to come straight along to my office.'

By the time Sir Peter got to his office Charles Walters was there waiting for him. Walters felt like asking him where the hell he had been, but restrained himself. Since the Barton Industries share price had started falling an hour ago the telephone lines had been jammed. Nathan Sanson had managed to get through on an ex-directory line, but Barton Industries brokers had suffered along with the press and Uncle Tom Cobley and all who had been trying to get through to find out what was going on.

'What is it Charles?' He could not keep the irritation out of his voice. He needed peace and quiet and time to himself to decide what to do about the twin threats Martin Chandler had delivered, and he did not have much time.

'You mean you haven't heard?' Walters was unable to keep the note of incredulity out of his voice.

'Heard what?'

'Our share price has fallen through the floor.'

It was something of an exaggeration but it conveyed the main message very effectively.

'What, why?' Peter Barton hardly comprehended what he was being told. His mind was a chaos of unwelcome thoughts.

'We don't know. Our brokers say there has been a big seller in the market, but they don't know yet who it is. It's probably irrelevant anyway. Nathan says that unless our share price recovers pretty quickly, and by that he means by this time tomorrow, our bid for Amalgamated is as dead as a dodo.'

'Have you been on to Switzerland? They haven't reneged on us have they?'

'They were on to me within twenty minutes of the price falling wanting to know what the hell was going on. They

288

also took the opportunity politely to remind us of our obligations under the guarantee that we would make up any losses they might suffer.'

'I hope you reminded them of their obligation to us to buy to support our share price if it showed signs of weakness, and asked them what they were doing about it?'

'No, Sir Peter, I didn't. The level of selling and the fall in the share price was of such a magnitude that they would inevitably have said no. What is more I do not consider we could justify putting Barton Industries in jeopardy by undertaking further contingent liabilities on a large and unquantifiable scale.'

Barton was about to explode. He raised his hands to shoulder height and let them fall to his side in a gesture of defeat.

'Get Sanson round here. We must get a start and see what we can salvage from this mess.'

'He is already on his way.'

'OK, give me five minutes.'

Sir Peter Barton slumped in his chair. He knew he was defeated. A strange thing, fate. He had always been a winner and now, within an hour, he had become a three way loser. Maybe not a three way loser, it all came to the same really. He had failed to acquire Amalgamated and he had seriously weakened Barton Industries in the process. How this had happened was irrelevant. He knew in his heart of hearts that even had the share price collapse not happened he would have capitulated to Martin Chandler. At least he could now capitulate for a reason that was already glaringly obvious to everyone. He might as well call Chandler now. No, let him sweat a bit longer. Leave him until three o'clock.

Sir Peter Barton, for all his inability to control himself in matters personal, had an iron control in matters of business. There was no point in wasting time regretting the past. Now was the time to deal with the present. There was the little matter of what to do with all those Amalgamated shares he owned. He certainly could not afford to keep them.

✰ ✰ ✰

Martin had not gone straight back to Amalgamated House. He had not enjoyed his encounter with Peter Barton. He somehow felt unclean. Maybe he didn't have a sadistic streak after all. He couldn't actually bring himself to feel sorry for the man, but neither did he feel any sense of triumph. He found a small pub where he could have a quiet drink by himself before returning to Amalgamated House to announce his triumph. He felt oddly unexcited, but did not dwell upon the cause.

Amalgamated House was in a state of rampant excitement. There had been no formal announcement, but there was nobody who considered it other than a foregone conclusion that the Barton Industries bid had failed and that, as a consequence, the Amalgamated bid for Axehouse had succeeded. Martin Chandler stepped into this atmosphere in the same blissful ignorance that half an hour before Sir Peter Barton had stepped into his quite different, and equally unexpected, atmosphere.

He sat at his desk waiting for his telephone to ring. He had given Ann strict instructions that he did not want any calls put through to him unless they came from Barton Industries. He had also asked her to request Robert Brodie to come and see him. It did not take long. Brodie did not try to deny the allegation that he had been working clandestinely for Barton Industries. Within ten minutes he had left Amalgamated House never to return.

Two fifteen. The telephone rang. Martin picked the receiver up before the bell had the slightest chance of ringing again. It was Ann on the other end.

'I'm sorry Mr Chandler. It isn't Barton Industries. I have Inspector Rawlings on the phone. I thought you would probably wish to speak to him.'

Martin was in too good a mood to be cross, and Ann was quite right, he would not have wanted to fob off Inspector Rawlings. He was still worried about the threat, the more particularly as it had in the first instance come through Sarah.

'Hello, Inspector.'

'Ah Mr Chandler. I have some good news for you. Our friend slipped up with that last letter of his. He chose a piece of writing paper from immediately under the previous letter he had written. A hand written letter. It left a series of nice indentations which gave forensic very little trouble in deciphering the address on the letter head. We have made a visit to the address and a gentleman is now helping us with our enquiries.'

'What was he after Inspector?'

'Exactly what he said as a matter of fact. It seems he is in deep financial difficulty and had taken a big gamble on the outcome of your bid for Axehouse General and the Barton Industries bid. It was vital to his scheme that you lost. He is as harmless as a fly. He would have done nothing to you or your family even had we not caught him.'

'Thank you, Inspector. That is a big weight off my mind.'

He rang Sarah immediately and gave her not only this piece of good news but forewarned her that, before the day was out, there would almost certainly be more good news. He told her to pack a bag and come up to London for a celebration.

The telephone didn't ring again until five past three that afternoon, and it wasn't Peter Barton on the other end.

'Mr Chandler, Charles Walters here of Barton Industries. Sir Peter Barton has asked me to inform you that at three fifteen this afternoon Barton Industries will be announcing the formal withdrawal of their offer for the shares of Amalgamated Products.'

Walters did not wait for a reply.

Martin let out a most untypical whoop of delight and rushed into Ann's office, grabbed her by the waist and gave her a smacking kiss.

The rest of the day was a whirl of activity. A mixture of uninhibited celebration and getting on with the essential things that needed to be done. The bid for Axehouse was declared unconditional, the withdrawal of the Barton Industries bid for Amalgamated having guaranteed its success.

Sir Richard Brookes, the chairman of Axehouse General, had graciously called Martin to congratulate him on his success and had arranged a meeting for the next day to start planning the future. Best of all Martin had had one of the most enjoyable evenings with Sarah he could remember. He had booked a suite at the Connaught and a table in the Connaught Grill. The superb meal had only been surpassed by the enjoyment Martin and Sarah had found in each other afterwards back in the suite.

☆ ☆ ☆

Tuesday 9.00 a.m.

'Miles Wartnaby on the phone Mr Chandler.'

'Thank you Ann. Put him through.'

'Hello Miles, how nice of you to call.'

'Hello Martin and congratulations.'

'Thank you Miles. It was a tough battle and there were times when I thought we would lose.'

'Oh, yes. Congratulations on that as well.'

'I beg your pardon Miles. What else is there to congratulate me on?'

'Becoming part of BCI, Martin.'

'What! What on earth do you mean?'

'Well it's like this Martin. Sir Peter Barton had a slight embarrassment. He had an awful lot of shares in Amalgamated, and he couldn't afford to keep them. I don't like to see a chap down so I bought them from him, or at least to be more accurate, BCI bought them from him at nine o'clock last night. Nice chap, he let me have them at a very reasonable price, fifteen pence below last night's closing price actually, and that figure was itself well down on the day's opening price. Added to the shares in Amalgamated that BCI and I personally already owned, and taking full account of the shares you will be issuing to finalise the purchase of Axehouse, that brought me to forty five per cent of Amalgamated. Five minutes ago I bought enough in the market to bring me just over the fifty per cent mark. Just as soon as we can clear the formalities BCI will be making a cash offer for the remainder. I don't think there is any doubt that it will sail through without a murmur. Oh, and don't worry, I am sure I can find you a nice little job within the expanded BCI. Loads of status but requiring no more than an average demand upon your

292

time. There will be plenty of time left for you to spend with Sarah. No weekend working and no need for a London apartment.'

Martin Chandler was speechless.